UNCHOSEN RULER

MAFIA WARS - BOOK SIX

MAGGIE COLE

PULSE PRESS

This book is fiction. Any references to historical events, real people, or real places are used fictitiously. All names, characters, plots, and events are products of the author's imagination. Any resemblance to actual events or places or persons, living or dead, is entirely coincidental.

Copyright © 2021 by Maggie Cole

All rights reserved.

No part of this book may be reproduced in any form or by any electronic or mechanical means, including information storage and retrieval systems, without written permission from the author, except for the use of brief quotations in a book review.

PROLOGUE

Hailee O'Hare

In my world, bad boys have always been off-limits. It never mattered how attracted I was to them. Every man I felt drawn to who fit the definition, I avoided like the plague. It didn't matter how many times they asked me out or how much pressure my friends put on me to stop dating the safe, boring guys. I had my rule for a reason, and I wasn't about to break it.

The guidelines I set for dating were all due to my childhood. Stability wasn't something I experienced early in life. My mother fled with my sisters and me to Chicago. She did it to get away from my father, who was an abusive criminal. No matter how much time passed, my mother never stopped worrying about him finding us.

The year I turned twelve, everything changed. That's when my father went to prison for murder. My mother morphed into a new person after she told us. Her stress lifted, and it's like she could finally breathe again. However, that didn't mean any of us forgot.

There are times I still have flashbacks of the violence that reigned over our house. Those moments serve as reminders to never let anything I can't control into my life. Also, to always choose the safe route because nothing in life comes free. Everything has risk. Managing it is the only way not to get hurt. Dating a bad boy was a surefire way to go directly into the danger zone, and that wasn't an option.

Then Liam O'Malley set his sights on me. The moment our eyes met, it was like an earthquake ripping through my core. No matter how much I tried to stay away or told him we couldn't be together, I always found myself running toward him. Once our worlds collided, there was no way to escape each other.

Everything about Liam is one hundred percent bad boy. Unbelievably sexy. Fearless. Protective beyond all rationale. Possessive, unlike any man I've ever known. And a hard-core convicted criminal. But that isn't all. He's the only son of the head of the O'Malley crime family. And the Irish clan's successor. The O'Malleys rule all of Chicago and are enemies with too many other crime families to count.

That one fact should have been dangerous enough to keep me away, but it didn't. And my mother never told me everything about my lineage. She never disclosed to my sisters or me who we were or what our bloodlines made us a part of. To this day, I wonder if I would have stayed away from Liam or he from me had either of us known. There's no way to tell for sure. My head says we would have. The honest side of me says if Romeo and Juliet couldn't, we didn't stand a chance.

There would have been no way to stop us from being together.

Then there's the question about what would be different in my life had I known.

Would anything?

Would everything?

The truth unleashed makes me a hypocrite. *Do unto others as you would have them do unto you* is spelled out on my classroom wall. It's in front of me all day, every day. Each morning, my class recites it, and we discuss it. I always tried to live by it. And it always felt easy.

That is, until now.

The thing about secrets is they don't always stay buried. Sometimes they come to life. It doesn't matter if you want them to or not. The moment it hits you who you really are and what your birthright bears, you're at a fork in the road. You have to choose the direction to take, even when both have risks more significant than anything you could ever fathom.

They say good triumphs evil. I used to believe it, but I'm no longer sure. How can it when to get what you want, you have to go against everything you've ever preached and destroy anything that stands in front of you? Do you morph from good to evil? If that's the case, does it give you the ability to overlook things in the future you always thought in the past were wrong?

There isn't a lot I'm sure about anymore, except one thing: Liam O'Malley isn't a choice. He's the air I breathe. Staying an innocent, good girl is no longer an option.

1

Liam O'Malley

LIGHTS FLASH THREE TIMES. THE PRISON TURNS SILENT, AND my palms sweat. Time seems to stand still until the guard yells, "O'Malley," destroying the silence as men hollering fills my ears.

I stand in front of the door, waiting for it to open one last time. I'm getting out of this hellhole, but nothing prepared me for the flipping in my stomach.

Why am I nervous?

It's been fifteen years.

What's it going to be like on the outside?

The stale air I've breathed for years seems normal. The humming and brightness of the fluorescent lights and white walls made my skin crawl when I first got locked up. I thought I would never get used to them, but they are no longer foreign. Men I've befriended, those I hate, and some who don't mean anything to me, I pass. There's only one person whose eyes I meet on my way out.

Finn.

He's in the last cell before I step out the door. His green eyes are hardened, probably like mine. He says nothing, nor do I. We don't have to. For my entire stay here, he's been my rock. He was incarcerated a few years before me, and once I entered the prison, he made it clear to all that I was the future ruler of the O'Malley clan. It gave me immediate respect, protection, and also enemies. At twenty-five, I was hardly a man. Finn was only thirty, but those five years and time in the slammer I didn't have made him wiser than me. My father told me to listen to Finn before I got sentenced, and it was the best advice he could have given me. In a few months, Finn will be out, too. And we have a new plan for how the next generation of O'Malleys will survive.

I give him a nod. He returns it, and the guilt that I'm leaving him behind fills me. He got here first for the same crime I committed, but his punishment for murder was longer than mine. It's another hard reality about how unfair life is. There is no equality for criminals or life. It doesn't matter why you committed whatever heinous act you did. Some skate free, while others pay. Finn and I both paid our dues longer than many in one of America's worst penitentiaries. Leaving him here seems cruel.

I tuck all emotions I have deep inside me. Finn taught me how to stay in control of my body language at all times. The look in his eyes tells me not to falter now.

The guard leads me through the door. It's somewhere I've only been once, fifteen years ago, when I was led into this cesspool. I'm taken to an area to remove the orange jumpsuit I've worn since arriving. The clothes my mother mailed via the prison rules are in a zipped plastic bag. I put them on and throw my jumpsuit and shoes in the laundry bin.

"Sign here," the guard at the desk says.

I sign my name on several forms without even looking at the information. I don't care to read it. My mother will probably nag me about it. It's something I used to hate, and now, I'm looking forward to it. I'm sure it'll bug me soon enough, but until something is taken away, you don't realize how much you'll miss it.

He hands me the papers. "Don't come back." He points to the door. "You're free to go."

I don't answer him. I've never seen him before and don't care to ever again. He can take his shitty job and shove it up his ass. Anyone who'd choose to work in this hellhole, knowing what secretly goes on here, doesn't deserve an ounce of my time.

In four steps, I'm out the door, but so is the other guard who escorted me from my cell. The fresh air hits me. It's something I've not breathed in years since they expanded the prison and turned the outside rec area into another building. The sunlight hits me first, mixing with the chilled oxygen, and I shut my eyes for a moment, just letting it hit my face.

"Bet that feels good," the guard says.

I open my eyes and ignore him, too. I've had to look at this prick for too many years. The sins he's committed while being paid by the State of Illinois are too many to count. I walk toward the gate, and as soon as it opens, I have to hold back my emotions again.

"Liam!" My mother sobs, pulling me into her arms the minute I step through.

I embrace her as tightly as I can, trying to get her to stop crying, but it's pointless.

"Son," my father says, patting my back, then going into a coughing fit.

I pull away from my mother. "Dad, are you okay?"

He continues coughing into a handkerchief for a moment. His face turns red and his eyes water. "Let's get out of here."

Inhaling a large breath of clean, cold air, I follow my parents to the car and get inside. My mother sits next to me, my father across from us. For several hours, we travel north to Chicago. I stare out the window, trying to make sense of how things have and haven't changed since I was last free.

Throughout the ride, my father continues coughing. At one point, bright red speckles his white cloth.

"Dad! Have you been to the doctor? You're coughing blood," I state.

He and my mother exchange a look. I may have been gone fifteen years, but I know that look.

"What's going on?" I ask.

"Nothing. How does it feel to be free?" my mother replies, nervously taking her eyes off my father.

I turn to my dad. I repeat, "What's going on? Are you sick?"

"He's fine. He just—"

"Don't sugarcoat it, Ruth. The man's been in prison. He's not a child who will wilt," my father growls.

"Darragh, this isn't the time," my mother claims.

"Someone better tell me what the hell is going on," I order. My gut drops when my mother looks out the window and twists her fingers in her lap. Something is seriously wrong. I can see it on her face and feel it in the air around us.

My father's face hardens. He blurts out, "I have terminal lung cancer." He removes his brown plaid, tweed cap and sets it on his lap.

What the...? Unable to put words together, I stare at him.

"It's good they released you on parole. If you had to serve the final year of your sentence, I would've been dead before you got out."

My pulse increases and my mouth goes dry. "Excuse me? Did you say a year?"

The pit in my stomach grows as he shrugs. "Probably less. So we don't have any time to waste. You have a lot to learn so you can run things."

Blood draining from my face creates a chill in my spine. "Dad—"

"I don't want to hear it. There's nothing anyone can do. I've been to dozens of specialists that your mother dragged me to see. It's a done deal. Now the best thing we can do is get you up to speed and capable of running things."

I gaze at my mother, who's still facing the window. I reach for her hands and put my other arm around her. She quietly shakes and attempts to keep her sadness in check.

My father pins his steely gaze on mine. His voice is as cold as his eyes. "There's a lot to be done, Liam. The O'Malleys are vulnerable right now."

Alarm fills me. "What's the threat?"

My father takes out his pipe and lights it up, inhaling a lungful of smoke. He cracks the window and slowly releases it.

"Should you be smoking?" I ask.

He snorts. "Don't nag me like your mother. I'm dying. It's a fact. Let me smoke in peace."

How is this possible? My father has always been the strongest man I know. I haven't spent any time with him in fifteen years, minus a few minutes once a month during visitation, and now he's dying?

I have to step into his role.

I'm not ready.

I have to be.

The rest of the car ride is somber. My mother says nothing. I don't remove my arm from around her or take my hand off hers. My father stays in his unemotional state, filling me in on issues we have going on with the other crime families, specifically the Rossis, Petrovs, and Baileys.

My cousin Killian and the Ivanov brothers started a silent war with the two largest crime families and our enemies, the

Rossis and Petrovs. We're monitoring the war to keep it balanced, allowing them to kill each other off and stepping in when one side gets too much power. The issues with the Baileys are nothing new. They're another Irish crime family. Since the beginning of time, our families have been at war, fighting for control over the drug and gambling trade.

By the time we get to Chicago, my head is spinning. My father reels everything off quickly. It all overwhelms me, but I don't show him any weakness. It's another thing I learned in prison. Anything but strength gets you killed.

The car pulls up to our house. My cousins Killian, Nolan, and Declan are there, among other O'Malleys, but they're the ones I care about the most. Each of them has been like a brother to me before I killed the thug who murdered their father. For fifteen years, they visited me and never missed an opportunity to see me. But one person I want to see as much as them isn't here. I glance around the house. It's been updated and bears no resemblance to the former decor of my childhood. Everything is modern and fresh. It's beautiful, but a tiny bit of disappointment fills me. I've dreamed of being home in my old house. This is new and unfamiliar. It's five thousand times better than where I spent the last fifteen years, but I still wish something was the same. I don't dwell on it though. "Where's Nora?"

"We didn't invite her," Killian says.

"Why?" Their other sisters, who I don't give a shit about, are in the kitchen. They never cared about me the way Nora did. She and I were always close. The only reason she stopped visiting me was that I didn't like the prisoners checking her out. Where I was at was no place for a woman, even in the visiting room. My mother insisted on continuing to come.

Nora tried, but her brothers convinced her it was what I wanted and too dangerous.

"Let's go talk," Killian says and hands me a beer.

"Is she all right?" I ask, worried.

Declan nods. "Yep. But let's talk."

I don't take the beer. "I can't. My parole officer—"

My father grunts behind me. "You're an O'Malley. No parole officer is going to be checking up on you or making you pee in a cup. I made sure of it."

I spin. My father holds out a shot of whiskey. I take it, and he says, "I've waited a long time for you to be home, son. To your future. To the O'Malleys."

"And may you find a lovely woman and give me some grandbabies," my mother chirps.

I groan, and my cousins snicker behind me. I toss back the whiskey, and it burns my throat as it slides down. Killian hands me the beer. I take a large mouthful, cooling my warming insides. He motions to the other room. "Let's talk about Nora."

We go into the den, and my chest tightens. I've hardly processed my father admitting he's dying. Nora better not be sick or hurt. I turn to my cousins. "Someone better tell me why Nora isn't here."

Nolan holds his hands in the air. "Chill. She's fine. She's just..." He nervously glances at his brothers.

"What?" I demand.

"She's pregnant," Declan states.

"She's having a baby?" I ask.

They all affirm.

Happiness fills me. "That's great! So why isn't she here?"

Another look passes between them. Killian says, "It's Boris Ivanov's baby."

Too shocked to say anything, I study their faces. Not marrying an Irish man is not something my father or the majority of the O'Malleys would be cool with unless there were some arrangement. I finally find my words. "Does my father know?"

"Yeah. The Ivanov brothers agreed to an alliance to control the war," Killian informs me.

"I see. But Nora is happy? She and the baby are healthy?" I ask.

"Yeah. She's the happiest I've ever seen her right now."

"And you're all good with this?"

"Yes. We need you to be, too."

"I don't have any issues with it," I proclaim.

All three brothers look at me with surprise. Declan crosses his arms. "You don't?"

"No. Being locked up makes you think about what's important and not. I assume Boris is treating her right?"

"Of course," Nolan says.

I take a big sip of my beer. "As long as she's happy. When can I see her?"

"Tomorrow. I'll set it up," Killian replies.

"Good."

The rest of the night, I attempt to carry on conversations with family members I haven't seen in fifteen years. It's difficult. My senses seem to be on overload. Every woman I speak to has a different perfume on, itching my nostrils. Men have cologne overpowering me, too. It all makes my skin crawl. Topics others find normal make me feel like a complete outsider. And I'm fully aware every O'Malley is assessing me, wondering if I'm capable of leading the family.

When the party ends, I'm relieved to go to my old room. It's updated as well. The new bed feels oddly soft and luxurious compared to what I've grown accustomed to in prison.

The next day, Killian takes me to Maksim Ivanov's penthouse. Nora's there with a woman named Anna, who's Dmitri Ivanov's wife. Another woman, Maksim's girlfriend Aspen, is in the bedroom recovering from a snake bite. We have lunch, and it's the first time I feel normal since my release, yet I also can sense Nora is hesitant around me.

Maybe I'm imagining things?

No, she's definitely worried I'm going to screw up.

Over the next month, I get more acclimated to society. I'm either with my father, learning O'Malley business and meeting his important contacts, or Killian, Nolan, and Declan are with me. I speak to Nora a few times and also get reacquainted with the Ivanovs.

My Nana left her pub to Nora when she passed. The Baileys started a fire, and she had to remodel the entire place. The day of the grand reopening arrives. It should be nothing but happiness, but like every day, dozens of issues pop up.

I'm starting to feel as if my life only consists of putting out fires, learning everything my dad says I need to in order to take care of our clan, and implementing the plan Finn and I put together with the insider information we obtained.

The packed pub makes my skin crawl. All I want to do is congratulate Nora, have a beer, then get out of the pub as soon as possible. And then, my heart almost leaps out of my chest.

The most stunning woman I've ever seen is sitting in a booth with Nora, Anna, and some other women. Her smile lights up the room. Kindness radiates off her. Innocence best describes her aura, and I already know she's way too good for me or any other man in this bar. Her long, blonde hair, blue eyes peeking out under thick lashes, and pink, pouty lips take my breath away.

I don't know what they're saying, but a blush fills her cheeks. For the first time in what feels like forever, I'm sure about something.

I have to meet her. As I beeline toward the table, my gut flips.

What do men say to women these days?

I swallow the lump in my throat. "Nora, are you going to introduce me to your friends? All stunning lasses, by the way," I add, staring at the gorgeous creature in front of me.

"Umm..." Nora picks up a glass of water and takes a long sip. The woman's cheeks burn to the color of Nora's red hair.

Anna steps in and makes introductions. I hardly hear anyone's name, except hers.

Hailee.

The sexiest voice I've ever heard comes out of her mouth. "Nice to meet you."

The waitress comes over. "Nora, I don't mean to interrupt, but Darragh said to come get you. He's talking to Boris near the back."

Nora hesitates but replies, "Oh. Okay. Thanks." She rises, and I pull her chair back.

"I'll keep your seat warm while you're gone." I wink, hoping she'll help me out if I need it later in the night, then refocus on Hailee.

"Sure. I'll be right back," Nora claims.

I don't take my eyes off Hailee and tell Nora, "Take your time." I sit in the chair Nora vacated. "Are you Irish, Hailee?"

She smiles. "Yes."

"What's your last name?"

"O'Hare."

"O'Hare. O'Malley. Both good names. So what were you ladies discussing?"

Hailee's face turns almost purple. "Noth—"

"Licking furry pussies," Skylar states.

I chuckle. "Is this some strange trend I'm not aware of?"

"No!" Hailee exclaims.

"Hailee's online boyfriend asked if he could sample hers." Kora smirks.

Hailee groans and puts her hand over her face. "Stop it! You know I wax!"

Disappointment fills me. I raise my eyebrows. "Boyfriend?"

"No, she doesn't have one," Anna cuts in and grins.

Thank you, Anna!

Relief replaces the gnawing in my gut. Hailee's blue eyes shyly meet mine again. "That's good. I might have to kill him for being so disrespectful to you."

2

Hailee

LIAM DISAPPEARS WITH ADRIAN IN THE BACK ALLEY. After more teasing from my friends, I excuse myself to the restroom. My reflection displays my flushed cheeks, and the more I think about Liam, the redder they turn.

I need to get a grip.

He's a bad boy. Stay away.

His expression, which morphed from cocky playboyish to brooding, fills my mind. Every inch of him is sculpted. He has arm sleeves of tattoos. His greenish-blue eyes are stunning against his chestnut hair and short beard. And his large hands...

I take a deep breath, reapply my lip gloss, and put a cold, wet paper towel over my cheeks. When I'm finally looking my normal color again, I step out of the bathroom and run into Liam's chest.

He slides his hand on my back, and tingles run down my spine. His deep voice matches every part of him that's so fiercely male, I can't help but think about how it's not fair to the rest of the population. He admits, "Just who I was coming to find."

My insides do a happy dance.

Pull it together. It's just another hot guy.

There's nothing that makes him anything like another ordinary guy.

Jesus, he smells good. I inhale the woody scent and tilt my head up, feeling my cheeks burn all over again.

His intensely focused expression reappears, and it's on no one but me. "Do you come here a lot?"

"No. This is my first time."

"I guess we'll have to change that, then."

My insides quiver. *He's perfectly wrong for me. Every part of him screams danger.*

And hot sex for hours full of stops on the O train.

As if I know what that's like.

Ugh. These thoughts aren't helping.

I force a smile. "Nora and Anna did a great job with it. It's beautiful."

"Yeah. I remember what it used to look like before the remodel." He glances around, and a hint of sadness passes over his face, but it's gone as quickly as it appeared. He turns back to me.

I hold my breath, unable to move out of his grasp. "You've been gone for a few years?" I ask. Anna told me he just returned home recently.

He hesitates. "Yes. Hey, have you had enough of the party yet?"

"Ummm..."

"You want to get out of here?"

I swallow hard. I should say no and end this conversation, but I ask, "Where do you want to go?" Several women come into the hallway. I step against the wall to give them room. Liam protectively keeps his arm around me and steps closer so his body presses against mine. My pulse beats hard in my neck.

His jaw clenches. His eyes dart between my eyes and mouth. "Anywhere with fewer people."

"Are you not a people person?" I nervously tease.

He shrugs. His eyes burn into mine. "Hard to talk in this environment, isn't it? Besides, it looks like Kora is the only friend of yours left."

I glance toward the table. She and Sergey are the only two sitting there. Skylar's pink hair peeks through the window next to the back of Adrian's head. Aspen might well have vanished.

"I'm supposed to ride home with my friends."

Did I seriously say that? How lame am I?

His lips twitch. "Text your friends you left. I have a driver and will give you a ride home."

My heart races, and I'm close to breaking out in a sweat. More people come into the hallway. He steps as close as possible and leans into my ear. "We can stay here if you prefer."

The most intoxicating scent on earth flares in my nostrils. His hot breath on my neck is a blowtorch igniting every ounce of my blood. Not once in my life has my body ever reacted so strongly to a guy.

He's not a guy. He's a man.

Stay away. He's trouble.

Against my goody-two-shoes self, who's screaming at me to run and hide, I blurt out, "We can go."

His eyes light up. "Yeah?"

"Sure." *What am I doing?*

He says nothing more, grabs my hand, and leads me down the hall and out into the alley. As soon as we step outside, he texts his driver and instructs me, "Tell your friends you don't need a ride."

More nervous flutters take off in my belly. I flirt by saying, "Are you always this bossy?" and immediately reprimand myself.

"Only when I want something or, in this case, someone." He's so confident and honest, I'm not sure how to reply. Most of the guys I've been with play games. That doesn't seem to be Liam's approach, which I like, but it also scares the crap out of me. Regardless, my face is once again on fire.

I must look like a stupid high school girl.

His car pulls up, giving me a brief break from his sexy, smoldering stare down. He opens the door and motions for me to get in. I slide across the seat, and he follows me, then shuts the door.

"A lot's changed since I got back in town. Where can we go?" he asks.

My place?

Hell no. Somewhere safe.

His place?

Jeez. No. No. No.

"There's a cafe called Late Nights that has live music near my apartment. It's nothing too loud. Does that work?" I ask.

"Perfect." He rolls the divider window down and instructs his driver then closes it. He turns to me. "What do you do for a living, Hailee?"

"I'm a teacher."

His expression morphs into approval. "What grade do you teach?"

"Kindergarten."

He grins. "That was my favorite grade. No homework, lots of games and art projects."

I laugh. "You didn't like school, did you?"

"I loved school until about third grade. Then it stopped being fun and became all about the work."

I tilt my head. "Well, that makes me sad to hear."

"Sorry. Just being honest."

I nod. "It's okay. I wish I could create a school where kids had different options to learn the same material. Then it would be fun. So many children I know would like to learn instead of dreading it. Every year, it seems as if the state rules get harder for us to teach effectively."

"What do you mean?" he asks.

"It's all about how many kids pass the standardized tests. It isn't as bad for me as some of my teacher friends who have older grades, but everything has become about the state exams. There are a lot of things kids aren't learning. If a child doesn't learn a certain way, it's hard for them. It can affect their self-esteem and create a lot of anxiety for them, too."

"That sounds like a big headache for your profession."

I can't deny it. "It can be. But I adore my students."

"I can tell you care about them. I bet your kids love you, don't they?"

I snort. "That would depend on the day."

"Oh, come on now."

"Most of the time they do," I admit.

The car stops. Liam gets out and reaches into the car to help me out. When I'm on the sidewalk, he doesn't let go of my hand. His body is a warm pillow of hard flesh, and I sink into it. He guides me inside. There are two musicians set up in the corner, singing indie music. The lights are dim compared to the daytime. He leads me to the back corner and pulls out a chair then motions for me to sit.

The server comes over. He puts two drink menus down. "Welcome. I'm Timothy, and I'll be your server. Are we looking for something alcoholic or nonalcoholic?"

"I've already had my limit tonight. Can I have an iced tea?" I reply.

"Sure. And you, sir?"

Liam hands the server the menus. "Same. Thanks."

The server leaves, and Liam refocuses on me. "Have you lived on this side of town a long time?"

"For a few years. Where do you live?"

He taps his fingers on the table. "I'm going to sound like a total loser right now."

I lean closer and tease, "Are you one of those guys who live in their parents' basement, watching porn all day and trolling social media?"

He bursts out laughing. "Not the basement. I don't know what trolling is, and I haven't seen porn in years. But I'm living with my parents until I find a new place."

"You just got back in town?"

He shifts in his seat. "Yeah. I've been gone awhile."

"Where?"

Once again, he hesitates, as if he's not sure how to answer my question. "Down south near the state border."

"What made you come back to Chicago?"

He ponders my question again. I'm not sure if Liam is an over-analyzer or uncomfortable with my questions about himself. He finally replies, "It was time. My father is teaching me everything I need to run his business. Is your family in Chicago?"

"Yes. My mom and three sisters."

"Three?"

"Yep."

"Are you close?"

"Fairly."

"Do you look alike?"

I shrug. "You can tell we're sisters."

"And your father? Is he in town, too?" he asks.

The pitch in my stomach I always get whenever I think of my father perks up. "No. I haven't seen him since I was a child. None of us have a relationship with him, and we don't want one."

Liam studies me. "His loss."

"Yep," I curtly agree.

He puts his hand on top of mine and traces my fingers. "Sorry for bringing him up, then."

Zings race up my arm. "It's all right. So you live with your mom and dad. Any siblings?"

"Nope. Just me. And I'm only at my parents' temporarily," he quickly reminds me.

I laugh. "Don't worry. I'm not judging you."

"I'm judging me," he states.

The server sets our drinks down. "Do you need anything else?"

"No, thank you," Liam says.

"Okay, great. I'll check on you later." The server leaves.

"So you're Nora and Killian's cousin?" I ask.

"Yeah. You know Killian, too?"

My cheeks heat, and I cover my face. *Why did I bring his name up?* "We've met. Nora keeps trying to play matchmaker with Killian and me."

Liam freezes. He slowly removes his hand off mine. "Have you gone out with Killian?"

"No! I don't even have his number. She keeps trying to push him on me," I blurt out.

"Well, that's going to stop," he confidently says, then sits back in his chair. He takes a sip of his iced tea.

My stomach flutters increase tenfold. He stares at me, as if I'm the only person in all of Chicago. His gaze is so piercing, I have to tear my eyes away to breathe.

"What school do you work at?" he asks.

I take a sip of the cold drink. "Freedom Elementary."

He raises his eyebrows and whistles. "That's a rough area."

I shrug. "It's the kids who need the strongest foundation. They have everything working against them. On average, less than half the kids I've taught make it past their sophomore year."

"You have kids you taught old enough to be in high school?"

I laugh. "Sure. My first few classes I taught. I'm old."

His expression fills with doubt. "How old are you?"

"Thirty-seven."

He snorts. "That isn't old."

"What about you?"

"Turned forty a few months ago."

"Ohhh. What's it feel like to be over-the-hill?"

Why am I flirting?

I need to stop and not lead him on.

Why am I even here?

Liam replies, "Freeing."

"What do you mean?"

He pinches his eyebrows together. "Nothing. So what do you do for fun?"

"Hang out with my friends. We practice yoga together on the weekends. I also like to hunt for deals and refurbish things or redecorate for next to nothing."

He leans closer. "Sounds interesting. Where do you do this 'hunting?'" He puts his fingers in quotes and wiggles his eyebrows.

"It depends on the time of the year. I shop in secondhand stores in the winter. When it warms up, I'll go to garage sales or outdoor flea markets."

"What do you do with all these things you find?"

I take another sip. The song ends, and the cafe erupts in clapping. I add my applause to be polite but have hardly listened to anything they sang. Liam is the only person I can focus on. "I resell most of the things. I have a little slush fund building."

"Wow. That's impressive."

"Not really. It's just a hobby."

He leans forward again. "Sounds to me like you're resourceful, creative, and have an entrepreneurial streak in you."

"It's just for fun."

"Still impressive."

I drink more iced tea. "So, what kind of business does your father have?"

Liam nervously shifts in his seat. His elbows are on the table. He crosses his arms and taps his biceps. The piercing looks he gave me previously are nothing compared to how he stares at me now. He lowers his voice. "Before you met Nora, did you ever hear of my family, Hailee?"

My chest tightens. All the reasons I already know I shouldn't be sitting here with him surface. I choose my words carefully so I don't insult him or say something that isn't true. "I've heard of the O'Malleys, yes."

"And what did you hear?"

Heat rises for the hundredth time tonight in my cheeks. I glance past Liam, but no one is near us. "My understanding is that the O'Malleys are a crime family."

He licks his lips and studies me. "And what do you think about that?"

"Is it true?"

He slowly nods. "Yes. But I'm working with my father and Nora's brothers to change things."

"What does that mean?"

"I'm sorry, but I can't go into details."

My heart races. I don't like what this means. If he's trying to change things, I can appreciate his effort, but it's a strong enough reason to get up and leave right now. Liam confirmed that he represents danger, and it's a risk I shouldn't take. If only I could get my feet to move.

He traces my fingers, which does nothing to motivate my body to do what I rationally should do. "Why aren't you married, Hailee?"

I sit up straighter. "Sorry?"

"You seem like a woman who would be married with ten children and a few furry animals."

I laugh. "So stereotypical."

He raises his eyebrows. "Am I wrong? Or do you have a bunch of kids and pets you aren't telling me about?"

I turn his question on him. "Why aren't you married with ten children and a few furry animals?"

He once again pauses, gathering his thoughts and making me wonder if he's an analyzer or doesn't like answering my questions. "I would have if my life had gone differently."

"Yeah, well, me, too."

He opens his mouth then shuts it.

"I should go. I have to prepare for my lessons tomorrow."

"Did I offend you?" he asks.

I shake my head. "No. I'm behind. This week has been super crazy, and I've gotten barely anything done."

"Do you need help?"

"Help?" I ask.

"Yeah. Is there anything I can do?"

I'm taken aback by his offer. "That's sweet of you, but it's all stuff I need to deal with on my own."

He rises and tosses cash on the table. "All right. I'll take you home."

"I can walk. It isn't that far."

He scrunches his face, as if I'm crazy. "No."

I roll my eyes. "Are you going to be like Adrian now?"

His face falls, and his eyes turn to slits. In a low voice, he asks, "Adrian?"

"Yeah. He wouldn't stop telling me how unsafe my neighborhood is."

His jaw clenches. "I guess I'm confused since I saw him leave with Skylar, and maybe you are all cool with that or something, but did you date Adrian?"

My head jerks back in shock. "Eww. No. He gave me a ride home from the hospital when Aspen got bit by a snake. And Skylar was with him."

Liam releases a big breath. "Good to know."

I'm not sure how to respond. I rise, and Liam puts his hand on my back and guides me out of the cafe. We get in his car, and I tell the driver my address. He drives two blocks and pulls up to my building. Liam steps out.

I get out and look up. "Thanks for the drink."

"I'll walk you inside."

I should argue. I've already spent more time with him than I should have. It's pretty clear he's interested in me, and I shouldn't give him hope. He's way outside of my comfort zone. Anything with him would be a huge risk. He even admitted his family is into bad things, yet I say nothing and let him lead me inside. Neither of us speak. The elevator opens, and the silence continues. Blood pounds between my ears. I'm more nervous than I've been in a long time. His woodsy scent fills the small area. I avoid looking at him, and I'm relieved when the door opens.

He leads me to my unit. Against the warning in my head, I consider inviting him in but find the determination not to. I unlock my door, spin, and smile. "Thanks again. It was nice meeting you."

He doesn't hesitate. "It was. Can I have your phone number?"

I bite on my lip. He cocks an eyebrow, giving me a set of puppy dog eyes. I cave. "Okay. Give me your phone."

A smile erupts on his lips. My insides quiver harder. I've never met a man who looks sexy no matter what his facial expression.

I shouldn't give it to him, but I text myself from his phone and hand it back to him.

"Thanks, Hales. I'll see you soon," he says, as if there's no way it's not happening.

"Hales?"

"No one calls you Hales?"

"No."

"Good. I will. Have a good night." He winks, turns, and I watch him stroll to the elevator and step inside. I shut my door and lock it.

What did I just do?

This is a recipe for trouble.

My phone vibrates. I remove it from my purse and look at the screen. My heart skips a beat.

Liam: *Thanks for hanging out with me tonight. It's been a long time since I met a nice woman.*

I should ignore his text and get my schoolwork done. Instead, I reply.

Me: *I haven't met anyone nice in a long time, either. Thanks.*

Liam: *Don't work too hard.*

Me: *I won't.*

Liam: *Night.*

Me: *Goodnight.*

I attempt to turn the voice in my head off; the one telling me to send him a text we can't see each other anymore. I spend the next few hours getting my work done then put on my pajamas and crawl into bed. I stare at the text conversation, and dots appear as if he's texting me. I bite on my smile, waiting to get a message, but the screen turns blank and nothing comes across.

Disappointment fills me. I shouldn't encourage him or want him to give me any attention. I toss and turn for hours. I finally fall asleep. When I wake up the next morning, I get ready and go to school.

Around noon, when my students are at recess, one of the employees who works in the office knocks on my door. I open it, and she holds out a huge bouquet of roses. She smirks. "Someone loves you."

I gape at the dozens of long-stemmed red roses.

She laughs. "Are you going to take them?"

"Oh. Sorry. Thanks."

"Sure." She hands them to me and leaves.

I go to my desk and open the small envelope. It's handwritten, and my guess is Liam personally signed it. The card reads:

Hales,

I hope you're having a great day.

Liam

My heart stammers. I gaze back at the bouquet and count seventy-seven flowers. I glance at the time and pull my phone out of my purse.

Me: *Thank you for the flowers. They're gorgeous.*

Liam: *Not as much as you.*

My heart beats faster.

Me: *Seventy-seven?*

Liam: *Yep. Your age and my age combined. I think we can be good together.*

We.

Together.

I rock in my chair, trying to think of how to reply. I avoid responding to his comment again.

Me: *Are you having a good day?*

Liam: *I am now.*

My butterflies go crazy. The bell rings, and I reply.

Me: *I have to go. The kids are coming back from recess. Thanks again.*

Liam: *Have a great rest of your day.*

I spend the rest of the day attempting to concentrate on my students, but all I can think of is Liam and wonder when I'm going to see him again. And I can't get out of my head the thought of what the seventy-seven roses represent.

3

Liam

Besides the few minutes I spent in the flower shop ordering Hailee's flowers and writing the note, my father has consumed all my time. Meetings with government officials, allies, and clan members who run different parts of our businesses have my head spinning. Every man I sit in front of looks at me the same way.

Hesitant.

Fearful.

Pissed off.

I am their future unchosen leader.

Prison taught me lots of things, but Finn always made sure he took my lessons a step further. No one knows how to read people better than him. He spent too many hours to count trying to teach me how to listen before reacting. He showed me how valuable it is to watch another man's body language and utilize the emotions in their eyes to understand their thoughts. The only thing I had while locked up was time. Finn made sure I used it well, and there's nothing I don't miss.

When I get home, it's after midnight. I stare at my phone, holding myself back from texting or calling Hailee. It's a school night. I don't want to wake or disturb her. The more I reread our text chain, the more I'm tempted to message her anyway.

I finally throw my phone in the drawer next to my bed so I can't screw it up before it begins. It only sends my mind into a further spiral.

Hailee's too good for me. I knew it the moment I laid eyes on her. I should have told her at the cafe I was in prison. The debate in my head said to let her get to know me then tell her, so she isn't scared to be around me. She was already hesitant. I could tell I made her nervous, and when the topic of my family came up, I saw how uneasy it made her.

I tried to answer her questions without lying, but I skirted around the truth. Now, I'm not sure when the right time will be or how to even tell her. Eventually, I'm going to have to come clean.

Everything in my life feels so overwhelming right now. So much has changed in fifteen years. My parents aged. I was always so relieved to see them or my cousins when they visited me in prison, I never really noticed. Now, I can't escape any part of reality.

My father's cough seems to get worse. All day long, he has fits. Sometimes there's blood. Not always, but every hack reminds me he's dying. It's bad enough I'm losing my father. Running the O'Malley clan when I'm not ready is another form of a cruel joke.

Every relative of mine, except for Killian, Nolan, and Declan, thinks I'm incapable. I see it in their eyes. I don't blame them. My father has his hands in so many different pots, I don't understand how he manages it all.

It's why I need to make sure Finn's and my plan goes off without a hitch.

The blackness in my room, I still haven't gotten used to. In prison, there was always a faint glow. I should put a nightlight in my room or something so I can sleep better, but I don't. I'm back in the real world now. Whatever I need to do to be normal again is what I'll do. Plus, nightlights are for kids, not forty-year-old men. What would I say to Hailee? "Hey, let me turn on my nightlight?"

I groan and scrub my hands over my face in frustration. The last thing I need to be thinking about is a woman or whether she's ever going to even let me touch her. I've got enough on my plate. The added anxiety popping up whenever I think about how I could even get to that place with Hailee doesn't help.

Before prison, I had plenty of girlfriends. I never worried about any of the details. I knew how to ask a girl out, take her on a hot date, and get exactly what I wanted. Now, I question everything. Anything I used to do doesn't seem good enough for Hailee. Some of the things just seem young and foolish.

I need to talk to Killian.

The only people in the world I've confided in for the past fifteen years are Finn, my father, or Killian. I had short bursts of time with everyone but Finn. I knew I would miss him, but I didn't know how much. I keep thinking about how he's still in that hellhole and I'm in a bed with a luxury pillow top mattress.

I don't sleep. At four in the morning, I throw on workout clothes and run to our family's gym. When I get there, no one else is there. I pull on boxing gloves and rotate between kicking and hitting bags.

"You're here early," Killian calls out.

Sweaty and out of breath, I turn. "Couldn't sleep."

Killian hands me a bottle of water. I take off a glove and down half of it, and he says, "Your left hook needs work."

"Get in the ring and we'll see about that."

He grunts. "Sorry. It's conditioning day. Uncle Patty is going to have me jumping rope all morning."

"Have fun with that. Hey, I wanted to ask you something."

Killian stretches his arms above his head. "What's that?"

My chest tightens. He better not say yes, or I'm not sure what I'm going to do. I'm already obsessed with her, but I also don't violate bro code. "Did you have a thing for Hailee?"

He stops moving and raises his eyebrows. "Nora's friend? The kindergarten teacher?"

"Yeah."

"No. She's hot, but she's way too innocent for my tastes. Nora wasn't happy I had Becky at her pub opening. I got an earful, but I intentionally brought her so Nora would take the hint. Why?"

I shift on my feet. "She said Nora was pushing you on her. I just wanted to double-check you weren't interested."

Killian crosses his arms. "Liam, you need to get laid. I told you, Becky has plenty of friends who are hot and will be totally into you. You're asking for trouble with Hailee."

I forget everything Finn taught me and let my emotions take over. I bark, "And why is that?"

"Did you not hear me say, innocent and kindergarten teacher? Becky's friends—"

"I don't give a shit about Becky's friends. I only needed to know if you were into her. Glad to know you aren't. Next question. What's a good place for a date these days?"

Surprise fills Killian's face. He pins his gaze on mine. "You're seriously going to pursue her?"

I angrily reply, "Yeah. You have a problem with that?"

He holds up his hands. "No. I just think you're going down a hard road."

"Yeah, well, that's my choice to make. Are you going to help me or not?" I pick up a towel and wipe the sweat off my face.

"Easy. Of course I'll help you. Find out what kind of food she likes, and I'll tell you what restaurant to go to."

I tilt my head and stare at Killian. "That's the best you've got?"

He looks at me as if I'm crazy. "What's wrong with dinner?"

"It's not very original, is it?"

"You took girls out for dinner in the past."

"Yeah, well, Hailee isn't a girl, is she?"

Killian shakes his head and sighs. He walks over to the mat and sits on it. He bends over and touches his toes. "Dinner is safe. Take her to dinner. When you realize she's way too naive for an O'Malley, you can drop her off at her door and leave it at that. I'll hook you up with one of Becky's friends."

This is going nowhere. The more Killian talks, the more pissed off I get. "Whatever. Thanks for nothing." I stomp out of the gym with Killian calling after me. I run home and shower. My phone buzzes.

Killian: *Find out what she's into and go do it. If she wants you to watch a chick flick and cry into your popcorn, just do it. If she thinks flying acrobats on trapeze are awesome, find a circus. Be you, Liam. Dating is the same as before. But just be careful. A girl like that can stomp all over you when she learns the truth about who we are.*

His message pisses me off, but I also know he's trying to watch out for me. Few people have my back.

Me: *Noted. Thanks.*

I re-read his message and Hailee's. Nothing stands out. I replay our conversation from the cafe. When I go downstairs, my mom is cooking breakfast.

"Morning," she chirps then hugs me. It's something she does every time I walk into a room. I'm not sure when she'll return to not doing it, but I don't mind, especially if it brings her some happiness when my dad is dying. "Eggs and bacon?"

"Sure." I pick up a coffee cup and fill it. The hot liquid slides down my throat, and I lean against the counter. "Mom, do you have a busy day planned?"

She puts a paper towel on a plate and adds the bacon to it. "Your father has a doctor's appointment later this afternoon. Mary Kelly and I are going to church this morning then lunch. Do you want to come?"

I snort. My mother can keep her Catholicism to herself. I already know I'm damned and there's no return. "Sorry. I've got plans."

"Oh?"

"Nothing exciting." I take the plate from her and set it on the table and sit.

My mother sets a plate of eggs and toast in front of me, and my father comes into the room. He lights up his pipe, and I try to hide my disgust. That shit is responsible for killing him, and he's still smoking it. And now I have to deal with it during my breakfast.

"Darragh, I said no smoking at the table," my mother reminds him.

He grumbles and disappears out the back door.

My mom sits next to me. I concentrate on my breakfast so I don't have to talk. I'm halfway through my plate when my father walks inside.

"Liam, I need you to go to Elgin today."

I set my fork down and look up. Elgin is about 35 miles northwest of Chicago. "Why?"

"I want you to meet with Niall and Shamus."

The hairs on my arms rise. "Erin and Nessa's husbands? Why?" Nora, Killian, Nolan, and Declan barely talk to their sisters. Their husbands aren't anyone I prefer to hang out with, either. But they also live in the city. I'm not sure why my dad wants me to go on a tour of the suburbs.

"They believe they're running the show. It's time you show up and remind them who runs this clan and who will in the future. They're at the safe house."

My stomach flips. Having to show my status in the O'Malley family isn't something I particularly enjoy. Some of my relatives I had a good relationship with prior to prison now see me as the kid who's sliding into a role he didn't earn. I can't say I blame them. Niall and Shamus are arrogant jerks. They married into the family and have always been dickheads. Now I get to remind them they aren't blood and what that means for them on the totem pole in our business. I sigh. "What time are we leaving?"

My father drinks his coffee. "I'm not going."

"What?"

"You can handle this on your own."

"Are you serious?"

"Yeah. Take Knox as your driver, and Grady, too. They'll back you up." My father bites into his toast.

I wipe my mouth and rise. I put my plate in the dishwasher and take a few deep breaths while staring at the frost on the ground.

My father clears his throat. His smoker's voice rings in my ears. "The only way to take what is yours is to demonstrate your power. If you don't, you will lose it. This is your birthright."

It's nothing new. I've always known what my role in the clan is. Not once did I think I would have to run things fresh out of the slammer and at forty. I always assumed my father would live until he was an older man, not die in his sixties.

Suck it up. There is no choice.

Finn needs to get out of jail. Then I don't have to deal with this shit from Niall and Shamus. All this crap my father is involved in that I don't care for, I can end. There is a better way. Times have changed, and I need Finn.

"Yeah, Dad, I know. Consider it handled." I leave the room and text my second cousins, Knox and Grady, to pick me up. I pace my bedroom while waiting, not wanting to get into a discussion with my father or mother.

There's a knock on the door. My mother calls out, "Liam?"

I open the door. "What's up?"

She smiles, and my gut drops. It's the face she puts on when she wants to convince me of something I don't want to do. "Are you sure you don't want to go to church first? You haven't attended since you came home. I spoke with Father Antonio. He said he could give you confession and then you'll feel more comfortable returning to mass."

I need my own place.

Stay calm. She means well.

"Mom, we've been through this. I'm not going to church or confession."

"God will forgive you if—"

"No, Mom. Don't ask me again. I need to go." I lean down and kiss her cheek, trying to avoid the disappointment in her expression. I step past her and am halfway down the stairs when my phone vibrates.

Hailee: *These made me smile when I walked into my classroom today.*

A picture of the roses I sent her follow.

Me: *Why don't you send me a picture of you?*

Another text comes in from Knox saying they're outside. I put on my coat and leave. As soon as I get in the car, another text pops up.

Hailee: *Is that your way of asking me for a dirty photo?*

My pulse increases. I stare at the phone in shock for a moment. Is this a thing I'm not aware of? Is Hailee a naughty girl?

Me: *Should I double-dog dare you since you're in school?*

A few nerve-racking minutes pass. I wonder if I sent the wrong thing, then I get a video. My dick hardens so much, I curse myself for asking. I'm going to have blue balls all day, and I've already had them for the last fifteen years.

Hailee's in a form-fitting, yellow sweater. She's at her desk, turned backward in her chair so all the kids' desks are behind her. She wiggles her eyebrows, unbuttons a few of her tiny buttons, displaying a pop of her cleavage, then moves the camera to the flowers. "Thanks again for the flowers, Liam."

Fuuuuck.

I need to figure out how to take her out.

I watch the video several times but then get antsy, wondering how to respond. I roll the divider window down. "Guys."

"Yeah?" Grady asks.

This is so embarrassing.

Deal with it. I can't afford to screw this up.

I swallow my pride. "If a woman sends you a sexy video, what do you send her back?"

"Dick pic," Knox says.

"Come on," I say, not believing them.

"Yep. Dick pic for sure," Grady affirms.

"I'm not sending her a dick pic," I say, annoyed.

"Hey, you asked. That's how it works," Knox says.

"Suit yourself. But don't ask if you don't want real answers," Grady adds.

I roll the window up. These two have to be pulling my chain. There's no way women are into that.

Me: *What do you send a woman who sends you a sexy video?*

Killian: *Dick pic.*

Me: *Are you pulling my leg?*

Killian: *No. Want to see some of the ones I've sent women?*

Me: *Fuck no.*

Killian: *Suit yourself. Of course, you'll probably be jealous.*

Me: *Guarantee you I won't.*

Killian: *What body part did she send you?*

Me: *None of your business.*

Killian: *Dude, you need to chill. I'm trying to help.*

Me: *Not discussing my woman's body parts with you.*

Killian: *She's your woman now?*

Me: *Yep. I've claimed her. Now tell me you're joking about the dick pics.*

Killian: *Nope. Women dig it. At least they do with me, but I'm hung like a horse.*

This conversation is getting me nowhere. I glance down at my groin, considering what to do. I replay the video several times.

Get some balls.

I pull up the video feature on my phone and wiggle my eyebrows the way she did. I angle the phone and undo my belt, pull down my zipper, then bring the camera back to my face. I wink and turn the video off.

I watch it, not knowing what to think but feeling like a creeper.

It's not a dick pic.

It's close.

Jesus. Why does everything have to be so different?

Me: *Please tell me now if you're lying about dick pics.*

Killian: *Bare it. But make sure you're hard first. Women don't want to see your flaccid little peter flapping in the wind.*

Me: *I'm flipping you the bird right now.*

Killian: *They have emojis for that.*

Me: *What the fuck is an emoji?*

A little yellowish-orange cartoonish thing pops up on the screen.

And now I've seen it all. Who thinks of these things?

Too much time on their hands.

I gather my courage and send the video off to Hailee. By the time I get a text back, my palms are sweating.

Hailee: *Is there sound to this? My kids are starting to come into the classroom.*

Me: *Nope.*

Several more minutes pass. I tap my hands on my thigh, glancing between the quickly passing Chicago skyline and my phone. No messages come in. We pull into the driveway of our safe house. I shove my phone in my pocket and get out. The uneasiness I always feel whenever I have to throw my weight around erupts. This is the first time I've done anything without my father next to me.

The three of us go into the house. Several of our men are there, running receipts from bets and placing others. They all look up. Some of them I haven't seen in years and are happy to see me. Others, not so much. I ask, "Where are Niall and Shamus?"

"In the office." A guy I've never met motions to the door.

I don't bother to knock. I open the door, step inside, and Knox and Grady follow.

Niall and Shamus look up from their desks. Both their eyes turn to slits. Shamus says, "What are you doing here?"

I sit in the seat across from him. Knox and Grady sit across from Niall. "Came to check in and pick up the receipts and cash."

"It's not collection day," Shamus claims, scowling.

I sit back and cross my arms. "It is now."

"What's this about, Liam?" Niall asks.

"He doesn't answer to you," Knox replies. "Now get the receipts and cash as he asked."

"I'm calling Darragh," Shamus says and pulls out his phone.

I rise. "You do that. You've got two minutes to give the receipts and cash to my cousins. If two minutes pass and I don't have them in my possession, this will be the last time you'll ever step foot in this house. Are we clear?"

"You motherfucker. Don't you come in our house—"

I lean across the desk and grab Shamus by the shirt. "Your house? This is an O'Malley house. *My* father's house. Your two minutes are running out. And if you think my father is ruthless, you have no idea what I'm capable of, so make your decision." I release him and leave. I go directly to the car and wait.

Within a few moments, Knox and Grady come out with several bags of cash and a briefcase of receipts. I pull out the ledger, and it's a mess. Dates are missing. Amounts are estimated. Nothing is in order as it should be. Those bastards are skimming off the top.

I call my father.

His smoker's voice hits my ear. "Liam, do you see why I sent you?"

"Why have you let this go on? Everything is out of order."

He chuckles then goes into a coughing fit. I hold the phone away from my ear and wait until he can speak again. "If you want men to respect you, you've gotta clean house. I left it for you to sort out. It's time everyone in the family learns what kind of ruler you are."

I close my eyes and hit my head against the back seat. Nothing ever gets past my father. Everything he does has a reason.

"Liam, take care of it. Nothing in life is free. If you want something, you have to earn it. This is your time to show the O'Malleys you're capable of leading them. Your birthright makes you my successor. If you want our men to love and trust you, you have to do what others are too scared to do." The sound of my father lighting up his pipe fills the line.

There's nothing to say except, "I'll handle it." I hang up and stare out the window. My father's words replay in my mind.

The car stops in traffic. I glance across the car and out the other window. A huge flashing neon sign reads: Flea Market. New items every week, and, Open until 9 P.M.

My father's words ring in my head again.

Stop being a pussy.

I glance at the time and roll down the divider window. "Freedom Elementary."

I pull up to Hailee's school. I watch as kids get on the busses and others walk home. I wait until it's past five and then my heart somersaults.

Hailee walks toward my car in an icy-blue peacock coat. Her long, blonde hair blows in the wind. She has a large backpack slung over her shoulder.

When she gets several feet in front of the car, I roll my blacked-out window down and call out, "Hales."

Her eyes widen. "Liam. What are you doing here?"

"Get in." I open the door and slide over.

She sets her bag on the seat then gets in. I pick it up and put it on the seat across from us. "That's heavy. What are you carrying in there?"

She smiles. "Everything. Are you going to tell me what you're doing here?"

"Taking you to the flea market."

4

Hailee

"Flea market?" I ask Liam, my pulse beating hard in my neck. I obsessed over him all night. It drove me nuts I didn't hear from him since I got the flowers. As soon as I saw them this morning, I threw caution to the wind and had to text him.

His greenish-blue eyes drill into mine. "Yep. Open until nine. New items every week. Thought you'd be into it."

My insides flutter. "Where is this at?"

"Elgin."

"You want to drive to Elgin in rush hour traffic?" I ask, still trying to contemplate a man like Liam going to a flea market with me. I've had one boyfriend who went once with me, and he complained the entire time. After that, I decided it was pointless to ask any guy to go with me. It ruined my fun and distracted me from the hunt.

He nods. "I'm free the rest of the night. Are you?" His typical fierce gaze morphs into puppy dog eyes that send my loins into overdrive. Liam's a concoction of confidence you don't want to mess with or question, but I can sometimes see a slight nervousness. I regretted sending him that video this morning because all day, I snuck peeks of his video. Several times, I got caught not paying attention and had to ask my students to repeat themselves.

Everything about him is beautiful and strong. There's also a vulnerability about him. Something seems fragile within him. I don't think the rest of the world gets to see it. I take a deep breath. "I don't have any plans. But do you want to do something else? I doubt the flea market is your thing."

His face lights up. "Nope. I'm ready to get out the camouflage and hunt."

I laugh. "Camouflage?"

"You'd look hot in some camo." Liam knocks on the window three times, and the car takes off.

Heat rises to my cheeks.

He rolls his head so his face is next to mine. "What are we going to look for?"

His woodsy scent fills the air. His face is so close to mine, my mouth waters. I'm suddenly sweltering and need to take my coat off, or I'm going to break out in a sweat from the heat of his stare and all the indecent thoughts I've had since I laid eyes on him.

I unbutton my jacket as I reply, "No idea." His eyes travel to my hands, and I freeze, thinking about the video I sent him.

What am I doing?

He's so out of my league.

Why is a bad boy taking me to a flea market?

His flaming orbs refocus on my face. "Did you have a good day?"

"Yeah. Did you?"

"I am now." He assesses me again then returns to his normally seated position.

I bite on my lip, relieved he backed off, my butterflies going so crazy, I feel slightly queasy. If he stayed that close to me, I might have done something I'd regret. My logic seems to be nonexistent around him. When I think about my lack of control to tell him it's a bad idea for us to pursue anything, it petrifies me.

Should have thought about that before I sent him that video.

I'm starting to wonder why I even need to contemplate starting something with him. That scares me even more.

He picks up my hand and studies it. My heart beats harder, and in an amused voice, he says, "Why are your fingers tinted blueish-green?"

"It was finger paint day. There was an accident." I fail to mention why it happened. I couldn't stop thinking about him and his sexy-as-sin wink and large hands unzipping his bulging pants.

"Were there any casualties?"

I wince. "Nope. Everyone survived, but little Jamar and Tamika are going to have to scrub their hair tonight."

He raises his eyebrows. "Did you have to break up a fight or something?"

"Mmm...more like they decided to be each other's art project, and I wasn't paying attention." I cringe, thinking about how I let my loins interfere with my teaching.

Liam chuckles. "Sounds like they had a fun time."

"Thank goodness it's washable. Maybe I should bring body paints to the next class," I joke.

"Body paint? Is that a thing?"

"Well, not for kids, normally. I think they call it 'adult finger painting.'"

Liam cocks an eyebrow and tilts his head. "And what does that entail?"

"You haven't heard of the latest trend?"

"Nope. Fill me in."

"Okay. They have nontoxic, edible paint you can pretty much put anywhere on your body. People pick a few colors, put it on each other, then have sex on a cotton canvas. Then they hang it in their house as a souvenir of their umm...activities." My cheeks grow hotter.

Liam stares at me with an amused expression on his face. "Have you done this?"

"No."

"Huh. And this is sold in stores?"

"I'm not sure. I saw it on the internet."

He moves his face closer to mine again. "What were you searching that you came across this?"

Every inch of my skin erupts in flames. I swallow the lump in my throat and admit, "My friends send me a lot of links to things."

"Really? What kinds of things?"

"You met them. I'm sure you can use your imagination," I quickly state.

"I'm not very imaginative. You're the creative one in this relationship. Why don't you fill me in?"

Relationship? My heart beats faster from the thought of being in a relationship with Liam. Is it even possible? The idea adds to my embarrassment of having to disclose to him anything my girlfriends texted or emailed me.

He presses. "Come on, Hales. I won't tell anyone. Your secret is safe with me. What did they send you?"

I put my hands over my face. "Ugh! Okay. Fine. I'll tell you. We kind of have this game going on."

"About?"

I turn more in my seat. "So, the four of us all try to outdo each other on the strangest things we can find. Such as toys. Or fetishes. Or comments random people make on blogs or other online forums about things they've done. Or strange things guys say to us online. It's been going on for years."

The corners of his lips turn up. "And do you then act upon these things?"

"Sometimes they do," I blurt out.

"But you don't?"

Jeez. How did I get into this conversation?

"I haven't."

"Why not?"

I skirt around the question. "Some of the stuff is kind of over the top?"

"Like what?"

"Bodily fluids. Things that should only go in the toilet."

Liam wrinkles his nose. "Good to know you're not into that. What else?"

"I don't really understand the furry animal craze."

Confusion fills his expression. "You mean beastiality?"

"No. However, that's gross, too. I'm talking about when people get dressed up in furry animal mascot costumes and have sex."

His eyebrows pierce together. "This is a legitimate thing?"

"Yeah. It's growing in popularity. You haven't come across it online?"

He hesitates then says, "No."

"Well, it's super strange to me. I can understand role-play, but the furry costume is creepy," I blurt out.

He licks his lips and stares at me.

"What?"

He scans my body. With a cocky expression, he asks, "What kind of role-play are you into, Hales?"

"I'm not!" I reply as my face burns so hot, I think I might need to crawl in a hole and never come out.

"No?" he asks, as if he's sure I am.

The truth is, I've never had anyone do anything crazy to me. The guys I date are all straitlaced, vanilla as they come. My friends are always telling me to date the bad boy, but I've never given in to the temptation.

In a teasing tone, Liam says, "So, your friends all try these things, but you never have?"

"Well, not the super-strange things. But some of the stuff they have," I admit. Time to flip this conversation off my super-boring, currently nonexistent sex life. "Why are you so interested in this? Do you have a bunch of crazy fetishes you've tried out?"

His lips twitch. Green flames glow in his eyes. "No. But I thought your naughty teacher video was pretty hot."

Jesus, help me.

I've never sent anyone a video of myself like that before. I'm still unsure why I chose to create and then send it, especially when I'm not supposed to even be in this car with him. To add to my embarrassment, I blurt out, "I've never made one of those before."

Why can't I shut my mouth today?

Satisfaction forms on Liam's face. It's swift and cocky, and I totally fall further for him. "Good. Let's keep it where I'm the only one who gets those types of videos."

Time to change the subject. "So, are you divorced, or have you always been single?"

His face hardens slightly, and I wonder if I hit a nerve. "Always single. What's been your longest relationship?"

And we're back to me. "Two years."

"What happened?"

I shrug. "My mom approved of him, so I think I stayed with him longer than I should have. He's a nice guy. We didn't really have much in common. What about you?"

The same look enters his expression. "A year."

"What happened?"

He slowly inhales. "Life." The car stops, and he looks out the window. "That was quick." He opens the door and steps out. The cold air feels good from the heat of everything—the car, the conversation, but mostly just being in his proximity. He reaches in, takes my hand, and helps me out. Like the previous night, he puts his arm around me. It's protective. It's possessive. It's the gateway of everything my independent self never thought I needed or wanted. Somehow, I don't want to ever lose this feeling, and I'm not sure how this can be possible when I just met him.

Liam guides me into the building. He leans down and murmurs in my ear, "You didn't tell me how this works. Do we negotiate or pay whatever they ask?"

Zings fly through my neck and straight to my toes. I glance up. "Always negotiate."

"Great. I'm going to watch you in action, then. Show me what you got, Hales."

I laugh. "We have to find something first."

He glances around the large space full of aisles of items. When he turns back, he drags his finger across my forehead and tucks a lock of my hair behind my ear. "Lead the way."

We spend hours looking at different items. Some things are antiques. Others are junk. No matter what booth we stop at, Liam puts in as much effort as I do. It surprises me. All night, we laugh and talk about random things.

We get to the last aisle before something catches my eye.

I grab Liam's arm and freeze.

"What?" he asks.

"Do you know what that chair is?"

He glances at the wooden structure. "Should I?"

I glance up at him. "You call yourself Irish and don't know what that is?"

"Sorry, Hales. You'll need to fill me in."

I step closer to it and run my fingers over the scratched walnut. There's no seat or back. Intricately carved cherubs, vines, and fruit dance on the headrest.

"It's broken," Liam states.

"Can I help you?" a man behind us asks.

I spin. "How much for the chair?"

"Two thousand."

Liam laughs. "No, really. How much?"

It's actually a fair price. Restored, this chair can go for over ten thousand dollars. It's an early nineteenth-century Palatial Carved Irish Throne. But I'm not paying that much.

"I'll give you two hundred dollars," I tell the man.

"For a broken chair?" Liam bursts out.

"Do you know what this is, ma'am?" the man asks.

I play dumb and give him my most naive look. "No."

"It's an antique."

"Of what?" I innocently ask.

"It's an RJ Horner."

"It's broken," Liam repeats.

The salesman pushes his glasses on his nose. "Sir, do you know who RJ Horner is?"

Liam points to where the seat and back should be. "This is a piece of carved wood right now and nothing else."

"Sir—"

"How long have you had it?" I ask.

The salesman turns to me. "A few years."

"I'll give you three hundred."

Liam whistles. "That's a lot of money for a piece of broken wood, Hales."

"Sir, this is a Horner," the salesman reiterates.

"If I pick it up, is it going to fall apart?"

"It's an antique. You should handle it with care," the man states.

"Sir, you've had it for years. How many offers have you had for it?" I ask.

He scratches his bald head. "I'll give it to you for a thousand."

"Are you delusional?" Liam asks.

"Hey! I'm in business, and I know what that chair is worth refurbished."

"But you haven't done anything with it. And no one has bought it. My final offer is five hundred dollars. Take it or leave it," I say.

"Sorry. It's worth more."

"You're crazy," Liam says.

I smile at the salesman. "Okay. Thanks for your time." I turn back to Liam. "Ready?"

He puts his arm around me and scowls at the salesman. "First rule of business: Know when to cut your losses and move on. Let's go, Hales." He guides me down the aisle.

Ten. Nine. Eight. Seven. Six.

"Wait!"

I spin. "Yes?"

"I'll take the five hundred," the salesman says.

"Great! Do you deliver?" I ask.

He nods. "Yes. Where to?"

"Chicago, near the south side."

"It'll be another hundred for the delivery fee."

"No. Hold the chair and my guys will come get it tomorrow," Liam instructs.

I look up at him. "You don't have to—"

"I need payment tonight," the salesman chimes in.

I dig into my purse, and before I can find my wallet, Liam slaps five hundred dollars in the salesman's hand.

"Liam. I can—"

He puts his finger over my lips. He addresses the salesman. "Can you wrap it up so it doesn't get any further damage, or do my guys need to bring stuff?"

"No, I'll wrap it."

"Great."

The salesman hands Liam a ticket. "It's all yours. Have your guys bring the ticket to claim it."

Liam escorts me away and leans into my ear. "That was fun. You stole it!"

I stop walking and glance up at him. "Do you know what it is?"

His eyes twinkle. "No. But he wanted two G's, and you got it for five hundred."

I laugh. "How do you know it's even worth the five hundred?"

"Because you wouldn't have offered it if you weren't sure."

"How do you know?"

"This is your thing. You're not an amateur."

"Attention, guests. We are closing in fifteen minutes. Please make any final purchases and make your way to the front of the store," a woman over the loudspeaker says.

Liam puts his arm back around me. "Let's go. I'm hungry. Are you hungry? Do you want to grab dinner?"

"Sure."

The automatic doors open, and we walk out into the cold night air. He says, "Okay. I don't know where anything is anymore, so you'll have to pick the restaurant."

"Okay. Are you picky?"

"No. Are you?"

"Not really."

We get in the car and he asks, "So why is that chair special?"

"It's an early nineteenth-century Palatial Carved Irish Throne by RJ Horner. Once I get done with it, I can sell it for over ten thousand dollars, maybe even twenty."

He puts his hand to his ear. "Sorry, can you say that again?"

"It's worth the two thousand dollars he wanted," I state.

"The broken chair?"

I laugh. "Yep."

"Wow. How do you know this?"

I shrug. "Years of hunting. My mom used to take my sisters and me when we were kids. She's the one who showed me how to refurbish and fix things."

"Fix what things?"

"Basics around my house. I can do electrical, plumbing, and all sorts of stuff," I admit.

"Seriously?"

"Yes."

He slides his arm around me. "You just became the coolest girl ever, little lamb."

No man has ever called me Hales, or little lamb, or spent time doing something I enjoyed without complaining or sulking. Liam was engaged the entire time. My resolve to stay away from him flies out the window. If this is a bad boy, I'll take him. "You were a good sport. Thanks."

"It was fun. Where do you want to go to dinner?" His phone vibrates, and he groans. "Sorry, Hales. I have to take this."

"It's okay."

"Dad—" His body stiffens. Liam's face hardens, and he stares at the ceiling. "Fine. I'm an hour away." He hangs up.

"Something wrong?"

He turns to me. "I'm sorry. Something came up with work. Can we do dinner another night?"

Disappointment fills me, but I can't be upset with him. "Sure."

He sighs. "I'm sorry, Hales."

Like many things today, I do something I normally never would. I straddle him and put my arms around his shoulders. I lightly drag my nails on the back of his neck.

Surprise registers on his face. His breathing shortens. His large, warm palm goes under my sweater and splays on my spine. He weaves his other hand through my hair.

I smile. "Thanks for surprising me."

He curls my hair around his fist. His lips are an inch from mine. "Thanks for getting in the car."

"Did you think I wouldn't?"

"I hoped you would." His gaze travels to my lips. He murmurs, "I like you, Hales." When his eyes meet mine, they're a fireball of lust mixed with vulnerability.

"I like you, too."

He tugs at my hair in a way I've only fantasized a man should do. The moment his lips hit mine, I'm a goner. It's not a gentleman's kiss. It's rough and possessive and so controlling, my breath is stolen. His hot tongue slides in my mouth, as if he's experienced a famine and I'm his first meal. His lips press hard against mine, as if he's afraid I might vanish and disappear. And I do. I melt into him and forget that we're two people.

Every moment of our kiss shows me everything I've been missing. Liam's a tidal wave, and I'm in the middle of the current, unable to escape the power of his hold over me.

One kiss leads to another. His hand slides down my back and into my pants, palming my ass. My knees sink farther, and I'm soon grinding on his hard erection.

I don't notice when the car stops until the door opens.

"Shut the door," Liam barks, and his driver obeys.

"Sorry, Hales."

"It's okay."

"No, it's not. I'll talk to him. He should knock when I'm with you."

I bite my smile. It's a bit overboard, but I find his reaction rather adorable.

He kisses me again then groans. "I have to go."

"I know." I return to his lips and several minutes pass before he pulls back. "Let me walk you upstairs."

"Okay." I roll off of him, instantly missing his arms around me.

He steps out of the car, helps me out, then leads me into the building to my unit. He kisses me outside my door. "I'll call you tomorrow, okay?"

"Sure."

He hands me my backpack and opens my door. "Lock up."

"I will."

He gives me one last kiss, pats my ass, and I go inside. After I catch my breath, I throw on my pajamas and get into bed. I watch the video he sent me several times.

There's so much about Liam that's a mystery to me. Now that I've crossed into unknown territory, I figure I should find out whatever I can about him.

I'm still smiling when I type Liam O'Malley of Chicago into the search. Every cell in my body turns cold. I sit up in bed.

At first, I think it must be a mistake. I know Liam has a dangerous vibe about him, but how can this be? One article after another pops up stating Liam O'Malley, twenty-five, convicted of second-degree murder with a sixteen-year sentence. The state tried to charge him with first-degree but at the last minute changed it to second. My insides quiver, and my mouth turns dry. Tears well in my eyes until the screen turns blurry.

It's him. He killed another man at a bar in front of all to see. His arrest photo and several from court all show a younger Liam. In one photo, Nora and her brothers are several rows behind him. She's sobbing while Liam stands and has a hardened look on his face.

What have I gotten myself into?

Why didn't he tell me?

He lied to me.

No. He didn't lie.

He didn't tell me the truth.

Some of his hesitations now make sense. A roller coaster of emotions and thoughts fly through me. And I'm so confused about how I could still want someone who did something so heinous and couldn't even tell me the truth.

5

Liam

I'M NOT SURE IF I'VE EVER FELT GIDDY BEFORE, BUT I SUDDENLY find myself a forty-year-old convicted felon who feels silly as a schoolgirl. My night with Hailee was perfect, except for my father's phone call. I hate leaving her, but I tear myself away and go.

I slide in the car with a smile plastered on my face. The interior still smells like her sugary scent. I lean my head back against the seat and close my eyes, replaying our ride to her apartment.

Jesus, that girl can kiss. She felt so good in my arms. Letting her go sucked, but maybe it's better this way. I'm not sure if we would have stopped, and I don't know what the rules for dating are anymore.

I meet my father at the building our family owns. It's an old warehouse on the outskirts of town. Many things take place here. Tonight, my father's called a meeting of the top men in the clan.

The happiness I feel fades as soon as I step inside. Dozens of men sit in chairs, including Nora's brothers. Niall and Shamus sit next to one another with nervous expressions on their faces.

My father motions for me to come to the front. When I'm next to him, he says, "It seems we have some thieves in our presence."

The room goes silent. Killian, Nolan, and Declan all send me a questioning look. They're still new to the O'Malley dealings. Our Nana made my father promise to keep them out of the business when I went to prison. Until their brother Sean was set up by the Baileys and killed by the Rossis, they took no part in our criminal activities. Sean's death changed everything. The night Killian went with the Ivanovs and took out Lorenzo Rossi and his thugs started the war. I supposed they might feel as overwhelmed or confused as I do at times. But when I look across the room, the only men I truly trust are them and my father.

"Liam discovered it. Since we know the rules, I'll step aside and let him determine what should happen."

My gut flips. Every time my father puts me on the spot, without any warning, I feel sick. I keep my scowl on my face and try not to show any surprise or weakness. In a loud, confident voice, I boom, "When a man steals from the O'Malleys, who do they take from?"

Every man in the room, including Niall and Shamus, yells out, "Our children."

"Yes. Shamus, tell me why we collect money. Does it all stay in my father's or my pocket?"

His jaw clenches. Red creeps into his cheeks. He barks out, "No. It gets split among the clan."

"Niall, what else do we do with the money?"

His hardened, brown eyes pierce into mine. He clears his throat. "We give it to members of our clan who are struggling."

"That's right. So when someone steals from us, it's not my father or me they cheat." I point around the room. "It's all of us. Your wives. Your children. Your blood."

Men shake their heads in disgust. A true O'Malley doesn't steal from the clan. Niall and Shamus married into the family. My father gave them roles based on trust. They've broken a sacred rule. My father said he's known they've been stealing for over two years. He could have dealt with this sooner, but everything he does, he thinks through. It's something I've worked on in prison with Finn. The value of me showing my power and role in this family is more significant right now than two years' worth of missed earnings.

"Raise your hand if you've accepted money from my father in the last year for a need your family had that was outside of your salary," I order.

About half the men in the room raise their hand, including Niall and Shamus.

Motherfuckers. Stealing and still coming to my father to take from our family members who needed it more.

"And who here got bonuses every quarter last year?"

The entire room raises their hands.

"Who sold something, or worked extra hours, or waited for their bonus instead of asking my father for money because you didn't want to take more from those in the clan who may need it more?"

Half the room raises their hand.

"Who is it?" my uncle Patrick, who trains Killian and anyone else who boxes, yells out.

The rest of the room erupts in the same shouts.

I put my arm in the air. "Quiet."

The room silences.

"The men responsible for this crime should step forward now, or your fate will be much worse." I cross my arms and glare in the direction of Niall and Shamus.

They stay seated, attempting not to look guilty, but it's all over their faces. If they weren't married to my cousins, they wouldn't have had such a high position in our family. They took the gift my father gave them and stomped all over it. They didn't honor our family, and now, the only way to make this right is to make sure they receive the consequences.

"Last chance," I say.

No one in the room moves. The rage I see on the faces of my family intensifies. The fear in Niall and Shamus grows, but they must still be holding on to hope that my father or I am too stupid to know what they've done.

I tap my fingers on my biceps, counting to ten in my head, giving them one last opportunity to come forward. If they do, they will live. It won't be pretty, but the clan will take some mercy on their lives. When I get to ten, they've secured their fate.

"I'm sure I'm not the only one in this room who feels ill we have thieves in our house. It gives me no pleasure to bring this forth to you. Niall and Shamus, your cowardice sealed your fate."

I don't need to say more. The men on the discipline committee jump out of their seats so fast, a few of their chairs fall. Niall and Shamus attempt to deny the allegations, but it's pointless.

The committee drags them into the next room. Over the next few hours, a blood bath occurs. Any O'Malley who has ever wanted to take a blow to them gets a chance. My father and I stand aside, watching things, never saying a word. Since I've already chosen Killian, Nolan, and Declan as my advisory team, they stand next to me with scowls on their faces. My father's team—my uncles—stands next to him or sits in chairs, too frail to be on their feet.

When morning comes, and there is no more life left in Niall and Shamus, our cleanup committee destroys any evidence the event ever occurred. They chop up their bodies and put them in a meat grinder. The disposal committee scatters their remains in Lake Michigan.

The clan will ensure their wives and children are taken care of. They may have profited from their thievery, but it's not their fault. The O'Malleys won't turn our backs on our blood.

When I finally get home, I shower and crawl into bed. I attempt to get the horror of the evening out of my head and return to the place I was when I left Hailee, but it's nearly impossible.

I try to call her. Nora's wedding is in a few days and I wanted to ask her at dinner to go with me, but I didn't get a chance. She doesn't answer. I remember she told me she had the day off work and was going to Nora's dress fitting. I finally send her a message.

Me: *Hales, I was calling to see if you want to go to Nora's wedding with me. Call me.*

A few minutes pass, and my palms sweat.

Hailee: *Sure! I'd love to!*

Yes!

Me: *Great! I'll call you tonight.*

I order two guys to pick up her chair at the flea market, and they come to the house to get the ticket. When they leave, my mom comes into the hallway and puts on her coat.

"I'm going to church. Will you go with me?" she asks again with hope in her eyes.

I sigh. "Mom, you need to stop asking me. There's no redemption for me."

She puts her hand on my arm. "Liam, Father Antonio assures me—"

"Enough, Mom!" I bark and instantly regret yelling at her when her face drops. I soften my tone. "Please, stop asking me. It's not going to happen."

She pats my arm and quietly leaves. Guilt fills me that I can't be the son she wants. And it's not just the fact I'm a felon. Last night's debacle only proves there's only one place I'm going and it's straight to Hell.

My phone rings and I answer it. "Hey, Nora."

She asks, "Where are you?"

"Home. My mom and dad went somewhere, thank God. My mom is driving me insane. I need to get my own place," I admit. I'm grateful I have a place to stay, but I need to sort my life out.

"I'm two minutes away. Can you come with me somewhere?"

"Sure. Where are we going?"

"I have a surprise for you."

I grunt. Surprises aren't my thing since going to prison. The last thing you wanted was to not know what someone was going to spring on you. "Should I be worried?"

She chirps, "No."

"Okay. I'll sit in nervous anticipation." We say our goodbyes and hang up. I wait for her with my stomach flipping. It shouldn't. Nora would never do anything bad to me, but old experiences are hard to forget.

As soon as her driver pulls into the driveway, I go outside. I slide in next to her and ask, "What's going on?"

"You'll see."

The car pulls out, and my nerves stay awake. The driver parks outside a bungalow not far from my parents'. I glance out the window. "Who lives here?"

Nora beams. "You'll see. Get out."

I chuckle. It's nice to spend time with her, especially since I don't feel like we've returned to how things used to be between us. "Anyone tell you how bossy you've gotten?"

"I'm Irish and pregnant. Don't mess with me," she jokes.

I chuckle and we get out of the car and walk to the front door. She digs in her purse, pulls out the keys, then unlocks the door.

We step inside the empty house. Outdated floral wallpaper has yellowed in several areas. Old brown carpet is the same throughout the house, and the rooms are choppy instead of an open floor plan. The kitchen has oak cabinets that are in good condition but haven't been in style for twenty years. The laminate countertops and appliances could use an upgrade. She turns to me. "This is my house I used to live in before I moved in with Boris."

I scan the room. The bones are good and it just needs someone to knock out some walls to open it up and update it. "It's nice."

"It needs some work. My brothers kept bugging me to fix some things, but I kept blowing them off. I didn't know what

I wanted to do with the design. It drove them nuts. I'm pretty sure you can utilize their skills and yours."

Confused, I ask, "What do you mean? Do you need to fix it up to sell it? It looks move-in ready to me. Unless something is going on that won't pass the inspection?"

She grabs my hand and places the key in it. "This is yours. If you want it."

Emotions overpower me, and I blink hard. I gape at her. It's the most generous offer on earth, but it's too much. As much as I want out of my parents', I don't want to take from Nora. I slowly say, "Nora, I can't take your house."

"You aren't taking it. I'm giving it to you," she insists.

I inhale sharply. "It's very kind of you, but I'm not taking your house. This is from your blood, sweat, and tears, not mine."

She acts like she didn't hear me. "The mortgage is paid off. Taxes are due twice a year and paid for the next twelve months as well as the insurance. I'll sign a quick claim deed tomorrow."

"Nora, I can't—"

"Liam, do you have somewhere else you're moving to?"

I say nothing and clench my jaw. I have no plans and don't even know how I'll get out of my parents' place. My father makes sure I have money, but I don't have a lump sum sitting in an account to buy a house, nor will I qualify for a mortgage with no work history. Plus, my father's money isn't exactly on a tax return.

She smirks. "Do you secretly love your mom nagging you all day long?"

I snort. "Nope."

She squeezes then releases my hand. "Good. Anna is a pretty amazing designer. I'm sure she'd whip up some awesome plans for you. My brothers will help you fix it up, and we've got accounts at the furniture places. Is there anything else you need that I'm forgetting?"

"Nora, it's too much," I claim, still stunned and touched she's offering me her house.

She tilts her head. "Do you know why I stopped calling you in prison?"

I snort hard and focus on the ceiling. Nora has always been the sister I never had. It hurt when our calls stopped. I attempt to keep any disappointment out of my voice. "I figured you were living your life."

"No. I didn't even know until today," she quietly claims.

I refocus on her, not understanding.

"I kept thinking Sean is dead whenever I thought about you, which didn't make sense because you were in prison. You didn't have anything to do with it. But I finally figured it out today."

I don't speak, wondering what she means.

She starts to cry, and my heart almost breaks. "It hurt. So bad. My father, Sean, Nana...I knew they weren't coming back. But you were alive, and I couldn't see you. Every day you were in hell, and there was nothing any of us could do to get you back. You were there because you did what we should have done...what I almost did, the night you shot him."

My chest tightens. "What do you mean?"

"I heard you and Killian talking. I knew what you were going to do. I took Daideó's gun. I sat in the parking lot, but I couldn't do it. I left and... it had to be only minutes before you got there. I should have been the one in prison, Liam, not you." She sobs.

I wrap my arms around her. "No. You should not have done what I did. I made the wrong decision. Not killing him but how I went about it. You used your head."

She glances up. "Take my house. I want you to have it. I saved it. I didn't know why. Boris said to sell it or keep it, and something told me not to sell it. I want you to have it."

"Nora—"

"Please. Tell me you'll take it."

I hesitate.

"Please," she begs.

I begin to cave. "Are you sure about this?"

"Yes. It will make me happy."

"Okay. Thank you." I hug her tighter and kiss the top of her head. I survey the room. "You know what's going to drive my mom crazy?"

"What?"

My grin widens. "Trying to figure out how to top this gift."

She laughs and wipes her face. "Yep."

"Seriously though. Thank you. This is beyond generous."

Her face falls, and she takes a deep breath. "There's something else I need to tell you."

A bad feeling replaces my joy. "What?"

"It might hurt you."

"I'm listening."

She hesitates.

"Tell me," I demand.

"Hailee researched you online last night. Kora is the one who responded to your text."

My heart sinks. I'm such an idiot. I forget how everything is all online nowadays. I should have come clean with Hailee at the start and not been a coward. "That's my fault. I wasn't sure how or when to tell her."

Sympathy fills Nora's face. "I'm sorry."

"Is she scared of me?"

"I'm not sure. Things got kind of heated. I think I might have gone a little Irish on them."

Despite my disappointment, my lips twitch. I can see Nora going a bit crazy. "Okay. Thanks for telling me."

She studies me.

"Why are you staring at me?"

"You really have changed, haven't you?"

I shrug. "There's only one thing I'm sure about anymore."

"What's that?"

"I'm never going back inside," I tell her, and I mean it. No matter what I do, I'm going to use my head.

We talk for a while longer and then leave. I thank her again before getting out of the car and going back inside my parents' house. I pace my bedroom, trying to figure out what to do about Hailee. Maybe it's the wrong move, but I finally decide talking face-to-face is the best thing, no matter my fate.

I have my driver drop me off at her apartment. Someone is walking out of the building, so I go directly to her unit. I knock on the door and wait.

Several minutes pass. I text her.

Me: *Nora told me what happened. Will you open the door so we can talk? I'm not going to pressure you either way, but I owe you an explanation.*

I wait another minute, and the door finally creaks open. A nervous expression fills Hailee's face. Her eyes are slightly red, and I hate myself even more.

I softly say, "Hey. Can I come in?"

She hesitates and finally steps back and opens the door more.

I restrain from touching her. I want to tug her into my arms and tell her how sorry I am, but I don't know if she's scared of me. I don't want to put her in an uncomfortable position.

She shuts the door and fidgets with her fingers, staring at me.

"Can we sit down?" I ask.

She points to the couch.

I motion for her to go first, and she does. I follow and sit on the opposite end to give her space. My insides quiver as much as they did the day I got sentenced to sixteen years in prison. I just met her and already know I don't want to lose her, but I'm not sure if the damage is repairable or not. I gather my thoughts and clear my throat. "I'm sorry I didn't tell you. I was going to, but I wasn't sure how to tell you or when."

She bites on her lip and nods.

"I tried to make sure whatever I said wasn't a lie, but I understand I left out some pretty big details and shouldn't have," I admit.

She scrunches her face and looks down. She returns to twisting her fingers in her lap.

I blurt out, "Are you scared of me, Hales?"

She pins her blue orbs on me. "Should I be?"

My stomach flips. "No. I would never hurt you or any woman. But are you?"

She slowly shakes her head. "No."

A tiny amount of relief shoots through me, but I know I'm not anywhere near where I need to be with her. "Ask me whatever you want to know, and I'll tell you."

Her lip trembles, and she turns on the couch with her knee against the back of the seat. "Okay. I read everything, and

Nora told me why you killed the man you did. Do you regret it?"

I release a breath and close my eyes for a moment, then open them and meet hers. "I'm not going to lie to you. I don't regret killing him. I'd do it again. I regret how I did it and losing fifteen years of my life."

Her face doesn't change. I'm not sure if my admission made things worse or if she's giving me any credit for being honest. My stomach never stops flipping. The ticking of the clock on the wall seems to get louder as the silence between us continues.

She finally asks, "So you would only kill him, or would you kill someone else again?"

My pulse beats so hard in my neck, I wonder if she can see it. "If someone hurt someone I love, I would tear them to shreds and destroy them."

She inhales sharply, and I curse myself for not delivering my truth more tactfully.

"You don't want me to sugarcoat things, do you?" I ask.

"No. I want the truth."

"I'm giving it to you. I know this is a lot to ask you to accept, but this is me. And I already know you're too good for me, Hales. You're a good person, and I'm not. But I will always be the best person I can be when it comes to you. If anyone tries to hurt you, they'll pay."

She swallows hard. "Liam, I spent the first few years of my life in a violent household. My father..." She turns away from me and wipes her face. Several minutes pass, and I continue to hold myself back from invading her personal space. She finally looks at me. "He's in prison for murder. My mom fled with us in the middle of the night. She lived in fear of him finding us for years. This…this is a lot for me to accept."

My heart sinks for her and what she's been through but also for what she's telling me. I already knew it was a lot, but this extra bit of information is a spear driving our truths deeper into my heart. "I like you. A lot. I want to get past this, but I know I can't make you okay with it."

She keeps blinking, and her lips quiver like her voice. "I like you, too, but I just..." She shuts her eyes. "I don't know if I can do this with you."

Panic, hurt, and the inability to breathe annihilates me. They are words I didn't want to hear, but I knew before I came over it could be my reality. But, she also didn't say for sure she couldn't be with me, so I hang on to any amount of hope left. "I understand."

"I'm sorry about the text. I didn't—"

"Hales, you don't need to apologize. I'm the one who screwed up. I should have told you. I just didn't know how. I didn't expect to meet you, and I didn't have a plan. I'm sorry. If you want to go to the wedding with me, then I want to take you. If you can't, I understand."

She takes a shaky breath. "I want to, but I just don't know if I can, Liam."

The clawing at my heart intensifies. "Fair enough. Why don't I give you time to think it over, and you can tell me when you decide?"

"Is that fair to you? Don't you want to ask someone else if I say no?"

I shake my head. "No. I'm not interested in anyone else. But if you already had a date or bring someone else, I'll deal with it."

"I wasn't bringing anyone."

I don't have a right to be relieved, but I am. The thought of seeing anyone else with Hailee makes my blood boil. "Okay. I hope you decide to come with me, but if not, I understand."

"When do you need to know? The wedding is only a few days away."

"There's no time frame. Whenever you're comfortable."

"Are you sure?"

"Yes. If there's anything I'm sure about right now, it's that I want you in my life. So if you need time, I'll give it to you."

She looks away again, and tears fall down her cheeks.

I slide over and tug her into me. I shouldn't touch her, but I can't handle watching her cry anymore. Her entire body shakes, and she whispers, "I'm sorry."

"Shh. Stop saying that." I stroke her hair and kiss the top of her head, wanting to make everything terrible between us go away but clueless about how to do it.

She retreats and wipes her face.

I rise. "I'm going to go now. If you have any other questions, call or text me."

"Okay. Thank you." She walks me to the door.

I want to kiss her—it could be my last opportunity—but I don't. There's nothing else I can do. My past and future are unavoidable. The notion I could ever have her, and she'd be okay with it, was reaching for the stars. Giving her space to figure out if she can accept me is the only avenue I see.

As I walk out of her apartment, I can't shake the growing pit in my gut. I'm asking for her to accept too much. It's a request I struggle with, and if I haven't figured out how to deal with things, how is it fair for me to ask her to embrace all that I am and all that I will become?

6

Hailee

Since Liam left my apartment, I haven't talked to him. He hasn't texted or called me. I'm relieved. Every second I'm not teaching, I think of him and what I should do.

The day of the wedding arrives. I haven't given him an answer. Every ounce of me wants Liam. I've never felt a pull to any man as much as I feel toward him. Yet, I can't seem to tell him I'll go to the wedding with him. I'm still processing how to accept all he admitted to me.

I go through the motions and get ready for the wedding. I pace my apartment, still torn. I've ignored my friend's calls and texts. The day of Nora's wedding dress fitting, I lied to them. I told them I hadn't gone out with Liam and don't know why. But if I talk to them, I'm going to admit I did spend time with him. All these feelings I can't seem to get rid of I'll blurt out, and I'm not sure I can handle that right now.

My phone rings, and I stare at the screen. *Liam.* My stomach flips. I answer. "Hi. I'm sorry. I—"

"Hales, my car's outside. I'm not in it. My driver will bring you to the wedding, no strings attached," Liam says.

I go to the window and stare down at the street. His black sedan is next to the curb.

"I ummm..." I blow out a big breath of air.

"It's okay. You don't have to say it. And I don't want you to feel strange around me, either, okay? I have to go. If you want to save a dance for me, that's cool. No pressure either way. Bye." He hangs up, and I wipe the tear falling down my cheek.

Why does he have to be so sweet?

I go into the bathroom and touch up my makeup then leave my apartment. I step out of my building, and Liam's driver gets out and opens the door for me. As soon as I slide in the car, I smell him. It makes everything hurt all over again. I hardly know him, and I miss every piece of him I got to know.

He's a murderer, and he said he'd do it again in the future.

But he won't ever hurt me. No matter what, I know this in my heart.

Did my mother think this about my father?

Jeez. The last thing I need is to hear her opinion on this.

Even if he never hurts me, killing is still wrong.

The debate continues, and I arrive at the church. I avoid my friends and Nora. I can't deal with anyone right now, so I take a seat. My insides are a shaking mess. I suddenly question why I came and didn't just stay home.

The wedding is supposed to start at noon but time passes. I get antsy. The church is full, but I've seen no one I know. Kora slides into the pew next to me, and Skylar steps over me to sit on my other side. Boris's brothers appear on the altar. "Hey," I say, surprisingly relieved to see them.

They both put their arms around me. Kora says, "We've missed you."

I smile. It's time to put our little altercation aside. They shouldn't have taken my phone and texted Liam I would go to the wedding with him, but they didn't mean any harm. "I missed you, too," I admit.

Music starts. Boris arrives at the altar. Adrian appears and sits next to Skylar. I glance toward the O'Malley side, and Liam is staring at me.

Holy hail Mary!

He's stunning in his tux. The same intense look he gave me the night he stared me down in the pub is on his face. He offers me a small smile, and I return one. My heart beats so hard in my chest, I think it might burst. The music changes, and everyone stands.

I rise and attempt to look at Nora, but I can't help locking eyes with Liam again. He's a few rows in front of me, so I try to concentrate on the wedding, but all I see are his broad shoulders and thick chestnut hair.

When the wedding is over, they dismiss us by rows. He

leaves first, and when I get to the back of the church, he's waiting. "You look beautiful, Hales."

My flutters spark to life. "Thanks. You look really nice, too."

"Can I give you a ride to the reception?" He gives me his puppy dog eyes, and my heart melts. I'm unable to tell him no.

"Okay."

He puts his arm around me and guides me through a side door, to avoid the crowd, and directly into his car.

Uncomfortable silence fills the air. The scent of him alone makes me hot. Liam O'Malley, in a tux, staring at me like he wants to eat me up, makes me squirm in my seat.

He finally breaks the silence. "Thanks for getting me out of there."

I softly laugh, partly due to nerves. "You don't like crowds, do you?"

"More like my mother and church."

I raise my eyebrow. "You don't believe in God?"

"Quite the opposite. I'm an O'Malley. We're Catholic. I fully understand my place in Hell. No amount of confession will save me no matter what Father Antonio tells my mother," he states, staring out the window.

My chest tightens. "I'm Catholic, too. My mom used to make us go to church when I was a child, but I don't anymore."

He turns to me. "Then you understand why my mother's wishes aren't realistic."

"I never really understood confession, to be honest," I admit.

He studies me, opens his mouth, then closes it.

"Say whatever you want, Liam."

He places his hand on top of mine. "It's good to see you."

"It's good to see you, too."

Lines form on his forehead. He hesitates, swallows, then licks his lips. "Should I keep hoping you need more time and will be okay with my situation, or did you already decide there's no way you can see me again?"

My stomach flips. "I don't want to lead you on, Liam."

His face falls and he clenches his jaw. "Meaning you already made up your mind?"

"No. But I can't tell you I'll get there and—"

He puts his finger over my lips. I gasp from the spark it ignites through my body and right into my soul. "I'll wait. As long as it takes, I'll give you. If you tell me no, I'll accept it. But if any part of you is still contemplating it, I'll wait."

The car stops, and he removes his finger from my lips. I stay silent, wishing he would be a jerk and give me a reason to hate him.

Hope fills his expression. "What if we hang out tonight and don't call this anything? Just two friends at a wedding together? Would that be okay?"

My eyes fill with tears. I wish this weren't so hard. I wish I could get past things. I wish he didn't have to be so kind and charming, or wasn't the sexiest man I've ever laid eyes on. I wish I didn't feel such a strong connection to him. It would make everything clearer. I nod. If I speak, I'm going to lose it, and I'm trying to hold it together.

He picks my hand up and kisses it. "Thanks."

I'm unable to tell him I can accept him, and he's thanking me.

What the hell is wrong with me?

It doesn't erase the situation.

He opens the door and helps me out. Within seconds, he's escorting me through a sea of people, confident, strong, so protective, I can't help but love every minute of it.

Since Nora's pregnant, she wanted the reception right after the wedding so she wasn't too tired. She had Anna help her design it, and the room looks like you're outside under the stars. Liam escorts me everywhere, never once leaving my side. I'm grateful, since all my friends have their men. He introduces me to every person we come across.

After dinner, I need to use the restroom. I come out of the bathroom and freeze. Liam's back is toward me. A woman with long red hair, a killer body, and perfect-looking everything is in front of him. She reaches for his bicep, and he shrugs out of her grasp.

"Don't touch me, Megan," he seethes.

"You don't have to be so upset. I didn't know you were out—"

"What would it matter?"

"Liam, I know I didn't handle things the right way. We were young," she claims.

"We were engaged. You agreed to marry me. I was still in the county jail, waiting for my trial, when you got with Danny," Liam accuses.

My pulse increases. *He was engaged to this woman?*

"I know. But everyone makes mistakes. And Danny and I aren't doing well. It's because I never forgot you. Now that you're out, we can start where we left off. I'll leave him and—"

"Are you out of your mind? You fucked my cousin within a month of me getting arrested. You've been with him this entire time. Now you're going to leave him?"

There's a lurch in my stomach. How could this woman be so cruel? No matter how old they were or what Liam did, she was going to marry him. If she loved him, she wouldn't have run to his cousin within a month. And I know how Liam feels about dating his friends' past girlfriends. I can't imagine how badly he had to hurt during an already-difficult time.

She puts her hand on his cheek, and I almost throw up in my mouth. She claims again, "Liam, we can start fresh."

He grabs her wrist and holds it away from him. "Don't ever touch me again. You were with me for my place in my family. You never loved me. I won't be stupid twice."

"I did love you."

He releases her. "Get away from me, Megan. Don't ever talk to me or expect anything from me. There's nothing from you I want. When you see me at family events, you better avoid me like the plague."

"Liam, please. Listen to me." She steps closer and lowers her voice so I can't hear.

Screw this.

I slide between them and reach for Liam's face. It's hot from his anger. He glances down at me, and all I see in his eyes are years of pain and betrayal.

"Excuse me, we were talking," Megan says.

"Hey, baby. I'm ready for my kiss now," I tell him.

Surprise enters his eyes. I swallow and stand on my tippy-toes until my lips are on his.

His one hand palms my ass. The other slides to the back of my head and tugs at my hair. The throbbing in my lower body intensifies as his mouth ravishes mine.

He spins me against the wall and tongue fucks me while pressing his hard erection into my stomach. I barely hear Megan spit out a few nasty words and leave.

"What are you doing to me, Hales?" he murmurs and sticks his tongue back in my mouth.

I whimper and pull him closer, unable to stop, or let go, or continue to ponder if we should or shouldn't be together. Everything hits me at once. I've always played it safe. It's never made me happy. When I'm with Liam, I feel alive. I'm taken care of and his priority. And I've never been with any man who's so fiercely loyal or kindhearted.

"Hales—"

"Take me home, Liam."

He retreats an inch from my face and stares at me. The green in his eyes flares against the brown.

My veins pulse with my blood. I add, "Come with me and stay the night."

He pushes a wisp of hair off my cheek. The pounding of our hearts beat against the other. His warm flesh presses deliciously into mine. The corners of his mouth slightly curve. "Do you want to dance first?"

"Not unless we're both naked."

He grins and pecks me on the lips. "Whatever you want, little lamb."

7

Liam

"Hales, I have to stop at the store," I tell her then dive back into her delicious mouth.

"Why?" she mumbles then pulls my bowtie.

I groan as she grinds her wet heat on my cock. I bunched her dress to her waist earlier. Her bare ass is as smooth as a baby's bottom. I squeeze her cheeks, happy she wore a thong. "I have to get condoms, unless you have them."

She freezes. "Umm...did anything happen to you in prison?"

"Hell no!" I growl.

She winces. "Sorry. Umm...have you had sex since you got out?"

"No."

"So you're clean?"

"Yeah."

"Okay. Well, so am I, and I'm on the pill."

My dick gets harder. "What are you saying, Hales? Be very clear."

She arches an eyebrow. "Do you want to skip the condom?"

"Fuck yes," I tell her as I fist her hair and tug it back, feasting on the soft skin of her neck. "I think you're my dream woman, little lamb."

She softly laughs and massages my scalp. Everything about her causes sensory overload. Her sugary smell makes me think of fresh-baked cookies. It's a smell I missed and forgot about over the last fifteen years. And it makes me so goddamn hungry for her. Every touch she gives me creates a buzzing euphoria that reaches into my bones. The look in her eyes—finally confident that she wants me—is so powerful, it could make me come on the spot. Every time she whimpers in my mouth or ear, I have to remind myself to wait until we get to her place to do what I've been dying to do since we met. If she didn't taste so damn good, it might make it easier for me, but her mouth and skin have me dying to taste every inch of her.

The car stops, and I don't realize we're at her place until my driver knocks on the door. It's a mistake they made once and never will again. When Hailee's with me, they'll make sure they don't ever get a glimpse of any part of my woman or our private time.

"We're here," I mumble into her mouth. I slide my finger over the slit of her ass.

"Mmm. It's not that far, right?" She circles her hips on my cock. The heat penetrates through my pants, and I say a prayer I don't come too early and disappoint her. Then my stomach flips with nerves.

Fuck. I haven't done this in fifteen years.

Get out of the car. The break will be good.

"Hales, if you don't get your hot little body off me, I'm going to sling you over my shoulder and carry you through the building."

She laughs again. God, I love listening to it. All I want to do is prove to her I'll be the man she needs and deserves even though I'm flawed beyond redemption.

She drags her finger over my pants and presses on my shaft. "If you do that, I'll have to mark your behavior chart."

I pull back and arch an eyebrow. "My behavior chart?"

She bats her eyelashes. "Mmhmm. Then you won't get to choose your prize from the treat box."

"What's in this treat box?"

She wags her finger in the air and tsks. "You have to earn it to see what's in it."

I roll her off me and lunge over her so I'm straddling her. I pull her dress down over her hips. "Upstairs. Now."

Her blue eyes twinkle. She swallows hard and traces my lips. "You're so bossy."

"If you don't get that sexy ass of yours upstairs, you're going to be embarrassed when you see my driver next."

"Oh? Why is that?"

I lick her bottom lip and pull away when she tries to kiss me. "Because of how loud you're going to get."

She pushes her face closer to mine. "Who says I'm a screamer?"

"Oh, you're a screamer, little lamb. At least with me, you will be."

"Is that a challenge?"

The cockiness I used to have with women, that I haven't felt in years, returns. It feels good. "Yeah. When I prove to be right, you're going to wake me up tomorrow with those plump lips and sinful tongue of yours on my cock."

She smirks. "Who said I won't have them on it tonight?"

Fuuuck.

Nope. I'll come and it'll be all over.

"Your mouth isn't touching my dick until I've been inside your tight little pussy."

She widens her eyes and gives me an innocent expression. "Who says I'm tight? You haven't touched me yet. Do you want me to spread my legs so you can check me out?"

Jesus, I love this woman.

I grunt and lean into her ear. "I'm huge, sweetheart. I've seen more dicks in the last fifteen years than you'll ever see, and they don't compare. I already know you're a good girl, but when you take me, and you'll take all of me, there isn't going to be any room left inside you."

She inhales sharply but recovers quickly. "I hope you aren't all talk, big daddy. My pussy is going to be disappointed if you don't slam it hard into me."

What the...?

Fuuuuck!

I roll off her, open the door, and get out. I reach in for her, quickly guide her into the building, then return to making out with her in the elevator.

So much for the cock break.

When we get to her front door, she fumbles with the lock. As soon as we get it open and step inside, I pick her up and throw her over my shoulder.

"Liam!" She laughs and smacks my ass.

I shut and lock the door, pull her dress up, and bite her ass cheek. The scent of her arousal fills my nostrils, and I about lose it.

She shrieks.

I smack my hand over where I bit and then rub it, walking toward where I assume the bedroom is.

She slaps my ass again, so I stop and bite her, then suck on the spot until she has a red mark. "If you smack me again, I'm going to tie you up so you can't move."

She freezes, and I continue toward the bedroom door. I step toward her bed when she smacks my ass even harder.

I toss her on the bed and lunge over her. "I warned you, little lamb."

Blue flames flare in her orbs. She breathily says, "Do it."

I pause, shocked once again by this woman everyone thinks is too innocent. "You like to be tied up?"

She shakes her head. "I don't know. Do it and let's find out."

The fact no one's ever done this with her makes me harder. My little lamb's going to be mine. Restrained for me to do whatever I want to her.

I pull her up to her feet then spin her around. Her hair is pure silk. I move it to the side, slowly unzip her dress, and kiss her neck. "I'm going to go sit in the chair, and you're going to strip for me."

She reaches for my thighs and grips them. Her tongue slides across her lips, and she turns her head. "Then will you tie me up?"

I tug her hair, kiss her lips, and move my hand to her sex. "I'm going to stare at your naked body until you blush. Then I'm going to tie you up and eat that tasty pussy of yours until you can't handle it anymore."

Her eyes flutter shut, and she takes a few short breaths. "Liam, go sit in my chair."

I take off my tux jacket and drop my pants so I'm only in my boxers. It's so hot in here, I might need to crack the window in the middle of winter. I sit in her chair and wait.

She does something on her phone, and music comes on. I have no idea what song it is, but it's some sexy hip-hop. Or maybe it's only sexy since she's moving to it and slowly sliding her black dress down her body.

When her dress is on the floor, she spins and leans over the bed. She puts her hands on the mattress, turns her head, and pins her gaze on me, then circles her ass in the air. I move my hand to my cock, lightly stroking it through my boxers, watching as she rises and slowly slides the sides of her thong down to the ground. She tosses them to me. I sniff them while never taking my eyes off her, groaning in anticipation.

"You're sexy as hell, little lamb," I tell her.

She gives me a sultry smile, removes her bra, then drops it on the ground and saunters over to me, swaying her hips. Her eyes drift to my cock, and she pulls the bow tie out of my collar. She holds it in front of me. "Use this. To tie me up."

I snatch it out of her hand and pat my thighs. "Come here."

She straddles me. I drag my finger over her breasts. She shudders and her nipples turn hard. "You're gorgeous, Hales. Every inch of you is perfect."

She leans closer, and I spend the next few minutes licking and sucking her chest until she's writhing and grinding her wet heat on my swollen cock. I lean up and kiss her then carry her over to the bed.

The iron headboard is in a crisscross pattern. It goes all the way to the ceiling and has numerous bars to tie her to. The four wooden posters are another avenue to restrain her. "If I didn't know any better, I'd say you chose this bed so you could be tied up, little lamb."

Her face heats. She chokes out in a raspy voice, "Please, Liam."

My dick twitches every time she says my name. "Remove my clothes."

Her hands slide up my shirt and tremble slightly as she unfastens my buttons. She kisses my chest as she finishes then slides the material over my shoulders. She releases my boxers.

She glances down at me and swallows hard then gapes at me.

"I wasn't lying, little lamb. Now get on the bed and face the headboard. I'm going to relax you real good so you're ready for all of me."

She takes a deep breath, pecks me on the lips, then does as I ask. I get behind her, take the bowtie, and weave it through the top of the headboard. "Hands clasped together above your head."

She obeys, and I secure her wrists. I lean into her ear, take a nibble, and murmur, "I think naughty teachers need some discipline, don't you?"

"Yes. Please. I've been so naughty."

Jesus. She's so into this.

"You'll watch me the entire time. If you close your eyes or look up, I'm going to stop. I'll slide you off my face, and you won't feel my tongue back on your pussy all night. Understand?"

"Yes. Liam?" She turns to look at me.

"Yeah?"

"You already feel so good next to me."

I groan and kiss her. "Yeah. You're heaven on a platter, little lamb." I twist her hair and tie it so it's not in her face. I want to see her breasts and face as I feast on her. I kiss the curve of her neck and down her spine.

"Liam," she whispers.

I get to her ass and kiss each cheek then shove my arms between her legs and spread them open until there's no slack and she's stretched as far as she can go.

I turn on my back and slide under her. I inhale her scent as deep into my lungs as I can and glance up.

Her blue eyes are heavy with desperate need. I stick my tongue out. In slow motion, I touch the tip of my tongue to her clit and roll it.

She gasps and her mouth forms an O.

I lazily stroke through her, witnessing every change in her expression.

"Liam," she whispers again, her face flushed with heat.

It's been so long since I've had a woman anywhere near me, much less on top of me, riding my face. But I don't ever remember anyone tasting this good or looking as sexy as she does.

I slip my tongue inside her tight channel. Every time she clenches her walls against me, I smack her ass.

She grinds on my face and fingers as I rotate what is in her and on her. Her skin becomes dewy. Her clit throbs in my mouth. Her moans and pleas and cries get louder.

When she comes, her face is the most beautiful thing I've ever witnessed. She comes down from her orgasm and tries to lift her body away from me, but I hold her down.

Then I show her how an O'Malley really eats out a woman.

"Liam! Fuck!" she screams as I lick, suck, and bite like a starving beast. But that's me. I'm a depraved soul who's been starved and deprived all these years, and she's going to take every ounce of me, whether it's my mouth, fingers, or cock.

"Li-am!" Her voice shakes so much, she barely gets it out. Tears drip out of her eyes and land on my forehead, mixing with my sweat.

I clamp down on her, and she screams, then squirts her juices all over my chest. It's only then that I stop. She's still looking at me, trying to catch her breath, her cheeks as red as a tomato. Her body is lithe and shaking.

I kiss the insides of her thighs and slide out from under her then push her knees together. My skin presses against hers, and she whimpers. I shimmy my hands up her arms and kiss her neck. "You did good, little lamb. Now, be the naughty girl you are and ride my cock this time."

She turns her head, and I slide my tongue in her mouth. She hungrily kisses me back. I retreat, and in a quick motion, I grab her hips and spin her. A large gasp fills the air.

I meet her eyes. "You didn't think I was going to let you stare at a headboard the first time I shoved my cock in you, did you?"

Her lips twitch, and her hot breath merges with mine.

I kiss her swollen lips then arrogantly demand, "You got me dirty. Lick me clean."

She arches an eyebrow.

I give her one back then glance at my chest and back at her.

She smirks then bends as far as the restraint will allow her, and licks my chest, moaning, as if it's the best meal she's ever had.

I weave my hands in her hair and tug her head back. Fire flares in her eyes. "My body needs you, little lamb." I don't release her hair, yet she lifts her hips and inches onto me.

Her wet heat almost annihilates me. It's the kingdom of heaven every good Catholic is striving to end up in. If I died right now, I'd be a happy man, and she's barely past my cap.

"You got more to go, Hales. Get my cock in you, or I'm going to do it for you."

She stops moving and swallows. "Do it."

I groan. She's a temptress disguised as an angel because I'm sure she works for the devil. I grab her hips and, like the greedy son of a bitch I am, shove her down until her tight, wet, heat sheathes my cock and her body hits my pelvis.

"Oh God!" she screams, her lips trembling. Her back arches and arms attempt to move.

I stroke her hair and put my lips next to hers. "Shhh." I kiss her, letting her adjust around me, and try to regain control of my erection so I don't come too soon.

Like every kiss she gives me, it's an intoxicating hunger that makes me feel like a needed man. It doesn't take long before she rocks on me, moaning in my mouth.

"You feel so good, Hales. Just like that. Don't stop," I order her. I glide my tongue against hers and slide my hand up her arm.

"Oh God. Liam..." she pants and moves faster on me.

I release the tie from the headboard and lace my fingers through hers, keeping them as straight in the air as possible.

She squeezes my hands, and a riptide of tremors rolls through her.

"Liam," she barely gets out as her blue eyes roll.

My balls tighten. My toes curl, and adrenaline begins to pool in my cells. I give her a chaste kiss. Sweat rolls down our skin.

I move her hands over my head and grab her hips then thrust her over me faster as she screams.

Her walls clench on my shaft so tightly, I violently pump my seed into her.

"Fuuuuck! Hales!" I growl.

She clings to me, and I tighten my arms around her as we try to catch our breath. Minutes pass. She slowly pulls her head away from my neck.

I stare at her. My beautiful, red-faced, blue-eyed, perfect little lamb.

She slides her hands over my cheeks and kisses me. For the first time since going to prison, I finally feel like I'm home.

8

Hailee

Liam's hands slide through my hair and grip my head. He mutters, "Jesus, little lamb." He opens his eyes, breathing harder. He pins his gaze on me, and I smirk at him, with my mouth full of his hard cock.

It's not an easy thing to do. He wasn't exaggerating about his size. And a bet is a bet. Liam O'Malley turned me into a screamer. All night, he continued to keep me in O town. My voice might be gone for all I know. And I'm loving every minute of waking him up this way. It's as if he flipped a switch in me, and anything I've ever thought about doing, I'm able to act out with him. I've never been vocal about sex. Not once have I ever begged a man or had anything near the amazing sex we had all night. Prior to Liam, I thought all those things were wives' tales. I assumed my friends were overstating how good it could be. And I've never felt comfortable talking dirty or being so confident in the bedroom.

I'm finding it rather freeing. I want to explore every part of Liam, and I want to make him feel what he does to me. I squeeze his balls, run my tongue over his cap, then deep throat him while controlling my gag reflex.

"Fuuuck." His fingers twitch on my scalp, as if he's trying to control himself from pushing me down on him.

I place my hands over his and push my face toward his pelvis, and he groans. "You're my dream girl, Hales," he says, which he said several times last night. Flutters fill my gut again, and I moan as his pre-cum hits my tongue.

He reaches for my armpits, flips me on the bed, and cages his hard flesh over me. My heart thumps hard in my chest as green heat flares in his eyes, focused on me. "Morning." His tongue becomes a sword, aggressively attacking my mouth. Tingles erupt under his fingers as he drags them on the side of my torso. My legs have a life of their own and instantly spread to take him in. His hand goes under my thigh, and he shoves it up, then sinks his erection in me.

"Liam!" I cry out and dig my nails into his shoulders.

"Shh," he whispers, fisting my hair harder. He returns to ravaging my mouth and begins thrusting.

Heat consumes me. His body fills mine, and I'm no longer my own person. It's Liam and me, bodies so perfectly in sync, I wonder how we ever survived without the other.

"Harder. Split me in two," I taunt him, wanting something I never knew existed before he consumed me.

He groans, then slams into me, over and over, while I shudder with every delicious assault. His lips and teeth travel along my neck. He mumbles, "You naughty little lamb."

"Oh God! Oh God! Oh God! Oh God!" I scream so loud, the neighbors can probably hear it. A tidal wave of adrenaline rolls through me, and I claw at Liam's back. My eyes roll, sweat coats my skin, and he bites the pulse in my neck.

White light fills my vision when he growls, "Hales!"

His erection swells, pumping viciously, and all hell breaks loose in my body again. He collapses over me, keeping his body weight on his forearms and knees, and buries his head into the curve of my neck. His hot breath beats onto my wet skin.

My body continues to quiver beneath him. I slowly inhale more oxygen. I don't release him and kiss his dewy forehead.

He glances up, gives me a chaste kiss, then rolls off me. His strong arms slide under me, and he tugs me against his chest. My stomach growls, and he chuckles. "I think I need to feed you. Should we go to breakfast?"

"Okay. There's—"

A loud ring cuts me off. He groans and reaches for his phone. "I have to take this."

"No problem. I'm going to shower."

He hits a button, kisses me on the forehead, and answers. "Dad. What's going on?"

I rise, he slaps my ass, and I jump. I glance back, and he winks. My heart skips a beat. Everything about Liam is sexy.

I check out his perfectly sculpted torso for a moment then tear my eyes off him. I go into the bathroom and turn on my shower.

Once the water turns warm, I step in. I'm finishing rinsing the shampoo out of my hair when Liam sneaks in behind me. I jump when he slides his arms around me.

He chuckles. "Sorry to scare you."

I spin. He's beaming. "Why do you appear extra happy right now?"

His grin widens. "Two reasons. One, I'm in a shower with you. Two, my cousin Finn is coming home tomorrow."

"Where's he at?"

His face drops. "He's in the same prison I was."

My pulse increases. "Oh. Umm...was he there with you for a long time?"

"He's been there longer than I was. I wouldn't have survived if it weren't for him."

I swallow the lump in my throat. I force a smile. "Congratulations. I'm sure you've missed him."

He nods and tugs my hair. He dips down to my face. "I have. But you don't need to be scared of him. Finn's like me. He would never hurt you or any woman."

I release a breath I didn't know I was holding. "I'm sorry. I didn't mean—"

"Hales, it's okay."

I bite on my lip.

Liam scans my face. The longer he stares at me, the more nervous I become. He finally says, "I'm going to promise you something. I want you to understand that my word means everything to me."

"Okay."

He traces my jawline. "If we're ever around anyone who I don't trust, I'll tell you. But there are only a few people I would entrust with your life without thinking twice. Finn is one of them. Nora's brothers and the Ivanovs are the others. If anyone ever tries to harm you, I'll kill them."

My chest tightens. I have mixed feelings about Liam's vow to me. Part of me loves how he will protect me. Another voice in my head won't shut up about how murder is wrong. "Liam, I don't want you doing something that will have you back in jail."

His eyes darken. I get a chill from how cold they become. "I'm never going back there, little lamb. No matter what, I'll never be stupid like I was before."

"What do you mean?" I blurt out.

"I'm not the same person. I won't make dumb mistakes." He pecks my lips. "Can we stop at my parents' so I can get fresh clothes before breakfast?"

"Sure."

He assesses me again. Nervousness fills his expression. "Are you rethinking us right now?"

"No. I just...I'm getting used to things."

He swallows hard. "You still haven't come to terms with who I am, have you?"

How do I answer such a loaded question?

He shuts his eyes then opens them while releasing a breath. "Am I going to get a call or text when I'm not with you that you can't accept this?"

I slide my hands up his chest and into his hair. There's no thought or analysis. "No. I'm not trying to make you feel bad, either, Liam."

"I didn't say you were."

The pounding of water on the tile is the only sound. We don't tear our eyes off the other, each lost in our own thoughts and worries. I wish it could be easy to accept Liam's truth and move on. At this point, I have to find a way. I've already stepped into the forbidden zone, and there's no going back.

"I don't want to lose you, Hales."

His words and vulnerability affect me. I've been with weaker men who can't tell me what they want or how they feel. If you saw Liam on the street, you would guess he'd be unable to express himself, like those men. But he isn't. Not with me. And I know in my heart it isn't a side he shows everyone. I tease, "Am I a keeper since I kept my end of the deal and showed you my blow job skills?"

His lips twitch. "Remind me to make that bet again in the future."

"I knew it!"

He kisses me lightly on the lips. "It's everything about you."

"Stop worrying. I already made my choice, and I chose you." It comes out confident and strong. The voice in my head nagging me about morals I bury deep for the time being. "Let's finish and get dressed. I'm hungry from all the calories I burned all night."

He wiggles his eyebrows. "I can work you out later if you want to burn some more."

I laugh. "If you don't get any bad marks on your behavior chart, maybe you'll get rewarded."

"Does this include the treat box?"

"Maybe," I chirp.

He kisses me again then we finish our shower and get dressed. He puts his pants and dress shirt back on and leaves the top few buttons unfastened.

I hold out the tie. "Can we keep this?"

He snatches it from my hand. "Maybe I'll make a special treat box for you."

"Ooh. Getting creative, are you?"

He winks, and his phone buzzes. He glances at it. "My driver's here."

We leave and go to his parents'. I met them briefly at the wedding. They were both nice when I met them, but now that Liam and I are together, nervous butterflies fill my stomach. I haven't met or hung out with anyone's family in a long time.

The car stops outside the house, and Liam escorts me inside. His mom and dad are sitting in the family room. His dad is reading the paper, and his mom is knitting a baby blanket. They look up in surprise when we enter the room.

"Mom. Dad. You remember Hailee?" Liam says.

They stand and greet us. His dad kisses me on the cheek, and his mom embraces me.

"We're only here for a minute. I need fresh clothes," Liam announces.

His mom takes my hand. "Hailee, come sit down."

I let her lead me to the couch. She moves her skeins of yarn and we sit.

"I'll be right back," Liam says, and I nod. He leaves the room.

"Hailee, it's nice to see you again."

"You, too. Your home is beautiful, Mrs. O'Malley."

Her face lights up. "Thank you. Please, call me Ruth. And I spent the last year remodeling it. Darragh finally gave me the go-ahead to do all the things I wanted."

I glance around the family room. The sunlight pours through the window. Creams, gold, and rich browns fill the space. Everything is fresh and new. "You did a great job."

She smiles wider. "Thank you! Do you work, Hailee?"

"Yes. I'm a kindergarten teacher at Freedom Elementary."

Surprise registers on her face. "Wow. That's a rough neighborhood."

I shrug. It's the comment everyone makes when I tell them where I work. "Yes. But the kids are awesome. Who are you making the baby blanket for?"

"Nora. Darragh and I both think she's having a girl. She carries the baby the same way her mother carried her when she was pregnant."

I pick up the blanket. It has pink, blue, green, and yellow in it. "This is beautiful."

"Do you have children, Hailee?"

"No. Just my kids in class."

She pats my hand. "Liam would make an excellent father."

My chest tightens. I'm all for kids, but I just met this woman.

"Ruth. Don't scare Hailee out of the house," Darragh reprimands.

I smile gratefully at him.

"I'm just stating a fact," Ruth says. She puts her hand on mine. "Hailee is an Irish name. Are you Irish?"

"Yes."

"Catholic or protestant?"

"Umm...I grew up Catholic."

She beams. "Wonderful. I go to church every morning and confession is on Saturday. You'll probably be in class for weekday mass, but you can come to confession this weekend with me if you want?"

My gut tightens. *Is this woman for real?* Heat ignites in my cheeks. I'm not ashamed I don't go to church anymore, but I'm not sure how to respond without offending her. "Well, I umm..."

"It's at ten a.m. Mary Kelly comes with me, and we go to brunch after. Did you meet her at the wedding yesterday?"

"I'm not sure."

"Hales, you ready?" Liam booms then comes into the room.

I rise, relieved he's back and ready to leave. "It was nice seeing you again."

"You, too, dear. Have Liam give my phone number to you. You can send me your address. I'll swing by and pick you up."

I gape at her, unsure how to respond.

"Pick Hailee up for what?" Liam asks, his eyes turning to slits.

Ruth chirps, "For confession on Saturday. You could come, too, Liam. We'll go to—"

"Mom, neither Hailee nor I are going to confession. Stop trying to get me to go," he barks.

Ruth's face falls. She purses her lips together.

Liam puts his hand on my back. "Come on. I'll see you later."

"When will you be home?" his mom asks.

"Not sure. I'm forty, remember, Mom?" Liam snaps.

"Don't talk like that to your mother," Darragh scolds.

Liam scowls and shakes his head. He guides me out of the house so fast, I barely have time to say goodbye. As soon as the car door shuts, he turns to me. "I'm sorry. I shouldn't have left you with her. She means well. I think she's gone a bit crazy because of my dad dying, and—"

"Your dad's dying?"

The car turns silent. His face hardens, weaved with pain. He finally says, "Yeah. He has lung cancer."

"Liam, I'm so sorry."

"It is what it is. No one can do anything about it. I'm sorry about my mother. I'm her only son, and I've been gone and—"

I shut him up with my lips and straddle my body over his. His arms wrap around me, and I inch as close to him as I can. When I end our kiss, I run my hand through his hair. "I'm sorry about your father. That sucks."

He admits, "Yeah. It does. My mom means well, but she's driving me crazy. She's going to flip when I tell her I'm moving out."

"Where are you going?"

He hesitates but says, "Nora surprised me the other day and gave me her house."

I gape at him.

He chuckles. "I think that's how I looked."

"Wow. That's an awesome gift."

"I know. I feel guilty taking it, but she insisted. I spoke with Boris, and he thought it was a great idea, too."

"Well, I definitely want to see it."

Excitement fills his face. "I'm going to remodel it. Anna said she'd help me with colors and materials. I can use her designer discounts. Nora's brothers will help me implement, but I'm horrible at making things match."

"I'll help you if you want. I love that stuff."

"Really? You would?" he asks.

"Yeah! If you're serious about me sticking my nose into your project."

His face lights up. "I'm totally serious about you sticking your nose into my business."

I laugh.

"Do you want to see it after breakfast?" he asks.

"Sure! Do I get to help knock out walls, or are you only doing cosmetic stuff?" I ask.

Amusement appears in his expression. "You want to help do the work?"

"Duh. I even have my own tools. I told you I know how to do electrical, plumbing, and other things."

He kisses me again. "That's sexy hot, little lamb."

The car stops, and Liam kisses my hand. We get out and go inside the restaurant. It's a popular spot, but the line isn't long. The hostess soon seats us at a booth. I slide in, and Liam sits next to me. He puts his arm around my shoulders and leans into my ear. "So when do I get to see what's in the treat box?"

I softly laugh. "Mmm, maybe—"

"Hailee?" My mom's voice rings in the air.

I turn to see her and my sister, Gemma, staring at me. My mom has her who-is-this-guy look on her face, and Gemma has a smirk.

My stomach flips. "Mom. Gemma. What are you doing here?"

My mother glances at Liam then back at me. "We came to eat breakfast."

A brief moment of silence fills the air. Liam holds his hand out. "I'm Liam. It's nice to meet you."

"Oh! Sorry. This is my mom and sister, Gemma. This is Liam."

"Liam. It's nice to meet you." My mom smiles and shakes his hand.

"Do you want to sit with us?" Liam motions to the other side of the table, and my nerves vibrate. I'm unprepared for this.

"Don't mind if we do," Gemma, who's the family troublemaker, says as she slides into the booth before I can object. "Liam, where did you come from?"

I groan. "Gemma!"

"What?"

She leans forward as my mom sits next to her. "Liam, do you have any brothers?"

"No. He doesn't," I say. I love my sister, but I'd prefer for my other sisters, Ciara or Ella, to be here right now. Gemma reminds me of Kora at times, and I can never guess what she might say. I'm the oldest, she's a year younger, and my other two sisters are twins and eighteen months younger than Gemma.

"I only have cousins." Liam flashes his panty-melting smile.

Gemma wiggles her eyebrows. "Are they single?"

"Gemma!" I put my hand over my face.

Liam chuckles. "Some are."

The waitress arrives at the table. "Hi! I'm Katie, and I'll be your server. Can I start you off with coffee?"

We all flip our mugs, and she goes through several specials, but I barely hear it. All I see are the questions on my mother and sister's faces. We rattle off orders, and the server leaves.

My mother clears her throat. "Hailee, how did you and Liam meet?"

"At an event."

"Oh?" My mother raises her eyebrows.

Liam doesn't seem fazed. "My cousin remodeled her pub after a fire and had a grand reopening."

Gemma's face brightens. "Your cousin owns a pub? Is he the single one?"

"No. *She* isn't," I say in an annoyed voice.

"Was everyone okay from the fire?" my mother asks.

Liam nods. "Yes. We got lucky."

"That's good to hear. What's the name of the pub?"

"O'Malley's. Have you heard of it before?" Liam asks.

The color in my mother's face drains. She glances at me then back at Liam. "You're an O'Malley?"

Liam stiffens. "Yes. Do you know someone in my family?"

My mother says nothing then shakes her head. "No." She refocuses on me. "How long have you two been seeing each other?"

My chest tightens. "Not long," I answer. My mind spins, and I shift in my seat.

Does my mother somehow know who Liam is?

It was fifteen years ago. Would she have remembered if she heard something on the news with all the crime that occurs in Chicago?

My sister is unfazed. "I've passed O'Malley's before. I've never gone in. Hailee, you should take me there sometime."

"No!" my mother blurts out then turns red. She looks down at her coffee mug. She's gripping it so hard, her knuckles turn white.

Liam glances at me, but I'm not sure what's going on. How could my mother know anything about Liam? It happened so long ago.

"Why not?" Gemma asks.

"Drop it," I tell her.

Gemma furrows her eyebrows. "Why?"

"Gemma," I mutter under my breath.

Liam removes his arm from around me and puts his hand on my thigh.

I glance at my watch. "Liam, I think we're going to be late. We should go."

He meets my eyes and nods. He pulls cash out of his wallet and tosses it on the table. "Breakfast is on me. It was nice meeting you Gemma and Ms. O'Hare."

My mother slowly looks up and meets his eyes. She forces a smile. "You, too." She refocuses on me. Her face is more nervous than I've seen in years. "Hailee, can you call me tonight?"

"Sure."

"Have a nice day," Liam says and leads me out to the car. When we get in, he looks at me. "What just happened?"

I shake my head. "I don't know."

9

Liam

The clawing in my gut hasn't stopped since I met Hailee's mom. I'm not sure why she acted freaked out when I mentioned my family name. After I show Hailee the house, we go to the pub and have lunch since we haven't eaten. But she's quiet and just going through the motions. When we get in the car, it's midafternoon.

"Are you okay, Hales?"

She smiles, and it's the same tight-lipped one her mom wore. It looks forced. She says, "Yeah."

I lean closer to her face. "Are you going to lie to me now?"

She shuts her eyes and sighs. When she opens them, she stares at the ceiling. "At some point, I knew I might have to explain things to my mom, but I'm not ready. And the only thing I can think is that she must know. She must remember your trial on the news or something from fifteen years ago."

My gut sinks. I ask the question I already know the answer to. "And she'll never approve of us? Well, I should say me with you."

Hailee's face scrunches. She slowly turns toward me. "I don't know, Liam. I would hope she wouldn't let what my dad did rule her ability to see what I see in you, but I don't know. I'm...I don't even know how to discuss this with her."

"Do you want me to meet her with you? I can explain things."

Hailee shakes her head. "No. I think it's best if I talk to her alone. Can you drop me off at my place?"

Every fear I have seems to grow exponentially. I roll the divider window down and tell my driver to take us to Hailee's. When it's closed again, I pull her onto my lap. I hold her head so she can't escape looking at me. I speak slowly but firmly. "Whatever I need to do to help smooth things over, I will. I don't want to lose you, Hales."

She strokes the side of my head. "You haven't done anything, Liam. Whatever my mom knows, it's not her business. She doesn't know you or have a right to judge you. You served your sentence. I'm sorry about this morning."

"You don't have anything to apologize for," I state then repeat, "I don't want to lose you."

She kisses me, and I put everything I have into that kiss, but she still doesn't tell me I won't lose her. When I drop her off at her apartment, she promises she'll call me after she talks to her mom. I leave feeling as if I'm leaving my life behind.

The rest of the day, I sit on pins and needles. I don't hear from Hailee, and at ten, I try to call her. It goes to voicemail. So I text her.

Me: *Hales, can you call me?*

Hailee: *I just got home. It's been a long day, and we didn't sleep a lot last night. I have to teach tomorrow. Can I call you after work?*

I scrub my hand over my face. I contemplate going directly to her apartment and banging down the door until she lets me in. My rational side talks me out of it.

Me: *Okay. Get some rest.*

Hailee: *You, too. Night.*

I don't sleep. The next morning, my driver arrives at four a.m. to go downstate and pick up Finn. Killian is already in the car. I read and re-read Hailee's and my text messages, watch the video she sent without the volume on, and pretty much stay in the torture zone until seven a.m. hits.

Me: *Morning. Did you sleep?*

Hailee: *A little. Did you?*

Me: *Honestly? No.*

Hailee: *Okay, I lied. I didn't, either.*

I call her. It rings twice and she answers. There's background noise, so I can't hear her very well.

"Hales, where are you?"

"On the bus."

"What bus?"

"The city bus. I'm on my way to work."

The hairs on my arms rise. I never thought to ask Hailee how she gets to and from work. The thought of her walking to the bus stop in her neighborhood doesn't sit well with me, but the one her school is in freaks me out. Anyone could easily hurt her. "I'll have a car waiting to take you home when you get out of work tonight."

"What? Don't be silly. The bus is fine," she insists.

"No. It's not. Knox will be waiting if I'm not back in time."

"Liam—"

"Don't argue with me, Hales. This isn't up for discussion," I bark.

"Don't act like you're the boss of me, Liam," she angrily snaps.

Rage boils in my blood. I squeeze my hand in a fist. I avoid Killian's questioning expression, and in a low, controlled voice, I state, "This isn't the issue to make an independent, feminist point about."

"Excuse me?" Hailee seethes.

"You heard me. The car will be waiting for you."

"Well, it'll be sitting there all night since I'm taking the bus home."

My skin crawls. "No, you aren't."

"Watch me," she belts out.

"Hales, if you—"

"I have to go, Liam. Boss your guys around or something." She hangs up.

I stare at the phone in shock. "She just hung up on me."

Killian grunts. "Told you she was high maintenance."

"Shut up. No, you didn't. You said she was innocent." I call back, but it goes to voicemail.

Me: *Pick up the phone, Hales.*

I don't hear back from her. After several minutes, I call again. Once again, it goes to voicemail.

Me: *This is childish.*

Several more minutes pass.

Me: *Are you seriously going to ignore me?*

More time passes.

Me: *If you don't call me right now, I'm calling the police to make sure you're okay. Then I'm calling the school. Make your choice, and don't test me, Hales. I'm warning you.*

A minute passes.

Me: *You have two minutes, and then I'm dialing 911.*

Ninety seconds go by when I get a text.

Hailee: *Stop being psycho. I was walking into school. I don't wave my phone around during my commute.*

Me: *You should wave a gun around in that neighborhood.*

Hailee: *This is totally inappropriate. I have to work. Don't harass me the rest of the day.*

Me: *Harass you? Because I want to make sure you're safe?*

Hailee: *I survived without you up until now. Nothing's changed. I'll be fine.*

My pulse beats so hard, I get dizzy.

Me: *What the fuck does that mean?*

Hailee: *What does it sound like it means?*

Me: *Sounds like you're acting like I'm not in your life.*

Hailee: *Jesus, you're dramatic.*

Me: *I don't know what you're trying to prove, but this is the wrong way to go about it.*

Hailee: *I'm at work. I'll talk to you later, Liam.*

Me: *Yeah, tonight.*

Hailee: *No. When I say.*

I growl in rage and start texting her back when my phone rings. "Great." I answer the phone. "Make it fast, Dad."

His smoker's voice hits my ear. "Why? What's got you tied up on the way downstate?"

I blow out a big breath and almost smack Killian for his smug, amused expression. I firmly say, "What do you need, Dad?"

"Your mom wants to know what you want for dinner tonight. She's going grocery shopping."

This is my fucking life.

"Nothing. I'm a forty-year-old man. Do you think you can reiterate that to her?" I bark, sick of my mother smothering me and feeling like I have no control over anything.

"Don't be disrespectful," my father warns.

"Liam. Chill," Killian mutters.

I scowl at him. "I need to go, Dad." I hang up. I know I'll hear about it later, but I don't care right now. I toss my phone on the seat.

Killian shakes his head. "I told you going after that girl was asking for trouble."

"Shut. Up," I warn through gritted teeth.

"Jesus. You're totally pussy whipped already."

"I swear to God, if you don't shut your face, this car is going to be a bloodbath."

Killian snorts. "Bring it." His phone rings, and he glances at it, then sends it to voicemail. It rings again, and he does the same.

After the fourth time, I ask, "Who's trying to call you?"

He annoyingly replies, "Becky."

"Why aren't you answering it?"

He shifts so his back is to the window. He stretches his legs, and they hit the door. "I told her I didn't want anything serious with her. She suddenly can't seem to abide by our agreement. So I ended it with her last night. I'm about to block her if she doesn't stop calling me."

I lean closer and point. "And you want to talk shit about Hales and me?"

He scoffs. "Do I look all pissed off with my panties in a twist? No. I don't wear panties. You sure as hell look like you do right now."

"Fuck off, Killian."

He grunts. "Seriously, you need to chill out, Liam. We've got bigger issues right now. Deal with it when you get home."

The car stops, and our driver knocks on the divider window. I stare at the building I lived in for fifteen years and only escaped less than a few months ago. The burning in my stomach starts and climbs up my esophagus. I stare at the razor wire and gate.

The entryway to Hell.

"You all right?" Killian asks.

I don't answer. I get out and wait in the cold air next to the car. Killian steps beside me, and we say nothing.

When the gate opens, Finn steps out. His green eyes pierce into mine. A hardened expression fills his face. A tidal wave of emotion rolls through me.

He's been my rock for so long. I would have died by now if it weren't for him. These last few months have been a concoction of confusion in so many ways. But now, it's my turn to make sure he gets everything he deserves and not an ounce less. And once we make happen what we've been planning, he's going to finally have the life he should have instead of the shitty one he's been living.

10

Hailee

The intercom beeps in my classroom. The disembodied voice of Marcia, the school secretary, booms through the speaker. "Hailee, you have a visitor."

It better not be Liam.

I'm on my lunch break and still fuming from our earlier text exchange. I'm more than capable of getting myself to and from work. If he thinks he's going to tell me what to do, he has another thing coming.

I press the button. "Who is it?"

"Your sister, Gemma. I'm on my way to Mrs. Smith's classroom to drop a few things off. Do you want me to escort her to you?"

What is she doing here?

"Yes, please."

I rise and pace my classroom. When I went to my mom's house last night, it didn't go too well, but I also didn't get very far.

My mother's face was full of fear. She said, "Hailee, the O'Malleys are a crime family. That pub used to be Liam's grandmother's. His father is the head of the clan. You need to stop seeing him, immediately."

I crossed my arms. "No. I'm not going to break up with Liam."

My mother's face turned pale. "Hailee, this isn't a topic to fight me on."

"I already know everything about him. You're going to have to accept him and what he's done," I told her.

Her eyes turned to slits. "What has he done?"

My gut twisted. *She doesn't know?*

Then why is she freaking out? Is it purely because of the O'Malley reputation?

I didn't have a chance to respond or ask her how she knew all this. My mother's boyfriend showed up with dinner. Gemma came out of the other room. Some weirdo at her apartment complex bought a bunch of cockroaches, termites, and mice as pets. The guy didn't even bother to keep them caged up. They infested the entire building. Gemma moved in with my mom while the landlord takes care of the problem.

"We'll talk about this later," my mother muttered.

As much as I wanted to ignore the topic and pretend nothing was going on, I stayed, in the hopes we could talk after dinner and get it over with. Before I knew it, it was dark and almost ten. I realized I wasn't going to get much farther with her boyfriend and Gemma there.

The door opens, interrupting my frustration and worries. Gemma steps inside my classroom and closes the door. "Jeez. It's like an airport around here. I almost throat-punched the security guard who took my metal nail file and box cutter out of my purse. She's holding them hostage until I leave."

I put my hands on my hips. "This is a school, Gemma. You can't bring weapons in here."

She waves her hand in the air. "Oh, please. I thought she was going to handcuff me when the metal detector went off. Personally, I think she wanted to frisk me."

"What is wrong with you?" Sometimes, I wonder how we're related. I'd ask her why she has a box cutter, but Liam is right about this neighborhood being unsafe.

She beams and chirps, "Let's change the topic to more interesting things."

"Gemma, what do you want? I don't have time for your games."

She twirls her strawberry-blonde hair around her finger. "Is that the welcome I get?"

I tilt my head and glare at her.

She wiggles her eyebrows. "You've been holding out on me, Hailee."

"What are you talking about? And why are you at my work? Don't you have your own job to be at?" I snap.

She strolls over to the table and pulls out one of the little chairs meant for the kindergarten kids. It's sturdy, and adults can sit on it, but it's lower to the ground. She pats the seat next to her.

I sigh and sit next to her.

"One, I have a day off. Two, I'm here so I can get details. Three, I didn't think you had it in you. I looked up your bad boy, Liam O'Malley, last night. He's a hard-core felon." Her eyes are bright with excitement, and she leans closer and lowers her voice. "How hot is the sex? Did he take out all his years of pent-up sexual frustration on you?"

Heat rushes to my face. I gape at her. My sister has always been the wild one, but this is a bit over the top, even for Gemma. "This isn't funny. Mom's having a fit. Did you two sit and talk about Liam and me all day?" I scold.

Her face falls. "No. Mom wouldn't tell me what was wrong and told me to drop it. Then she acted strange all day. She was so nervous, her hands were shaking at breakfast, and she could barely eat. I looked it up myself."

"And now you're here, at my work, gloating?"

She smirks. "Gloating? No. Giving you props? Hell yeah. It's about time you got rid of those boring guys you always date. I mean, that last guy you brought home was a nerd without the benjamins."

"What does that mean?"

She jerks her head back, as if in shock. "You know. Complete class-A geek. No money. If he was loaded, I could see why you would put up with it. After all, he did call his butt a fart-box, which might be hot naked since he had that fine bubble ass going on, but jeez. He was a downright dork with no bling. Now, Liam..." She breathes out a big breath of air and fans in front of her face. "He's Mr. Yum Yum with an extra side of make me super squirty. When can I meet these single cousins?"

My patience is about worn thin. "This is totally inappropriate right now. Do you realize you're out of line and in my kindergarten classroom? And FYI, it's not normal to be excited about guys who just got out of prison or go looking for one."

"Says the girl who's knocking boots with a murderer."

Anger sears through me. Gemma can push anyone's buttons, and I'm not in the mood. "You can leave now."

"Oh, come on."

"I'm at work."

"On your lunch break," she points out.

"I was working."

"Whatevs. I can't stay in Mom's house all day. And all my friends are at their jobs right now."

"Why aren't you again?"

She ignores my question. Her face turns serious. "I need a huge favor."

I sit farther back in my seat. *Here we go.* "What?"

"Can I move in with you until my apartment remodel is complete? I can't take another day of Simon."

The hairs on my arms rise. "Why? What's wrong with Mom's boyfriend? She's happy, and I like him."

"Nothing, except he and Mom are annoying me. I keep imagining them having sex, and..." She wrinkles her nose.

I make the same face. "Ewww."

"Tell me about it. I keep walking in on him whispering things in Mom's ear and her giggling. I feel like a third wheel. *Please* let me stay at your place. I'll even do your laundry." She puts her hands in the air, as if she's praying.

Normally, I wouldn't care. But now that I've hooked up with Liam, I'm not looking for a roommate. "The last time you did my laundry, my sheets turned pink."

"But they are so much better pink, aren't they?"

"Ask Ciara and Ella if you can stay at their place."

"Nope. They'll drive me nuts with their double-trouble twin powers. You know how they are. Come on, Hailee. Please. Save me from another night of thinking about Simon's wrinkly balls."

I wince. "Ugh! Why do you have to give me visuals?"

"Now you know how I feel. So you'll let me stay? After all, if you get tired of me, you can go to Liam's."

With his mother? I don't think so.

I snort. "So I'm supposed to leave my house so you can move in?"

She shrugs. "No. I'm just giving you options. It's only temporary. Please," she begs again.

"No. Sorry. You'll have to deal with it."

"Ugh. Haileeeeee," she whines.

"Sorry."

The two-minute-warning bell rings, and she jumps and covers her ears. "That is way too loud."

I groan. "Gemma, you've gotta go. Mom's place is your best option right now."

She rolls her eyes and pouts. "Fine. But you owe me now."

I scoff. "I owe you? For what?"

"Not letting me stay and making me deal with Mr. Wrinkly Balls groping Mom. When are we going on a double date with one of Liam's cousins?"

"What? Gemma, I'm not—"

She slides down on her knees and looks like she's praying again. "Please! I feel like there are no good men in this city."

"You don't know anything about them."

"Ummm...do they look anything like Mr. Yum Yum?"

"Do *not* call my man, Mr. Yum Yum. Now get up, I have to get my kids." I reach for her hand and help her up.

"Please, Hailee. I'll help you with all your teacher projects for the next year."

"Don't sound so desperate, Gemma." I walk to the door and step into the hall.

She follows me. We walk toward the gym. It's sleeting outside so recess was inside. She replies, "Call me whatever you want. Just tell me you'll set it up."

We approach the front of the school. I force a smile. "This is where we part, Gemma. Next time, don't bring any weapons."

She groans. "Fine. I'll get my friends, and we'll stalk the pub."

I freeze and lower my voice. "Gemma, what has gotten into you? You're talking crazy."

"No, you're selfish. It's okay for you to be with Mr. Yum Yum, but I'm not supposed to find anyone. I'd help you if I knew of any—"

In my sternest voice, the one I usually reserve for my kindergarteners, I say, "Gemma, I have to get my kids. We'll talk about this later."

In Gemma's mind, that means I said yes. She hugs me then kisses me on the cheek. "Awesome. I'll text you. And think about me moving in and how much fun we'd have!" She bounces over to the security guard, Lucy.

I mouth, "Sorry," and Lucy shakes her head at me, then scowls at Gemma. I pick up my kids from the gym and take them back to class. I try to shake Gemma's visit out of my head, but I can't. In some ways, I'm relieved she's cool with Liam's past. At least one person is on my side. On the other hand, when Gemma wants something, she doesn't stop until she gets it. Her current revelation that she thinks it's cool to date a murderer, as if it's no big deal, bothers me. She could get hurt. Gemma believes she can handle anything, but one of these days, I fear she's going to get severely injured.

The snow continues to come down so hard, I can't see out the windows anymore. When the final bell rings, I put my kids on the buses, walk many of them over to the after-school program, and help those walking home bundle up with the scarves, gloves, and hats I bought for most of them.

On days like these, I usually take an Uber, but I'm still upset about my previous text conversation with Liam. To prove he's not going to order me around, I decide I'm sticking with the bus. I finish my work, fill my backpack, and bundle up. It's after six, and the streetlights are on when I step outside. A cold blanket of white wetness flies around me, and I can barely see.

This was a dumb idea.

Too late now. It's only a block away.

I go several yards and hear Liam shout, "Hales."

My stomach flips. I spin into his chest. Before I can say anything, he grabs my backpack and steers me toward his car.

"Liam! Give me my bag!"

"I will, once you're in the car." He opens the door. "Now, get in."

"You're out of line," I attempt, but it comes out weak. A warm car sounds pretty nice right about now. Regardless, my stubbornness won't let me take the easy route.

Liam grabs my chin and dips down so his face is inches from mine. His eyes are full of angry green fire. They glow, almost like a crazed animal. Snow covers his lashes. Through gritted teeth, he enunciates, "Get in the car. Now."

"Don't order me around, Liam," I bite back.

"I'm not telling you again, Hales."

"I'm—"

"Ms. O'Hare! Is this man bothering you?" Lucy calls out.

Liam raises his eyebrows but doesn't tear his gaze away from mine.

I spin. "No, Lucy. Everything is fine, thank you. Go back inside."

She hesitates and eyes Liam over, with her hand on her gun holster. "Are you sure?"

"Yes. I'll see you tomorrow." I get in the car so she doesn't attempt to shoot Liam or call the police.

Liam follows. The car takes off the second the door shuts. I spin on him and accuse, "What do you think you're doing?"

He takes a controlled breath then faces me. In a quick move, he lurches over me, pins my arms behind my back, and restrains them with metal handcuffs.

I try to get out of the cuffs but can't free myself. "Liam! What—"

"You want to disobey me? Fine. We'll play this game," he growls.

"This isn't funny. Let me out, Liam."

"No, little lamb. You'll get out when I say you're ready to get out." He presses his lips to mine, and I turn my head.

"Liam, I'm warning you—"

He grabs my chin and holds my face in front of his. He kisses me again. I try to keep my mouth shut, but he slides his tongue through the seam of my lips. His delicious tongue rolls around my mouth until my heart is racing and I'm panting. He pulls back. His eyes still have the same crazed look, only hotter. Within seconds, he puts a blindfold over my eyes.

"Liam!"

His hot breath hits my ear. "You've pushed me too far, Hales. And naughty little lambs need to learn lessons."

11

Liam

THE CAR PULLS INTO THE GARAGE. I PULL HAILEE OUT OF THE back seat then throw her over my shoulder.

"Liam!" She squirms, but without the use of her hands, she can't do much.

Regardless, I smack her ass harder than I have in the past. But she also has pants and a coat over it. "Stop fighting me," I growl. Then I nod at my driver to leave. He backs out, and I hit the button for the garage door to close.

"Liam! You're freaking me out! Let me go!" she cries out.

I squeeze her thighs tighter and step into the house. The rage I've been feeling all day over our text conversation and the fear from not getting verification she isn't going to let her family come between us is at a high. Now that she's in front of me, there's no going back. My little lamb is going to learn who the boss of this relationship is when it comes to her safety. "I'm freaking you out? Imagine if it were some lunatic thug who had you thrown over his shoulder. Then what would you do? Hmmm? Tell me, Hales."

"You're the only lunatic right now."

"Keyword being now," I grumble then go into the bedroom. After I dropped Finn and Killian off, I came here. The mattress was delivered earlier in the day, along with the sheets and food. I spent forty-five minutes setting things up. I had a feeling Hailee wasn't going to back down. After I secured ropes through the ceiling beams and bed legs, I went and waited for hours outside her school, stewing over her disobedience regarding her safety.

I flip on the fireplace. It's the only light in the room. There's a blizzard outside, which only irritates me further. I sit on the bed and straddle her over me. "You could have frozen to death, little lamb."

Her ragged breathing and pouty lips make my cock hurt. The flush in her cheeks deepens. She's the most beautiful woman in the world, but I'm learning she's stubborn as hell. Well, I can be just as hard-nosed. She asks, "Liam, what are you doing?"

I give her a chaste kiss. She doesn't back away and comes toward me for more, but I hold off. I stroke her cheek. "You know the initial feeling you had when I handcuffed you and covered your eyes?"

She slowly admits, "Yes."

"What if that was someone else?"

"Liam, I've used the bus for years. I—"

"You weren't mine, though, were you?"

She bites her lip and sighs. I kiss her chin where it meets her neck, and she shudders.

"Tell me, little lamb, how would you fight back right now if I wasn't me?"

She stays silent.

"It's dark. Cold. Too dangerous for you to take chances. I have enemies, but even if I didn't, you should know better than to take that type of risk. And I won't have this conversation again." I slide my finger over her lips. "You're going to agree I'm the boss when it comes to your safety."

She tilts her head, and her jaw clenches. Oh, my little lamb is so headstrong. I love it and hate it at the same time. Now, I'm going to have to break her.

I unzip her jacket and remove her hat and gloves. I unwrap her scarf and toss everything on the floor. "I'm going to take off one of your handcuffs so I can remove your jacket. If you fight me, I'll slice your coat and the rest of your clothes in half, understand?"

"Liam. Don't!"

"It's your choice. I'm warning you." I take my pocket knife out and open it. I put the flat steel blade on her cheek.

She gasps and freezes.

"What if this wasn't me holding this knife? Do you understand what could happen to you?" I ask her, my heart beating a thousand miles a minute. I hate thinking about any of this, but I've lived with the evilest of men for fifteen years. Until I prove my point, I'll keep going. "Are you ready to be a good girl so I can remove your clothes?"

She doesn't answer. I can almost see the wheels in her head spinning. Her pride won't allow her to give me what I need to hear.

"I need an answer, Hales. Do you choose the good girl whose clothes stay intact or the naughty one, so I have to slice every piece of fabric off you? It's your choice."

She continues not to answer me.

I move her hair to the side and press the flat part of the blade on the back of her neck. I lean into her ear. "Three. Two."

"Liam! This is ridiculous. You made your point. Release me," she orders.

I drag my finger over her hairline. "I don't think I have, little lamb. This will be over when I say it's over. Now, last chance. Good girl or naughty girl?"

She still won't answer. I hold my chuckle inside at her inability to cave. She definitely has Irish in her.

I take the knife and, in one slice, split the front of her sweater.

"Liam!"

"It's your choice. I think it'd be a shame to ruin this beautiful coat you have."

"Liam, please," she whispers.

I fist her hair and tug her head. I put my face so close to hers, our lips touch. "Please what, little lamb? Please don't cut your coat because you're going to be a good girl and not fight me? Or please keep slicing until there's nothing left that's wearable?" I dart my tongue along her lips, and she whimpers. "Last chance to save it. Three. Two. One."

"Wait! I'll be good. Please don't destroy it!"

I kiss her and shove my tongue in her mouth when she gasps. I keep her head firmly planted, and she succumbs, kissing me back and rocking her hips on my erection. I groan and retreat. "I'm putting you on your feet. When I remove your handcuff, if you attempt anything, we're going to have issues. Don't test me, Hales."

She takes a deep breath. "Okay. Please don't cut my coat."

"Be a good girl and I won't." I peck her on the lips, put the knife on the bed, and place her on her feet. I slide my hand in my pocket for the key and unlock one cuff. I slide her jacket and ripped top off her arm then grab the rope and secure it around her wrists.

"Liam, what are you doing?" she frets.

"Shhh," I murmur against her lips and continue to restrain her. I slide my hand down her naked skin, and she shivers. "Ready for the other one?"

She swallows hard. "Liam, where are we?"

"My house. No one's here. No one's coming. Even my driver left. It's you and me, little lamb, and until I get what I want from you, neither of us are leaving."

"What do you want?"

I tilt her head up. "You know what I want."

"No. I don't," she claims.

I peck her lips. "Don't lie to me, Hales." I release the other handcuff, slide the material off her arm, then tie her up. Her arms stretch toward both walls. I step back and stare at her then run my finger over her see-through black bra, stroking her hardening nipples.

"Liam," she whispers, her chest rising and falling faster.

"I know this gets you off, little lamb. But if it were anyone else, it wouldn't. You'd be flipping out right now, wouldn't you?"

She doesn't say anything, but I get a nod this time.

I circle my arms around her and hold her face to my chest. I say in her hair, "Enemies are all around us. I won't allow you to be careless, Hales. Your actions have consequences, and in this relationship, you don't get to argue with me about your safety. It's not your right to question my motives. My words aren't ever suggestions, and you will give me full control over this. The time where you made choices is now over."

She freezes. It doesn't surprise me. Hailee's independent, and it's one of the things I find attractive about her. But she's handing the reins over to me on this issue.

"You don't like what I said, little lamb?" I taunt her.

"I'm not going to be like one of those women who let you walk all over them, Liam," she fires at me.

And there's the pushback I expected. I dip to her face. "Keeping you safe is not walking all over you."

"I know how to protect myself."

"No, you don't. Your bottle of mace isn't going to do shit if someone wants to come after you," I hurl back. I release her pants, kneel in front of her, and sniff hard. I kiss her wet panties.

She squirms, and a harsh breath flies out of her mouth.

I finish removing her pants so she's only in her bra and underwear.

I stroke her slit. "You're wet, little lamb."

Goose bumps break out on her skin. Her cheeks flush, and I grab her hips, then bite through her panties. "Liam! Oh God!" she screams as I edge her closer to an orgasm. But then I stop and study her face. "Naughty girls don't get to come. And you were very naughty today, weren't you?"

"No. I wasn't. I have a right—"

The sound of my hand hitting her bare ass, courtesy of her thong, echoes in the room. She yelps, and I bark, "You don't have any rights in regards to your safety. That's my job. Get it through your head, Hales."

She breathes hard and furrows her eyebrows.

I reach for the other rope and tie her ankle.

"Wh-what are you doing?" she nervously asks.

I don't answer, secure her other ankle, then increase the tension until she can't stretch her body any farther.

"Liam," she breathes.

I step back and study my beautiful, naughty little lamb. I unzip my pants and stroke my cock a few times then smear my pre-cum on my thumb and stick it in her mouth.

She sucks on it without me even ordering her to, which only intensifies the buzzing in my veins. "Mmm," she quietly moans.

I pull my thumb out and rub it on her lips. I press my body against hers, slide the blindfold onto her forehead, and give her a moment for her eyes to adjust. "Do you know what I thought when I stood outside the prison, waiting for Finn to come out today?"

She blinks twice. Her long lashes expose her blue eyes. Her voice comes out raspy. "No."

My chest tightens, and the burn I felt earlier in the day crawls up my esophagus. "All these years, I lived in the epitome of Hell. It was a cesspool of the vilest men on earth. I was shackled, stripped of my freedom, and forced to do things I didn't want to do. There was no choice. I had to submit. And that's our problem. You don't know how to give up control, little lamb, do you?"

Her lips tremble, and her eyes glisten. She doesn't answer me. The longer she stares at me, the more her orbs fill with tears.

I cup her cheeks. "If anyone understands where you are right now, it's me. I even respect it. But know this. Fighting me, not agreeing to give me control, is only going to make this harder for you. Until you submit, you'll stay here, spread out, at my mercy, unable to make any choices. And I will break you until you're begging me for dear life, little lamb."

Fear crosses her face, and I know we're now on our way. "You said you would never hurt me."

I palm her ass and push her body into mine. I tug her hair harder than normal. She gasps, and I kiss her until she's hungrily kissing me and whimpering. I pull away and stroke her hair. "I'll never physically harm you, Hales. I'm doing this so no one else ever will, either. But when I break you, it's going to hurt, and you're going to beg me for everything that comes after it."

12

Hailee

"Liam! Please!" I beg, unsure how long I've been at his house, under his mercy. My limbs are shaking. Sweat coats my skin. My underwear and bra cling to me to the point it's uncomfortable. The fire is the only light in the room, and sometimes I have none, depending on if Liam decides to put the blindfold over me or not. Currently, it's on. And every part of Liam's tongue, fingers, and even cock has been in me at times.

Not once has he allowed me to come. It's an excruciatingly delicious pain in a way I've never experienced before.

His hot breath hits the curve of my neck. "Tell me I'm in charge of your safety, little lamb. All this will go away." His lips add more zings to my ready-to-explode body.

I must be a masochist. No matter how much I want to be free, I won't give in. I've taken care of myself for my entire adult life. There's nothing wrong with the bus. I'm not going to give anyone total control over any area of my life, no matter if what Liam is saying may have some truth. If I give him this, what's he going to ask for next?

And this is over the top. Several times, I wonder if he's crazy and if I've welcomed the devil himself into my life, even though Liam claims this is about keeping me safe. Then I change my mind and think it's the hottest thing anyone has done to me, and that makes me wonder if I'm the crazy one.

"You don't have a right to do this," I weakly reply.

"Stop fighting me, Hales." His finger slides inside my panties, and he teases me for what feels like the hundredth time.

Why does he always feel so good?

If he doesn't take my undergarments off, I'm going to die.

"Please, take them off." He keeps moving them to the side then replacing them. It's making my skin crawl.

"If someone had kidnapped you, you wouldn't be asking," he barks.

"Liam..." I lose control and get emotional. Against my will, tears soak the blindfold. If anyone else did this to me, I would be scared out of my wits and wanting to die. I choke out, "Please, stop. You're hurting me."

He steps behind me so his naked body is flush to mine. His erection presses against my spine and his arms encircle me. He slides his fingers back on my clit. "This is hurting you?" He swirls his finger, and I tilt my head back onto his chest, so tired of being on the edge of coming without him taking me over it.

"Yes," I whisper.

"No, I'm not hurting you. I'll never hurt you. I'm protecting you. All you have to do is tell me I'm in charge of your safety decisions. Vow to me you won't fight me about it ever again." He turns my chin and deeply kisses me, and right when I'm about to come, his hand freezes. It's like he knows my body better than I do. "Give me the power. I'll make you feel so good, little lamb."

I blurt out, "I can't."

"You can."

My body betrays me, and I cry hard. I hate myself at this moment for showing him my weakness. "I can't."

"I won't let anything happen to you. You're mine to protect. Why can't you give this to me?" he murmurs in my ear.

"What else are you going to take from me?" I sob, finally admitting to him what I'm petrified of. It would be easy with Liam to let him make all the choices in my life, and I would lose myself and who I am.

He spins to the front of me and palms my head to his chest. "Shh."

I keep sobbing, and he removes my blindfold. He holds my cheeks. His face is inches from mine. "I'm not taking anything else. Nothing, little lamb. Nothing else. Deep down, you know this is for the best. I can't function if you don't give this to me. I need to know you're safe at all times."

"I hate you," I whisper.

Pain briefly flashes in his eyes. "No, you don't. You hate admitting I should make these decisions for you. But I'm right. And don't ever say you hate me again. You're the missing part of my heart, Hales. And I'll give you anything you want, but you *will* submit to me on this one thing."

I close my eyes and barely get out, "I need these off. I'm so hot. My skin's crawling."

"I know. That's how I felt all day thinking of you walking to and from the bus stop, in neighborhoods that aren't safe. It's like a bug is under your skin and you can't get it out, isn't it?"

"Yes."

He tugs my hair back. His lips press against mine. He reaches for something and says, "Stay still."

I don't move. I really can't. There's no slack in the ropes.

He holds up the knife then quickly slashes the straps of my bra and the part sticking to my cleavage. It's so wet it doesn't fall, and he pulls it off me.

"Oh God!" I never thought anything could feel so freeing.

He kisses me again, and I roll my tongue against his. My bare breasts press against his chest, and he groans. "Do you want your panties off?"

"Please," I beg.

"Give it to me. Tell me one time that you won't ever argue with me again about your safety, and I'll remove them. I'll untie you. Then I'll make every part of you feel good, little lamb. Just tell me."

I can't do it anymore. The freedom I feel from my bra alone is like the first hit of a drug. I have to have more. I cave. "Okay. I won't argue ever again. Take it. Please cut them off."

He takes control of my mouth while slicing the back of my thong. His hands pull the fabric through my legs to the front of my body, and he cuts the side. He peels it away and tosses it on the floor. "Feel better?"

"So much," I cry out, and more tears fall down my cheeks.

He crouches down and releases my feet, but my legs are like noodles. He holds me close to him, whacks the rope with his knife, and my arms fall over his shoulders. He picks me up and takes me to the bed.

"Liam," I sob.

"Shh. Everything is okay. Let me take care of you now, little lamb." He brushes the clump of wet hair off my face. His lips destroy me. My mouth. My breasts. My pussy is so overloaded, I come the moment he flicks his tongue on me.

But I have hardly any voice left. And my cries lodge in my throat, barely making any noise. My fingers pull at his hair, and his deep groan echoes in the air.

He lurches over me, thrusting inside me in one movement and covering my gasp with his mouth. His tongue tastes of my orgasm. It fucks me at the same speed as his erection. And I cling to him, unable to stop quivering, with endorphins annihilating every atom in my being. The tears never stop. Adrenaline continues to pound me like a jackhammer.

He promised he would make me feel good, but nothing could compare to how this feels. It's like a full-on onslaught of every high you could ever experience.

"Fuck, Hales," he mumbles in my mouth as I scratch him so hard, I draw blood. It only makes him thrust into me harder and faster.

"Liam!"

"You're mine, little lamb. Tell me I'm not going to lose you."

I scrunch my face. After all this, why is he even talking this way? I don't reply from shock.

"You never told me yesterday I'm not going to lose you. No matter your family or mine, you tell me right now, it's you and me. I need it, Hales. Tell me." His eyes fill with something I've never seen before.

Is that what he's been worried about?

Didn't I tell him he wouldn't lose me?

No, I didn't.

I kiss him. "You and me, baby."

A growl comes out of him. I don't know if it's relief from pent-up worry or some other emotion, but it flies out of him. He dips his face to my neck and buries himself in the curve. "Jesus. You're such a good little lamb. Fuuuuck!" He pumps his seed in me, and it's like a machine gun going off.

I lose control of anything that's left. My body goes to a place I've never been before. It's as if I'm floating. All I see are stars. When the chaos ends, and the sound of the room is filled with us trying to catch our breath, it feels like a long time passes before Liam lifts his head off me.

He strokes the side of my wet head. His green eyes glow in the dark. He pecks me on the lips then pierces his gaze into mine. In a soft voice, he says, "Don't hate me for doing that."

It's not thought out. I don't hesitate. I draw my hand back and slap him as hard as I can across the cheek. The air fills with the sound of my palm hitting his skin. The end of the rope, still tied around my wrist, swats his neck.

Time seems to stand still as he keeps his face toward the wall. He takes deep breaths and finally licks his lips. My chest tightens as he slowly faces me.

My voice cracks but gets stronger as I speak. "That's all you're getting control over. Don't ask for anything else. I won't be a mindless Stepford wife. I'm capable of making decisions."

I expect him to be upset that I hit him. Instead, his lips curve into a smile. His eyes turn so hot, they're glowing. "No, little lamb. You aren't a Stepford wife. You're my queen."

A new, scary thought hits me hard about who he is.

He's the future king of the O'Malleys. And I'm already so far in, I don't question if it will happen or not. I couldn't leave Liam if I tried. That makes me someone I never thought I'd be. And I wonder if I'm really capable of being an O'Malley queen.

13

Liam

Several Weeks Later

THE SOUND OF THE CAR DOOR SLAMMING REMINDS ME I NEED to cool it. I take a few deep breaths to simmer my building rage. I just left Obrecht's. Adrian's ex-wife, who has always been trouble, showed up in town. She's making deals with the Polish mob in the Ivanov name. I've never liked Dasha, but she's gone past the point of no return. She's running drugs for them. Her dealings interfere with O'Malley business. I don't do drugs, and I don't like my family's involvement in them. Things are also changing. Many states are legalizing different ones, which means our business isn't as lucrative as before. There are numerous reasons why I'm working so hard to change the path of my family's future income. I want out of that industry, but until I pull off Finn's and my plan, Dasha playing drug dealer for the Poles in my territory isn't going to fly. She's also putting my family at risk. And a threat to the Ivanovs puts Nora and the baby in danger, and I'm not letting anything happen to them.

If that were the only thing going on, I wouldn't be so pissed right now, but Adrian and Obrecht just warned me to stay away from Hailee, without using those words. As if I could. I don't need them or anyone telling me my little lamb is a good person and a better woman than I deserve. I already know that. Nothing will change the facts. But there's no way I'm giving her up.

They're such hypocrites.

My guess is over the last fifteen years, they've killed more men than I have. Adrian was my best friend when he came to the States. We hit it off playing sports in physical education class, and before I knew it, I was teaching him, Obrecht, and his mom how to speak English. Adrian became the brother I never had. Then Dasha came into the picture, and I got involved in my father's affairs. We gradually split apart. His offer to grab a beer before I left sounds good in theory, but he doesn't trust me.

Who am I kidding?

No one except Nora and her brothers and Finn have full confidence in me. Some of the Ivanovs seem to be coming around, but I have a long way to go. Every moment of the day, I'm in a constant battle trying to make better decisions and regain the trust I used to have with people. It's exhausting. I wonder if I'll ever be able to regain it. You would think I did something personal to them. I've never harmed any of them—only the man I killed who murdered my uncle. Yet, all I see when I look at them is distrust.

The car stops and Finn gets in. It's a sunny day, and the first signs of spring are showing. He takes off his sunglasses and cleans them. The inked snake that weaves through the bones on his hand flexes. He asks, "Why are you scowling?"

I grunt. I almost tell him it's nothing, but Finn raises his eyebrows. I've never lied to him, and he can always see through me. If anyone can understand how I feel, it's him. "I can handle the 'I don't trust the felon' bullshit, but I draw the line where Hales is concerned."

His eyes turn to slits. "What was said?"

There's no point rehashing it. I force myself not to wallow in my misery and waste Finn's time. "Nothing I don't already know. Anyways, how are we going to get the dirt we need on Jack Christian and Judge Peterson?"

Frustration fills Finn's face. "I can't get access. They're clean as a whistle, except for the club. And you know I can't get in with my felony."

Acid creeps up my esophagus. It started happening recently and seems to increase throughout the day unless I'm with Hailee, except when she's stressing out about her mom's continued attempts to get her to stop seeing me. The only reason her mom will give her is that I'm an O'Malley and we're a crime family. I don't want my little lamb at odds with her mother. I keep hoping time will make things better.

When Jack's company goes public, it'll be on the stock exchange. It will forever change the O'Malley future. And that bastard and the judge deserve everything they have coming to them. However, if we can't get dirt on these pricks, I'm unsure how we can take them down.

"We need someone else. Declan would be good. Or Nolan. He's quieter and more inconspicuous," I offer.

Finn shakes his head. "You all were at my trial. We can't take any risks even though it was over two decades ago. I'm laying low, especially when Jack and the judge are together, but even those times make me nervous."

"Did you find any leads on Brenna?"

Finn's face turns harder than usual. "No." He glances out the window.

"Dad hasn't found anything, either. But we'll keep looking. She's out there somewhere."

Finn lowers his voice. "What's her life like? What if I find her and I blow up everything she has going on? I don't want to destroy her twice."

"You won't," I assure him.

"You don't know for sure."

"Finn—"

"I have to go. Figure out a plan B. We need to get into the club. Once we do, everything will go as planned. Then, I have something to offer her when I find her." He opens the door and leaves before I can respond.

My phone rings. Obrecht's name flashes on the screen.

"Miss me already?" I answer.

His voice lacks all emotion, as it usually does when he's speaking to me. "We've got an issue we need clarification on."

"What's that?" I ask, tired of it but knowing I have no choice but to prove to everyone I've changed. In the past, I acted before I thought things through. That's no longer me.

"Not over the phone. Where are you?" he replies.

I glance out the window and recognize the storefront we're passing. Hailee's getting out of school soon and I'm picking her up. I glance at my watch and say, "A few blocks. I can turn around. Meet me when I pull up. I don't have a lot of extra time."

"Fine." Obrecht hangs up, and I tell my driver to return to his building.

Adrian and Obrecht get in the car. The moment the door shuts, Adrian accuses, "Why is one of your guys following Jack Christian?"

My stomach flips. "What business do you have with Jack Christian?"

"We've been trying to find dirt on him. You?" Adrian replies.

"Figuring out how to take him down once his company goes public and gets listed on the stock exchange."

Adrian's eyes turn to slits. "Why?"

"That's O'Malley business. Why do you need info on him?"

"He's in the middle of a divorce. Kora's representing his wife. He threatened both of them. I'm pretty sure his wife has already seen his wrath."

The timing on this can't be more perfect. I ask, "You need enough leverage for him to finish the divorce?"

"That's my guess, but Sergey wasn't specific."

I tap my fingers on my thighs. "Are you willing to share your intel with me? After you get what you need?"

Adrian shrugs. "Sure. I don't mind seeing the bastard further destroyed."

I scratch my chin. No red flags are popping up about why Adrian and Obrecht wouldn't get approved for the club. I finally say, "You need to become a member."

"Of what?" Obrecht's eyes flash his distrusting glare.

The acid burns in my gut. I attempt to ignore his look. "There's a private club. It moves locations and events are pop-up style. Jack never misses. My guy can't get in because of his record. Neither can I, plus, I'm an O'Malley. They don't let anyone linked to crime families inside. It's mostly politicians and businessmen. But you two, well, you would be their ideal candidates. You've got money and your name isn't associated with anything bad. Plus, it's easier to hide in a group than by yourself if you're trying to get proof of things while you're there."

"So it's a sex club?" Adrian asks, scowling.

My pulse increases. Finn and I need this, or we're going to lose our window to make it happen. "Yeah. You get a notification an hour before your entrance time. If you don't arrive at the exact time, you don't get in. There are no other warnings. Once you're inside, everything goes. You two up for it? I guarantee you'll get everything we both need on Jack."

Obrecht grunts. "Why do I have to get pulled into this? It's Adrian's assignment."

"There's another man I need dirt on, too," I admit and brace for his backlash. "As I said, a group is less noticeable than a lone wolf in these types of situations. Once you pound the hammer down on Jack, you won't get back in."

"So now I'm doing O'Malley jobs?" Obrecht grumbles.

He's getting too predictable. I shake my head. "No. We're exchanging favors. You got a problem with that?"

"What do we need to do to get a membership? Sergey's all over my ass, and I'm tired of my guys following this dickhead," Adrian admits.

I raise my eyebrows at Obrecht. *Time to admit you need my connections, asshole.*

Obrecht scowls. "Fine. Don't get used to me working for you. Who do you need dirt on?"

"Judge Peterson."

His face hardens further. He glances at the ceiling, shaking his head, then pins his steel gaze on me. "Who's the guy with the hand tattoo?"

"Finn O'Malley."

"Who is he?"

"My cousin. He went inside before you immigrated. He got out a few months after I did."

More distrust crosses Obrecht's expression. "What was he in for?"

God, I hate this. You can do your time, but it doesn't erase the stain, even with other criminals. "Murder. You want me to set up your membership or what? The woman who runs it will allow me to vouch for you."

"But she won't let you in?" Adrian suspiciously asks.

I swallow the acid rising in my chest. "My record doesn't allow me entry for a lot of places. Doesn't mean she's not in my pocket."

"Fine. Do what you have to do. Get us in. We'll get your info for you, but I don't work for you, Liam. Neither does Adrian," Obrecht states.

"Yeah, I'm clear on what this is," I seethe. I'm not looking for the Ivanovs to work for me. We have an alliance. Some of them, Obrecht especially, can't seem to understand I take that seriously.

Obrecht nods and they get out. I drive off and stop at my parents' house. I walk inside, and my dad hangs up the phone. "Liam. Your mother is going to be upset you missed her."

As expected, my mother wasn't happy when I moved out. I'm remodeling things at my new place, but I decided to live in it and work around it. It's better than her smothering me. Plus, after a few days of being trapped inside the house during the snowstorm, Hailee and I put a plan together on what to remodel first so it was the least inconvenient. She impressed me with her construction knowledge and reiterated she wanted to help. She had a social media site where she had pinned different photos to boards. There were a lot of great ideas, and I told her to choose everything. Whatever my little lamb wants so she enjoys being at my house, I'll make happen.

When I shrug, my father shakes his head. He lights up his pipe. After he takes a lungful of smoke, he slowly exhales. "Your mother is going to need you when I'm dead."

The burning in my stomach reignites. "You think I don't know this?"

His cold green eyes pierce mine. "She needs something to make her happy right now. She's having a tough time."

Guilt eats at me. "I love Mom, but I can't live with her. I'm sorry she's upset—"

"I'm not talking about that."

I cross my arms and sit in the chair. I sigh. "What do you want me to do, Dad?"

"You haven't invited her to your new house."

"She's been to Nora's house before."

"It's not Nora's anymore. Don't you think your mother deserves an invite?"

"I'm remodeling it. I thought I'd have her over after."

My father erupts in a coughing fit. When he finishes, the blood spots appear larger than normal, or maybe it only seems that way.

Sometimes it's easier just to do what my dad wants. I cave. "I'll ask her if she wants to come over."

He nods. "Today would be good."

"I'll call her when I leave. Hey, I've got to pick up Hailee soon. I need to get Adrian and Obrecht a membership for the club Jack and the judge go to. Can you work on that?"

Suspicion crosses my father's face. "Why did they agree to do O'Malley business?"

"They need dirt on Jack, too. I convinced them to get it on the judge for me while they were at it."

My father sits back in his seat and scratches his head. "You just invited trouble into your plan."

My stomach flips. I firmly reply, "No. I just solved our dilemma."

My father takes another deep drag off his pipe. I sit in nervous anticipation as he exhales. "Did you make it clear no one touches Jack until after his company has gone public?"

"They just need it to move Jack's divorce along. We get what we need, and so do they. It's a win-win," I inform him.

He leans forward. "Son, nothing is ever straightforward. Make sure they are crystal clear that nothing happens to him until the bell on the stock market rings and those shares pop up on the screen."

I shift in my seat. No matter what decision I make, I always seem not to have all the pieces together. My father finds a lesson in everything. Every time he teaches me something else, I have to push the nagging thought out of my head.

What if I don't learn everything before he dies?

His phone rings, and I rise. "I have to get Hales. Can you get them into the club?"

"Yeah. I'll let you know when they're approved."

"Thanks." I pat his back and leave.

I'm arriving at Hailee's school when Killian texts.

Killian: *Pub tonight?*

Me: *I'll ask Hales. Who's going?*

Killian: *My brothers and Finn said he'll try.*

Me: *I'll let you know.*

The busses take off, and I text Hailee.

Me: *I'm outside but no rush. Killian said my cousins are all at the pub tonight. Want to go?*

A few minutes pass then I get a response.

Hailee: *I'm wincing asking this. Can I bring Gemma? She had a day off and volunteered in my classroom. She was super helpful and is with me right now.*

Gemma sounds like a handful, according to Hailee. I haven't spent any time with Hailee's family besides the few minutes at breakfast. She told me Gemma knows about me and is cool with my past. Hailee also made her agree not to mention anything to her mom, so we still don't know if her mom is aware I was in prison. She holds firm to her statement that the O'Malleys are a crime family.

Me: *Yep. Tell Gemma drinks are on me.*

Hailee: *You might regret that. Please limit her.*

Me: *Do you want me to give her drink tickets?*

Hailee: *Not a bad idea.*

Me: *I'm sure she isn't that bad.*

Hailee: *You've never seen her in action.*

Me: *Looking forward to it.*

Hailee: *Honestly, it's not pretty. We'll be out in ten minutes, okay?*

Me: *No rush, little lamb.*

Hailee sends me a kiss emoji. I call my mom and invite her to see the house this week. She sounds happy, so I check one thing off the list. Hailee and Gemma come out of the school building. Hailee gets in the car and I pull her onto my lap and kiss her. "Did you have a good day?"

Her eyes sparkle, and the little jolt of happiness I get whenever I'm around her springs to life. "It was. Gemma was a big help."

I glance past Hailee. "Where is she?"

Hailee turns and groans. "She's talking to Knox. Or should I say flirting?" Hailee sticks her head out the door. "Gemma! We need to leave! Get in!"

I chuckle.

Hailee shakes her head. "She never stops."

Gemma slides into the car and shuts the door. She beams. "Hey, Liam! What's Knox's situation?"

Hailee groans. "Gemma!"

"What? He's superhot with a bit of penitentiary vibe. No offense, Liam. And don't worry, you've got it, too." She winks at me.

Well, at least someone is digging my record.

"Gemma!" Hailee reprimands again and slides off my lap.

I put my arm around her and kiss her head. "Gemma, I think you're the only person on earth who's excited I was in prison."

Hailee elbows me. "Don't encourage her."

"Ouch! Easy there!" I tell Hailee.

Gemma grimaces. "Sorry. I didn't mean anything offensive. It was a compliment."

"It's okay. Your sister digs the penitentiary vibe, too," I tease then pull Hailee closer. At least Gemma doesn't give me the same feeling everyone else does. She shouldn't think prison is cool. If she is seriously looking for a guy who's been in prison, then I'm going to need to sit her down and have a little chat. However, I assume she's joking. I'm happy she isn't scared of me though. In some ways, she reminds me of Dmitri Ivanov's wife, Anna. Since we met, she's been nothing but sweet to me, and I know she knew from the moment she met me, I was in prison. So it's nice to have someone not judge me.

Hailee puts her hands over her face. "Seriously. Don't encourage her."

Gemma playfully kicks Hailee. "Don't be a downer, Hailee."

I roll my head so my face is next to Hailee's. I smirk. "Yeah, Hales. Don't be a downer."

She grabs my chin. "Are you trying to annoy me?"

I peck her lips then turn back to Gemma. "Did Hales make you do crazy stuff today?"

She chirps. "Nope. We kept it pretty tame. Oh, except when Carlos and Mark decided to use their scissors as swords. That was fun. It's a good thing safety scissors don't have sharp edges!"

Hailee snickers. "Gemma also got asked out."

"By who?" I ask.

Hailee sinks into my chest. She sings, "Mr. Bonwilder."

"Who's that?"

Gemma rolls her eyes. "A super boring dude who teaches in the class next to Hailee. He always stares at me whenever I come in, often at my boobs. He asked me at lunch. And he's so not my type."

Amused, I ask, "Why is that?"

"You're so mean. Barry is super sweet. And he's a great teacher," Hailee claims.

"Don't be calling another man sweet," I tell her.

Gemma laughs. "Trust me, Liam. You have nothing to worry about unless Hailee decides she'd rather be with Mr. Dork-fest Boob Pervert."

"I thought you liked the perverts," Hailee teases.

"Ha ha! Funny!"

"That's not nice to say about Barry though," Hailee chastises her.

"But true. He wears knit button-down sweaters with suspenders underneath, for crying out loud. And has he eaten lately? The guy is skinnier than your school kids."

Hailee playfully kicks Gemma's leg and laughs. "That's so—"

"True! Admit it!" Gemma cries out.

"Fine. You're right. But he's nice."

"You sound like Mom now. If I have to hear about getting a nice, dependable guy one more time, I'm going to scream. I don't need boring in my life," Gemma drones.

"I'm nice and dependable," I state.

"Yes, you are," Hailee agrees.

Gemma leans forward. "You left out boring, which is why you aren't in the same box as Barry. Now tell me about your single cousins, Liam. They'll be there, right?"

Hailee rolls her eyes and kicks Gemma again. "You said you'd behave."

Gemma's eyes widen. "What? I am!" She looks at me and waits.

I chuckle. "Killian is a boxer and pretty outspoken. I'm closer to him than Nolan or Declan. Nolan is a few years older. He's a bit quieter and has a crazy-high IQ. He's one of the smartest guys I know and big into algorithms."

"He sounds boring. Is he a nerd?"

"Gemma! That's so not cool. Nolan is nice," Hailee claims.

Gemma smirks. "Killian sounds way hotter. Okay, who else do you have?"

"You can't talk bad about my boys," I warn Gemma but say it in a teasing tone.

"Ugh. Fine. Nolan sounds amazing!" she declares with a big smile. "Now what other hotties are related to you?"

Hailee shoots me an annoyed glance, and I hold back more laughter. Gemma's refreshing in some ways. She speaks her mind, which everyone might not appreciate, but I do. And at least she seems not to be scared of me or disapprove of Hailee's and my relationship. Since she's Hailee's sister, it makes me appreciate her more. I wish I could figure out how to help their mom give me a chance, but I'm still unsure of the best avenue to take. "Declan is the oldest. He's really into tech, too."

"How?" Gemma asks.

I shrug. "He has some mad hacker skills."

"Oooh! Now that's hot. And he's older? Like how old? Are we talking 'be my dirty daddy' material or 'too wrinkled to go there?'"

Wow. This girl might be a tad crazy.

Hailee gets down and dirty.

Behind closed doors.

Hailee's face turns red, and she scowls. "Oh. My. God! Gemma! You seriously need to listen to yourself one of these days!"

"Whatevs. Liam? Which is it?"

"Mmm...not sure. I'll let you judge that one."

She sighs. "Fine. Do you have any more cousins?"

"More than I can name. But the only other one who might be there is Finn."

"He's single?"

"Technically."

"What does that mean?"

My chest tightens. "Nothing. I'm not even sure if he'll show up."

"What's his story?"

"He just got out of the prison I was in."

Gemma's eyes light up. She wiggles her eyebrows. "Really? I definitely want to meet him."

"Oh my God!" Hailee mutters, further mortified.

And she isn't just joking. Time for a chat.

I remove my arm from Hailee and lean forward. In my firmest tone I say, "You should not be looking for a guy who has been in prison. Most of them are monsters. You could get hurt or killed."

She gives me a defiant stare. "So Finn is a monster?"

"No. But that doesn't mean you should go looking for trouble."

"I can handle myself."

In a firm voice, I warn, "Gemma, you're a gorgeous, nice girl. I'm pretty sure you can get any guy you want. Stay away from the ones who have been in prison."

She smirks. "You sound like our mom."

"I'm worried about you. This isn't cool," Hailee frets.

The acid in my stomach crawls up my chest. "Your mom isn't wrong."

The car stops in front of the pub. Gemma jumps out, and Hailee gives me a nervous glance. I kiss her quickly then motion for her to get out. I lead both women into the pub and to the bar. Darcey, Nora's manager, is behind it.

"Hey, Liam and Hailee! Good to see you. What can I get you?" she asks.

"Hales? Gemma?"

"I'll have an Irish Fix," Gemma says.

"What's that?" Hailee asks.

"It's good. Try it."

Hailee shrugs. "Make it two, then."

"Guinness for me." I glance around the crowded bar, trying to find my cousins.

Gemma grabs my sleeve. "Please tell me that hottie is Killian or Finn. He doesn't look old enough to play Daddy."

Wow.

I get over my shock and follow her gaze. "Nope. That's Nolan."

"What?" Confusion fills her voice. "He looks like a total bad boy, 'please take me behind the bar and do indecent things to me,' kind of man."

"Yep," Hailee chirps.

"Hey!" I chastise her.

Hailee laughs. "What? It's true. Nolan's smoking hot."

I lean into her ear. "I'll take you behind the bar and show you what's up and who's smoking hot, little lamb."

Hailee gives me her innocent little smirk, and my dick twitches. If Gemma weren't with us, I'd take her out back right now. Instead, I wave to Nolan.

He makes his way toward us. Darcey sets our drinks down. Gemma clinks glasses with Hailee and downs half of it.

"Liam. Your dad said to tell you it's confirmed." Nolan pins his eyes to mine.

A chill runs down my spine. Our guys in prison murdered Bruno Zielinski's sons and pinned it on the Rossi family. We designed it to break the alliance between the two crime families. It also guarantees a battle between them. My father doesn't seem to make mistakes, but I still ask, "It went our way?"

Nolan nods.

Gemma clears her throat next to me.

Nolan assesses her until her cheeks turn bright red. Then he embraces Hailee and kisses her on the cheek. "Hailee. How are you doing?"

My little lamb smiles, lighting up the room. "Good. You?"

"I don't have any complaints."

Gemma straightens. She sticks her hand out. "I'm Hailee's little sister, Gemma."

"By a year," Hailee mutters.

Nolan scans her body again. He takes her hand. "Nice to meet you. I'm Nolan." He drops her hand and spins toward Darcey. "Hey, Darcey. Can I get a bottle of water?"

"Sure. You aren't drinking tonight?"

"No. I'm only staying for a bit. I have work to finish."

"Well, that doesn't sound like fun," Gemma taunts.

Nolan takes a sip of his water and shrugs without glancing at her.

One of the servers comes behind the bar. She beams. "Hi, Nolan!"

"Hey, Molly."

"Thanks for fixing my mom's laptop," she says.

"No problem. Glad it's working again."

"Hailee, is this your sister? You look a lot alike." Molly redirects a friendly smile at Hailee and Gemma.

Hailee confirms, "Yes. This is Gemma."

Gemma steps next to Nolan. She gives Molly a dismissive smile and focuses on him. I don't miss Molly's irritated expression. She's been friends with Nolan since we were in school. Gemma puts her hand on Nolan's arm and bats her eyes. "So you're a computer guru? I thought you'd be the boxer, at first glance." She squeezes his biceps.

He stares at her with a neutral expression. "Yeah? Well, I'm not. Nice meeting you." He turns to Molly. "Are my brothers in the game room?"

14

Hailee

My sister has always been the wild child of our family, but she's taking it a bit too far. I don't understand her sudden attraction to felons or the over-the-top-look-at-me behavior. She's usually fun and outgoing like Kora, but there seems to be a recklessness about her. She's drinking more than I've ever seen her drink. Watching her in action with Liam's cousins only makes my skin crawl.

"Time to get off the table, lass," Killian orders.

Gemma sits on the corner of the pool table, with her legs crossed and cleavage hanging out. She's drunk way too much, and it's only eight o'clock.

"But Nolan hasn't said please yet." She shoots daggers at Nolan. He's not giving her the attention Killian, Declan, and Finn have. The more he doesn't respond to her, the more embarrassing she gets. It's not like Gemma to call out guys who don't give her the time of day. Then again, most guys drool over her, so maybe it's a first for her, and I just have never thought about it.

He steps next to her, leans down, and says something in her ear. I can't hear it, but she reaches for his shirt and fists a handful of material.

In a loud voice, Gemma slurs, "You don't know who you're messing with."

"Yeah? Who's that?"

I groan and turn to Liam. "Can we please take her out of here?"

"Your sister knows how to keep it interesting," Finn replies with an amused grin and finishes the rest of his beer.

I cover my face and lean my head against Liam's arm. "Please."

He slides his arm around me. "Do you—"

"What did you just say?" Nolan barks.

The hairs on my arms rise. I drop my hand and look at my sister. Nolan has a snarl on his face. Both of his hands are on the table next to my sister's hips, and his face hovers inches from hers. I've only met Nolan a few times, but I've never seen him angry before.

Killian and Declan's faces are both colorless. They gape at Gemma, and my gut drops.

I jump up. "Gemma. What did you say?"

Nolan doesn't tear his eyes off her, matching her glare, but I don't miss her lips quivering. In a low, menacing tone, he repeats, "Say it again."

The room becomes so quiet, the sound of my heart pounds in my ears. Gemma attempts to slide off the table, and Nolan grabs her by the throat and makes her look at him.

"Nolan! Let her go!" I yell.

"Nolan!" Liam growls and pulls at his arm. He glances at Killian and Declan. "What the fuck is wrong with you two? Why are you just standing there?"

The brothers seem to snap out of it. "Let her go," Declan barks.

Nolan releases her neck, steps back, and seethes, "Get out."

"Nolan! What has gotten into you?" Liam snaps.

I step between him and Gemma. She's trembling and trying to hold back tears. I reach for her. "Come on."

"You need to leave, too," Nolan fires out.

Liam tugs him back and slams him against the wall. He gets in his face. "What did you just say to my woman?"

"Liam!" I scream.

Finn pulls Liam away, and Killian and Declan step in front of Nolan. Each brother scowls.

"How could you bring them into our house?" Nolan seethes. His eyes look as crazed as Liam's. But hatred fills Killian and Declan's. I'm at a loss for words. What could Gemma have said that would create such a reaction?

"You better watch your mouth," Liam barks.

Nolan enunciates, "Get them out of here."

Liam moves toward him, but Finn grabs him. He orders, "Easy."

"What are you doing?" Liam asks Nolan.

He points to my sister and me. "Ask the Bailey sisters."

Bailey?

I glance at Gemma, and her tears fall. I'm so confused. Why would she tell Nolan our last name is Bailey? And why is Nolan so upset? I firmly say, "My sister is obviously drunk. Our last name is O'Hare."

"How long have you been spying on us?" Nolan barks.

"I swear to God, Nolan, if you don't stop these accusations, you're going to leave in a body bag," Liam hurls.

"It's true," Gemma whispers.

My insides shake harder. "What are you talking about?"

"I'm going—" She puts her hand over her mouth and runs out of the room.

I follow her through the pub, yelling her name. She gets to the bathroom, and as soon as she enters the stall, she throws up. I hold her hair, confused about everything that is happening and not understanding what any of this means.

When she finishes getting sick, she spins on her butt and leans against the stall. I hand her wet towels, and she wipes her mouth. New tears fall. "I'm sorry." Her face is red and sweat coats her skin.

I push her hair off her face. "Gemma, I'm so lost right now."

"I saw him," she whispers.

"Who?"

She sobs harder then gets back on her knees and gets sick again. "I'm sorry," she cries out and rolls back on her ass.

I help her clean up again then pull her to me and hug her. "Gemma, it's okay. Tell me what's going on."

"I-I'm not supposed to. I don't know why I did that out there. I...oh God! He's evil. I saw it in his eyes. And she's so cruel. How can our sister be so mean when we're blood?" she sobs.

"Shh," I say to calm her, even more frustrated over these things she's saying that I can't comprehend. When her chest returns to a more normal breathing pattern, I pull away. "Gemma, what did Ciara or Ella do that was cruel?"

She shakes her head. "Nothing. They don't know."

"Know what?"

She squeezes her eyes shut. Her lips tremble harder, and her voice cracks. "Who they are. Who we are."

"Gemma, who are they?" She loses it again, and I pull her close. I stroke her head until she calms and ask again, "Who are you talking about?"

She wipes her nose. "Our father. His other daughter."

I freeze. My insides quiver so hard, I swallow down bile. Everything she said spins in my head, including she saw his eyes. I try to gather my thoughts before I speak. "Where did you see him?"

"I didn't want to. She made me," she cries out.

"Gemma, this isn't making any sense. I need you to explain this."

"He said we have to take our roles in the family."

Dizziness hits me from the fear swirling in my bones. I hold my sister tighter. "What does that mean?"

"He's a Bailey. We're Baileys. Our time is running out."

I shake my head. "I don't understand what that means."

She puts her head on the stall wall, and pain crosses her face. "Our father is Rory Bailey. He has a few months until they release him from prison. Our sister is Orla Bailey. She's running the clan but can't have kids. Our father says we have to take our roles in the family. He has men lined up to marry us."

My stomach twists. "What are you talking about?"

Her green eyes widen. "It's true. She made me go with her to see him."

"When?"

"A month ago. She's...she follows me everywhere. She said she would kill Mom if I told anyone." She closes her eyes, but the tears never stop.

A chill digs into my bones. So many questions are flying at me. Flashbacks of my mother bloody and bruised, and me holding Gemma, Ciara, and Ella in a closet, trying to keep them quiet so my father wouldn't find us or hurt my mother worse, fill my mind. "We have to talk to Mom."

"We can't. I shouldn't have told you. You don't understand. The Baileys are..." Gemma swallows hard. "They're mob, Hailee. But none of them seem like the O'Malleys. Orla is the madame at their whorehouses. She took me there. If we don't marry who our father wants, he said he'd put us in there. They...oh God! We're them!" She breaks down, and I pull her as tightly to me as possible.

I don't understand this. How could our mother not tell us we were part of this? How did this Orla woman find Gemma?

Gemma wipes her face. "Liam will protect you. I-I need to find someone to protect me, too. Please. I don't want to ever see them again."

"Shhh." I do my best to calm her, but my hand is shaking as hard as she is. "We need to get out of here, Gemma. Let's go home."

"Where? She infested my building. It wasn't another tenant. She did it. I-I can't go to Mom's. It's too hard not to tell her," she sobs.

"Gemma, we have to talk to her."

Gemma grabs my arm. Fear fills her face. "You can't. Orla will kill her. She isn't like us, Hailee. Please! You can't tell anyone!"

I put my hand on her cheek. I've never seen her so upset. She may have drunk a lot, but she's never looked so scared or sounded so hysterical. "Okay. I won't. Let's go home. We can't stay here all night."

She slowly allows me to help her up. I'm about to open the door when she puts her hand on it, stopping me. "He wants to see you, Hailee."

My stomach churns so fast, I cover it. "I'm not—"

"Do you think Liam can kill them? Especially her. She's...Hailee, she's so horrible." She falls apart again.

I freeze. Blood pounds between my ears. Air becomes hard to take into my lungs. My mouth becomes dry. I open it, but nothing comes out.

Gemma's eyes are so scared, I get new chills. "She's everywhere. On my phone. In my building. At my work. Anywhere I go, she shows up. I'm going to go crazy."

I embrace her again. She sobs against me, and a puddle of her tears soak my shirt. I say the only thing that comes to mind. "Let's go. We'll talk to Liam about how to protect you."

She finally allows me to lead her out of the restroom, but a new reality meets us. Liam and his cousins are standing against the wall, waiting for us. They all have the same piercing gaze. New horror fills me. Betrayal and hatred swirl in their expressions, but Liam's feels the worst. And I finally understand this isn't just about Gemma and me.

15

Liam

Acid burns my throat. The air in my lungs seems not to exist. My heart seizes so forcefully, pain overpowers everything. If I could squeeze my fists any tighter, I might break the bones in my hand.

My little lamb is a Bailey. Not just any Bailey. The daughter of the head of the clan, Rory Bailey. How is this possible? Gemma has to be lying. Nothing is coming to mind about why she would concoct this story. Yet, I can't wrap my head around it.

The Baileys rule the southern part of the country. It wasn't always that way. Over the years, the war between our families created a border. Our grandfather met with the head of their family to stop the bloodshed. They created a treaty. The Baileys got the southern half of the country, and we got the northern part.

It should have solved our silent war. For a few years, things calmed. Both parties kept their word. Then our grandfather died. The running of their clan fell into Rory Bailey's hands. He and his brothers had just arrived from Ireland and didn't have any intention of keeping the status quo. Everything he did proved he was a new level of vicious. My father had just stepped into power and was unprepared. In no time at all, the agreement fell apart. Rory didn't even wait a week after taking over before he started moving in on our territory.

A new war began. The man who murdered my uncle—the one I killed in revenge—was Rory's cousin.

Rory's ego was too big, and he thought he was untouchable. He went down for a double homicide. For over twenty years, he's sat in a jail cell, on the floor above where I slept for fifteen years. It was the warden's attempt at keeping peace in prison. Baileys lived on the fifth floor. O'Malleys on the fourth. It worked for some things, but inside the concrete walls, the threat of violence between the families was a daily occurrence. Everywhere I went, I watched my back. It wasn't a secret Rory wanted me dead.

Rory might be locked away, but he's continued to call the shots. His brother Mack implements all his orders. Over the years, the Baileys have become more violent. In addition to their drug and gambling earnings, human trafficking has become a big income for them. Thinking about it makes my stomach churn. The more money the Baileys get, the more powerful they become.

Every ounce of control I have not to tear down the bathroom door is now on display. Several times, I step forward, and Finn pushes me back against the wall.

"Wait," he advises.

"You let the enemy come into our house," Nolan seethes.

"Quiet! We don't know if the woman is even telling the truth," Declan claims.

I sniff hard and turn. All I see are Killian's eyes in hot flames. I have no right to pray, but I find myself begging God for it not to be true. Then my mind wanders to what it means if my little lamb is a Bailey and if she could be a pawn sent to spy on me.

She never saw me until I approached her at Nora's reopening.

It could have been part of the plan.

Jesus. It's Hales. There's no way she's a Bailey. Gemma is lying.

Why would she lie?

What if their blood is tainted?

"Sean and our father are dead because of the Baileys," Nolan fumes.

"Enough," Declan reprimands.

The door opens, and a lump forms in my throat. The acidic bile fills my chest, and I lock eyes with my little lamb. Her blue orbs flare with so many emotions, I can barely breathe. Is it that they've blown their cover? Is it fear of what we will do? Is it confusion?

I thought I knew Hailee, but I suddenly feel as if I don't know anything about her. If she is a Bailey, then how can I ever touch her again?

Tears stain Gemma's cheeks. Her eyes are red. She's shaking harder than Hailee. My little lamb protectively keeps her close to her side as if to shield her from us.

Us. The O'Malleys.

Them. The Baileys.

More bile rises at the thought, and it takes everything I have to swallow it down. Two beautiful women, with the blood of Satan swirling in their veins. How is it possible?

"Is she lying?" I force myself to ask.

Hailee defiantly sticks her chin in the air. Her glare makes my stomach churn faster. "My sister isn't a liar."

"But you are?" I hurl, bracing my hands against the wall, trying to stop the rage and hurt spiraling through me.

"We didn't know!" Gemma cries out and sobs.

Hailee tugs her closer. "Why are you so angry about this? We're the ones who should be upset. We're the ones who just learned we're part of some family we've never heard of."

"Are you kidding me?" Nolan growls, and Gemma jumps.

"Nolan," Declan warns under his breath.

Hailee's eyes dart to each of my cousins then land on me. Her lips tremble. She quietly asks, "Liam?"

"Your family helped murder our brother. It was after they killed our father. Let's start with that," Nolan barks.

Gemma gapes at Nolan then turns to Hailee. "We need to go."

Hailee furrows her brows. She finally tears her gaze from me. She turns to Gemma and quietly says, "Let's go." They take two steps, and I step in front of her. "The door is that way." I point to the back exit.

Fear fills both women's faces. Disgust hits me. My little lamb is scared of me. It isn't something I ever wanted. And I might be more confused than she is about what Gemma revealed.

If she isn't trying to trick me.

Jesus. It's Hales.

She didn't deny it. She's a Bailey.

Hailee tightens her arm around Gemma. "We aren't going in the alley. We're going out the front door. Now move, Liam."

Blood pounds between my ears. It may be the sickest I've ever felt. "No. My car is parked out back. You're coming with me."

Gemma's voice shakes. "You're going to hurt us now? Because we're part of a family that we don't want anything to do with?"

"Don't fall for it," Nolan orders.

"Watch your mouth," I bark back.

He steps toward me, but Killian grabs the back of his shirt. He yanks him backward.

"Get off me!" Nolan shouts.

"I said to calm down," Declan orders. He and Finn exchange a glance. They form a wall around Nolan.

Finn motions toward the door. "Go."

I put my arms around Hailee and Gemma and guide them past my cousins and into the alley. Knox opens the back door of the vehicle. I order, "Get in."

Gemma gives Hailee a questioning look. My little lamb hesitates.

My stomach twists tighter. They think I'm going to do something terrible to them. I can't believe these thoughts are running through the mind of the woman who was my everything until a few minutes ago. I hate I'm not sure if she still is or will be in the future. I quietly say, "I'm not going to hurt you, Hales. We can't stay here right now. Let's go."

Her blue eyes peer out under her long lashes. "How do I know you won't hurt us?"

Emotions I don't want to deal with attempt to break through the surface. "I'm not the one who's changed, little lamb."

Hurt fills her eyes. "You think I have?"

"Didn't say that," I reply with my heart pounding against my chest cavity.

Her eyes turn to slits. "Didn't you?"

I avoid answering her. "Get in."

"Where are you taking us?" Gemma demands.

I don't take my gaze off Hailee. I'm searching for something, anything that will reveal the truth about her knowledge in this matter, but the same defiant, fearful expression stays present. "My place. We need to talk."

"What if we don't want to go?" Gemma asks. Her voice sounds strong, but her body hasn't stopped shaking.

I look over my shoulder at the door then at Gemma. "Would it be better to go to your mother's? After all, I do have questions for her."

"No!" Gemma cries out, and her face crumbles.

Hailee turns to her. "Get in the car, Gemma."

"But—"

"Please. Do what I ask."

Gemma sniffles and nods. She gets in the car, and Hailee turns to Knox. "You get in the car, too, please."

He glances at me, and I motion for him to get in. Hailee shuts the back car door, and Knox closes the front. We stare at each other in silence for a brief moment.

Hailee clears her throat. "I-I didn't know, Liam. Before tonight, I never heard of these people. I'm sorry for what they've put your family through, but you have to believe me."

I want to tell her I believe her. That no matter what, we'll get past this and nothing will break us. But the Bailey name alone makes me feel so much hate, I don't know how I can look the other way. There are too many questions and too much bloodshed between our families to pretend everything is fine without doing my due diligence. I finally admit, "I want to."

She blinks hard. "But you don't?"

"I didn't say that."

"Stop using your noncommittal bullshit on me, Liam," she angrily spouts. She rips the door open. "Gemma, get out."

"Hales—"

She spins. "They've threatened my sister. They want to kill my mother. My father, who I didn't even know the name of until tonight, has plans for Gemma and me. They scare the shit out of me. And if you aren't going to help us, then I don't have anything else to say. I don't answer to you, Liam."

I slam the door shut and step forward so she's against the car. I fist her hair and tug it back. She gasps, and all the years the Baileys stole from my family reach a boiling point. Maybe it's some sick, twisted karma that Rory Bailey's two daughters are in front of me, needing protection from him. Satisfaction creeps into my bones that I've fucked his daughter in too many positions to count. But it's a fleeting, selfish feeling. It reconfirms I'm a bastard, because the only thing that matters is I get to the bottom of the truth. Looking into Hailee's eyes, I already know she could never lie to me about this. I don't know what his plans are for her, but at this moment, it doesn't even matter. "You forgot something, little lamb."

Her eyes glisten in the moonlight. She chokes out, "What?"

"You're mine. And you do answer to me. I'm in charge of your protection. So get your ass in the car. When we get to my house, you and your sister will tell me everything you know. Then I'm going to call the shots. Not you. Not Gemma. *Me*."

"Liam—"

"He can want you all he wants, Hales. He's not getting you. If you told me you knew all along, he still wouldn't get you. I would chain you up and keep you hidden from everyone. You'd never escape. I'd make sure of it. I could say it would only be to hold over him, and God help me, I would enjoy every second of knowing how much it eats at him to know that I have you. But the craziest part is, as much as I despise the blood that flows through your veins, it's only a small crumb about why I would keep you."

She swallows hard. Her breath merges with mine. "This is some sort of sick revenge for you, isn't it? The fact you've had me, and I'm that vile man's daughter."

I lean closer and brush my lips against hers. "I said small crumb. The rest of the loaf he doesn't get to taint."

"So I'm your pawn against my father? That's all I—"

"Jesus, you need to listen better, Hales," I growl.

She bites on her lip. Her forehead creases with wrinkles. "I'm not playing your game."

"No?" I drag my finger down her cheek. "From the brief discussions we've had about him, I always got the impression you hated your father."

"I do. And especially now," she blurts out.

I trace her lips with my finger. "Are you going to stand here and tell me you don't like sticking it to your father by fucking an O'Malley, now that you know there is bad blood between our families?"

She deeply inhales and doesn't reply. She tries to look away, but I hold her chin.

I lean into her ear. "Admit it, little lamb. Admit you love me, but you also are going to love fucking me and knowing how much your father would hate us being together."

"You're sick," she whispers.

I kiss her but don't deepen it. "Yeah. I'm sick. I'm also in love with a Bailey. So I'm going to enjoy every warped second of it. And I promise you this, when I get through with him, there will be nothing but dust blowing in the wind."

Her expression never changes, but it doesn't fool me. Things I couldn't figure out about Hailee now make sense. Her stubbornness. The fight within her. And my naughty little lamb who looks so innocent but really isn't.

"Admit you're just as depraved as me. This new reason to love me is an added bonus you're going to enjoy. I'm right, aren't I?"

Time seems to stand still. Heat flares in her eyes. She finally whispers, "Yes."

16

Hailee

The ride to Liam's is quiet. Gemma sits across from me and keeps giving me nervous looks. Liam possessively has his arm around my shoulders. My body wants to sink into him as if everything is the same. But I'm not sure if it ever will be again. Liam confessed his love for me, and it should have been one of those romantic moments. Instead, we were talking about twisted things. To my surprise, I loved how it all came out. I must be a lunatic for not feeling disgusted. All I keep doing is replaying it in my mind and reprimanding myself for the flutters I keep feeling.

I should also be concerned he revealed he would chain me up if I had known who my father is, but all I feel is my body throbbing over his deranged, obsessive comments. I've already experienced what he's capable of doing to me when he tied me up after our argument over the bus, and my most intimate nerves are pulsing at the thought of him doing it again. The vision of me in chains, at Liam's mercy, keeps popping up, and heat rushes to my face. I hate that every part of me is happy he would do whatever he needed to keep me. So between the revelation about who I am and my thoughts, which keep surprising me, I wish I could close my eyes and pretend this night never happened.

I'm still grappling over everything Gemma revealed. Anger is building in me. My mother hid from us the identity of our father. She always said it was for our protection. Since we remembered living in fear, my sisters and I never pushed her. We were grateful she was strong enough to leave him.

Now, the truth feels deceptive. It appears to have put us in harm's way. We were unaware of what could happen, and now we're left to figure out how to stay safe and free from his grasp. And who is this Orla woman Gemma keeps saying is our sister?

There's so much I don't understand. I've never seen my sister scared like this before. It takes a lot to rock Gemma. The things she revealed tonight make my stomach pitch. I'm not sure how to stay safe or protect anyone in my family.

We pull into Liam's driveway and another car parks behind us. Lights fill the car. The door slams. Liam glances out the window. His lips hit my ear, sending shivers down my spine. "I'll handle this. Take your sister inside."

"Who—"

There's a knock on the windshield and Liam motions to my side of the car.

"Let's go, Gemma." I open the door and get out then reach in to help her.

Gemma says, "Thanks. I—"

"We need to talk, Liam." Nolan's voice hits my ear.

Gemma freezes and turns.

Liam gets out. "Not tonight. We'll talk tomorrow."

"No. I want to know why she said what she did."

"We already know why," Liam claims.

"No. We don't know why. We know what she said, and that's it. I want to know why she said what she did to me," Nolan seethes.

"I'm sorry! I shouldn't have," Gemma cries out.

"Gemma," I quietly warn. I don't want to rile Nolan up any more than he already is.

"Hales, take your sister inside!" Liam firmly orders.

"Come on." I attempt to guide my sister away, but her eyes don't leave Nolan's.

"Tell me," Nolan says.

Liam tries again. "Nolan—"

"Were you targeting me?" he asks.

"What? Nolan, go home. Don't you dare harass my sister," I bark.

"Stay out of this," Nolan replies.

"Don't talk to my woman like that," Liam warns.

"Your woman is a Bailey," Nolan growls.

"You have a five-second warning and then I'm going to—"

"I'll tell him why!" Gemma belts out.

The air turns silent. Nolan's green eyes seem to glow hotter next to Liam's. Nolan grits out, "Tell me."

My sister shifts on her feet. "Can I tell you without Hailee and Liam?"

"What? Gemma, no!" I insist.

Liam agrees, "Yeah. I don't think—"

"Fine. Get in my car," Nolan orders.

I tug Gemma to me. "No. She's not—"

"Stop!" She shrugs out of my grasp. "He has a right to know. I shouldn't have said it."

"What exactly did you say?" I ask.

"Nothing you need to know." She walks toward Nolan's car, and I stare at her.

I point to Nolan. "If you hurt her—"

Nolan spins toward me. "I don't hurt women. I'm an O'Malley, not a Bailey. You should learn the difference."

"You grabbed my sister's neck," I point out.

Nolan shakes his head. His expression turns cocky. He keeps his eyes on mine and calls out, "Gemma, did I hurt you?"

My sister clears her throat. "No."

"Did you like it?" More arrogance fills his orbs.

I glare at him. "You're an—"

"Yes," my sister announces.

I jerk my head and gape at her. "What is wrong with you?"

"Don't be a hypocrite, Hailee. I'm sure Liam is no saint around you." She opens the door and slides into the car.

"What does that mean?" I ask.

Liam chuckles.

I turn toward him. "Why are you laughing at me?"

"I'll show you." He takes my hand and pulls me into the house. The moment the door shuts, he spins me against the door and puts his hand on my neck the same way Nolan did it to Gemma.

My heart races faster. Blood pounds in my ears. My lungs attempt to take in more air but can't seem to.

He tilts his face in front of mine, staring at me. His lips hit my jaw, and he kisses up to my ear. "I think Gemma knows more about what she likes than you do. I'm going to have to work on showing you."

I don't speak, trying not to think about Liam and his hard body or the way tingles are rushing down my spine. We have a lot to talk about. I need to decipher what all this information means.

"So much makes sense about you now," Liam mumbles.

I hold my breath. "What do you mean?"

He brings his face to mine, giving me one chaste kiss. "You've got some Bailey traits in you, little lamb."

My stomach flips, and I feel sick. I don't know much about the Baileys, but what I do know I don't like. "Don't say that."

He moves his hands to my cheeks. His thumbs graze my lips. "Do you want me to lie to you?"

"I'm not them."

His lips curl. "Oh, but you are. Your blood is theirs. The stubbornness and fight in you come from them. I didn't understand how you could be so fearless of me, but now it all makes sense."

I ask a question I'm scared to know the answer to. "How can you say this, then tell me you hate them and still want to be together?"

His eyes blaze into mine. "I'm not giving you up, little lamb. You may be part of them, but you're also *not* part of them." He tucks a lock of my hair behind my ear. A sinister smile appears in his expression. "And like I stated earlier, I'm a sick bastard. There was no way I was ever letting you go before tonight. This...well, this is better than anything I could ever have done to your father."

My stomach nervously flips. I should run from Liam right now. Everything about this is a blinking red light. I hate my father. It's clear Liam does as well but for different reasons I know nothing about. I'm not sure if I want all the details. Instead of running, I swallow the lump in my throat. "Doesn't this worry you? At the very least, aren't you concerned about what my father may do to my family and me?"

His face falls. "Now that I know who you are, no one will come near you or Gemma."

"What about my mom and other sisters?"

"They all have O'Malleys watching them right now."

My mouth turns dry. I stare at Liam. "Wh-how?"

He drags his finger almost nonchalantly over my jawline. "I take care of what's mine, little lamb. And I told you I had enemies. Your family got my protection the moment we got together. If anyone tries anything, my men will stop them."

The uncomfortable feeling I can't shake intensifies. Liam warned me he had enemies. I could never have imagined they were my blood relatives. There's comfort and uneasiness knowing he already had his men watching over my mother and sisters. Something else pops up in my mind. "How did you not know about Orla if you have O'Malleys trailing Gemma? It's been almost a month since we got together."

Liam's face turns white. "When did she last meet with her?"

I shake my head. "I don't know."

"Then let's—"

The door flies open, and Nolan storms inside. Gemma is close behind him. He holds out his hand. "Give me your phone, Hailee."

"What? No!" I'm still unsure about him after he got so angry with Gemma.

"Hailee, give it to him," Gemma orders with fear in her eyes.

"Why?"

Her eyes widen. She whispers, "Please. And stop talking."

A chill runs down my spine. Her previous admission Orla knew her every move and was in her phone enters my mind. Liam doesn't hesitate. He reaches into my purse and hands my phone to Nolan.

"Code?" Nolan demands and swipes the screen.

"Six-Eight-Two-Nine-One-One," I reply.

He spends five minutes going through it and finally hands it back to me. "It's clean."

"Clean?" I ask.

"They don't have a tracer on you."

I glance at Gemma. "They had one on your phone?"

She nods. "Nolan just removed it. I had the microphone off since I was paranoid, but they were tracking me and had access to my emails and text messages."

My stomach pitches. "Gemma, when did you talk to Orla last?"

She scrunches her face. "She calls me every day, several times."

"Saying what?" Liam asks.

Gemma's eyes fill with fresh tears. "Reminding me that when our father gets out of prison, I have to marry the man he has chosen for me." Her lips tremble harder. Her tears spill on her cheeks. "Telling me your day is coming, and she knows you've betrayed our family by sleeping with an O'Malley."

A wave of cold flows through my body. The look on my sister's face infuses a lifetime of fear into my bones.

Liam pulls me tighter to him. "She's not coming near Hales, nor you. When did you see her last?"

Gemma pauses for a moment. "Maybe a month ago. She was following me all the time. At least a few days a week, she'd appear. The last time I saw her was a few days before my mom and I ran into you and Hailee at breakfast. Since then, she only calls. But I also stopped going out of the house. If I'm not with Mom or coming to see you, I don't leave."

"What about your job?" I ask.

Guilt fills Gemma's face. "I quit. I-I kept making mistakes. She would show up or send one of her thugs to surprise me at work. I just wanted it to stop."

I gape at her, speechless. Gemma had her dream job, working for one of the top advertising agencies in the country. She spent years working her way up the ladder and was only a promotion away from a vice president position.

She glances at the ceiling, and shame fills her face.

I step forward and pull her into my arms. I quietly ask, "Did you tell your boss, Gavin, why you were quitting?"

She pulls back. "No. What would I say? My psycho half-sister is stalking me and my incarcerated father is getting out soon and wants me to marry one of his mob thugs? She will stop at nothing to destroy my life. I couldn't continue making rookie mistakes at work. It wasn't fair to my team, but I couldn't pull it together. Her people were everywhere—the delivery guys, the food cart employee, the Uber or taxi drivers. Anywhere I went, they showed up. It became easier to stay home at Mom's. I'm going stir crazy, but at least I don't have to see them."

Guilt eats at me. I wish she would have told me what's going on. She begged to stay with me, and I didn't let her. I blurt out, "I'm sorry I told you no. You can move in with me."

"No," Liam states.

I spin to him. "I'm not—"

"Neither of you are living on your own. You'll both move in here. I'll watch over you."

I point to the mattress in the corner of the open space from the walls that came down a few days ago. "There isn't even one bedroom right now."

"Gemma's coming with me," Nolan states.

I turn to him in shock. "What are you talking about?"

He crosses his arms. "She knows a lot more than what she's disclosing right now. She's going to tell me everything she knows about anyone associated with the Baileys."

"You aren't kidnapping my sister," I claim.

Nolan's eyes turn to slits. "The attitude toward me is getting old."

"Don't talk to my woman like that," Liam barks.

Nolan focuses on him. "Don't let your dick cloud your judgment. They're Baileys. We're at more risk because of your relationship. Whatever she knows, she needs to disclose."

Liam steps toward him. "I said—"

"I'll go with him," Gemma blurts out.

"What? No!" I exclaim.

"He's right." Gemma turns to Nolan. "If I go with you, nothing will happen to me? You'll protect me from them?"

"As long as you don't lie to me. If you utter one untruth and I find out, I'll throw you to the wolves like a piece of raw meat," Nolan threatens.

"Jesus. You are not going with him. Liam," I say, looking at him for help.

"I don't lie. It won't be a problem. Let's go. I'm tired," Gemma interjects.

"Liam—"

"Let her go. Nolan, if she lies, you bring her to me, not the Baileys," Liam orders.

"I don't lie!" Gemma insists.

"Good. We won't have any issues, then." Nolan opens the door and motions for her to go.

"Gemma!" I try one last time.

She spins. "What do you want me to do? Go back to Mom's? Go to your place? I'm not safe anywhere. At least if I go with Nolan, I'm protected."

"Liam already has O'Malleys watching you. You don't need to go with him," I blurt out.

Betrayal fills Gemma's face. "You allowed him to have people watch me, and you didn't tell me? No wonder why I'm so paranoid. I've got Baileys and O'Malleys following me. You should have told me."

"I only told her before you walked in. Unlike the Baileys, you won't notice them. We aren't trying to scare you. It's only for your protection," Liam informs her.

Gemma shuts her eyes then shakes her head. She opens them and replies, "I'll talk to you tomorrow, Hailee."

"Gemma!" I reach for her, but she shrugs out of my grasp.

"Don't! I'm tired. I'm sick of talking. I'll see you tomorrow." She walks out the door and Nolan follows her.

"Nolan, if you hurt my sister—"

He spins, scowling. Anger emanates off him. "I'm not repeating this again. I'm not who you have to worry about. Liam, set your woman straight." He leaves.

Liam shuts the door. "You don't need to worry about Nolan. He won't hurt her. She'll be safe with him."

It's meant to calm me, but I can't shake the thought, how will any of us ever be safe again?

17

Hailee

"Orla?" my mother gasps.

"You know her?" Gemma asks.

My mother squeezes her eyes shut, as if reliving a painful experience. "Yes. Your father had an ongoing affair with a woman named Riona. Her daughter is Orla."

"Mom, how could you keep all of this from us?" I accuse. My twin sisters Ciara and Ella haven't said much after Gemma and I told them we're Baileys.

My mother stares at me with no color left in her face. She quietly replies, "I warned you to stay away from Liam and the O'Malleys."

"Don't you dare put this on Liam or his family," I reprimand.

"The O'Malleys are the only option we have for protection," Gemma insists.

My mother's eyes widen. "Your father and his thugs will kill them if he finds out you have anything to do with them."

"He already knows Hailee is with Liam," Gemma blurts out.

My mother's hand covers her mouth. Tears form in her eyes. She closes them for several moments then steps in front of me. "You have to break it off."

My insides quiver. I stand straighter and firmly reply, "No."

She puts her hands on my shoulders. "You don't understand. A full-out war will occur. No one is more powerful than the Baileys. You will never be safe again and—"

"So I break up with Liam and marry the gangster my father has lined up? Is that what you want?" I angrily fire back.

"And what do you think Liam is?" My mother's eyes drill into mine.

"He's nothing like the man you fell for," I remind her. She isn't an innocent angel, either, when it comes to her past dating life. I know nothing about it, but from what I've tried to forget and what Gemma and Liam told me about our father, I don't see how she could have ever loved a man so vile.

My mother turns away, and her hands shake.

The normal sympathy I would show toward my mother is nowhere. I've always been proud to be her daughter, but I suddenly don't understand how she could have ever made the choices she did. All night, I tossed and turned. I barely slept, replaying all the details I learned about whose blood runs through my veins. I ask, "How could you think you could hide this from us, and we wouldn't find out?"

She continues not to face me. "I-I didn't think he knew where we were. I was so careful. I changed our last name. Anyone I knew when I was with him, I no longer spoke with, including my closest friends and family. Everything I did was to protect you from him and his clan."

I wish I could control the anger I can't seem to shake. I spit out, "They're the mob. I'm sure they know everything."

My mother spins. The same rage I'm feeling is on her face. "And what do you think Liam is a part of, hmm? I begged you to break up with him. I told you about his family, and you still stayed with him. What makes you think it is okay to continue seeing the future head of a crime family?"

Rage spins so fast, I hurl back, "I guess the apple doesn't fall far from the tree, right, Mom?"

Pain ripples through her expression. The room turns silent, and my heart beats faster. She finally bites out, "You don't know what you're getting yourself into."

"Maybe I don't. But at least you didn't have to tell me about Liam. I already know everything he's capable of. Hurting me isn't part of it. But regardless of my relationship with him, it doesn't negate the facts. The minute we were adults, you should have told us the truth about who we were. They stalked and threatened Gemma for months, so badly she quit her job," I reveal.

My mom gapes at Gemma then her tears fall. She puts her arms around my sister. "I'm sorry, baby. Why didn't you tell me?"

Gemma scrunches her face. Her voice shakes. "Orla said she'd kill all of you if I told anyone."

"Then why are you telling us?" Ella shrieks. Out of all of us, she's the one who's the biggest scaredy-cat.

Gemma pulls out of my mom's embrace. "The O'Malleys are protecting us. They were as soon as Hailee started dating Liam. Nolan said you all need to be aware and tell them if you see anyone suspicious following you, but their men are watching over us."

"Who's Nolan?" my mother asks.

"Liam's cousin."

My mother swallows hard. She lowers her voice. "Please tell me you aren't dating an O'Malley, too."

A line forms between Gemma's eyebrows. She puts her hand on her hip. "No. But I'm staying with him."

Confusion fills my mother's face. "What does that mean?"

Gemma sticks her chin out. "He's going to protect me."

"Why? And for what in return?" Suspicion laces my mother's voice.

I nastily interject, "Why do I get the feeling you would rather we be with the Baileys than the O'Malleys?"

Betrayal fills my mother's expression. Her anguish fills the room. "You don't know anything about the Baileys or O'Malleys."

"You didn't tell us," Ciara snaps.

My mother spins toward the twins and cries out, "It was for your protection."

"A lot of good it did for Gemma," Ciara points out.

My mother closes her eyes again. "I thought I was doing the best for you. I didn't want you to know anything about who your father is. It's not a world I want you in."

"But it's part of us. We deserved to know the truth instead of being blindsided," I state.

My mom walks to the window and stares out at the Chicago skyline. My sisters and I exchange glances. Several minutes pass, and my mother turns. "We need to leave Chicago. Now. You can't take your phones or anything traceable. I'll go to the bank and cash out my accounts. No one leaves, and you only take what's on your backs. When we get wherever we're going, we'll buy new things."

"What? No!" I cry out.

"Are you crazy?" the twins say in unison.

"Orla will track us down and kill us!" Gemma exclaims.

My mom picks up her oversized brown purse. "This isn't a choice. I'll be back as soon as possible. Do not do anything stupid." She walks toward the door, and we all follow her.

"Mom, stop!" Gemma pulls on her arm.

My mother's voice gets loud. "No! You don't know what they are capable of. Do not test me on this." She opens the door, takes a step out, and Liam steps in front of her with his arms over his chest. Nolan stands next to him.

Liam's eyes turn to slits. In a firm voice, he says, "Go back inside, Jane."

My mother freezes. Her hands shake again, and she grips her purse strap so tight, her knuckles turn white.

Liam's tone becomes calmer. "I'm not here to hurt you, but go back inside."

Time seems to stand still. Liam and my mom's eyes stay locked in battle until tears fall down her cheeks. She finally speaks but her voice cracks. "You-you need to go."

Liam raises his eyebrows. The green in his eyes grows brighter until they look like a wild animal's glowing in the dark. "I'm sorry, but I can't. Go inside, Jane."

My mother doesn't retreat. I reach for her arm. "Mom."

She stands straighter. "You need to stay away from my daughters. Both of you."

Liam shakes his head. "That won't be happening. Now please go back inside so we can discuss this situation."

"Mom," I try again, squeezing her biceps.

Her eyes never leave Liam's. Her voice grows stronger. "I won't have my daughters be part of your world."

A flash of hurt crosses Liam's face, but it disappears quickly. "They are already in it. All of them were born into it. But it doesn't have to be what you experienced."

A laugh flies out of my mom's mouth. Tears fall fast and drip off her chin. "Is that—"

"This isn't safe to discuss in the hallway. For your daughters' safety, please go back inside," Liam says.

"Mom! Come inside," Gemma demands.

I tug on her arm, and she finally retreats into the apartment. Liam and Nolan follow and shut the door. Liam motions to the living room. "Please, sit. We need to discuss how to keep all of you safe."

"They will kill us. *All* of us," my mother warns.

Liam tugs me close to him. In a no-nonsense voice, he states, "They aren't coming close to any of your daughters or you. My family will protect all of you, but we need to set some ground rules."

"You don't know who you are dealing with," my mother claims.

"I know exactly who I'm dealing with. And the only ones dying will be the Baileys," Liam states.

My mom's eyes widen. She stares at me. In a quiet, pleading voice, she says, "This isn't what you want for your life."

Liam's body stiffens next to mine.

I lean in closer to him. "Liam is who I want. Whatever comes with him, I'll deal with. I'm not naive or a child, and this isn't up for debate."

Silence fills the air. Disappointment fills my mother's expression.

Liam finally breaks the awkward quiet. "I know the monster you married. I was in prison with him for fifteen years, but I knew of him even before then. I'm not him. I'll never hurt Hailee. You have my word."

His words don't seem to satisfy my mother. She looks between us, and all I see is helplessness, frustration, and fear.

"Can someone tell me how you're going to keep us safe? I'm not into all this mob crap and like my life as it is," Ciara declares.

"Seriously?" Gemma scowls at her.

"What? It's true."

Nolan clears his throat. He points to the couches. "Please sit down."

My sisters obey, but my mother stays planted.

Nolan gently says, "No one can change this situation. All we can do is move forward."

My mother turns to him, as if noticing him for the first time. "Who are you?"

"I'm Nolan O'Malley."

"What do you want with Gemma?"

Nolan glances quickly at my sister. Then he pins his gaze back on my mother. "Information. Rory Bailey orchestrated the death of my father. The Baileys are coming after all of us. The O'Malleys will keep you and your daughters safe. But Gemma is going to tell me everything she knows, even the little details she thinks are insignificant."

My mother's lips tremble hard. "So my daughter is your prisoner?"

Gemma cries out, "Mom! Stop! That's not—"

My mother spins fast and cuts her off. "You do not know what you are doing or what these men are capable of. This isn't a game or a wild night out, Gemma."

Gemma's eyes fill with tears. "You don't think I know that? They've destroyed my life in the last nine months. I've lived in fear, quit my job I worked my ass off for and was good at—no, I was amazing at it—and now I've become a hermit to the point my friends won't even talk to me. My half-sister infested my home so badly, I can't ever walk in there again without the feeling of rats crawling on me because the one night I took a sleeping pill, I woke up with them all over me. Every night, I get in bed and can barely sleep. My stomach feels like an acid pit eating at me all day. So don't stand there and tell me what I know or don't know. I'm fully aware this isn't a game, Mother."

Horror fills all of us. It erupts on our faces, and Liam tightens his arm around me. My mother covers her mouth with her hand and whispers, "I'm so sorry. I didn't know. You should have told me."

"Like you should have told us who our father is?" Gemma fires back.

My mother breaks down in sobs, and Gemma brushes past her.

"Gemma!" I follow her into her bedroom and pull her to me.

Her body shakes. "I'm not letting Mom take us who knows where. They'll find us. I know what Orla is capable of, and we'll all end up in the whorehouse or dead."

"Shh. We aren't running. We're going to do whatever Liam says."

Gemma pulls back. "Nolan hates me. But at least I slept last night, knowing someone was watching over me. Plus, he had other O'Malleys keeping watch over his house."

I wipe the tears off her cheeks. "Was he mean to you? If he was, I'll get Liam—"

"No. It's my fault he hates me anyway."

"What did you say to him?"

"I don't want to repeat it. Don't ask me again."

I sigh. "Fine. But if he's nasty to you in any way, you'll tell me, right?"

"Of course. But I don't think he would hurt me," she claims.

"Liam swears he never would, but all I keep seeing is him grabbing your neck."

Gemma sarcastically laughs. "You're a hypocrite sometimes, Hailee."

"What are you talking about?" I defensively reply.

"Liam hasn't done that to you? Or some other crazy shit?" She arches an eyebrow.

My flutters erupt thinking of last night when he spun me into the wall after we got into the house and when he tied me up for hours when I tried to defy him and go home on the bus.

"Yep, that's what I thought. You act like a Goody Two-shoes, but I know you, Hailee. We aren't so different like you think," she claims.

"Meaning what?" I ask but don't need to. I already have an idea about what she's going to say.

Her lips twitch. "You're with Liam. You finally went for the bad boy. I see how possessive he is. I'm pretty sure nothing with him is ordinary in or out of the bedroom. I might be a year younger, but I'm not naive. Just be careful. Bad boys don't stick around forever."

My heart races faster, thinking about the possibility of Liam leaving me one day. All of Gemma's previous asshole boyfriends who broke her heart fill my mind. I blurt out, "Liam isn't like that."

A sad, agonized look passes in her eyes. "He would be the first. I hope he proves me wrong."

There's a knock on the door, and we spin to find Liam in the doorway. His gaze tells me he heard what Gemma said. "We need you both in the other room."

Gemma's cheeks flush. "Sure. Sorry." She rushes past him.

I take a deep breath and move toward the door, but Liam steps in front of me. My heart pounds harder. I stare at his chest, trying to think of anything but him someday breaking it off with me.

He tilts my chin so I can't avoid him any longer. In a firm voice, he says, "She's wrong, little lamb. You know this deep down. My love for you isn't wavering."

Relief fills me.

His thumb strokes my jawline. He opens his mouth, shuts it, studies me, then says, "I need to hear you say you believe me. That no matter what, you won't ever question my devotion to you."

I reach for his head and move his face an inch from mine. "I believe you."

His face stays solemn. "Your mother hates me. Tell me it's not going to cause you to question us."

I wish I could deny my mother's feelings and distrust toward Liam, but I can't. However, I do know there isn't a choice in being with him. Instead, I tease, "If I can handle your mom scheduling me into confession and not running, I think I've proven I can deal with my mother's disapproval."

He stays silent, staring at me.

I do the only thing I can think of to squash his concerns. I press my lips to his, giving him everything I have, trying to show him I'm not running due to anything we're facing. I'm a Bailey, his archenemy, and he still loves me. If he can accept me for my faults, I can love him unconditionally for all of his.

In our kiss lies a promise. We don't have to say it. I feel it. When his mouth leaves mine, he says, "Let's get this over with and get out of here."

I stroke his cheek. "What are we doing the rest of the day?"

"Killian and Declan are working on the walls. I need to help them."

I trace his lips. "While you do that, I'll get the treat box ready."

He arches an eyebrow. "Do I finally get to see this treat box?"

I coyly reply, "If you earn it."

"And what would earning it involve?"

I softly laugh. "You'll have to wait and see."

He smiles, pecks me on the lips, and takes my hand. "Let's go talk to your family." He leads me out to the other room, and I stand in front of him. The entire time, he's behind me, with his arm wrapped around my waist.

Over the next hour, Liam and Nolan make it clear they will have eyes on us at all times. They discuss what to do if a Bailey contacts any of us. Nolan disengages the microphone and location features on our phones. He shows all of us how to check our cells for basic trackers.

No matter how much Liam and Nolan try to help my family, my mother's expression never changes. Her distrust in the O'Malleys runs deep, and I wonder if it will ever change.

The only thing I'm confident in is Liam and me. Everything about our families means we shouldn't be, yet every part of us fits perfectly together. I don't understand it, but I'm determined not to dwell on how it's possible or how it can't end up in disaster. And maybe that's where I go wrong.

18

Liam

Several Weeks Later

"Because I said he couldn't," I tell Obrecht. My cousins, Boris, and I are meeting with him at Nora's pub. I just reiterated that nothing is to happen to Jack Christian until his company goes public. Obrecht found out Boris knows what we are planning and isn't happy no one will tell him why I'm not disclosing everything to him. It's not that I distrust Obrecht, but he's got a big chip on his shoulder where I'm concerned and isn't showing any signs of giving me his trust anytime soon, so I'm not showing him the cards to changing my family's future income streams. Plus, when we take Jack Christian down, Judge Peterson gets destroyed. And that makes it super personal for us O'Malleys. I'm not telling anyone, except those I have to.

The tension becomes thicker. Obrecht shifts his gaze between me and Boris. "Are you taking orders from Liam now?"

Boris snorts. "Hell no. Don't overreact, Obrecht."

I slam my hand on the table. Obrecht's attitude toward me is beyond old. "Jesus. When are you going to realize we're all on the same side and stop acting like I'm going to destroy everyone around me?"

He sarcastically laughs. "You sit here and don't give me full disclosure. What am I supposed to think?"

"You're supposed to trust all of us, including me," I growl.

"Yeah, well, trust needs to be earned, doesn't it?" he spouts.

Yep. That goes both ways, you bastard.

No matter what I say or do, I can't seem to win Obrecht over, and I'm sick of trying. But I don't know what I did to have him distrust me so much. I know Adrian and I had some issues before I went to prison, but we were best friends for years. "What did I ever do to you, Obrecht? Do you want to fill me in? I'd love to know."

"I'm not getting into this," he states.

I sneer. "Why not? Now's as good of a time as ever."

"Fine. You want to get into this, I'll tell you. I don't like all the shit you pulled Killian, Boris, and Adrian into when we were kids."

My stomach flips. It seems like whatever I do, my reputation from when I was barely a man bites me in the ass. "Kids. The keyword being kids. I'm a forty-year-old man now."

He snaps back, "Yeah, well, I also remember you trying to pull all of them into the murder that got you thrown in the slammer for fifteen years. You haven't been out in this world like we have. You're all ready to lead the O'Malleys into whatever this big scheme is you have up your sleeve. All I know is your track record isn't too good. So excuse me if I don't give you my full faith."

Boris starts, "Obrecht—"

"No. Do you think for one minute if an Ivanov were in trouble, Liam would be sticking his neck out to help us? Unless there's something in it for him, I'm not betting my money on him."

Are you fucking kidding me? I'd put my life on the line and die if it meant saving an Ivanov.

"You're wrong," Boris claims.

"Liam's always been loyal," Killian growls.

He faces me. "Are you going to sit here and tell me you'll put your life at risk for an Ivanov if there isn't something in it for you?"

I try to control the rage burning in my gut. The acid I can't seem to stop from eating at my stomach grows stronger. "Yeah. I would."

Obrecht sniffs hard. "Bullshit. Watch yourself, Boris. This alliance we all have, it feels a lot more like a one-way lane to me than a two-way street."

"You're out of line, Obrecht," Boris says.

"When the day comes where Liam does something for one of us with nothing in it for him to gain, I'll recant my statement. Until then, I'm going to watch my back. Have a good day." He shakes his head and stomps out of the pub.

"Have your little temper tantrum," I mutter under my breath.

"Don't," Boris warns.

"Oh, you're going to stick up for him now?" I reply.

Boris crosses his arms. "Not telling my brothers and cousins what is going on isn't going to help you regain anyone's trust."

I avoid responding to his comment. It's true, but I'm not ready to take any additional risks with this situation. "If he touches a hair on Jack's head before his company goes public, we're going to have problems." Finn and I were on the same cell block as a former stock trader named Micky. We didn't think much of it until one night when he drank too much of the alcohol he secretly fermented. Jack and the judge's name came up. He rambled on and on about how he would take them down. After that, we learned everything we could about how the market works, what he knew about Jack's company, and his competitors. We formed a friendship, and the three of us began concocting a plan. When my father visited, I filled him in, and he did the groundwork we couldn't while inside prison. For several years, my father helped hedge fund managers and other wall street gurus take care of career and personal issues. Many of those problems our family created. Now, they owe us for saving their asses. A few years ago, our prison buddy got pneumonia and died. At that point, we were already thick into our plan.

When Jack's company goes public, we're going to short the stock. As it falls, we'll profit off it, but because of laws, we had to get a lot of men in our pockets, so it's not linked to the O'Malleys. The money will funnel into untraceable offshore accounts and then be laundered through several more accounts until it disappears into thin air. It will set up the current generation of O'Malleys for life. From that point forward, we'll have funds to build the tech company Nolan and Declan will run, among other companies. Our family will finally have legitimate revenue sources and will get out of the drug and gambling business.

Boris rises. "I don't like keeping things from my brothers and cousins. There are six of us you should trust with your life. You're putting me in a bad situation. I'm giving you a week to tell Maksim. After that, you'll leave me no choice. I've gone along with this longer than anticipated. Tell Maksim, or I will, Liam."

I point my finger at him. "Don't cross me or give me orders, Boris. I'm in charge of this ship."

He grunts then shakes his head. He glances at Killian. "Remind your cousin I don't take orders from him."

"You two want to stop your pissing match now? We've got important shit to take care of. Let's go, Nolan," Declan grumbles, and they get up and leave.

Boris and I continue to lock eyes.

"I'm done, too. I've got a lunch date," Killian boasts.

I turn to him and raise my eyebrows. "With who?"

"Becky."

"I thought you broke it off with her?" Boris questions.

Arrogance fills Killian's face. "She says she understands the rules. My balls are turning blue and my dick's going to be her lunch. We'll see if she can follow the rules this time, but I already warned her."

"Good luck with that." Boris gives me one final warning. "One week. Figure it out, Liam."

I scowl at him, and he leaves. Killian rises. "We don't need this animosity between the Ivanovs and us. Just talk to Maksim."

"Go get your blowjob and leave the decisions to me," I snap. "Have fun with Becky. Sounds like a train wreck waiting to happen."

"Yeah, well, my cock's ready for the train wreck today. Later." Killian leaves.

I get up, step outside, and go to the tattoo parlor. When I walk in, Bones, who I haven't seen since before I went to prison, stops inking the man on the table.

"Well, I'll be. If it isn't the devil himself." He stands, grabs my hand, and slaps my back. "Didn't know you were out."

"Few months. You got time to ink me up?" I ask.

He grins. "Sure. Give me five minutes to finish. Take a seat."

I sit, and he returns to working on his client. When he finishes, he asks, "What do you want me to do?"

I tap my forearm. "I want two Celtic hearts. One is upside down and one right side up. In the middle, I want you to add a Celtic H."

Bones raises his eyebrows. "Eternity. What's the H for?"

"My girl, Hales."

He whistles. "You never got an M for Megan."

I groan. "Did you have to bring her up?"

"Couldn't believe Danny and her hooked up the minute you got arrested. You dodged a bullet with that one," he states.

My stomach pitches anytime I think about how my cousin and ex-fiancée betrayed me. I may not have been close to Danny, but it's a line no man should cross. "Let's drop it."

Bones nods. "Done. Let me do a quick drawing and make sure it's what you want."

"Cool."

We engage in small talk while he's drawing the tattoo. I approve of his sketch then spend the afternoon getting my new ink. He wraps it, and I roll my sleeve over the bandage. When I get home, it's around dinnertime. Hailee is at the house. I nod at my guys parked in the street near the driveway and go inside.

The new kitchen got installed a few days ago, and Hailee's cooking dinner. She has music on and doesn't hear me come in.

I sneak behind her and put my arm around her waist. She jumps, and I nuzzle her neck. "What smells so good?"

She tilts her head and pecks me on the lips. "I'm making a sweet potato Shepherd's Pie."

"Sweet potato?"

"Yeah. Ciara got me hooked on it. It'll be ready in about thirty minutes."

"Well, it smells good. How was school today?" I ask.

Her eyes gleam. "Normal. Nothing exciting. But I got home early and made you something."

"Oh?"

Her lips twitch. "It's on the counter."

I release her and turn to the island. A green poster board has each day of the week on it, boxed in with gold glitter. My name is at the top. The end of each week has a column titled Total. Hearts are drawn and filled in with Kelly green glitter around it. The bottom row has letters, the equal sign, and numbers. A closed, velvet pink box sits next to it.

"What is this?" I point to the box.

"Your proper treat box."

Hell yeah! The last time she talked about the treat box, it was a ticket to wake me up with one of her blowjobs.

"And this?" I point to the poster board, trying to play it cool.

She smirks. "It's your behavior chart."

Jesus, I love this woman. My blood pounds harder. "How does it work?"

Her coy expression fills her face. It's another thing I love about her. The world sees her as an innocent kindergarten teacher. When I see that expression, I know my freaky, dirty, sexy little lamb has something up her sleeve. She runs her finger down my arm that didn't get the tattoo today. "You get to earn points for your good behavior."

I point to the bottom of the chart. "What does N/O mean? Since there's a zero, I assume it means I did something wrong?"

She pouts and bats her eyes. "It means you didn't give me an O for the day. It also cancels out all your other points you've earned up until that day for the week."

I drag my finger over her breast and circle her nipple. It hardens under her barely there mesh bra, which makes my dick twitch. "We wouldn't want that, would we?"

"Nope," she says, popping the p.

"O equals five points. I think I know what that means," I cockily say and mentally plan on earning at least one hundred points tonight.

"Yeah, but it's for noncreative, basic ones," she replies.

"Such as?" I ask.

She tilts her head and sticks her finger in my mouth. I suck it as she replies, "Anything vanilla."

I glance at the chart, she pulls her finger out of my mouth, and I undo the button on her shirt and ask, "What does B equals ten mean?"

"For every ten minutes you make me beg, you get ten points."

Oh, my dirty, little lamb.

I continue unbuttoning her shirt and ask, "And R equals fifteen?"

Her eyes brighten. "Restraints get extra points."

My pants get tighter. "G equals twenty?"

"G-spot Os."

I lick my lips then continue studying the chart. "A plus C equals thirty?"

"Anal with clit orgasms."

I freeze. I've never approached anal sex with her before. I guess nothing she does should surprise me, but for some reason, it does. My heart races faster. "You'd let me?"

She traces the clover tattoo on my neck. "Is there anything I've not let you do?"

Fuuuuck.

I glance back at the chart. "C-H equals bonus five?"

"Chains," she innocently says.

I run my finger over her navel and stop at the top of her pants. "Real metal chains?"

"Yes."

"You'd look hot as fuck, little lamb," I admit to her.

She leans into my ear. "You could do it with the A plus C."

I shove my hands down the back of her pants and palm her ass cheek. My erection hardens so much, it hurts. "So I can combine points?"

"Yep."

Heat courses through my veins, and I suddenly feel really hot. I twirl her hair around my fist and tug her head back. Her blue flames sear into mine. I ask, "And what is S-P-J for fifty?"

She licks her lips and widens her eyes. "Squirting pussy juice."

Jesus.

A rippling groan rumbles through my chest, and she smirks. I ask the final question, "M equals bonus five?"

"Anything with your mouth deserves extra credit, don't you think?"

"How many points do I need to get something from the treat box?" I ask, wondering what's in it.

She wiggles her eyebrows. "Every five hundred points."

"Challenge accepted," I cockily boast.

"You think it will be easy?"

I snort then scoop her up and lay her on the new floor I installed yesterday. She squeals, and I cage my body over hers. "I'm ready to earn my points."

She raises her eyebrows in a challenging stare and taunts, "Show me what you got, Daddy."

I cockily snort, dip my lips to her collarbone, and make my way to her belly button. I unzip her pants. My mind starts spiraling with all the points on the chart. "How many points did you say I get for ten minutes of begging?" I shove her pants down and nip her panties.

"Ten," she breathes and grabs my hair.

The music and my blood pounds between my ears. I slip my fingers under the thin material and tease her clit then slide into her hole. I do everything to her until her panties are soaked. I lick and suck and penetrate every place possible, knowing she can't handle her underwear or bra on her when she's sweating and desperate to come.

"Take them off, Liam. Please," she begs in a raspy voice.

"I'm just getting started, little lamb," I mumble into her trembling pussy then bite on it.

"F...oh fu..."

I pull back. My thumb is inside her sex, my finger up her ass, and I press them together inside her while sliding against her walls.

"Liam! Oh God! Please!" Her insides clench hard against my digits.

I continue the same movement and bring my mouth to her breast. Her bra sticks to her skin, and I run my tongue on the mesh over her hard nipple.

She moans like a wild animal and tries to pull my shirt off me, but I don't let her.

"You aren't in control, little lamb."

"Please, I-oh...oh!" She screams as I press my thumb and finger harder against her walls.

It goes on and on. Her cries get louder. She screams out my name too many times to count. Her body quivers but doesn't go over the edge. The coat of sweat on her skin drips all over the floor as I rotate my mouth between her pussy and her breasts.

"Liam, please! I can't handle it anymore," she cries out.

"Oh dear!" My mother's voice fills the air.

I jerk my head up to see her gaping at us. Hailee's eyes fill with horror, and she attempts to cover her chest. I yank my shirt off and put it over her lower body. I growl, "Mom! Turn around!"

"Oh! Sorry!"

"What are you doing here?"

"I-I knocked, but no one answered. So I came around back and used the key Nora used to keep outside."

I had no idea Nora kept a key hidden there, but from now on, that's going to change. "So you just came in?" I pull Hailee into a sitting position and sit in front of her in an attempt to hide her nakedness from my mother.

My mom turns to look at me. "I heard the music—"

"Turn around!" I bark and reach behind me for Hailee.

She jumps. "Sorry. I thought you just couldn't hear me knocking."

"Mom, go outside to your car. I'll be out in a minute," I demand.

Hailee presses her forehead against my back, and I tighten my grip around her.

My mom's voice sounds hurt. "What? I just got here."

"Don't argue with me," I order, pissed she can't take the hint and obey me when she entered my house without warning and caught me being intimate with my woman.

She doesn't say anything and walks around the island and out the door.

I spin. "Hales, you okay?"

She nods. "Just embarrassed."

"Don't be. I'm sorry." I rise then pick her up off the floor.

"What are you doing?" she asks.

"Taking you to the bedroom. Let me deal with my mom. I'll be right back."

A shrill beep fills the air. Hailee says, "I have to take dinner out of the oven."

I peck her on the lips and walk into the bedroom. "I'll get it." I set her on the bed and lean over her. "I'll be back with food. But be prepared, little lamb. I plan on racking up a lot of points tonight."

19

MC

Hailee

THE MUSIC GOES OFF, THE OVEN STOPS BEEPING, AND THE sound of the door slamming hits my ears. I wait for what feels like forever until I hear a car start. Several more minutes pass. I remove my top, pull Liam's T-shirt over my head, then go out to the kitchen.

His palms are on the island. He's taking deep breaths with his eyes shut. He's still shirtless, and for the first time, I notice the bandage wrapped around his forearm.

I slide my arms around his waist. "Are you okay?"

His back stiffens. He pauses, then says, "Yeah." He spins and slides his hands through my hair. "I said I'd bring you dinner. Why are you out here?"

I can't help noticing the shift in his eyes. Sadness fills them, and I instantly panic. "Why was your mom here?"

He slowly exhales and looks at the ceiling.

I place my hand over his heart. It's beating faster than normal. "Liam?"

His jaw clenches. He blinks hard and finally looks down but at the top of my head. His eyes glisten, and in a neutral voice, he says, "She wants me to go to the doctor with her and my dad tomorrow. She thinks he's getting worse."

I reach for his cheeks and tilt his head down so he can't avoid me. "I'm sorry. Do you want me to go with you? I can use one of my personal days."

He shakes his head. "No. It's best if you go to work. There isn't anything anyone can do anyway."

Minutes pass in silence. I don't know what to say. I wish there were something I could do to offer some sort of comfort, but everything seems like empty words.

"Let's eat. It smells great." He takes my hand and kisses it.

I reach for his arm above where the bandage is. "Hey, what did you do to your forearm?"

His lips twitch. "I got a new tattoo."

"Really? What of? Can I see it?"

He glances at the clock. "After dinner, it'll be time for me to remove the bandage and wash it."

"You aren't going to tell me what it is?"

His eyes nervously scan mine. "It's two Celtic hearts. One upside down and one right side up."

"Like for eternity?"

"Yeah."

"Huh."

His face and voice turn to worry. "You don't like Celtic hearts?"

"I do. But I didn't picture you as a heart tattoo kind of guy," I admit.

"It's a symbol. And there's something else on it," he states.

"What?"

"I'll show you after dinner." He steps away and walks around the island. He reaches into the cabinet and takes two plates out then puts a serving of Shepherd's Pie on each one. He sets the food down, and we sit on the bar stools.

He takes a bite. "This is good, Hales."

"Isn't it? I was skeptical when my sister made it the first time." I put a forkful in my mouth, and the sweet potatoes mix with the beef and carrots in perfection.

He takes another bite then admits, "When I was a kid, my mom used to make Shepherd's Pie. When I got to prison, they had mashed potatoes a lot. It was all from a box. Nothing ever tasted good. Every time I saw the lump of white on my plate next to the mystery meat, I pretended it was my mom's Shepherd's Pie so I could get it down."

Liam never talks a lot about his time in prison, and I haven't asked him about it. The thought of him caged like an animal physically hurts. I put my arm on his back and lean closer. "Were you scared?"

He drops his fork and faces me. "Yeah. When I got there, I thought I would never survive. If Finn hadn't been on my cell block, I'm not sure I would have. Anything vile on earth existed inside those walls."

"And you met my father? Even though you were on a different cell block?"

His face hardens further. "Yeah. He tried to kill me the first night I was there."

"What?" My pulse quickens. I sit straighter in my chair.

He pauses then asks, "Hales, do you know who the man I killed was?"

"The one who murdered Nora's father," I state.

Liam licks his lips and studies me. "Yes. But *who* he was?"

Uneasiness fills my belly. I'm not sure why. "I read online his name was Danny Walsh."

He continues staring at me.

New nerves swirl in my gut. I ask, "What about him?"

"He was your father's cousin on his mother's side."

"Oh." I look at the food, unsure how I'm supposed to feel, but I don't feel anything warm and fuzzy for this blood relative of mine. I glance back at Liam. "What did my father do to try and kill you?"

He shifts in his chair. "We don't need to talk about it."

"I want to know."

He shakes his head. "No. I shouldn't have said anything."

"Liam, tell me."

His eyes turn to slits. "Why? What's it going to accomplish?"

"I want to know what my father is capable of," I admit.

"You already have the answers to that. You remember what he did to your mother. What more do you need to know?"

Liam is right. I don't need any more proof of what a monster my father is, but something in me wants to know. I quietly ask again, "What did he do, Liam?"

He grinds his molars and taps his fingers on his thigh, avoiding my gaze.

I wait for what seems like forever. Liam's body never moves, except for his chest from his deep breaths. I finally turn his chin toward me.

The hatred I see in his eyes makes me hold my breath. It stirs something deep within me, and right before he speaks, I recognize it from my childhood. The emotion in his eyes isn't just hatred. It's also shame.

He quietly states, "The prison owns you. The prisoners own the guards, and the guards own the prisoners. You don't know who's on whose side or what area is safe versus not. At any time, anything can change. I learned that from your father the first few hours I was there."

My insides quiver, watching Liam's expression and hearing his words. I know too well my father's wrath, which only came out when he was drunk and beating on my innocent mother. I reach up and cup Liam's cheek.

He sniffs hard. His jaw twitches under my fingers. The room seems to get colder, and he reveals, "Before they got rid of the outside area, you'd get an hour a day. I hadn't seen Finn yet. When they brought me to my cell, he was working in the laundry room. The guard told me to stand at the end of the line. I felt something was off, but there wasn't anything I could do. When I got to the door, the man in front of me stepped outside. The guard shut it and told me not to move or he would throw me in solitary confinement. I was facing the door, and I could hear him leave the hallway. Your father stepped behind me with a plastic bag and put it over my head. Two of his thugs held my arms."

I gasp and put my hand over my mouth. Tears fill my eyes.

Liam glances up at the ceiling. "Finn somehow came into the room. Four of our guys were with him, and it became an all-out brawl. Everyone except your father got thrown into solitary confinement for a week. After that, the warden moved the O'Malleys to the fourth floor."

I'm unsure what to say. The shame never leaves Liam. It wasn't his fault, but it's the same look my mother has had at times when she's spoken of my father's abusive actions toward her. I do the only thing I know. I rise and kiss him, grateful he's alive, while wishing more than ever my father was dead.

It's something I've felt since I was a child, before we escaped him. I was barely in school when we fled. The few times he was mentioned between my sisters or mother, it would reignite. Since Gemma revealed all she's gone through, it's stayed on the surface of my thoughts. I've had a hard time trying to get my father out of my mind, but I don't want to live in fear of him or let the thought of him control my life. Liam has his guys watching over me everywhere I go. The school is on strict lockdown. Liam's men keep an eye on who is coming and going. The moment I step outside, I go straight to Liam's car. Whenever he can be, he's in it, but sometimes it's only his driver and another one of his men. If Liam and I are shopping or eating at a restaurant, he's got numerous O'Malleys inconspicuously watching us, ready to take any Bailey down. And true to his word, Liam has the same measures on my sisters and mother.

I pull back from our kiss and blurt out, "I hope he dies a horrible death soon."

Liam hesitates then strokes my cheek. "Hales, I know this is your father. Are you sure you feel this way?"

I snort. "Yes. But does it matter?"

Liam studies me. "I worry you may hate me one day. It's still your father. When he gets out of prison, nothing will stop my men or me from hunting him down until he takes his last breath. The war has already started. It's gone on for years before we were even born. I can't get to your father in prison. Once he's out, he won't have the protection he does now. Yes, the Baileys will watch over him, but we will take him and anyone protecting him out."

A chill runs through my bones. Not at the thought of my father getting what he deserves but at the risk it puts Liam and his family in.

His face drops. He winces. "So you may hate me?"

"What? No!"

"You shuddered, and your face changed, little lamb."

I shake my head. "I'm worried about you and your family. Not them. They are monsters and don't get any of my sympathies. Blow them all up so they can't harm you or my family. Do whatever you have to. No Bailey will come between us, including my father. Just promise me, whatever you do, you won't end up back in prison."

"I'm never going back, Hales. You have my word," he vows.

I release a breath. "Okay. Finish your dinner."

"Bossy," he teases then pecks me on the lips.

We finish eating in silence. After dinner, I point to his bandage. "Time to show me."

He holds his arm out. "Go ahead and remove it."

I gingerly pull apart the bandage, and when it's fully unwrapped, my heart stammers. I gape at the Celtic hearts representing eternity and the Celtic H in the middle. A lump forms in my throat. I swallow it then glance up at Liam.

Nerves fill his expression. "What do you think?"

"Is the H for me?"

"Who else would it be for?"

My sight becomes blurry from tears. "It's beautiful. I love it."

"You do?"

I grab the pink velvet box. "Yes. In fact, I think you earned your first treat." I open the lid.

His lips twitch. He pulls out one of the fifty red heart-shaped pieces of posterboard I cut out and reads it. His grin grows, and he leans into my ear. His deep voice sends new chills through my spine. "I love how dirty you are, little lamb." He licks my earlobe.

"What does it say?" I ask, my heart racing faster.

He grunts. "Did you get everything needed for anything in this treat box?"

"Yes. It should be marked on the card where in the closet it's located."

His lips curve. The spark in his eyes heats into a beautiful, glowing green. He leads me into the bedroom. "Good. And don't ask me any more questions." He takes out his phone, turns on a hip-hop song, and goes into the closet. He comes back with a tie and sits on the accent chair then commands, "Strip."

I take my time, pulling his T-shirt halfway up my body, then releasing it so it's still on. I slowly eliminate my panties then toss them to him. I step in front of him, pumping my naked ass in the air.

"Grab your ankles," he demands.

I slide my hands down my legs, and he drags his fingers up them, then kisses my ass cheeks. Tingles ignite under my skin, zinging all through my nerves.

He pats me on the ass. "Finish."

I slowly rise, release my bra, then finally take the T-shirt off.

He curls his fingers in the air. I obey him, stopping in front of him, waiting for his command until he widens his legs and says, "Kneel."

I drop to the floor and lick my lips, still not sure what he chose from the treat box, but dozens of thoughts are running through my head about what it might be.

"Hands linked on your neck, little lamb." I obey, and he takes the tie and puts it over my eyes. He knots it once then moves my hair over my hands and weaves the silk over my wrists so I can't move them away. His hot breath hits my ear, and my pussy spasms when he says, "This isn't from the treat box. Before we do that, you're going to take all of me, Hales. Every hard inch of me, and I'm going to control this pretty little mouth of yours."

I breathe deeply, not able to see anything, my hands restricted on my neck, my elbows spread. The sound of his buckle and zipper hit my ear. A drop of my arousal drips down my leg. He fists my hair and tugs it then brings his face in front of mine.

His kiss is full of everything. The love and devotion he has for me. Our chemistry so undeniable, even the forces that should rip us apart can't. And the flutters I never seem to get rid of when he touches me, or even comes close, intensify.

"Get your pretty little mouth on my cock, little lamb," he growls.

I bend toward him and begin licking his shaft. He lets me explore for only a moment before he controls my every move, making me do everything he promised. I take him deeper and deeper until nothing is left and he's groaning and gripping my head.

He's about to come. The taste of his pre-cum is a drug I want more of. His cap hitting the back of my throat is a feeling I'm obsessed with but can't explain. He swells bigger and bigger, and right when I think he's going to give me all of him, he moves me off him.

I'm panting as his lips consume me all over. Then he murmurs, "Stay here and don't move."

Time seems to crawl. Blackness is all I see with the tie around my eyes, and the sweat on my skin turns clammy. I feel exposed with my hands tied the way they are, but he restrained me so tightly, there's no room to do anything but kneel and wait. The music continues to pound in my ears. When he finally stands behind me, a bolt of his energy courses through my veins.

He kneels and nibbles on my ear while dragging his finger down the curve of my waist. It's not as warm as the rest of him, and more thoughts shoot through my mind wondering what treat he pulled out of the box.

He tugs at the silk and releases my hands. As my eyes adjust to the room, which is now dark and lit only with candles, he pulls me up and spins me into him. "You've been discrete with your treat box items."

"You didn't go through the rest of the closet and see everything, did you?" I ask, not wanting him to know the other things I bought until it's time for whatever treat he pulls.

He pecks me on the lips. "Nope. I normally don't like surprises, but this is one exception."

I release a relieved breath. "Okay. Good."

He steps back with me in his arms until we're on something besides the wood floor.

I glance down. It's a canvas, and I let out a small laugh. "You picked the adult body paint card."

He takes his finger, covered in green paint, and circles my nipple. "I think my Irish girl needs a bit of green, don't you?"

I dip my finger into the gold paint. I drag it over his torso and stop at his belly button. "I think the king of the O'Malleys needs a bit of gold."

He holds up his arm that just got the new tattoo. He rewrapped it and put plastic over it. His finger is blue. He spreads it on my mound and says, "Of course, we should add some blue for your eyes."

"Is your tattoo going to be okay?" I ask.

"Yep. I'll take care of it after we finish. Now focus, Hales. This is going on that wall." He points to the wall across from the bed.

I dip my hands in the red and step forward. He tilts his head down, and I reach around him to palm his ass. His tongue slips in and out of my mouth so perfectly, I momentarily forget about anything but our kiss. Then he scoops me off my feet, kneels, and places me on the floor. He cages his body over mine then tucks my hair behind my ear, studying me intently.

I reach for his face. A mix of gold and red gets all over it. I laugh, and the animal I always see whenever Liam and I are together awakens.

He pins my wrists above my head. He teases my nipples with his tongue and lips until I'm moaning. My back arches into him. I spread my legs to wrap around him, but he releases me and grabs the paint jar. In thin lines, he drips green paint the length of my body. He sits on his knees and scans me, "You filthy woman."

"You made me dirty. Lick it off," I taunt.

Arrogance fills his expression. He slides a green finger through my pussy. It's slightly cold but warms quickly before his mouth and fingers attack me, as if he's on a mission to lick and wipe me clean.

"Holy...oh God!" I cry out.

"I'm finishing what we started, little lamb," he growls. He lessens the intensity, keeping me on edge until my sweat mixes with the paint and I'm clawing red and gold marks into his shoulders.

"Please," I whimper so many times, my voice turns hoarse.

It goes on and on until tears fall down my cheeks.

"I can't—" My body explodes with endorphins, and I come harder than ever before, ejaculating on his face.

He doesn't let me come down, lunging on top of me and shoving my thighs toward my chest. His hard erection slides into my spasming walls. He pounds into me a few times then pulls out.

"What's—"

He spins me so fast on my stomach, I don't finish my sentence. His arm slips under my waist, and he pounds back into me, leaning his body over mine. "Jesus, I love you, Hales."

"I love you, too. So much," I whimper.

He bites on the curve of my neck and growls, "I want your ass, little lamb."

"Take it," I tell him.

"Not now. The right way."

I don't know what it means. I've never done it before. Right now, my body is a cooked noodle, unable to do anything but feel Liam and his warm flesh.

His finger circles my clit, and I instantly orgasm again, crying out his name. A rumble from his chest vibrates on my back, and he tugs me closer to him. The force of his thrusts accelerates, and he hits me deeper, muttering, "Fucking filthy girl," over and over until I'm coming so hard on his cock, I can't hold myself up anymore.

"Liam!"

"That's it, little lamb. Fuuuuck!" His erection swells, and he violently pumps into me. I might die from the extra rush of endorphins hitting me everywhere.

He pants in my ear, and I roll onto my back. Our eyes sear into the others', breath merging, sweat and paint everywhere.

"You look like a rainbow threw up on a leprechaun," I state.

He laughs, and I do as well. He says, "Let's shower. I need to make sure none of this got on my tattoo."

"Especially since I love it so much," I claim, still shocked he got it and what it represents.

He beams then pecks me on the lips before pulling me up. We stare at the canvas before going into the bathroom.

He leans into my ear. "One hundred and five."

I raise my eyebrows.

He proudly states, "When we get out of the shower, you're marking my chart."

20

Liam

"Gemma. What are you doing here?" I ask in surprise. The O'Malley gym isn't a place we usually see women unless it's during a boxing match. It's around lunchtime. I wanted to get a workout in before I meet my parents at the doctor's office.

She stops punching the bag and spins. Sweat stains her clothes and drips down her skin. She takes her shirt and pulls it up to wipe her red face, displaying her toned abs. In a sarcastic voice, she replies, "Can't exactly work out at the gym I go to when Orla got herself a membership there, now can I?"

My heart rate increases. "When did this happen?"

She angrily shakes her head. "Last night. Nolan said it was all clear, but apparently, your guys aren't well versed in checking out women's locker rooms. I thought I was going to get my neck sliced off."

I turn to Nolan, who's jumping rope a few feet away from her. "Who was watching her? Why didn't you tell me?"

He stops and drops the rope on the floor. "Tiernan and Fergal. I told you they were too inexperienced for this."

I get defensive. "They've done security for my dad for over ten years."

"They aren't the smartest representation of the O'Malleys, now are they?" He grabs a bottle of water and downs a quarter of it.

"Gee, thanks for telling me I was in good hands and safe when you had concerns, Nolan," Gemma fires at him.

Guilt crosses his face, but it disappears quickly. "Go back to punching your bag. Get it out before we get home."

"I know what I'd be happy to punch. If you'll excuse me, I think I'll go work out in peace instead of near the man who would be happy if I got slaughtered in public." She and Nolan exchange more eye daggers then she stomps off toward the other side of the gym.

Nolan stares at her backside, his eyes in slits.

I repeat, "Why didn't you call me?"

He tears his eyes off Gemma's ass and crosses his arms. "I tried calling you. Since you didn't pick up, and the lights in your house were off, I took Gemma with me to your mom and dad's house. Darragh is switching up her security."

My pulse increases. It figures. The one night I turn off my phone to spend time with Hales, something happens. I try not to be pissed he went to my dad, but I'm sure I'll get a lecture later today when I join him and my mom for his doctor's appointment. I mutter, "Great."

Nolan drinks more water then asks, "What did you do to your mom, by the way?"

A bad feeling rolls through me. I don't need my mom playing the Irish victim to Nolan or my dad. "Why? What did she say?"

"She said you and Hailee kicked her out of your house?"

I groan. "One, Hales had nothing to do with it. Two, she walked in without any warning, thanks to Nora."

"What does my sister have to do with this?" Nolan bites back.

I shake my head. "She had an emergency key somewhere outside the back door. She should know better than to be so loose about her safety. It would have been nice for her to tell me about it as well."

Nolan's face turns redder with anger. "My brothers and I all told her not to keep a key outside."

I snort. "Doesn't surprise me. You know Nora. She doesn't listen to any of you most of the time."

Nolan grinds his molars. "Okay, so your mom walked in. What's the big deal?" He picks up a towel and wipes his face.

It would be easy to tell him what my mother walked in on so I don't look like a heartless prick, but I dislike talking about or anyone having privileges to Hailee's and my personal life.

I avoid answering him. "Who did my dad put on Gemma's security?"

Nolan calls out, "Gemma, we're leaving in fifteen minutes. Be ready to go." He turns back to me. "He said it would take a few days for him to move some of our guys around. Until then, I get to have the princess glued to my side."

I jab his chest. "Watch your mouth. She's Hailee's sister. And you're the one who said she was staying at your house. If you can't handle her, I'll make room at my place."

Nolan grunts. "You couldn't handle a day with that woman."

I snap, "She's coming home with me if you're going to be disrespectful."

"No. She's staying at my place."

"Why? If she's annoying you—"

"Because she's a Bailey, and I don't trust her. I'm keeping my eyes on her."

I step closer. I'm not naive enough to think Gemma is an angel, but she isn't looking to take part in anything to do with the Baileys. She should never have had to go through what Orla and Rory subjected her to. Gemma also accepted me from day one in Hailee's life. I like her and promised nothing would happen to her. "I better not hear you're anything but nice to her," I warn.

He huffs. "Don't get your panties in a twist. The princess has everything she needs."

"Stop calling her that," I growl.

"I have to get ready. Throw your weight around with someone else," Nolan instructs.

I change the subject, not into fighting today. All I want to do is get through all my daily bullshit and my father's doctor appointment, then spend the rest of the night with Hailee. "What did Orla say to her?"

Gemma steps next to me. "I violated a rule when Nolan turned off my location tracker on my cell phone. I got this lovely new cut when your cousins realized they hadn't checked that area of the gym out, and we ended up with a gun pointed at both our heads. I guess I should be grateful it was my leg instead of my neck, which is where she held the blade on me originally." She glares at Nolan.

"Not sure why you're looking at me. Liam decided who was watching you when I can't," Nolan fires back.

Acid rumbles in my gut, climbing up my esophagus. I scan her body in alarm. "Where on your leg?"

"My upper thigh. Near all my reproductive organs."

"Stop being dramatic. Your inner thigh isn't where your reproductive organs are," Nolan chastises her.

I glance at her leg, but she's wearing pants. "Are you okay? Did you go to the hospital?"

Her cheeks turn crimson. "No. Nolan said it wasn't deep and cleaned it up. I'm going to get changed." She avoids looking at Nolan and goes into the locker room.

"You aren't a doctor. She might need medical attention," I claim.

He groans. "Stop being overprotective. It's a small gash. She's fine. Trust me. She didn't have any issues last night or this morning."

I raise my eyebrows. "Issues?"

He avoids looking at me and starts walking to the locker room. "She's fine. I have work to do."

My phone rings and I yank it out of my pocket. I sigh and answer. "Hi, Mom."

Worry and disapproval fill her voice. "Liam. Your dad canceled his appointment. He said he's feeling better."

I stare at the ceiling, feeling the burn increase in my throat. I remind her, "You can't make Dad do something he doesn't want to do."

Her voice drops. "I thought if you came over for dinner tonight, you could talk to him. Get him to realize he needs to keep his appointments."

The last thing I'm going to do is order my father around. However, telling my mother this is only guaranteeing me another thirty-minute phone call. "Sorry, Mom. Hailee is making dinner tonight. I'll talk to Dad when I see him next, but don't expect me to perform a miracle. You know he isn't going to listen to either of us."

"Oh? What is she making?"

I smile. Hailee asked me what my favorite thing is and wanted to make it tonight. "Potato soup."

"Oh. Has she made it before? I can come over and show her—"

"No. She's good, Mom. Hey, I have to go. I'll call you later." I hang up before she can keep me on the phone or invite herself over. It's still a little too close to the incident last night for my or Hailee's comfort.

I go to the other side of the gym, where the heavy bags are. After my workout, I shower, get in the car, and receive a text.

Killian: *Nora is in labor.*

Me: *Awesome! Hales is out of school in a few hours. I'll meet you at the hospital.*

Killian: *Boris said it might take a while. She doesn't want us waiting around. He'll call once the baby arrives.*

Me: *Okay. Keep me posted.*

Happiness replaces the negative emotions I've felt since I dropped Hailee off at school this morning and dealt with all the O'Malley shit. It included a meeting with Nora's twin sisters, Erin and Nessa. They questioned me for over an hour at the pub about where their husbands are. I told them no one had heard from them or seen them, but we still had men looking. I also gave them each a few thousand dollars when Nessa said she didn't know the combination to their personal safe and needed money for groceries. I told them I would put them on a weekly allowance until Niall and Shamus return from wherever they are. I finally sighed in relief when Declan walked in and I excused myself.

I start to text Maksim we need to meet. Boris gave me a deadline, and after careful consideration, I realized he's right. Maksim needs to know why Jack Christian is off-limits until his company goes public. Another text pops up on my screen.

Finn: *We got a problem and need to meet.*

My gut burns again.

Me: *Where?*

Finn: *Come to my place.*

I instruct my driver and head over to Michigan Avenue, to Finn's current hotel. Since he got out of prison, he refuses to stay with any of our family members, including me. He bounces from one place to another, claiming it makes it easier to follow Jack, the judge, and whoever else we need him to watch.

I get up to his room, and when he opens the door to his suite, the fire in my chest reignites. His eyes are bloodshot. He has a crazed look in them. I shut the door quickly, and he motions for me to follow him.

We get to the living area, and I freeze.

Eric Baskin, a hedge fund trader who set up dozens of our offshore accounts and positioned us to profit from the fall of Jack's company, lies in a pool of half-dried blood.

I gape at his slit neck and finally turn to Finn. "How the fuck did this happen?"

Finn's eyes turn colder. "The bastard put our accounts in his name."

"What are you talking about?"

"Gianluca confirmed it with his guys in Switzerland. I called Eric and told him to come here. When he got here, I asked him to pull up our online accounts. He wouldn't. Declan had already hacked in and gave me new user info. Every single account we had with all our positions are in his name."

My stomach flips. Bile fills my throat, and it takes all the power I have to swallow it. I glance back at Eric's dead body. "Tell me Gianluca can get this fixed for us." He's our contact stateside who deals with all our Swiss accounts.

"He's working on it. He said his brother, Claudio, stated it's going to cost another million," Finn seethes.

"Another million! It's his fault this happened. He shouldn't have ever let anything happen to our accounts," I bark. Claudio is in Switzerland and is high up in the bank we're dealing with.

Finn sniffs hard. "He claims his boss allowed it. Gianluca couldn't do anything about it. The million covers taking out the boss, which also puts Claudio in that position going forward."

I grunt. "So we pay him to get him promoted?"

Finn lets out a long sigh. He points to the dead body. "Let's worry about that issue after we take care of this."

I pace the room with a million thoughts racing through my mind, assessing the situation to try and figure out how to take care of this mess so our tracks are covered.

"We need the hotel's security footage. I'm not going back inside," Finn states.

I nod and pat his back. "Stay here. Don't let anyone in. I'll handle this." I leave and text Nora's brothers.

Me: *Where are you?*

Killian: *Pub*

Me: *Declan and Nolan, too?*

Declan: *Yep. New coed just walked in. I'm ready to show her what a real man can do.*

Me: *Put your dick away. I'm coming to pick you up. Where's Nolan?*

Declan: *Way to kill my hard-on. Haven't talked to him all day.*

Killian: *Me, either.*

Me: *I'll be there in ten minutes. Be ready to get in the car.*

My driver weaves through traffic and pulls up to the pub. Killian and Declan are waiting and get into the car.

Declan says, "This better be good. Ms. Coed was on my lap doing shots and asking if I wanted to see her new piercings."

"You hacked into the Swiss accounts that Eric moved into his name?" I growl.

Declan's face falls. "Yeah. I gave the information to Finn last night."

"It didn't occur to you to tell me?"

"Finn said he'd handle it. I tried calling you, and your phone was off."

"Last night. I saw you today," I remind him.

He snorts. "You ran out of the pub and left me with Erin and Nessa as soon as I came into the room."

I spit out, "Damn it, Declan."

"What's going on?" Killian asks.

"Eric's dead. Inside Finn's hotel room."

Killian and Declan gape at me. Silence fills the air, and blood pounds so hard between my ears, I wonder if it's mine or theirs.

"Fuck," Killian finally mutters, breaking the silence.

"Yeah, fuck is right. How are we cleaning this mess up? And I need you to retrieve the hotel's security footage," I direct Declan.

"My laptop's in the office." He opens the door and gets out.

I stare at Killian. "Where's Nolan?"

"No idea. He isn't answering his phone. Do we need to talk to Darragh?"

My chest tightens and my heart races. "No. We're taking care of this. My dad will bring in the cops on our payroll. I don't think that's a good move. We can't take any chances screwing anything up. This is going to stay just the four of us."

Killian takes a deep breath. "Stop at the warehouse. We'll see what we need to take. Where's Finn?"

"In his room."

Killian locks eyes with mine. "He freaking out?"

I hesitate then say, "No. He's okay right now."

"If he goes into a—"

"I said he's fine."

Declan opens the door and gets inside with his laptop bag. I roll the divider down and instruct my driver to go to the warehouse. When the window is back up, Declan asks, "Is Finn—"

"He's fine," I repeat. I nod to his laptop bag. "Start hacking. I need all the footage they have in the last twenty-four hours."

He obeys. The three of us stay silent for the fifteen-minute ride out of town. The car pulls up to the old building, and I hit the remote for the garage door. Our driver pulls inside then I shut it. Killian and I go to the section where we keep our supplies.

We study the materials.

Killian asks, "Where is the body?"

"On the living room carpet."

"Fuck. He couldn't do it in the bathtub, could he?"

I grunt and grab a few gallons of bleach and put them in the trunk.

Killian crosses his arms. "Are you walking into the hotel with that?"

I scrub my face. "Okay, wise guy. Tell me how we're doing this."

He turns back to the shelf of equipment. "Hell if I know. Let's figure out what we're doing to get the body out of there first."

Several moments pass as we stare at the tools. Declan gets out of the car and says, "I got the footage and inserted a replay from the day before. No one will notice unless they're looking for it."

A tiny amount of relief fills me. "Finn and Eric were both on it?"

Declan nods. "Yeah. He's clear though."

"Okay. One problem solved. What are we doing with the body and carpet besides the bleach?" I ask.

Declan steps to the shelf and picks up another jug of cleaner. "No bleach. Trust me. You want this. It'll leave the floor in good shape, so no one notices anything, and remove all traces. Killian, grab the saws, tarp, and trash bags. We're going to need some suitcases."

"Done this a few times?" I ask, surprised by Declan's sudden direction.

"You can thank me later. Go in the closet over there. You'll find suitcases. How much does this guy weigh?" Declan asks.

"Maybe two, two-twenty," I state.

Declan ponders the information for a moment then says, "We'll take five. Three full, two carry-on sizes. Grab fresh clothes for the four of us from the closet, too. We'll bring the body back here and destroy the remains."

"Was it contained?" Killian asks.

"Yeah. I think it's just on the carpet. Finn must have already changed," I reply.

Declan grabs the UV light off the shelf. "Liam, get the box of cleaning supplies. We need to go through the entire suite. Who knows where Finn might have gotten some blood."

We do as Declan says and put everything in the suitcases. We get in the car and go to the hotel, rolling the baggage straight to the elevators.

Finn opens the door, and relief floods his expression.

"Don't kiss me since you're so happy to see me," Declan says and winks.

"Fuck, it smells in here," Killian moans, covering his nose.

"Don't be a pussy," I warn.

We quickly get to work. Killian and I unpack the cases. We put the tarp down and move the body onto it. Declan goes around the room with the UV light. He finds a few traces of blood in the bathroom and cleans it then shows Finn how to get the blood out of the carpet.

"Put some music on. I can't saw this dickhead up without something to take my mind off the smell," Killian says.

"You'd never survive prison," Finn says.

"Yep. He's a straight-up pussy," I taunt.

Killian scowls. "Not looking to spend time in the pen, and I think what you meant to say is straight-up pussy lover."

Declan puts on music and sits on the couch.

"What are you doing?" I ask.

He smirks and grabs his laptop. "Looping the feed to cover up we're here. I've found if you put the saw on an angle, it tends to go faster."

"Gee, thanks for the tip, Einstein," I sarcastically jab.

We get to work, and I suddenly realize it's dark outside. "Shit. I need to call Hailee." I look at the body. It feels like we haven't even gotten that far. Since we're in a hotel, we can't use a chainsaw due to the noise. Rigor mortis has set in, and every slice is like cutting through a piece of steel. All of us are sweating, and Declan and Finn are still working on the carpet, which is taking longer to clean than I anticipated.

I pull my gloves off and go into the bedroom and shut the door. I call Hailee.

She answers after a few rings. "Hey."

"Sorry, Hales. I'm tied up and I'm not sure when I'm going to be able to come home."

"You'll be gone all night?" she asks with a worried voice.

"Possibly. But don't worry. I'm safe."

She lets out a nervous breath. "Okay."

"What are you doing?" I ask.

She pauses then replies in a cautious voice, "Getting a lesson from your mom."

"What?"

"She heard I was making potato soup, brought a big pot, and now is telling me what I need to change in the one I made."

My stomach drops. "Shit. Hales, I'm sorry. Put her on the phone. I'll get her to leave."

Hailee's voice chirps, "No. It's okay. I guess we're going to have a freezer full of potato soup."

I shut my eyes and bang my head against the wall. "I'm sorry. She's having a hard time with my dad. She wanted us to come to dinner and—"

"It's all right. Just come home as soon as you can, okay?" she says sweetly.

My heart swells. I've always known she's too good for me, but in these moments, she always shines. Everything about today has been a stressful disaster. Just hearing her voice makes me smile, and I want to be home.

I finish my call, and we continue cutting up the body. It's after midnight by the time we get it in the suitcases, along with the tools and our dirty clothes. We shower and put on fresh clothes then leave the hotel.

Declan erases the security footage of us leaving the building the moment we get into the car. We head to the warehouse.

"Can we skip the meat grinder and fire up the incinerator? I'm over this. I know Darragh prefers the meat grinder, but I don't," Killian admits.

"Guess it's good he's not in charge on this one. Fire it up. I'm ready to go home to my woman," I state.

"You guys go. I'll finish this up," Finn volunteers.

"No. It's—"

"Go. Finn and I got this, don't we?" Declan asks.

"Yep. You kids go," Finn tries to tease, but I still don't like the crazed look in his eyes.

I study him and open my mouth, but Declan steps in front of Finn. In a stern voice, he says, "Go home to your woman."

I hesitate. I'm uncomfortable leaving Finn when he has that look in his eyes.

Declan gently repeats, "Go."

Killian bumps fists with them both. "If you need us to come back, let us know."

"We won't," Declan says. "If that coed comes back in the pub, keep your hands off her. I'm calling dibs."

"She's barely twenty-one. Even for you, that's young," Killian states.

"Can't help it if women of all ages want me," he claims.

"Jesus. I'm leaving on that note. Finn, where are you staying?"

"I'll get a new—"

"My place. This hotel shit is over. You can argue about it tomorrow," Declan declares.

Finn takes a deep breath. "Fine."

"I'll see you tomorrow?" I ask.

Finn nods. "Yeah. Sure."

I pat him on the back. Killian and I get in the car. When we pull out of the garage, he questions, "Finn going to be okay?"

I lock eyes with Killian. "Yeah. We're going to make sure of it."

21

Hailee

Light trickles in the bedroom when Liam walks in. He shuts the door, and blackness reappears. I faintly see the outline of his body. I ask, "Baby, are you okay?"

He pauses near the bathroom door. "Yeah. Go back to sleep. I need another shower."

"Another one?" I sit up.

He blows out a big breath of air. "Yeah."

"Where were you when you took a shower?" I ask, suddenly suspicious of what he was doing. Before he called, I spent hours wondering why he wasn't home. I spent the night with his mom, who critiqued my potato soup. She had no problem telling me what was missing and making me take spoonfuls of hers after mine until I agreed with her that mine was lacking whatever ingredient she deemed necessary.

His voice turns firm. "I can't tell you anything about tonight. Don't ask again, Hales."

I get out of bed and step toward him.

He growls, "I said go back to sleep."

"What were you doing that you need a shower? Do you have perfume or something on you? Lipstick maybe?"

He scowls and in a disgusted tone replies, "What? Of course not. Don't be crazy. I had work issues." He goes into the bathroom and turns on the shower.

"Crazy? Me? Liam O'Malley, if you were with another woman and I find out, I'll kill you," I warn.

He spins. A glowing fire ignites in his green eyes. He spits out, "I've had a long day, and I'm exhausted. I've never even looked at another woman since I laid eyes on you. Go back to bed, Hailee." He begins to strip.

I move closer to him. "No. Tell me where and why you would take a shower anywhere but here or the gym. And don't tell me you were working out, Liam. I'm not an idiot."

Red creeps into his cheeks. He crosses his arms. "Are we seriously having this conversation?"

"It's..." I put my hand on my hip and glance around the room, but there's no clock in the bathroom. "Whatever time in the morning, and you stroll in and tell me you showered somewhere else and need another one."

He takes a plastic bag out of his pocket, drops his pants, and starts putting his clothes in it. He barks, "Go to bed, Hailee. I'm not going to tell you again."

"Why are you putting your clothes in there?"

"Jesus," he mutters, and an annoyed sigh comes out of him. He puts his clothes inside the bag, ties it up, then tosses it on the counter. "I'm showering. When you come to your senses, let me know."

I snatch the bag off the counter.

He lunges toward me so quickly, I move against the counter. He yanks it out of my hand. "Do *not* open this bag. You *never* open one of these bags, nor do you touch them."

My heart beats in my throat, and I glare at him. "Why? What's on your clothes I can't see?"

He sniffs hard and shakes his head. "How can you possibly think I'd touch any other woman? I'm completely obsessed with you, and you know it."

"Then tell me where you were," I push. Liam cheating on me has never crossed my mind before, but I've had several teacher friends who caught unfaithful husbands or boyfriends. Even Aspen's ex-husband did. They always came home and took showers. I'm not going to sit back and play dumb.

"I'll never tell you where I was tonight. It's O'Malley business, so keep your nose out of it," he sneers.

I'm too angry to think about what he said. I fire back, "Don't talk to me like that."

"Don't accuse me of cheating on you."

I point in his face. It's something I teach my kindergarteners not to do, but the thought of Liam with another woman makes me lose any sense of politeness. "Don't slink on in here and give me visuals of you fucking some other woman in a shower, then tell me you have to take another one to get the rest of her off you!"

Betrayal grows in his expression. He steps back, opens the bag, and holds it to my nose. "Sniff."

I freeze and keep glaring at him.

He lowers his voice and in a firm tone orders, "I said, sniff."

I can't hold my breath any longer and obey. Something resembling a mixture of decay and chemicals fill my nose. I put the back of my hand under my nostrils and cough.

He takes the bag, twists it, then ties it back up. He tosses it on the counter, then demands, "Don't touch the bag. And you should know me better." Hurt floods his face.

Relief it doesn't smell like a woman fills me and also embarrassment I accused him of cheating on me. "What is it?"

"I'm done with this conversation. I told you it's O'Malley business. I'll never tell you where I was or what I was doing. It's for your protection. Everything I do regarding you, I think about your safety. I assumed you knew that. Now go back to bed." He walks into the shower and steps under the water.

I watch him diligently scrub his skin with the soap, and another thought pops into my mind. *Did he kill someone?* A chill runs through my body, cooling the hot rage I was previously feeling. He washes every part of his body, including between his fingers and toes. He tries to get his back, but he can only reach so far. After several minutes of trying, he puts his forearm on the wall, head against it, then positions the top of the soap bottle near his nose while taking several deep breaths.

I'm such a fool.

I pull my T-shirt over my head and toss it on the counter then step behind him. I wrap my arm around his waist and put my palm up. "Let me get your back where you couldn't reach."

An anxious breath comes out of his mouth. He doesn't move. In a betrayed voice, he asks, "How could you ever think I would do that to you?"

"I'm sorry. I have friends who got cheated on, and their men always took showers when they came home. It just set something off in me," I admit, tightening my arm around him.

He puts the soap down and spins. It hits me how bloodshot his eyes are. He says, "We aren't ordinary people, Hales. Everything you thought you were and the life you would lead died the day you met me. It happened before you ever knew you were a Bailey."

My pulse increases. I open my mouth, but nothing comes out. What he says is true, but I've tried to push away the thoughts of anything being different than the life or person I thought I was all these years.

He slides his hands through my hair, and his thumbs stroke my cheeks. Our eyes lock, and he declares, "It's you and me forever. No one else. The sooner you come to terms with who you are and what being with me means, the easier it'll be for both of us."

My heart pounds harder, and my stomach flips. I blink fast and stare at his chest. The water begins to turn colder and beats on my back. I shiver and admit what I've been trying to hide from myself and him since learning who my father is. "I don't know how to do that or who I am anymore."

He spins me so I'm against the wall and forces me to look at him. "You're mine to protect and take care of, little lamb. The same amazing person you've always been but not the naive woman others see you as. And that's one of your greatest weapons. Others will underestimate you. At some point in time, you'll understand all that you possess. God help anyone who tries to hurt you or come between us. You and I apart are dangerous enough. But we aren't individuals anymore, are we? We're twisted together. And do you know what happens when you twist anything together?"

I quietly blurt out, "It gets stronger."

"That's right. You can't break it. Even if it frays, it's still intact. So get all the thoughts of me fucking any other woman out of your head. It's not happening now or ever. When I come home like this, I'm trying to get death off me so it doesn't touch you. And I'll never tell you the details. So dig deep, little lamb. The trust we both require from the other isn't anything like what your friends define as trust. What others have is surface level, and that will never be us."

I only nod, since I'm afraid I might start crying. There isn't any doubt our love and relationship has too many elements other couples don't have to deal with. And everything about Liam is intense. Who he is as a person and in the O'Malley clan. What he has to do to fulfill the responsibilities of his family. How he will protect me and us at any and all costs. I've tried not to analyze the blood that runs through my veins, but I keep wondering if I have any of Liam's intensity. There's nothing hidden about the Baileys and their wrath. I can't deny they have to possess many of the same traits as Liam. Does that mean somewhere deep in me I do, too? If so, what does that mean?

He studies me. "You're scared of who you might be, aren't you?"

I whisper, "Yes."

His eyes turn gentle but are full of tension. I don't know if anyone besides me ever sees them like that. "It's okay, little lamb. Sometimes, if I overthink about the future and my place in my family, I go down the rabbit hole, too."

"You do?" I ask, surprised he questions anything about leading the O'Malleys.

"Yeah. I worry I'm going to screw up the lives of anyone I care about."

I blurt out, "You won't. You can't."

He lets out a short laugh. "Oh, but I can. Most people are placing bets that I will. But if I ruin yours, I'll never forgive myself."

"The only way you would ruin me is if you left me, Liam. You're right, I'm no longer just me. We're part of each other, and I couldn't exist without you."

His lips curl up. He dips down and kisses me with the full force of everything he is—a powerful yet vulnerable man that only I get to witness. He pulls away and asks, "Can you scrub my back? This water is freezing, and if you don't, my skin is going to be crawling all day."

I let out a shaky breath. "Yeah. Turn around." I wash his back then we get out of the cold shower and towel off. As soon as we step into the bedroom, my alarm goes off. I groan. "Ugh!"

He chuckles and pats my ass. "Get ready for work. I'll make breakfast. I'm starving."

"Did you eat last night?" I ask.

"No."

I smirk. "Well, your mom left plenty of potato soup."

He pulls me into him. "I'm sorry she just showed up here. I'll talk with her. Which one is yours?"

"I threw mine down the sink when she left," I admit.

He freezes. "Why?"

"It didn't seem good enough after she tore it apart."

He cups my cheeks. "Don't ever do that again, Hales. My mother means well, but no one should ever make you feel bad about anything you do for me." He gives me a chaste kiss. "Go get ready."

I do as he says, eat breakfast with him, then he insists on escorting me to school even though I tell him to stay home and rest. We pull up to the front doors of the building, and I turn to him. "Please tell me you're going to go home and sleep."

He hesitates. "I forgot to tell you Nora's in labor. She's been in it for a long time."

I trace the lines near his eyes. "Keep your ringer on, but get some sleep. You need it, Liam."

He kisses me. "I'll pick you up unless something comes up."

I caress his head. "Keep track of how many hours you sleep."

"Why?"

I wiggle my eyebrows. "I'll give you ten points on your behavior chart for every hour."

He chuckles. "Guess I've got a date with our bed, then."

I kiss him again then go into school. I can't get our conversation out of my head. I wonder how to figure out who I really am now that so much has changed, but there don't seem to be any answers.

———

When I get out of school, Liam picks me up. He's grinning.

I softly laugh. "Why do you look so happy?"

He pulls me onto his lap, and the car moves forward. His eyes twinkle, and he tucks a lock of hair behind my ear. "One, I'm happy to see you. Two, Nora had the baby."

"She did? Is it a girl?"

"Yes. They named her Shannon after our nana." A brief flicker of sadness passes in his eyes but doesn't last long. "Boris said she's perfect and even has a head full of red hair."

My heart soars. "Do we get to see her?"

"We're going to the hospital now."

I clap. "Yay!" My phone rings, and I dig into my purse and answer it. "Hey, Gemma."

Her voice sounds agitated. "Are you going to the hospital to see the baby?"

"Yes, why?"

"Okay. I need to talk to you when we get there."

My stomach flips. "Are you all right?"

"Yes. I'll talk to you soon. Bye." She hangs up.

I ask Liam, "Do you know why Gemma needs to talk to me?"

He grimaces. "Sorry, Hales. Things happened back-to-back yesterday. She had a run-in with Orla."

My chest tightens. "When?"

"Two days ago. She went to work out and Orla was in the locker room. She cut her thigh. It wasn't deep and—"

"Cut her?" I cry out.

"Calm down. She's fine. I saw her at the gym yesterday."

"How did Orla even get close to my sister?"

Guilt crosses Liam's face. "My dad is working on changing her security. Nolan isn't letting her go anywhere without him right now."

"What did Orla want?"

Liam shakes his head. "She told Gemma she broke a rule by turning her location services off on her phone."

"So she cut her?"

"Our guys rushed in."

My pulse continues to skyrocket. "Meaning what?"

Liam swallows hard. He stays silent, and horror overtakes my shock.

My insides quiver. A scary thought fills my mind. "Was she going to kill her?"

He pulls me tight to him. "I'm unsure."

An uncomfortable feeling expands in my gut. The image of my sister lying in a pool of blood fills my mind. I fight tears and blurt out, "I want her dead, Liam."

His body stiffens, and he locks eyes with me. I expect him to tell me he'll do it, but he doesn't. He studies me, and his jaw twitches.

"Why aren't you saying anything?"

"I don't kill women."

"She's not a woman. She's a vile monster who's out to destroy my sister and me."

He nods. "Yes. And she will be taken care of appropriately once we capture her."

Anger builds in my veins. "What are you waiting for?"

He lets out a deep breath. "It's not as easy as you would think. She has protection surrounding her when she appears. Most of the time, she's a ghost."

"Then have your guys shoot her from far away. Blow up her house if you have to," I tell him.

"Hales—"

"Don't Hales me. She's threatening my family and just cut Gemma with a knife. What would you even do to Orla once you capture her if you aren't going to kill her?" I spout.

He slides his hand in my hair. "Once again, I will never answer your questions. This is for your safety."

My lips quiver. "It's them or us, Liam. I keep thinking that Orla and my father need to die, or my sisters, mom, or I will. Maybe they'll even get to all of us."

He positions my face in front of his. "They won't get to any of you, little lamb. We will take them down, but until your father is out of prison, he's untouchable. My men are doing their best to track Orla right now."

I ask, "How did she get to Gemma?"

"We're looking into it, but it won't happen again. I spoke with my father before I picked you up. Two of our top guys are working in Michigan. He called them back to Chicago. They'll take over Gemma's security."

The car stops moving, and Liam releases me. "Let's go inside. This is a happy occasion. Too much of life isn't. Let's not let the Baileys ruin it for us, okay?"

I inhale deeply. He's right. Life should be happy, and lately, too many things are scary and uncertain. Every day, I see the stress on Liam's face and how he carries the weight of the world on his shoulders. Nora is the sister he never had, and he's been so excited for the baby to arrive. I don't want to put a damper on this occasion. I kiss him. "I hope the baby looks like you."

He raises his eyebrows. "Me?"

"Yeah. You got all the O'Malley good looks."

He chuckles, opens the door, and gets out. He reaches in and helps me out then leads me into the hospital. The waiting room is a mix of Ivanovs and O'Malleys, and everyone is in a cheerful mood.

Aspen, Kora, and Skylar are there. We all embrace and take turns holding Shannon. Gemma and Nolan arrive. The minute she sees me, she drags me over to the corner.

I give her a big hug, squeezing her tighter than I usually would. "Are you okay? Liam just told me Orla cut you?"

She furrows her forehead. Her blue eyes dart between me and everyone else. "I'm fine. But I need to know something."

The hairs on my arms rise, and chills race down my spine. "Okay. What is it?"

She lowers her voice. "Did Mom say anything to you about Orla's mother, Riona?"

I shake my head. Guilt fills me. "No. She's not said anything else besides what she revealed when we all met with her. I've not exactly been taking her calls, either. I blew her off again last night with an *I'm busy* text. Why do you ask?"

Gemma bites on her cheek and glances behind her shoulder. "Orla said something to me before the O'Malleys got to the locker room."

"About disabling the location services on your phone?"

Gemma nervously glances behind her again. "No."

More dread curls in the pit of my stomach. In a firm voice, I reply, "Gemma, what did she say?"

"I-I didn't tell Nolan or Liam."

"You didn't tell them what?"

Her breath hitches. "What she really said."

The air thickens as my chest tightens. "You lied to them?"

Gemma's eyes fill with tears, and she stares at the wall and blinks hard. She puts her hand over her mouth.

I wrap my arms around her. In her ear, I quietly demand, "Just tell me. We'll figure out what to do with the information, together."

Her hot breath hits my ear. In a whisper, she says, "I-I-I researched it. I think Orla is telling the truth."

I tighten my hold on her. "About what?"

"She told me she's going to destroy all of us. You, Ciara, Ella, and me. Only after the four of us suffer is she going to take Mom out."

My insides quiver so hard, I struggle not to get sick. I don't let Gemma go. "Why?"

Gemma's body trembles. "Everything matches, Hailee. The dates we left North Carolina line up perfectly."

I do my best to stay calm. "What matches?"

"The date her mother died. Orla..." Gemma grips my hand. "She-she said our mother killed hers."

22

Liam

It hasn't even been twenty-four hours since we saw the baby at the hospital before more threats pop up. It's wishful thinking to believe I could indulge in some family happiness for longer than a brief moment. But I'm an O'Malley, and it isn't reality. My dad and I are on our way to meet Finn when we get a message to meet at Boris's. The Ivanovs quickly fill us in about how Boyra Petrov somehow got into Sergey's house. He assaulted Kora and told him he now owns his brother Zamir's debt on the Ivanovs. He claims Sergey is going to pay it off.

Zamir is dead and missing. The Ivanovs killed him. Boyra showing up from Moscow is a surprise and deadly. After a brief discussion, my father claims the best way to watch Boyra is to focus on the Petrov whorehouses. He isn't like his brother Zamir who could have been a ghost. Boyra likes to show his face and he always spends the majority of his time in the whorehouses.

"I want Boyra to look at me when he takes his last breath," Sergey grits out.

"I said the O'Malleys are handling this," my father insists.

Sergey's face turns angrier. He steps in front of Darragh and growls, "He groped my woman. After he sliced her arm, he threw her on the ground and put his boot on her back while fondling her ass and threatening to put her in his whorehouse."

My father's eyes turn to slits. "And he will pay, but the O'Malleys will handle this."

"No. Let Sergey join us," I blurt out.

My father slowly turns to me. Shock and irritation flood his face. No one ever goes against his wishes. If they question him, they sure as hell don't do it in front of others. But I agree with Sergey. If someone touched Hailee, I wouldn't let anyone else tear them apart. And my father's health is deteriorating fast. He wants to act like he's fine, but he isn't. I need the Ivanovs on my side, along with their trust. Sergey still doesn't have any faith in me, so maybe this will give me some points on his scoreboard.

The tension in the air grows. My father continues to unhappily assess me.

I confidently remind him, "You said I needed to override your decisions when it was beneficial to the O'Malleys. This is a benefit for us."

My father's face changes. He seems appeased by my admission. "Fine. Where can I smoke?"

I cringe inside, wishing I could take his cancer pipe and toss it in the trash. I keep my mouth shut and let Boris lead him to the balcony.

"Always has to be something in it for you, doesn't it, Liam?" Sergey sneers.

My gut drops. "No. I said that to get my father to agree. If anyone did to my woman what you just described, I wouldn't let anyone else kill him."

Sergey's scowl doesn't fade.

"Jesus, Sergey. When are you going to realize we're on the same side? And my father won't be here much longer to guide me. At some point, I might need your help. I hope if that time comes, you do it because you want to help me, not because you feel obligated," I admit.

Shock overrides Sergey's hardened expression. "Darragh's dying?"

I sniff hard and don't reply. My insides shake with emotions I don't want to ever deal with but know at some point, I'm going to have to. There's no getting around it. My father's time is limited.

"Shit. I'm sorry," Sergey blurts out.

I swallow down the acid and bile climbing up my throat. I work hard to keep steady control of my voice. "It is what it is. Can we get on the same side? I don't see an alliance working out if we aren't."

He studies me, saying nothing.

I have no idea what he's thinking, but I'm tired of trying to figure it out. I turn toward Maksim. "I'm going to need help. I can't go back inside. My father doesn't have any advisors still alive. If I take advice from any of the O'Malleys who would be more than willing to give it, I'll destroy our clan. It's not a question of if but when."

Maksim's icy blue gaze assesses me. He finally says, "Besides this war, I don't want Ivanovs pulled into O'Malley business. I will be here for you and guide you if I can, as long as you agree to my terms. And that includes Boris."

I nod. Boris and I already talked extensively. We're on the same page. "I have no intention of doing anything of the sort."

Maksim pats me on the back, which creates a bit of relief in me. "You come to me at any time, then."

Sergey interrupts. "Tell you what, make sure I'm there to destroy Boyra, and you've got my support."

I attempt to withhold my smile. "As long as I get to watch you take the bastard out, consider it done."

Sergey nods, and my father comes inside, coughing. We leave and get in the car. I text my driver to meet me at Killian's and then text him I'm coming over.

My father turns to me and says, "You can't take any chances with the Petrovs. Don't ever show them any mercy or hesitation. They are on the same level as the Baileys."

"I already know that," I blurt out, a bit insulted he even questions my thoughts on the Petrovs. They may be the number-one enemy of the Ivanovs and not our first priority in the past, but we're aligned now. Shannon's blood is half Ivanov. That makes the Petrovs even with the Baileys, even slightly higher than the Rossis.

My father coughs a few times then says, "You can't let your emotions rule your decisions, son."

"I'm not."

"You are. You put yourself in Sergey's shoes and thought about Hailee. Adding additional men into the equation instead of moving swiftly and keeping this within the O'Malleys is a risk."

"I told you why—"

"Yes, but don't make a habit of it. Learn to use your ruthlessness, not your heart. There is no room for sentiment or love when you're dealing with other crime families. Those emotions will get you killed or cause you to make bad decisions for the clan."

"I'm trying to strengthen our alliance," I claim.

My father's face hardens. "We have three prerogatives. At all times, we have to think of the consequences of all three. Every move you make needs to help us stay in control of the war between the Petrovs and Rossis. It can't give any power to the Baileys. The O'Malleys, under your guidance, must destroy them. Each decision needs to keep us moving forward to establish the clan's future income stream without jeopardizing it."

Acid curls in my gut, and I clench my abs, trying to calm it. The spinning in my head creates a throbbing pain in my brain. The daily pressure I feel never seems to weaken or disappear. It's pointless saying anything to my father in my defense. He's right, and I can't deny anything he's saying.

The car stops in front of Killian's house. My driver waits on the curb. I reach for the door, and my father grasps my arm.

His expression hardens, and his tone is cold. Chills run down my spine. "Liam, you don't have the luxury of making mistakes."

"Yes, I'm aware."

"I don't think you are."

I release the door handle. "What does that mean?"

He taps my chest. "You haven't learned to control this yet."

Anger surges through me. All I've done my entire adult life is try to be good enough to step into his shoes. I finally admit, "I'm not you, Dad. I'm doing the best I can and—"

"This isn't about you doing your best. It's about digging down and finding the ability to rule with your gut and not your heart."

I almost laugh. All I feel in my gut is a hole burning bigger each day that passes. I sniff hard and stare at the ceiling.

He softens his tone. "You're smarter than I ever was at your age, Liam." He taps my head and gut. "Use these two things. Keep your heart at home with your woman and nowhere else."

I grunt, tired of all the stress of ruling the clan before I'm even the one in charge. I open the door. "Thanks for the pep talk, Dad. I'll see you later."

"Liam—"

"Lecture me later. We're finished with this conversation right now," I tell him and get out. I shut the door, and Killian steps out of his house.

"Why do you look so pissed?" he asks.

"Shut up," I grumble, not in the mood to dissect any of my conversation with my father. I slide into the car and instruct the driver to go to Declan's.

Killian slams the door. He rolls the divider window up. "Did you tell Maksim yet?"

"About what?"

"Why Obrecht can't touch Jack Christian? Boris just texted me to tell you that time is up."

I groan. "Tell him I'll do it today. Text Maksim and ask if we can meet him after we see Finn."

Killian sends the messages off. He raises his eyebrows.

"What?" I growl.

"You going to fill me in on whatever it is that made you move our meeting to now?"

I sigh. I tell him about Boyra Petrov and what happened to Kora and Sergey.

"Fuck, that's intense," Killian mutters.

"Yeah. My dad's notifying our guys to watch and report when he's at the whorehouses. He's not like Zamir, so he'll show his face. We shouldn't have a problem tracking him," I confidently state.

"Then why do you look so pissed?" he asks.

"Drop it," I instruct.

The phone rings, and I glance at the screen. I answer, "We're almost there."

Finn says, "Declan and I just left. Something came up."

My stomach twists. "Do I need to meet you?"

"Nope. Nothing you need to deal with or worry about. We'll try to catch up later tonight."

"All right." I hang up and call Maksim.

"Liam," he says after one ring.

"Can we meet now?"

"Sure. Swing by my place."

I hang up and instruct the driver to go to Maksim's. Within minutes, we arrive. Killian punches in the penthouse code. When we step off the elevator, Maksim is waiting for us. We go into the living room and sit on the couches.

"What's going on?" he asks.

I lock eyes with his. "I need to tell you how we're going to change the future income stream for the O'Malleys. Obrecht wants to kill Jack Christian. You can't let him touch Jack or Judge Peterson until his company goes public."

A line forms between his eyebrows. "Judge Peterson?"

"Yes."

"Is Finn keeping his distance? If the judge knows he's going after him—"

"He's extra cautious," I insist.

Maksim's eyes turn to slits. "Have you pulled Boris into this?"

I shake my head. "He knows what is going on, but he doesn't have anything to do with it. I swear."

Maksim leans forward. "And you're going to keep it that way, correct?"

"Yes. It involves his daughter's future, so it was only right I told him." I leave out the part about Boris and I having it out one night at the pub when he claimed the O'Malleys put Nora and his unborn child at risk by running drugs and gambling operations. He was hinting about not having O'Malley in Shannon's name, which is something he promised my father he would do, claiming it would be safer for her not to be associated with our crime family. That only made me angry, but we came to an agreement after a long conversation in the back alley. I assured him I would change things and disclosed what we had in the works. He vowed to have O'Malley in Shannon's name as long as I was serious about getting out of the addiction business.

"Fair enough. Now tell me why Obrecht can't kill that bastard right now," Maksim demands.

"Way to not beat around the bush," Killian inserts.

I ignore him. I explain to Maksim our plan to profit off the fall of Jack's company stock.

He stays quiet. When I finish, he sits back and pushes the pads of his fingers together. The feeling I said something wrong fills me until he says, "Where's Finn?"

"He and Declan are taking care of something. Why?"

Maksim tilts his head. "He's been out for over a month now. I've yet to see him. He refused to see me when I went to visit him after he got locked up."

"Why?" I ask. I was unaware of this. Maksim and Finn were tight. I always wondered why Maksim never visited him. I asked Finn once, and he said to drop it.

"That's between Finn and me. Now let me be clear about something else."

"What's that, Daddy M?" Killian teases.

Maksim and I both glare at him.

"Jesus. You two need to lighten up a bit," Killian mutters.

Maksim releases an annoyed breath and turns back to me. "From now on, you don't put my brother in a position to keep things from me. Whatever you tell an Ivanov, I better be aware of."

"Noted," I agree.

"And tell Finn, we're overdue. I want to meet with him this week. Not next week, this week."

"I'll tell him. But you know Finn. I can't make him do anything if he doesn't want to."

"Then you tell me where he's at, and I'll just show up," Maksim replies.

I groan and scrub my face. "Don't put me in that position with Finn."

Maksim points at me. "You had my brother keep important information from me. You owe me this, Liam."

"Listen, I—"

His phone rings, and he motions for me to stay quiet. He answers, "Sergey." Maksim scrunches his face, repeats Sergey, and rises. The color drains from his cheeks, and he motions for us to follow him.

We get in the elevator, and he puts it on speaker. There are several gunshots and Russian screaming. Sergey yells, "Fuck," then things get too muffled to hear anything.

"What just happened?" Killian barks.

Maksim snarls, "Boyra has them."

The elevator doors open, and Maksim calls his driver. "Follow me in your car. We don't know if we need it."

The ride to the outskirts of Chicago is fast and chaotic. Killian and I try to contact my dad, Finn, and his brothers.

When we pull up to the abandoned warehouse, Sergey is naked. His ankle and wrist are bound, and he's screaming, "Kora!"

Maksim rolls a thug off Kora. A pool of blood surrounds her. Boyra is dead on the ground several feet from her.

Without thinking, I pick up Kora and run to my car with her limp, blood-soaked body in my arms. I attempt to find a bullet, but I can't. Sergey jumps in my car naked, clutching his clothes. We take off for the hospital, both of us trying to locate a wound.

He keeps saying, "Wake up, my lapa."

We're close to the hospital when she barely opens her eyes. She whispers, "Sergey."

He does his best to keep it together, trying to comfort her. "Shh."

I stare out the window, trying to give them some privacy, but it's impossible.

We pull up to the hospital. He puts on his pants and carries her in. A team of people takes her from him and puts her on a stretcher. A nurse yells out, "She's going into shock."

My father comes into the waiting room with the police chief. They quietly talk with the Ivanovs and us. Adrian and my father leave to go to the scene of the crime and clean up with the police chief. We all want Kora and Sergey's name to stay out of everything. It's better not to have any crime family news in the press, and the police chief knows it.

After they leave, I get in my car and call Hailee. She's at school, and I've never called her before. She doesn't answer, and I text her.

Me: *There's an emergency. I'm at the hospital but coming to get you.*

Hailee: *What's wrong? Are you okay? Is Gemma okay?*

Me: *Yes. It's Kora. She should be fine, but I think you should be here.*

Hailee: *I'll get someone to watch my class and wait for you.*

When I pull up to the curb, she comes flying out of the building. I open the door, and her hand flies to her mouth. "Oh my God! Liam, what happened? I thought you said you were okay!"

I glance at my bloody clothes then remove my shirt. "Sorry. It's not mine. I'm not injured."

Her eyes dart between the shirt and me, and she starts to cry.

I pull her into my arms. "Shh. It's okay, little lamb. I'm fine. Kora will fully recover, too."

She pulls back. Her blue eyes overflow with tears, and her lips quiver hard.

I stroke her hair and kiss her forehead. I reiterate, "It's okay."

She shakes her head. "I-I need to tell you something."

My gut sinks. "What?"

"I-I should have told you last night when we got home, but I promised Gemma I wouldn't. But I researched everything today, and it's possible based on the dates."

The hairs on my arms rise. "What are you talking about?"

"I didn't think it could be true. And when you texted, I thought Orla did something to my sisters or my mom. And Gemma just called while I was waiting for you and...and..." She covers her mouth and closes her eyes. The tears never stop flowing.

I remove her hands from her face and cup her cheeks. "Tell me what is going on, Hales."

"Orla didn't say anything to Gemma about the location services. She told her my mom killed her mother, Riona."

I gape at Hailee. Riona Ryan was a mafia princess before her death. The rumor is she was ruthless and one of the most conniving Ryan women to ever exist. It doesn't surprise me how cruel Orla is, knowing who her mother and father are. The Ryans and Baileys have had an alliance for years. And I'm not shocked Riona was Rory's mistress. Dozens of marriages entwine their families.

"I-I think there's something else about my mom."

I wait, my chest tightening.

Hailee swallows hard. "I think my mom and Riona were sisters."

My stomach flips faster. "Your last name is O'Hare. Isn't that your mom's maiden name?"

Hailee shakes her head. "My mom changed it. I don't think it's her real maiden name. I can't find a Jane O'Hare anywhere in North Carolina. But I did find a Jane Ryan who had a sister named Riona. And Jane disappeared right after Riona's death. I don't think she married my father, either."

I choose my words carefully. "Your mom said she was married to your father?"

"Yes. Why?"

My heart pounds harder. I reveal, "She couldn't have been. Rory never married."

Hailee's eyes widen. "Why would she lie to us? What would the purpose be?"

I slide Hailee onto my lap. I attempt to keep my voice calm, but it's hard. "I don't know. But you should have told me what Gemma said last night."

Hailee wipes her face. "I know. But I promised Gemma and wanted to prove her wrong. I-I can't. And when she called, I thought it was about this, but it wasn't."

I'm scared to ask her, but I do. "What did Gemma call you about?"

Hailee's entire body trembles. "My dad is getting released in two weeks."

23

Hailee

THE DOCTOR SAID KORA AND SERGEY WILL FULLY RECOVER, SO that is a relief. Liam takes me home to get rest but has to go back to the hospital. When he gets home, we decide to go for coffee, since there is a fog delay for my school district. We run into Selena and Obrecht. They sit at our table, but things are tense between the two men. Obrecht brings up my teacher of the year award I received in the spring. When Liam questions me about it, Obrecht makes a snide remark about Liam being in prison when I got it. If I didn't love Selena so much, I would lash out at him for being so rude.

Something comes up, and Liam and Obrecht leave together. Selena and I talk for a while and then her therapist shows up, so I excuse myself.

Liam told me to go in Obrecht's car since they went in his. Liam's cousin Gavin is in the front with Obrecht's driver. I'm heading to school but can't get my mother's lies out of my head, so I call Nolan's phone.

She groggily answers, "Hello."

"Are you at Nolan's?"

"Yeah. Where else would I be? It's super early in the morning." She yawns, and there's a muffled noise in the background.

"Who's that?" I ask.

"Nolan."

"Why's he in your room?"

She avoids answering my question. "What's going on that you had to interrupt my beauty sleep?"

"I'm coming over."

"Now?" she frantically asks.

"Yeah. Is that a problem? We need to talk about the other night," I insist.

She groans and sarcastically remarks, "I almost forgot all the realities of our awesome family dynamics."

"See you soon. Bye," I chirp and hang up before she can protest. I roll the divider glass down. "Can you take me to Nolan O'Malley's instead?"

"Sure."

I roll the divider up and sit back in my seat. I send a notice to my school saying I'm sick. It's last minute, and I've never used a sick day when I wasn't before, but nothing about life seems normal anymore. So many thoughts are racing around in my head. I don't understand why my mother lied to us and continues to do so. The more she doesn't come completely clean, the harder it gets to control the boiling rage in my blood.

Within minutes, the car parks outside Nolan's house. Gavin escorts me to the front door.

Nolan opens the door. He's shirtless and barefoot, wearing only pajama bottoms. I try not to gape at his ripped, tattooed torso. There's no doubt he's an O'Malley, but everything about Nolan, I'm unsure of. On the one hand, I'm grateful he's protecting my sister. While the other part of me is always worried about whether he's being nice or a dick to her. Every time I see them, one of them seems pissed at the other, so I can't imagine how they are cohabiting together.

His cocky expression grows, and he arches an eyebrow. "My eyes are up here."

"Shut up," I blurt out and shove past him, trying to control the heat crawling into my cheeks. Before he ever met Gemma, I thought he was this sweet hottie. Something about my sister seems to bring out a different side of him. Or maybe I just never noticed. Either way, I don't need him gloating over me gawking at him. "Where's Gemma?"

The sound of the door shutting hits my ears. "Good morning to you, too, Hailee. Gavin, you want some espresso?"

"Nah. I'm good. Thought you didn't drink coffee?" Gavin asks.

"The princess requires it. She isn't a fan of my morning drink," Nolan reports.

"Smart girl. That shit is gross," Gavin replies.

"See, I'm not the only one who doesn't agree with raw egg smoothies." Gemma smirks, stepping through a doorway and into the room. She's wearing black silk pajama shorts and a matching button-up top.

I glance between Nolan and Gemma. "You two do know it's past eight, right?"

"Your point?" Gemma asks.

I roll my eyes. "The rest of the world is awake and has clothes on."

"Clothes are overrated," my sister chirps. She takes a mug and fills it with espresso. "Want one?"

"No, thanks. Can we talk in your bedroom?"

Her face falls. "Sure." She motions for me to follow her. I expect to go into the bedroom she came out of, but she leads me down the hall. The bed appears freshly made, and there are no signs of her things anywhere.

Suspicion fills me. "Where are your clothes?"

"Put away. What's going on?"

"Since when do you make the bed when you first get out of it?" I pry.

Her face turns pink. "I'm a guest. I'm trying to be polite. So, are you going to talk or ask me about house cleaning?"

I study her.

"Talk, Hailee," she warns.

I put my hand on my hip. "Why were you in Nolan's bedroom?"

"Shoot me for wanting to brush my teeth and running out of toothpaste." She tilts her head. "Is there something you came to talk to me about?"

I shut the door and whisper. "Are you sleeping with Nolan?"

In a firm voice, she asks, "Hailee, why are you here?"

I step closer. "I thought you hated each other?"

"I never said I felt that way. Did he say he hates me?" she asks with a hurt expression.

"So you are?" I ask.

Gemma crosses her arms and glares. "I'm going to leave the room if you don't get to the reason you called and woke me up so early."

I sigh and sit on the bed. "Fine. I can't find anything to prove Mom couldn't have killed Riona. But I think Mom lied about some other things."

Gemma sits next to me. She swallows hard. "Like what?"

I try to find the right way to tell her but decide there isn't any way to gentle the blow. "I think Mom is a Ryan and Riona was her sister."

Gemma's jaw drops. Several moments pass. She puts her hand on her stomach. Her face begins to turn green, and she slowly says, "So our father was screwing Mom's sister?"

My gut flips. "Yeah."

"Eww. How much grosser can he get?"

"I know."

"But..." She puts her hand over her mouth. "How could Mom kill her sister?"

It's a question I can't find any rationale for. My sisters and I would all die for each other. I shake my head and reply, "We need to talk to Mom. If she's Jane Ryan, she needs to explain why she continued to lie to us."

Gemma scrunches her face. "Why? What would be the point?"

I shrug.

Gemma rises and paces the room. She twirls a lock of her strawberry-blonde hair around her finger. "So we're part of these Ryan people, too?"

The air in my lungs becomes stale. I don't want it to be true. It's bad enough we have Bailey blood in us. This new information seems to hurt even more. "Yeah. And Liam told me our father never married."

Gemma freezes. "What? Why did she tell us she was married and divorced?"

"I don't know. She seems to be hiding so much, and I want to know what else she hasn't told us and why."

Gemma opens the closet and takes out a shirt and pair of jeans. "Let me take a quick shower. She had today and tomorrow off. Her boss decided to have the office repainted."

"Should I text her? Or should we surprise her?" I ask.

Gemma wrinkles her nose. "Text her. Otherwise, I'm sure Simon will be there, and who knows what we'll walk in on."

"Gross."

"You don't know the half of it. Listening to Mom giggle all day drove me nuts. I'm sure Simon moved in the moment I moved out. He was always there anyway," Gemma reveals. She pins her hair in a claw clip, goes into the attached bathroom, and shuts the door.

I text my mom that we're coming over and need to talk to her in private. Then I text Liam.

Me: *I called off work. I'm at Nolan's picking up Gemma. We're going to confront my mom. I think I'll go work on refurbishing the chair after, so I'll be at my apartment if you're looking for me later.*

I leave the bedroom. When I get to the main room, Gavin is nowhere. Nolan is sitting on the couch and talking to the server from the pub, Molly. I freeze before entering the room.

"My brother arrives Saturday. My mom wants to have a surprise party for him. Can you come?" she asks. Hope lights up her golden-brown eyes.

Nolan flashes the smile I used to see before he met Gemma. It's kind and soft and looks like the boy next door. "Sure. I talked to Colin last week, but he said he didn't know when he was flying out."

Molly's smile grows. "He called this morning. Well, I should go. I know Gavin is waiting for you outside."

I realize I'm snooping, and I step into the room. "Hi, Molly! He's with my driver."

She glances up. Her face falls, and she scrunches her forehead. "Oh. Hi, Hailee. I didn't know anyone else was here."

"Gemma's showering then we'll be leaving," I tell her.

Molly's face turns red. She looks at Nolan in question. "Oh. Sorry. I didn't know she was still here."

Nolan shifts in his seat. "Yeah. She lives here right now."

Molly looks at the floor then rises. "Right. Okay. I'll see you later." She starts moving toward the door, and Nolan follows her.

"Molly. Hold up."

She freezes, takes a deep breath, then spins. What appears to be a forced smile forms on her lips. She raises her eyebrows.

"Thanks for the cookies. I'll see you Saturday, okay?"

"Mmhmm. Bye." She turns and quickly leaves.

The door shuts, and Nolan stares at it and sighs.

"Are you screwing her and my sister?" I accuse.

He spins. "What? Are you kidding me right now?"

"No. I think it's a fair question."

He shakes his head in disgust. "She's my best friend's little sister."

"So, you're saying you aren't screwing her?"

He crosses his arms. "Not that it's any of your concern, but I promised her brother when he left for a job in Europe I'd watch out for her. She's my friend. That's it."

"Does she know she's only your friend?"

He scrubs his face and groans. "I'm not sure what it is about you O'Hare girls, but don't be spreading rumors around about Molly. She's a nice girl."

I point to the plate covered in foil. "I didn't say she wasn't. But women don't just bake cookies and bring them over to a man's house if they aren't into them."

"We're friends. She knows I like them and made extra. It's not a big deal," he claims.

"Last week, it was a pot of fish stew," Gemma snarls, walking into the room.

Nolan scowls. "This is getting old. Princess, why don't you and your opinionated sister butt out of my friendship?"

"Maybe you should stop leading the poor girl on if you aren't interested," I tell him.

"Right? Glad you see it, too," Gemma adds.

He groans. "What is with you two?"

"She likes you," Gemma claims.

"Yep," I agree.

"You two, stay out of my business. Where are you going?" Nolan asks.

Gemma huffs. "Guess your statement goes two ways, doesn't it? Let's go, Hailee."

"Gemma—"

"Don't start, Nolan. The new bodyguards are here, so I don't have to tell you my every move. Or do you have concerns about them, too?" She glares at him.

He studies her for a moment then shakes his head. "Have a good day, princess."

"Yeah. You, too, Prince Charming," Gemma snaps back and slings her purse over her shoulder.

"How do you two live together?" I question, glancing between them.

Neither answers my question. Gemma gives Nolan one final pissed-off expression, and we leave. Another car pulls up to the curb with two men, and we get in it. Gavin gets out of Obrecht's car and slides in the back seat with us.

"How many bodyguards do we need?" I tease.

"Liam will kill me if I don't go with you."

I can't help but smile. Gavin's right. I know Liam's overprotectiveness all too well.

We stay quiet for the ride. When we arrive at my mother's, Simon leaves. My mom pins her worried blue eyes on us. "What's going on? And why aren't you in school, Hailee?"

"There was a fog delay and then I decided this was more important," I admit.

"What is?"

"What's your real maiden name?" Gemma interjects.

The color in my mother's face drains. She says nothing, and her chest rises and falls faster.

"Mom. You need to stop lying to us."

Her eyes turn to slits. She snarls, "What did the O'Malleys tell you?"

I glance at Gemma. She gives me a questioning look, and I turn back toward my mother. "There's only one thing Liam told me. Orla told Gemma the other piece of information."

My mother shifts in her seat and taps her fingers on her thighs. "What did she say?"

"First, tell us who we are," I reply.

"Hailee—"

"Is your real maiden name Ryan?" Gemma blurts out.

My mother closes her eyes. Gemma grabs my hand. There's no doubt who she is. My insides quiver, and I ask, "So our mother is Jane Ryan, the missing mafia princess?"

Our mom's lids fly open. Pain fills her orbs. "I'm not her anymore."

"But you were and lied to us."

She winces. "You don't know what it was like to be a Ryan, given to a Bailey. I never wanted any of you to know about it or have any part of the Ryans or Baileys."

"Mom, why did you lie and say you were married to our father?"

A tear drips down her cheek. She wipes it away and says, "I was supposed to marry your father. He told everyone I was his wife, so in my eyes, we were married." She laughs and wipes her face as more tears spill. "My father might be sicker than yours. He lost a bet. My sister, Riona, and I were both in the pot. He handed us over to your father like we were nothing but objects to be owned. The ironic thing is, Riona liked it. She had every cruel and conniving trait my father possessed. She loved your father, and it became her mission to see how much she could torment me."

Gemma gets up and sits next to my mom. She tugs her into her arms. "You should have told us!"

"Why? What is the point? I don't want to relive any of it."

My heart hurts for her, but she also needs to come clean and tell us the full truth. I ask, "Mom, did you kill Riona?"

Tension fills the air. She stares at me until her face crumbles and she completely breaks down.

Gemma's eyes widen. She tries to comfort our mother.

I rise and sit on the other side of her and put my arm around her back. When she calms, I ask, "Mom, what happened?"

"I-I had to do it. She found all the money I saved to escape. She was going to tell your father, and he would have put me in the whorehouse. Riona would have raised you girls. I couldn't let her. She was so evil. I-I just lost it. She pulled a gun on me, and I lunged at her. I got it away from her. I-I could have walked away, but she would have come after me. So I shot her and made it look like it was a drug deal gone bad. Then I went home, put a sleeping pill in your father's drink, and that night we left."

Gemma and I spend a few moments attempting to comfort my mother, letting her admission sink in. The visions of my mother putting us in the car and the cold chill of that winter night pops up and digs into my bones.

I push it aside and continue, "Mom, there's something we have to tell you."

"What?"

"He's getting out in two weeks."

My mother gasps then jumps off the couch. "We all need to go, now. This has gone farther than I ever should have allowed. The O'Malleys cannot save you. And they are just as bad as the Ryans and Baileys. We need to get your sisters—"

"No! I'm not running. And I'm not leaving Liam. He's not a Ryan or Bailey, so don't put him in that bucket," I insist.

"I'm not going, either. If we run, we have no protection," Gemma claims.

My mother's hands shake. "You don't understand what your father is capable of."

"What about Simon? Are you going to just leave him?" I ask.

Anguish fills her face. More tears fall. She covers her mouth and says, "If your father gets out and I'm with Simon, your father will kill him."

"I'll get Liam to put bodyguards on Simon, then," I assure her, not even questioning it. Liam would never deny my request, and I know it.

My mother gapes. "Do you think I told Simon any of this? He would flip if he knew who I was and what I did."

Gemma cries out, "If he loves you—"

"This is the mob! It's not some ordinary prisoner getting out of jail. Trust me. Those thugs raised me. I *killed* someone. I'm not the person Simon thinks I am, and if he finds out—"

"Mom. Stop! I'm calling Liam, and we'll figure this out. You can't run from this anymore," I insist and remove my phone from my purse.

"Do not call an O'Malley. Don't you see? Your insistence on staying with Liam is going to make everything worse. And this is my fault. I didn't put my foot down hard enough. This thing you have going on with Liam and whatever you're doing with Nolan is over. There will be no more O'Malley protection. The two of you are coming with me. We're getting your sisters and leaving," my mother orders.

"What? No! You can't tell us what to do with our lives. We're in our mid-thirties," Gemma barks back.

A dark blue forms in my mother's otherwise-bright eyes. "Do not disobey me."

"Gemma's right, Mom. We aren't children. You can't make us."

My mom haughtily laughs. "Sure I can. I'm a Ryan. One thing a Ryan knows how to do is get what they want. So if I have to tie you up and throw you in my trunk, I will."

"Have you gone crazy?" Gemma lashes out.

I put my arm around Gemma's shoulders. "Let's go." I address my mother, "When you come to your senses, we can talk some more." I lead Gemma to the door and attempt to open it.

My mother's hand slams it shut.

"Mom! Stop acting like a crazy lunatic!" I yell.

"What do you think your father will be like? This isn't lunacy. You don't know what lunacy is," she fires back.

I reach for the door, but she bats my hand away.

"Mom!" I warn, trying to ignore the sting on my skin.

The crazed look in her eyes intensifies. "Go sit down. You aren't leaving until I'm ready to go."

"Get out of our way," Gemma orders and reaches for the door.

My mom slaps Gemma in the face. The sound echoes in the room.

Gemma shrieks in pain. She puts her hand over the red mark. For a brief second, I think she'll back down, but rage fills her expression. She attempts to push my mom out of the way.

I turn the handle and scream, "Move!"

Suddenly, Liam shoves his way through the door with Nolan in tow. Liam tugs me into him, and Nolan grabs Gemma and seethes at my mother, "You hit her?"

My mother's eyes seem to come back to the ones I'm used to seeing. It's like she didn't even realize what she did. She stares at Gemma. Nolan has his arm protectively around her, and his other hand is holding her head against his chest.

"Oh God. Gemma! I'm sorry! I..." My mother puts her hand over her mouth and breaks down again.

I'm torn between wanting to comfort my mother and trying to figure out what just occurred. I glance up at Liam, who's scowling at my mother. "We're leaving now. When you've calmed down, you can talk to your daughters. Until then, stay away. But know this, Jane Ryan. You and your daughters are under my watch, *my orders*. If you attempt to leave Chicago without my blessing, you won't get past your front door. Understand?"

My mother's face will haunt me forever. It's as if she finally is realizing there truly is nowhere to run.

24

Liam

"I think my mom's lost her marbles," Hailee frets once we get in the car.

"Let me see your cheek," Nolan softly says to Gemma.

"It's fine," she replies and looks out the window.

Nolan gently turns her to face him. "It's swollen and bruising. As soon as we get home, I'll get an ice pack for you."

Gemma's lips tremble, and she blinks hard, but a tear escapes anyway.

Nolan wipes it then puts his arm around her.

I tug Hailee closer to me and kiss her head. "Did she do anything to you?"

"No." She swallows hard and locks eyes with mine. "My mom said her father gave both her and Riona to my father when he lost a bet."

I ball my hand into a fist and then open it up and grip the edge of the seat. Nothing the Ryans or Baileys do should surprise me, but it's another disgusting reality of who they are.

"I know things got out of control, but I feel bad for Mom," Gemma says.

Hailee looks at her and nods. She quietly agrees, "Yeah."

Gemma's voice shakes. "I-I think she did what she thought was best to protect us."

Nolan's hardened expression meets mine. Unspoken words are loud and clear. There's no question that Jane's time with Rory was a form of hell on earth. She was brave to leave him. It's a miracle she and all four of her daughters are still alive. But she also was raised to hate O'Malleys. Whatever her family ingrained in her isn't going to die quickly, if ever.

Gemma clears her throat, and more tears fall. "Liam, you won't remove my mom's protection, will you?"

Hailee's body stiffens. She holds her breath, and anxiety plagues her face.

"No. The O'Malleys will continue to watch her. If any Bailey or Ryan comes near her, they will pay for it," I vow.

Gemma nods and turns back to the window, twisting her fingers in her lap.

Hailee curls into me. I stroke her thigh with my thumb, and she asks, "My mom thinks we should run. But they'll find us, won't they?"

My stomach clenches. The acid begins to bubble. Any thought of Hailee leaving Chicago makes me want to chain her up in the house and never let her out.

Before I can answer, Nolan does. "They had to have been watching you for years. It's not possible to escape them. For whatever reason, they left you alone all this time. Running again will only get you all killed."

Hailee shivers, and my gut flips at the thought.

The driver parks outside of Nolan's house. He gives me one final look then opens the door and reaches in to help Gemma out.

"Gemma, do you want me to come in?" Hailee asks.

Gemma shakes her head. She leans forward and hugs Hailee. "No. I'll call you tomorrow, but I'm going to talk to Ciara and Ella tonight. They need to know what's going on."

"I can go with you."

"No. I'll take care of it," Gemma volunteers.

"Gemma—"

"Can you please let me take care of one thing?" she snaps.

I hold my hands out. "Okay. If you change your mind, let me know."

Gemma nods and gets out. Once they're inside the house, I pull Hailee onto my lap. I slide my finger over her forehead and down her cheek. "I need to talk to my dad. Will you come to my parents' house with me?"

"Okay. I was going to work on refurbishing the chair, but I can do it a different day."

I give her a chaste kiss. My chest tightens. I hesitate then say, "What did your mother say about me?"

She licks her lips and furrows her eyebrows. Her nails graze the side of my scalp. She deeply inhales and tilts her head. "She said the O'Malleys are just as bad as the Baileys or Ryans. And that you can't save us."

I don't blink or unpin my gaze off her blue eyes. My heart pounds harder, and blood pulses in my veins. "I would die for you. No one, and I mean *no one*, will hurt you under my watch."

The corners of her lips slightly turn up. "I know. And I would rather die than leave Chicago and you. I also told my mother you aren't as bad as the Baileys or Ryans."

My pulse shoots straight to my head, and blood slams between my ears. I could let her continue to believe her misconception, but Hailee and I don't lie to each other. "Oh, but we are, little lamb. Whatever the Baileys or Ryans are willing to do to take us out, the O'Malleys won't think twice about doing tenfold. Any notion that we lack something your family has regarding their moral compass is wrong."

A line forms on Hailee's forehead. "You would add your daughters to the kitty in a bet and willingly give them to a man?"

"No. What I'm referring to is the wrath both the Baileys and Ryans will soon experience under my name, starting with your father's life."

A typical daughter would be upset upon hearing anyone threaten her father, but Hailee doesn't flinch. In a cold voice, she replies, "The sooner he's dead, the better."

I fist her hair and bring my face closer to hers. It's pointless discussing this anymore. So I change the subject. "Why didn't you tell me you were awarded teacher of the year for several years in a row?"

Pink floods her cheeks. "I told you this morning. It's not a big deal. It's just a stupid plaque and night for the administrators to get free drinks."

I tug her head back and lean over her face. "Don't do that, little lamb."

Her breath hitches. "What?"

"Act like you don't deserve the recognition for the amazing job you've done with those kids."

She stays silent.

I peck her on the lips then loosen my grip on her hair. I ask, "Why can't you give yourself some credit?"

She sighs. "I do the best I can within the confinements of the system. It's not the best I could do. If I were doing the best I could do regarding teaching, I could make a much bigger impact."

I study her for several moments, letting her words sink in. I finally tell her, "We're going to celebrate your awards tonight."

She opens her mouth then shakes her head. "It was months ago."

"Yep. We're still going to celebrate. And soon, I'm coming into big money. When I do, I'm giving you whatever you need to build and run your school," I declare.

Her head jerks back. "Wh-what are you talking about?"

"Just what I said. You told me you wanted your own school, so I'm going to make it happen. Wherever you want it, I'll build it. And you run things how you see fit."

She stares at me as if she doesn't believe me. She blurts out, "That's a ridiculous amount of money, Liam."

"Yeah. I'm sure it is. But we're going to have more than we'll ever need, I promise you."

She shakes her head, gaping at me. "I don't care about money."

"I know. But I have to make sure the O'Malleys survive."

Sadness enters her expression. She cups my cheeks. "That's a lot of pressure, Liam."

I stay quiet. There's no point in denying it. The growing hole in my gut reminds me almost all day long.

"Sometimes I worry you might crack," she admits.

"You don't need to worry."

She tilts her head. "I see all that you carry on your shoulders, Liam. I wish I could say I didn't contribute to it, and the only thing I did was help you take your mind off the world around you. But I know I've added to it."

I wrap my arms tight around her. "You're my sanity, Hales. The only time I laugh or have fun or forget about anything is with you. And I love you for it."

She kisses me then retreats and asks, "How did you know to come to my mom's today?"

"When you texted me, I had a bad feeling. I was pissed Nolan let you go there alone."

"Why?"

I take a slow, calculated breath. I slide my hand up her shirt and stroke her spine. "I know she's your mom, but she's also a Ryan."

In a defensive tone, Hailee replies, "She's not a bad person. What they put her through..." She turns away.

I move her chin back in front of my face. "I don't doubt it was horrible. Your mother was raised by one devil then given to another one. But there are things instilled in you when you grow up in families like ours. Her hatred for my family and me runs deep. So I don't know if she's ever going to accept me in your life. And that worries me, little lamb."

"I'm not leaving you, Liam. No matter what she thinks, it's not going to change my mind about us."

I release a breath. The car parks in my parents' driveway. I give Hailee a chaste kiss, then we get out and go inside the house. I guide her into the kitchen.

My mom is cleaning vegetables and stops. She hugs me and then Hailee. "Are you staying for dinner?"

I glance at the clock on the wall. "It's only noon, Mom. Plus, we have plans."

Her face falls, which makes me feel guilty.

Hailee surprises me and says, "Why don't we pick a day this week?"

My mom's face lights up. "Sure. Whatever day you want."

Hailee glances at the vegetables. "Can I help?"

"I'm washing these then need to cut them up."

Hailee picks the knife up off the counter. "I can do that."

My dad walks into the kitchen. He gives Hailee a hug and kiss on the cheek, then we go into his study. As soon as the door shuts, he says, "I called the twins up from Tennessee. They'll be here tomorrow. The rumor is Rory plans on coming to Chicago when he gets out in two weeks."

The twins are my cousins Dylan and Dean. They might be the most ruthless of the entire O'Malley clan. My father has them take out anyone and everyone who gets in the O'Malley's way. They have no limits. I haven't seen them since before I went to prison, but it puts some of my worries at ease, knowing they will be watching Rory's every move. "You're giving them the shoot-to-kill order, correct? I want that bastard and his brother Mack taken out."

My father fills his pipe. "Mack's involved with Jack Christian and Judge Peterson. It's best to keep him alive for the time being."

"Fine. Mack stays alive until after Jack's company goes public. But Rory gets taken out," I insist.

My father lights up his pipe and takes a long drag off it. He exhales and points to the chair. "Sit down."

Nerves flutter in my chest. I obey and wait.

"Son, are you one hundred percent sure Hailee, her mother, or her sisters aren't in bed with the Baileys?"

Rage climbs up my body so fast, I have a hard time controlling myself from reaching across the table and choking my father on his pipe. Instead, I clench my hands into fists and sneer, "Don't ever question Hailee again."

My father never flinches. "You just discovered her mother is a Ryan. It's prudent to do more due diligence."

I clench my jaw and grind my molars. After several attempts to calm myself, I reply, "I don't need to do any more due diligence. Now drop it."

"You're thinking with the wrong body part again."

I slam my hand on the desk. "Dammit, Dad. When I tell you I'm sure about something, don't question me. And the next time you have anything but something nice to say about my woman, you and I will have issues. Understand?"

His eyes turn to slits. "Watch your mouth."

"No. You watch yours. Make sure the twins become a hemorrhoid on Rory's ass. When they get a chance, they better take him out or tell me where to be so I can do it." I get up and leave the room. I go into the kitchen. "Hailee, we're leaving."

She spins with a knife in her hand. The blade is sharp and shiny. She smiles. "Can I finish slicing this tomato?"

"No."

Her eyes widen.

"Liam, you just got here," my mother whines.

I snap, "Not now, Mom. I don't need your guilt trip."

Hurt fills my mother's expression.

"Liam!" Hailee reprimands.

"We're leaving, now," I repeat and stomp out the back door. The cold air hits my lungs, but it doesn't cool me off. I'm getting tired of the lessons and constant questioning. It's bad enough half my family and the Ivanovs don't have any faith in my ability to make decisions. I don't need it from my father and especially not where it concerns Hailee. She's the only good thing in my life and the person I trust the most.

I get in the car, put my head against the back of the seat, and close my eyes. A few minutes pass, and the door creaks open. Hailee's muted sugar scent flares in my nostrils. Her body heat merges with mine, and she straddles me.

I open my eyes.

"Bad day at the office, dear?" she teases and bats her eyes.

Even though I'm still pissed, I chuckle.

Her face falls. "What happened?"

I usually keep everything work related away from Hailee. But everything seems to fly out. "I'm tired of having to prove myself and getting questioned all the time. Sometimes, I wish I wasn't Darragh O'Malley's son."

She studies me and strokes my cheek. "Maybe we should run away. Go live somewhere off the grid so no one can find us."

I grunt. "If it were possible, I'd do it. But I'm not stupid, little lamb. Everyone would find us. We're in this world, and there's no getting out."

Sadness and frustration fill her eyes. She leans forward an inch from my face then gives me a small smile. "Then I guess I'm going to have to make you forget about the world for the rest of the night."

It's another reason why I love her so much. She does exactly that. By the time we get home, I don't think about anything else, except her. I take her to a nice dinner to celebrate her awards. My stress and anxiety disappear. She ignites the flame of life within me, and it doesn't burn out until I drop her off at school the next day. The moment she gets out of the car, my chest tightens, the acid bubbles up, and I begin to feel suffocated all over again.

FOR THE NEXT FEW MONTHS, I SPEND MY DAYS DEALING WITH every O'Malley issue possible. Adrian's ex-wife Dasha is causing significant problems with the Polish mob. Obrecht is all over my ass about killing Jack Christian. I'm doing all I can to prevent him from pulling the trigger before Jack's company goes public, but I have constant anxiety he's going to do it. If he does, everything Finn and I worked for in prison will go down the drain. And when I look at my niece, Shannon, I think of her future and how we have to do better as a family. Then it makes me think about having kids with Hailee and how I owe it to her and them to change things.

The Petrovs and Rossis continue to lose power as the Ivanovs and O'Malleys keep each side balanced. Every time I come home from taking care of some thug, I've already showered but have to again. Hailee steps in with me. She takes over, scrubbing the death I can't shake off my skin.

Rory gets out of prison, and the twins keep a close eye on him. As expected, he moves to Chicago with his brother Mack. All the reports show Orla glued to her father's hip. There's so much security around them, my guys haven't had an opportunity to take him out. I often wake up in the middle of the night, thinking about how my little lamb isn't safe until we destroy the Baileys.

My dad's illness speeds up, but he continues to work every day, acting as though it doesn't exist and continuing to critique my every decision. The blood on his handkerchief is a constant reminder he won't be here much longer. I don't want to spend my last moments with him fighting, so I do my best to keep my mouth shut and do as he says.

I attempt to be a good son and visit with my mom, but she makes it hard to make her a priority. She never shuts up about me going to confession or church. Then there's the guilt trip about not inviting her over to my house often enough. It's usually during one of the multiple conversations I have with her to call before she comes over.

The feeling I'm failing in every part of life never leaves me. The only place I'm confident I'm succeeding is at home, with Hailee. Every night when I'm with her, she reminds me to breathe and helps me forget about all the bullshit, even if it's only for a few hours before my phone rings and I have to deal with more.

The day of Sergey and Kora's wedding arrives. I wake up alone since Hailee is in the wedding party and stayed with the girls. I call her guards, and they assure me she's safe. In all reality, she's probably the safest she's ever been, since all the other women have Ivanov bodyguards.

I get to the wedding and deal with more O'Malley issues then make my way to the bridal room to see Hailee. I turn the corner, and my gut drops.

My mother is blinking back tears. Her voice shakes, and she says, "I saw it when I was shopping and thought it would match your dress. It's freezing out. I thought you'd like it."

"It's not about what I like or don't like, Ruth," Hailee sternly says, as if she's talking to her kindergarten student.

"If you like it, what's the issue?" my mom asks.

"You went into our bedroom and through our closet. Then you made our bed and did our laundry. That's personal. You have to stop. Liam is a forty-year-old man, not a child."

A tear falls down my mom's face. She isn't usually a crier. Being the head of the O'Malleys, there isn't any leeway to show weakness. She wipes her face, and my heart races. She replies, "I thought you'd appreciate it. You both work so hard and—"

"You have to stop. I've had my own place for over ten years, and my mother has never once gone through my things. I can't take it anymore," Hailee cries out.

My chest tightens. My mother's makeup is a mess. Hailee looks like she wants to kill my mom. Neither Hailee nor I was amused about my mom coming into the house and doing what she did. I gave her a key because she forgot something and I had shit to take care of. Instead of grabbing it and leaving, she did our laundry. I meant to get the key back and kept forgetting. She came back when we were at work and did it again and put a shawl in the closet next to Hailee's dress, but Hailee didn't tell me it bothered her this much.

My mom puts her hand on Hailee's arm. "Hailee—"

"I think you both said your piece," I interject, stepping next to them.

"Liam, I was only trying to be nice," my mother cries.

"Oh, so I'm the bad person in all of this?" Hailee asks in a loud voice.

"No one said that. Chill out," I reprimand her.

Hailee's eyes turn into blue flames. She glares at me. "Seriously?"

"Just calm down. You're getting loud."

She gapes at me, and my father's voice makes my insides cringe.

"Ruth, what's wrong?"

I spin. "Everything is fine. Let's all—"

"Everything is *not* fine. Your mother doesn't just cry for no reason. You know this," my father barks.

"She's not exactly innocent," I respond.

My father steps forward and points in my face. "You seem to have lost your manners, son. This is your mother. Don't forget it."

"Oh, don't worry, she never lets me forget it," I sarcastically spit back.

"Ruth, you look beautiful," Finn's voice interjects. He shoots me a look, pushes between us, and hugs my mom.

She sniffles. "Thanks."

"Darragh." He nods at my father then spins. He pulls Hailee into a big embrace. "You look gorgeous. I think the women need you in the bridal room."

Hailee looks at him suspiciously.

Finn raises his eyebrows.

She sighs and walks away. I follow her to the door and reach for her arm. She spins into me and snaps, "What do you want, Liam?"

"Why are you mad at me?"

She puts her hand on her hip. "Seriously? You told me to chill out and didn't even stick up for me."

"I was trying to defuse the situation. We're in public."

She huffs. "Whatever." She attempts to turn, but I stop her and step so close, she retreats against the wall.

"You need to calm down," I demand.

Rage fills her face. "You have a lot of nerve, Liam O'Malley."

"What are you talking about?"

"Don't act stupid," she spouts.

"I guess I am. Fill me in," I angrily reply.

She shakes her head in disgust. "You say whatever you want to my mother, who hasn't once interfered in our life. The minute I say one thing to your mom about respecting our private space, you turn on me."

"I'm not turning on you."

"What would you call it?"

I snort. "It's not even the same thing. My mom likes you and is trying to help us. Your mother hates me and wants to run away to God knows where so you never see me again."

Her eyes grow hotter. "Thanks for having my back, Liam. Now get out of my way." She pushes my chest, and I step back. She goes into the bridal room and shuts the door.

I close my eyes and count to ten, breathing deep, not sure what just happened.

"Bad day?" Finn asks.

I open my eyes. "I'm never going to win that one."

"Then don't fight it. Let's go see Sergey and have a drink."

I don't move. "If my dad—"

"He's not going to be around much longer," Finn reminds me.

"No shit," I mutter, choking down the emotions creeping up in my throat.

Finn pats me on the back and leads me down the hall. I go through the motions with the guys. When the wedding comes, Hailee walks down the aisle but ignores me. In all the months we've been together, she's never done that. It pisses me off. When we get to the reception, she rotates between ignoring me and throwing daggers at me with her eyes.

Fuck this.

Several hours after dinner, I go into the side room and sit at the bar with Finn. He's clutching a tumbler of whiskey.

"Where's Hailee?"

"In the other room, acting like I don't exist or giving me a stare down like she wants to kill me," I reveal, sliding onto the stool next to him.

Finn taps the crystal glass. "Life's too short, man. Better fix that."

I blow out a breath of air and motion for the bartender to bring two more drinks. "She's out of line."

"I usually find it takes two to tango," he says.

"You going to lecture me all night?"

He chuckles. "Nope. I'm leaving soon anyway. The guys watching Jack and the judge need a break."

"We're so close. I can't wait for this to go through and prove to all the O'Malleys I'm not the moron half of them think I am," I admit.

Finn turns in his stool and stares at me.

"What?" The bartender sets the whiskey down, and I take a mouthful, trying not to cringe as it burns my throat.

His eyes turn to slits. "We spent all that time locked up, and you give a shit about what everyone else thinks?"

I don't respond. Something about Finn has always been wise. I only wish his words would take away my internal need for others to see me as capable.

He finishes his drink and rises. He leans down to my ear and taps my chest. "At the end of the day, the only person who needs to believe you're capable is in here. Everyone else can fuck themselves. The moment you stop worrying about what others think is when you'll be ready to lead. It won't matter what your dad or anyone else inside or outside of this family thinks. You'll know what actions need to happen. And that's what will save the O'Malleys from destruction." He squeezes my shoulder then adds, "Go talk to your woman. Make-up sex is pretty hot from what I remember." He winks and walks away.

I nurse my whiskey, thinking about what he said. I finish and go into the other room to find Hailee. She catches my eye near the bathrooms, talking to Aspen. I walk over and freeze behind her.

Hailee isn't a big drinker, but she's obviously had more than normal. I've never heard her slur before, but she does. "She didn't even see what she did wrong. And Liam thinks it's totally fine for her to invade our privacy. Well, you know what? I'm moving out. It's not like I officially moved in anyway. There are basic common boundaries you don't cross. Going through my things is bad manners, and I'm not living like that."

Aspen gapes at me. "Hailee, umm..."

"She touched my underwear and moved the treat box I made for Liam. It was open, too. I know she read it all. She probably had a heart attack and had to go to an extra confession." Hailee raises her glass to drink more, and I grab it from her. "What the—"

I spin her into me. "I think you've had enough."

"Give me my drink back."

"No."

The DJ announces it's the last song. I glance around the room and notice there aren't quite as many people here as at the beginning of the reception.

"Time to go," I claim.

"Have fun in your house alone," Hailee smirks.

I nod to Aspen. "Have a nice night."

She winces. "You, too."

I put my arm around Hailee's waist and lean into her ear. "You're either walking out of here, or I'll carry you out. So pick your poison." I move her toward the door.

"Liam—"

"Don't test me on this," I growl.

She glares at me but stays quiet until we get outside. When we get next to the car, she says, "I'm not going to your house. And you can't make me."

"Fine. I'll take you to your apartment. Now get in," I order.

She sticks her chin in the air then gets in the car. I slide in after her. When the door shuts, the car pulls out. We stay quiet for a long time. We're almost to her apartment when I turn toward her. "Wherever you want to sleep is fine, little lamb. But tomorrow, you're waking up next to me. When you open your eyes, you're getting over whatever this little temper tantrum is you're having."

Her face turns angry. "Me? You should talk to your mother. She's the one who—"

My phone rings, and I sigh. I answer, "Killian, I'm—"

"Get to the hospital. Adrian got shot."

25

Hailee

Liam hangs up the phone and rolls the divider window down. He says to the driver, "St. Joseph's and make it fast."

"Take me home, Liam. My house, not yours. And are you crazy thinking I'm going to church—"

"Adrian got shot. We're going to the hospital," he barks and hits the button for the divider window to go back up.

I freeze. I consumed too much alcohol, but I quickly sober up. I grasp Liam's thigh. "What do you mean Adrian got shot?"

Liam's face hardens. He snaps, "I don't know the details. But get over your antics."

I stay silent, staring at the dark glass in front of me. The car moves faster and weaves in and out of traffic.

Liam's hand moves over mine. In a low, calm voice, he says, "I don't need any more arguments tonight. Whatever I say goes. Do you understand?"

I meet his eyes. There's something unhinged in them. I've rarely seen it, but it's a mix of hatred and vengeance, along with still being pissed off at me. It frightens me. "Liam, what are you going to do?"

He clenches his jaw. His voice is so cold, it sends chills down my spine. "Whatever is necessary."

The driver pulls up to the entrance. We get out of the car. The air is crisp, and I hug my arms, suddenly wishing I took the beautiful wrap his mom bought for me. The ironic thing is I thought Liam bought it for me when I saw it in the closet and loved it. Then I learned it was from his mom, and she put it in our room without asking to come into the house. Out of principle, I wouldn't have anything to do with it. It all seems stupid now, and shame fills me that I spent the entire wedding upset and avoiding Liam. All I can think of is Adrian with blood all over him, fighting for his life.

Liam takes off his coat and drapes it over my back. I glance up at him, but he still has that look in his eyes. I want to beg him to forgive me, but it's not the time. Instead, I grab his hand.

He stiffens and guides me into the lobby. Gemma is with Nolan, Killian, and Declan. Obrecht and Selena are a few hundred feet away, huddled in the corner, talking.

"What's the situation with Adrian?" he asks his cousins.

"We don't know. We just arrived."

Hatred fills Liam's voice. "Dasha?"

"Adrian's ex-wife?" I blurt out. She's been a big problem between Adrian and Skylar.

Liam turns to me and warns, "No questions, Hailee. Don't push me."

I blink hard to stop the tears welling in my eyes. Liam's never been so harsh with me. But I've not been an angel tonight. I shut my mouth, and Gemma puts her arm protectively around my waist.

"Yes, she's behind it. Gavin got their license plate. We know where those thugs are," Killian seethes.

"Let's go talk to Obrecht," Declan advises.

Gemma and I exchange a worried look. The six of us walk toward them.

"Obrecht," Killian calls out.

Obrecht puts his arm around Selena and turns. The same hard look the O'Malleys have fills his expression, but I also see a man on the verge of breaking down and trying to hold it together. I realize all the O'Malleys are doing the same, especially Liam. The conversation we had months ago about how close he used to be with Adrian comes racing back.

Liam's eyes turn to slits. "How is he?"

Obrecht sniffs hard. "In surgery. They said he's losing a lot of blood."

"Where are the others?" Nolan asks.

"Down the hall in the waiting room."

Nolan states, "Let me take Hailee, Gemma, and Selena to the others."

Selena glances at Obrecht, and he kisses her forehead. "Go with Nolan. I'll be there soon."

I squeeze Obrecht's arm as we pass him. Liam avoids my gaze, and it's another blow about how he must have felt all night at the wedding. He tried several times to make things right with me. I just shot him dirty looks or avoided him. I kick myself for my stubbornness.

Gemma and I stand on both sides of Selena and hold her hands. Nolan leads us into the waiting room. Maksim says the hospital wants anyone who is able to donate blood to go to the on-site blood bank.

Obrecht comes back into the room angrier than he was outside. The O'Malleys aren't far behind, and he scowls at Liam so intensely, I get goose bumps.

I rise. "Liam, we need to go donate blood."

He studies me then puts his arms around my waist, and we go down the hall. When we get to the blood bank, I stop him before we enter. I reach up and cup his cheeks. It almost kills me looking into his eyes. I quietly choke out, "I'm sorry."

He stares above my head and takes a deep breath, grinding his molars.

Selena and Obrecht approach us. Liam finally meets my eyes. In an emotionless tone, he orders, "Go give blood."

My lips tremble. I don't attempt to say anything else and obey. Selena and I go back into the donation area. Since I drank so much, I'm ineligible to donate, which makes me feel worse. Selena didn't even finish a glass of wine at dinner, so they have her drink water and, after a breathalyzer test, allow her to donate. I sit with her for a few minutes. When I step out, Liam is giving blood.

He comes out, unrolls his sleeve and leads me to a corner.

"Did they let you donate?" I ask.

His broody expression never changes. He shakes his head. "No. I drank too much. Go back to the waiting room with Obrecht. Do whatever he or the Ivanovs say until I get back. Understand?"

Fear grips me. "Why? Where are you going?"

He shakes his head. "Don't ask questions you know I won't answer. Promise me you'll behave, Hailee."

Hailee. Not Hales. Not little lamb. Just Hailee, like I'm no longer his. And wherever he's going can't be anywhere safe. I'm not naive. He's going to kill whoever did this to Adrian. I've lost track of the times he's come home and done things he won't speak of, but for the first time, I'm petrified.

I swallow the lump forming in my throat and stick out my chin, determined not to cry. "I promise."

He studies my face then nods. "Go with Obrecht. Back up his story that there is a long line and only one phlebotomist on duty."

I open my mouth to question him, but he raises his eyebrows. I snap my mouth shut.

He doesn't kiss me goodbye. There's no hug or any sign of affection. The vengeance in his eyes grows deeper, and when his cousins come out from behind the curtains, they leave without another word.

I spend hours trying to keep it together. Bogden keeps coming in and out of the waiting room and talking to the Ivanovs. Darragh and Ruth sit together. I try to contemplate what to say to Ruth to smooth things over, but nothing seems appropriate right now. The doctor reports Adrian is out of surgery, and relief fills the room. But it's short-lived for me. I begin to pace, wondering when Liam is coming back and if he's safe.

Liam and Killian finally come into the room, but Liam avoids me. Darragh stands and coughs so bad, I worry he's choking. The Ivanovs huddle in the corner of the room with Liam and Killian.

"Where's Nolan?" Gemma asks, grasping my arm.

I shake my head but say nothing, staring at Liam. He takes out his phone and makes a call. Darragh approaches them, and while they keep their voices low, it's clear he isn't happy with Liam.

Liam says something to Darragh with a scowl on his face. He and Killian leave the room, but I follow him.

"Liam!" I call out, trying not to trip on my heels since he's walking so fast.

He freezes and says to Killian, "I'll meet you in the car."

Killian glances over his shoulder at me then back at Liam. He says nothing and walks out the door.

I put my hand on Liam's arm, and he spins. "Go back. Do not leave the eyesight of the Ivanovs."

I shudder when I see his eyes. At rare times, I've seen Liam's eyes crazed but never like this.

The tears I've held back all night fall. I reach for his cheeks, but he jerks his head back. "Go, Hailee. You don't belong near me right now."

"Liam," I whisper.

He studies the ceiling. "Go."

I reach for his cheek again, but he moves his head. "I need to leave. You need to go back."

"But—"

"Hailee. Come with me," Maksim orders and puts his arm around my shoulders.

Liam nods to Maksim and spins, never looking at me. Maksim leads me to the waiting room. After several hours, he takes Gemma and me to his house. Aspen shows us the guest rooms, but Gemma and I stay in the same room.

We both shower and put on T-shirts Aspen gives us. When we finally get in bed, Gemma whispers, "Where do you think they are?"

"I don't know."

"I heard the Zielinski name mentioned. Why would the Polish mob shoot Adrian if his ex-wife is involved? She's Russian, isn't she?" Gemma asks.

This is the first I've heard the Zielinski name associated with the shooting. I have no answers to give her.

Neither of us sleeps. It's late into the next evening when Liam finally picks me up. He has on a black T-shirt, black pants, and his hair is wet. His eyes are still crazed, not as bad as at the hospital, but the chaos is still swirling in them. I embrace him tightly. His body stiffens. He doesn't return my affection and firmly orders, "Let's go."

I follow him quietly to the car with my insides quivering. As soon as we get in the vehicle and the door shuts, I turn to him. He stares out the window, his hands in fists, and the nerve in his clenched jaw twitching.

I cover his fist and slide closer. "Liam."

He closes his eyes and exhales deeply.

"Liam," I repeat, putting my palm on his cheek.

He sniffs hard and finally turns.

I suddenly don't know what to say. Everything sounds petty and not good enough. His face becomes blurry from my tears, and I hear him sigh.

He tugs me onto his lap. I bury my face in his chest, sobbing. His strong arms circle me, and he kisses the top of my head.

We say nothing the entire way home. When we get inside the house, he goes directly to the bathroom, undresses, and turns on the shower.

I watch him scrub his skin then put his arm on the tile and smell the soap bottle how he always does. I strip and step behind him, wrapping my arms around his torso tightly. I kiss his back and cry out, "Please forgive me."

He drops the bottle and spins me so fast, I gasp. In an instant, his hot mouth is on mine. He slides his tongue into my mouth and reaches for the back of my thighs, lifting me off the ground, entering me in one thrust.

I kiss him back in a perfect storm of emotions that all night has been raging inside me. The fear I felt that I might lose him, my nerves about his safety, and the love I have for him that runs so deep in my bones I know I can't survive without him, all make me dizzy. And the regret I have for my petty actions toward him at the wedding swirl through all of it.

"I'm sorry," I sob again.

"Shh," he commands and presses closer to me. The warmth of his body is a sharp contrast to the cold tile on my back. I clutch my arms around his shoulders, gliding my fingers through his hair, trying to hold every part of him I can.

His hands grip the side of my head. He dips his tongue over and over into my mouth, matching the speed of his thrusts. Like always, he owns my body in every way possible.

The sound of the water beats on the tile. Steam fills the air, creating a foggy darkness. His green eyes glow through it, assessing me, as if I'm his prey to consume.

"You're mine, little lamb," he mumbles then slips his tongue back in my mouth.

Tremors fill my body. I dig my nails into his scalp, whimpering, unable to respond with words.

"Don't shut me out ever again," he growls, pounding into me harder until my eyes roll and I become limp, sandwiched between his hard flesh and the cold tile.

"Promise me," he demands.

"I-I promise," I barely get out.

He detonates inside me, holding my face in front of his and never taking his eyes off mine. His cock pumps ferociously, spewing his seed deep within me, and his labored breath merges with mine. Several minutes pass and he doesn't move. "I mean it, Hales. If you have a problem, you talk to me about it."

"I know. I'm sorry."

He nods. "I stopped at my parents' house and got the key back. My mother won't be coming in uninvited anymore."

For some reason, that makes me feel bad. I should be happy, but guilt plagues me. I blurt out, "I'll apologize to your mom."

He huffs. "My mother isn't innocent. You don't have to do that unless you want to." He steps back, releases me, then turns off the water. He grabs a towel and wraps it around me then puts another one around his body.

We dry off and get in bed. I stroke his head. "Liam, I need to know something."

"What?"

"Was the Polish mob involved in Adrian's shooting?"

His eyes turn to stone.

I quickly add, "I just want to know if they are after us, too?"

He sighs, strokes my back, then finally replies, "A threat against an Ivanov is a threat against the O'Malleys. I want to shield you from everything, but maybe it's better if you know who comes after us."

A chill runs down my spine. "There are more than the Bailey and Ryans?"

He grunts. "I wish they were my only problem. You don't ever trust them or a Rossi, Petrov, or Zielinski. Other families threaten us, but those issues are outside of Chicago."

I scoot closer to him. "And you have to deal with all these problems?"

He grinds his molars. "Yeah. But once my plan comes to fruition, there won't be as many threats. The O'Malleys will pull out of different businesses we have now, and that will eliminate a lot of issues."

"Like what?"

"Nothing I'll involve you in."

I open my mouth to speak, but he flips me on my back and cages his body over mine. He drills his eyes into mine. "You were a bad girl yesterday, little lamb."

"I know. I'm sorry. I—"

"Quiet!" he growls.

I gasp and swallow hard.

"Naughty girls get punished." He pins my wrists above my head with one hand and reaches for something in the nightstand drawer. His hot breath beats into mine. Metal handcuffs latch around my wrists.

My heart races faster, and my breath shortens.

In a low voice, he says, "I think I need to remind you who you belong to."

26

Liam

Several Months Later

"Here, change Shannon while I grab a quick shower." Nora hands me the baby as I walk into the penthouse.

The smell of a dirty diaper fills my nostrils and I turn my head. "Jesus. Did you save this until I got here?"

Nora laughs. "Nope. Shannon just knew Uncle Liam was coming and saved the best for you."

I hold Shannon in the air and stare at her. "You did this on purpose, didn't you?"

She scrunches her face and lets out a loud wail.

"Whoa! It's okay." I pull her to my chest and go to the changing table. "Where's Boris?"

"Showering. He'll be out in a minute. Hey, how was Jamaica? I feel like we haven't had a chance to talk. I can't believe it's been a few months since your trip," she replies.

I smile. Hailee and I went to celebrate Selena's birthday. Obrecht surprised her with the vacation and a group of us went. "It was awesome. Nice to get away and pretend we're normal for a few days."

Nora shoots me a smile but there's some sadness in it. "You work too hard, Liam. You should take more breaks."

I grunt. "Easier said than done."

She sighs then pats me on the back. "I know that feeling. See you in a bit." She hightails it out of the room.

I lay Shannon down on the table and quickly change her diaper. Her green eyes glisten, and she sniffles. "There you go, sweetheart." I fasten her onesie and carry her over to the couch. I sit down and bounce her on my knee.

She pulls at the green bow in her red hair. It slides out, and she begins to cry again.

I stroke her head. "It's okay. Mommy will be back soon. You're awfully upset today."

She cries louder.

"She didn't sleep all night," Boris says, walking into the room. He holds out his hands, and I pass Shannon to him. He picks up the pacifier on the table and puts it in her mouth.

She stops crying and curls into his chest.

"Pacifier. Does it every time," he claims.

"Noted." I shift in my seat. "I need a favor."

His eyes turn to slits. "What's that?"

My chest tightens. "Can Hailee and Gemma stay with you the next few days?"

"Of course. But why? Where will you be?"

I glance behind me to make sure Nora isn't in the room. I reply, "We're meeting with the Baileys."

"Are you crazy?" Boris blurts out.

I shake my head. "No. Rory sent a message to my father. I'd rather know what Rory is thinking than not."

"What if it's a trap?"

Acid curls in my gut. It's always a risk, but one worth taking to get into Rory's head. I add all the confidence I can muster into my voice. "It's not the first time the O'Malleys have met with another enemy crime family. We know how to prepare and not be blindsided."

Boris leans toward me. His eyes dart to the bedroom door then latch on mine. "What did his message say?"

"He wants to discuss our boundary lines."

A deep line forms between Boris's eyebrows. "He thinks he can come into Chicago and you'll roll over? Darragh isn't going to go for that."

I grunt. As far as everyone sees, my father is still running the show. Since I defied him and killed Adrian's shooters without waiting to set up either the Rossis or Petrovs, I've been calling the shots. Finn was right. The only thing that matters is I do what I think is right. Since that night, I don't ask my father for permission or wait for him to give direction. I do what needs to be done and tell him about it after. Lately, he doesn't even get out of bed for very long, so it's probably a good thing I stepped further into my role when I did. But no one knows how far his health has declined, except my mom and Hailee. To everyone else, the status quo is the same. I assure Boris, "Neither of us will. Even if Jack's company was already public, I still don't want him or his family within several states of here."

Boris protectively wraps his arm tighter around Shannon. "Agreed. Baileys need to stay in North Carolina, where they belong. If they think they can come into town and start throwing their weight around, they're going to have more than just the O'Malleys to deal with."

I rise and go to the window. It's a windy day in Chicago, and Lake Michigan is rougher than usual. The waves are several feet high. It seems appropriate for the rage coursing through my veins on a daily basis. Since Rory has been out of prison, I've been waiting for the twins to report they took him out or send me a location and time to do it myself. But neither has happened. The entire time Rory has been in Chicago on O'Malley turf but so well protected we can't go after him unless we have a complete shoot-out. While I wouldn't mind taking every one of his clan down, I don't want to put my men in harm's way. So far, he hasn't started to creep into our business dealings. Our lines of drugs and gambling are all secure for the time being. However, at some point, I know he's going to start moving in. This meeting is the first step for Rory to attempt to take what's ours.

"Please tell me you're meeting somewhere you chose," Boris states.

I spin and snort. "Don't insult my intelligence."

"Shoot his ass on the way in or out," Boris instructs.

I shake my head and point at him. "I expect more from you, Boris."

"What does that mean?"

I cross my arms. "I don't have the luxury of doing something like that in these meetings. If I do, there will be a war in the streets. He comes in escorted by our men, we talk, he leaves escorted by our men."

"What if it's a trap?" Boris repeats his fear.

"It's on our turf. It's not possible for him to trap us. An O'Malley would have to be a traitor for that to occur."

Boris's face hardens. He sniffs hard and stares at me. "We all know men can change sides."

"O'Malleys are blood. You can't change sides from your own blood," I insist.

Boris raises his eyebrows. "Isn't that exactly what Hailee and her sisters have done? Her mother, too?"

My heart pounds harder. "That's different."

"How?"

I look away and don't answer.

Boris's voice turns cold. "Not all your men are blood. You know this. Don't blindly give your trust like I did. There are weak men in every organization. My advice to you is to find out who those men are before the Baileys do. We would have prevented a lot had my brothers and I known who the traitors were."

I say nothing, not wanting to believe any O'Malley could turn on our clan but realizing Boris speaks from experience. He's one of the few people I trust, so I don't take his warning lightly.

"This is happening tonight?" Boris asks.

"Tomorrow. We're meeting in Indianapolis."

Alarm fills his expression. "Why there?"

"Rory thinks it's neutral, but we own the town. We're leaving tonight to make sure every point is secure," I relay.

Silence fills the air. Neither of us breaks our gaze. Boris finally asks, "You need our men on this?"

"No. I promised Maksim I wouldn't pull you or any Ivanovs into our business. I've got it handled."

"Liam—"

"We're good, Boris. I need to keep Hailee and Gemma here. If your guys can be on call for their sisters' and mother's security if needed, I'd appreciate it. There shouldn't be any issues, but in case something pops up..."

He nods. "Sure. I'll get with Adrian."

"Thanks. I'll bring Hailee and Gemma over around six." I step toward the door.

He calls out, "Wait. Nora said she needs to talk with you before you go. Let me go get her." He rises and takes Shannon into the bedroom.

I stare out the window, glancing down at the busy city streets. Boris's words about traitors fill my mind. I wish I could escape them, but I can't.

"Hey." Nora's voice rips me out of my thoughts. She runs her hand through her wet hair.

"What's going on?" I ask.

"Have you seen your mom lately?"

I exhale deeply. "Last week. Why?"

"I hadn't heard from her in a while. Shannon and I visited with her yesterday. She told me your dad isn't getting out of bed very much?" Nora's eyes glisten, and she bites her lip.

"She shouldn't be telling anyone—"

"Liam, it's me," Nora says in an insulted tone.

"Sorry. You're right."

She puts her hand on my bicep. "It's all right. Are you doing okay?"

I turn away from her and stare out the window at the waves. "It is what it is."

A moment of silence passes. Nora keeps her voice soft. "I think your mom is struggling, Liam."

I refocus on the building to the right. The guilt that always eats at me flies into my chest. I swallow the thick lump expanding in my throat. "I'm not sure what I'm supposed to do about that."

"Just go see her. It'll help take her mind off it for a while," Nora suggests.

I study Nora's face.

"What aren't you telling me, Liam?"

I close my eyes briefly. I admit, "Things haven't been good since Kora and Sergey's wedding. She and Hailee had it out, and I took the key back. I said some things I shouldn't have."

Nora slowly nods. "I see. Would this be about your mom invading personal space?"

"Bingo."

Nora smiles. "How are she and Hailee now?"

I shrug. "I've intentionally kept them apart."

Nora tilts her head. "You can't do that, Liam."

"Why? My mom stays out of our life. Hailee doesn't get pissed. It seems like a good plan to me," I state.

"That isn't a long-term solution, Liam. You can't shut your mom out. Is that what Hailee wants?"

"I didn't say that. This is all my decision. Hailee has asked a few times about my parents, but I'm not letting her near them. I have enough shit to deal with. I don't need family drama."

Nora puts her hand on her hip. "Your dad's dying. Take it from me, this isn't the time for you to stay away. Once your parents are gone, they're gone." She blinks hard, but a tear escapes, and she wipes it off her cheek.

I know everything Nora says is in my best interest. She wouldn't be butting in if she didn't think I was screwing up. "Fine. When I get back in town, I'll go see my mom."

"Where are you going?"

"I have out-of-state business to take care of. Hailee and Gemma are staying here for a few nights."

Concern floods her expression. "Be careful, Liam."

"I will. Keep Hailee and Gemma from freaking out."

Nora laughs. "Easier said than done. Maybe I'll invite your mom over for lunch."

"Nora—"

"What? It'll be fun."

"You're so Irish."

She beams. "Yep."

"For real, though, don't invite my mom over. I don't need Hailee upset, especially when I'm gone."

She rolls her eyes. "When did you get so dramatic, Liam? It's just an innocent lunch..."

"Yeah, right."

She groans. "You underestimate my talents."

I hug her. "Don't do it. Thanks for letting Hailee and Gemma stay. I'll see you tonight."

She squeezes me tight. "If you change your mind—"

"I won't," I firmly pledge then leave. I get in my car and glance at the time. There are always too many things in a day to do, but the combination of Nora and Boris's conversation sticks with me. I debate for a few minutes but finally tell my driver to head to my parents'.

When I get to the house, my dad is in bed. My mom carries a tray downstairs. It looks like it was barely touched. Food fills the plate, and the tea and water glasses are full.

"Liam. What are you doing here?" my mother asks. Her face looks more worn and tired than I remember.

I take the tray from her when she gets to the bottom of the steps. "I haven't seen you in a while."

She stays quiet.

"Are you doing okay, Mom?"

Her lips quiver, and she looks away. Her cheeks quickly become wet, and her chest heaves.

My heart breaks. I put the tray on the step and tug her into me. She sobs, and I hold her tighter. I blink hard to contain my own emotions. "Shh."

"I'm sorry," she cries out.

"Shh. It's okay. Everything will be okay."

"No, it won't. He's...he's..." Her body erupts in tremors, and I focus on the cross on the wall. I'm not sure why I look there, but I can't seem to tear my eyes away from it. It's the one thing that didn't change when my mother remodeled. Since I was a child, it has hung on the same spot on the wall.

Several minutes pass until she catches her breath. She finally pulls back and wipes her face. "I'm sorry. You shouldn't have to—"

"No. I'm sorry, Mom. I shouldn't be avoiding you."

More pain fills my mother's expression. I kick myself for my choice of words. She lowers her voice. It comes out as a statement and not a question. It's not angry or accusatory. It just sounds sad. "Hailee hates me."

I firmly reply, "No, she doesn't. I'm the one who kept her from coming over here with me."

She tilts her head. "I don't understand, Liam. If she doesn't hate me, why would you do that?"

I fight to look away from her, but cowards do that, so I keep my gaze on her green eyes. I realize I've been a coward since the wedding, and I detest myself for that. One thing I've always prided myself on is not being a coward. "In my mind, it was easier."

Tension fills the air. The ticking of the clock seems to get louder. My mother swallows hard. She takes a deep breath and quietly says, "Mary Kelly told me I overstepped. I just wanted to help. For fifteen years, I prayed several times a day that you were safe and you'd be home in one piece. I thought I was dying. Most days, I couldn't breathe. Your father, well, he had to continue like everything was normal. I've never felt so lonely. He was here, but we didn't talk about it. We couldn't. The happiest day of my life was when you stepped out of that hellhole." She shuts her eyes, and new tears fall. 'But now, I'm just losing everyone. And I'd rather feel what I did when you were gone than this. At least then, it wasn't your choice."

I've done a lot of horrible things in my life, but nothing compares to how I've hurt my mom. "Sorry doesn't seem like a strong enough word, but I am. I realize I made a mistake. I'm going out of town for a few days. When I get back, I'll do better. I promise."

"I'm not an obligation, Liam. You don't owe me anything."

My heart sinks further. "I know you're not. I want to see you. And you should know, Hailee's asked to come here several times. I've stopped her."

My mother furrows her eyebrows, and I know I've hurt her even more. I do the only thing that feels right. I step forward and tug her into me. "I'm sorry. And I've missed you. When I get back, we'll get together, okay?"

She sniffles and nods. "Okay."

I kiss the top of her head and pull back. "Is Dad asleep?"

"No. He's reading the paper."

"Okay. I'm going to see him before I leave."

She smiles. "Good. He'll like that."

I give her another hug then go upstairs to see my father. I knock on the door and try to cover the horror I feel every time I see him lately. In forty years, I've never seen him lying in bed until now. He's lost more weight, and the physically strong man I always knew seems to have withered away.

He looks up. "Liam."

"You have a minute?"

He motions to the chair next to the bed. I slide it across the floor closer to him. "How are you feeling?"

He arches an eyebrow. "Have you gone blind?"

My lips twitch. "No. You look like shit."

He starts to laugh, and it turns into a cough. After a long, drawn-out hacking session, he sets his blood-filled handkerchief down. His glistening eyes focus on me. "Is everything set up for your meeting?"

"Yeah. I'm leaving tonight."

He studies my face. "Don't let your guard down. At all times, you watch your back. He's a sneaky bastard."

"Got it. But I do have a question."

"What's that?"

"Boris made a comment today about traitors. How do I know we don't have any in our clan?"

His next words send a chill down my spine. In a cold voice, he replies, "You don't. Like I said, never let your guard down. At all times, watch your back, son."

"Great. I was hoping you'd give me some magical formula or something," I tease.

He snorts. "I wish. Now listen closely. When you meet with Rory, don't give him anything. The less you talk, the better. Listen to what he says, reiterate he's not doing business in our territories. Record the conversation, and we'll go through it together when you get back."

"Got it."

"One more thing, Liam."

I wait for him to continue.

"Come closer."

I lean toward him. He puts one hand on my head and the other on my stomach. "Use these. Whatever you do, don't use this." He taps my heart. "He's going to bring up his daughters. He wants them in their roles. He thinks he owns them. The worst thing you can do is react."

I struggle to inhale fresh air. The one thing I can't seem to control is my reactions to anyone threatening or even discussing Hailee.

We talk some more. I go downstairs and say goodbye to my mom. I get in the car and look at my watch. School would have gotten out. Hailee typically stays later, but I text her.

Me: *I need to pick you up now. If you have things you can do over the next few days at home, bring them with you.*

Hailee: *What's going on?*

Me: *Everything is fine. But you'll need to call off work for the next few days. I'm outside.*

Hailee: *I'll be out in five minutes.*

She comes outside and gets in the car. Panic floods her expression. "What's going on?"

"I need to go out of town. You and Gemma will stay with Boris and Nora."

"Where are you going?" she asks.

"You know better than to ask, little lamb."

She releases a frustrated breath of air. "Why do we have to go to Boris and Nora's? And why can't I go to work?"

I pull her onto my lap. "So I don't have to worry about you while I'm gone. And for this situation, I need to know you're safe. Now stop asking questions about this. I can't discuss anything else regarding it."

She pierces her eyebrows together and bites on her lip.

"You look cute when you're thinking hard," I tease.

"Stop it. This isn't funny. How long will you be gone?"

"A couple nights. When I get back, I need you to do me a favor."

She softens her voice. "Okay. What is it?"

"I want to go to my parents' for dinner. My mom isn't doing well. My dad's..." I stare out the window and compose my thoughts, shoving my emotions down. "He's not good."

"Liam, I've been telling you we need to go see your parents," she reminds me.

I give her a chaste kiss. "Yeah. I know you have."

"Okay. Do you want me to call your mom and arrange it?" she asks.

"Would you?"

"Of course."

"Thanks."

She slides her hand on my cheek. "Liam, why do I have a bad feeling about your trip?"

"Don't. You have nothing to worry about," I lie and instantly feel guilty. Hailee and I don't lie to each other. I may not tell her everything, but I don't ever want untruths between us.

"Then why won't you tell me anything?"

I fist her hair and tug it back so I'm looking down at her. She gasps, which makes me smile. "Keep your nose out of O'Malley business."

"This isn't funny, Liam. I'm wor—"

I slide my tongue in her mouth and kiss her until she's out of breath. I glide my hand up her skirt and trace the thin strand from her panties on her hip. "How much do you love this thong, little lamb?"

"Umm..."

"Get your ass on the other seat, take them off, and spread your sexy legs," I order.

A naughty smile forms on her lips. She backs away, sits on the seat across from me, and opens her legs. She drags her finger along her panties. She innocently asks, "You want these off?"

I lick my lips at the sight of the damp cloth. My pants become tighter. "Stop asking questions. I don't have time to punish you all night."

She purses her lips and takes her panties off. She holds her finger in the air with the thong hanging off it. "Now what?"

"Toss them here."

She flicks them at me, and I sniff them, then put them in my coat pocket. She pouts and opens her legs wider. "Is that all you wanted? You didn't have to pull me out of work early for that." She drops her hand and plays with herself.

Oh, my dirty little lamb.

I lunge between her legs and grab her hand. She continues to play with her clit, but I make her circle faster. I slide my tongue into her pussy, going as deep as possible, then flicking the tip as her walls clench me.

"Holy shit! Liam! Holy...oh...oh God!" she cries out.

I reach into my pocket and find the tiny bottle of lube I picked up at the store. Once my finger is coated in the slippery gel, I push past the hard ridge of her forbidden zone.

She gasps, and sweat breaks out on her skin.

I inch into her until my palm presses against her ass. My mouth stays locked on her pussy, my other hand guiding hers. She comes several times until I'm satisfied she's ready. Then I shove her thighs toward the back of the seat and cage my body over hers, pinning her legs with my shoulders.

Her orbs morph into blue, lust-filled flames. Our hot breaths merge, and my tongue, full of the residual of her orgasms, slips into her hungry mouth. I release my pants, pull my finger out of her, and replace it with my erection.

I groan as I slowly slide in her and mumble, "Jesus, you're tight, little lamb."

"Oh...oh..." Her mouth forms an O, and she opens and closes her eyes several times.

Her body grasps mine as I move in and out of her with a controlled speed. I lick her lips and take her hand and reposition it on her clit. "Just like before, Hales."

"I-I can't...oh...Liam, it's...oh God!" Her body begins quivering, and she struggles to keep her eyes open.

"Shh." I bury my face in the curve of her neck, inhaling her muted sugar scent and enjoying every sensation of her body spasming on mine.

Her hand circles between us, and a loud moan echoes in the car.

"That's it, little lamb. Show me what you got," I growl into her skin. I drag my fingers along the side of her thigh and begin thrusting harder.

Crimson floods her cheeks. A drop of sweat rolls down her chin and I lick it off. Salt mixes with the sweetness of her previous orgasms still on my tongue.

"Fuck, I love you," I mutter.

"Liam!" she cries out, and her body convulses so hard on me, I explode in her, burying my face once again in her neck.

We stay frozen, except for our breathing. The car stops. I pull out of her and release her legs and massage her quads. "Little lamb, are you okay?"

She nods, red-faced, blue eyes satiated, and her pink pouty lips curving up. Her chest rises and falls slower, and she reaches around me and locks her fingers behind my neck. She studies me. Then her face turns serious. "Liam, don't go."

Reality hits me. "I have to."

"I have a bad feeling about it."

I almost tell her there's nothing to worry about, but I stop myself. We don't lie to each other, and I don't want to start. The fact is, there are too many things that can go wrong. I might get blown to pieces the moment her father steps in front of me. Instead, I tell her, "It's a few days. You'll have fun with your sister, Nora, and the baby."

"Liam—"

"It's not an option, Hales." I kiss her on the lips. "Pull your skirt down so we can go inside. We need to pack."

27

Liam

In under three hours, we get to Indianapolis. It's dark, which is why I rolled into town at night. I want to experience what Rory and those other Bailey thugs will when they arrive for our meeting.

Declan and Nolan have their laptops out. Each one is checking in with our guys. Declan takes the right side of the street, and Nolan takes the left. Killian and Finn trail in an SUV behind us, looking at other possible holes in our security that could leave us exposed. We've got another fifty men waiting in different hotels for our instructions. Our clan members on the street have been here for two weeks, watching for any sign of a Bailey or even a Ryan. So far, neither has been seen in Indianapolis.

When we get to the meeting location, we do a sweep-through. To the public, it's nothing but an abandoned building. A corporation owns it, which on paper appears unattached to the O'Malleys, but my father has them in our pocket. We have the floor plans, pictures, and video footage of the inside, but several of our men are already there. They drove their vehicles inside, so it still appears dark and empty, should the Baileys or Ryans try to approach it tonight.

I step out of the SUV, and one of our top men, who is almost as ruthless as the twins, steps out of the shadows. His short, skinny frame wouldn't worry anyone from afar. When we were kids, someone gave him the nickname Leppy, saying he resembled a leprechaun. All these years, it stuck. He even started introducing himself as Leppy. In some ways, I think it helps him stay underestimated, which is a strength for him. Because if anyone messes with him, he'll slice you to shreds and enjoy every minute of it.

"Liam." He slaps my hand. "Glad you made it out."

I nod. Leppy was inside the prison with Finn and me for what we termed several tours. He'd come in for a few years, get out, then find his way back in. The last time I saw him was three years ago. "Good to see you're not back in."

He grunts. "The deal your dad made with whoever seems to have come in handy for me."

"Let's keep it that way. Want to fill us in?"

He points around the open space. "This is where we'll keep everything. It's open. There's an easy in and out for vehicles. The rest of the building, we have locked off and guarded. No one's made any moves in the last few weeks since we got here."

"And the back door and side entrances?" I ask.

Leppy walks, and we follow. "No one is getting in or out unless you're ten feet tall and have the power to remove those bolts." He points, and I look up.

Declan whistles. "That's the thickest piece of steel I've ever seen."

"You'll need a drill gun to remove it," Leppy adds.

"So all the exits have them?" I ask.

"Yeah. There are also identical pieces of steel on the outside," Leppy confirms.

"So, one way in, and one way out?" Nolan asks.

"Sounds like fucking prison," Finn mutters then pins his gaze on mine.

Leppy's voice grows colder. "There's one other way out, but it's not a door. And it isn't on the building plans."

The room turns silent.

"Don't tell me it's *Shawshank* bullshit and you want us to swim through sewage. I'm not down with that. I'd rather take a bullet," Killian claims.

Declan slaps him on the head.

"Fuck off!" Killian cries out.

"No one is taking a bullet."

I scrub my face, not into Killian's antics. "Knock it off. What's the way out?"

Leppy points up.

We all glance up at the beams, forty feet in the air. There isn't anything but the roof.

"Should I get my Superman cape?" Killian cockily remarks.

Declan's hand flies toward his head again, and this time, Killian ducks.

Leppy chuckles. He motions to the wall several feet away. "That's your way up."

Nolan looks at Killian. "Yeah, get your cape because Leppy seems to be high on acid or something."

"Jesus. Everyone shut the fuck up!" I growl.

"Chill out," Killian grumbles.

"This isn't the time for jokes. Leppy, stop being dramatic and get to the point," I order.

He walks to the wall, flips a switch, and a four-foot piece of concrete moves backward. A thick, twisted rope hangs off to the side. "Go stand on that platform."

The six of us do as he says. I look up at the pulley system that the rope weaves through. Beyond that, stars shine in the night sky. I raise my eyebrows at Leppy.

He points to Killian and Nolan. "Let the two loudmouths get us up there."

No one moves. I cross my arms over my chest. I arrogantly say, "You heard the man."

Killian and Nolan both give me a "fuck you" but start to pull on the rope. We begin to move up in the air.

"Those thugs will shoot us by the time we get up here," Finn points out.

Leppy shakes his head. "There's a flip on the inside to shut the wall."

"We'll get shot before the wall even opens," Declan says as Killian and Nolan grunt from the job of pulling on the rope.

"We'll put an SUV in front of it. The door will stay open. All you have to do is run and hit the closing switch if needed," Leppy claims.

"Liam, how many of our men will be in the building?" Declan asks.

"Two dozen, plus us," I reply.

Declan's eyes harden. His voice makes the hairs on my arms rise. "If we need to take this way out, that means our guys are dead. Including the ones on the way in."

I stay quiet, knowing it could be a reality. The pulley creaks, and we finally get to the top. Nolan reaches for the latch and locks it in place.

"Now what?" I ask. The wall in front of me is another twenty feet high, barricading the roof from anyone on the street.

Leppy nods behind me.

I spin. A rusty, black helicopter sits on a pad. "Where the hell did you get that?"

"The owner liked to fly in and out. He was a bit eccentric. He retired years ago and has dementia. He never married and has no family. It's been sitting here all this time," Leppy informs us.

Killian jumps off the platform. "Does it even run?"

"Looks like a deathtrap," Nolan mutters.

Leppy scratches his beard. "Craig looked at it. He replaced the gas lines and did some other things to it. He said it should be good."

Killian groans. "*Should* doesn't make me confident enough to get inside this tin can."

I stare at the aircraft. My chest tightens, and my never-ending gut acid starts to climb up it. "Who would even fly this? None of us are pilots."

Leppy smiles. "Keith will be here tomorrow night. He'll be ready to go at any time."

Oh shit. My gut drops.

Killian spins. "Crazy Keith? You want us to put our lives in the hands of a man who got kicked out of the military for stealing their aircraft and crashing it into a government ship?"

Leppy's face turns red. He angrily spouts, "You got another pilot you want me to bring in on this?"

"Anyone but Crazy Keith works for me," Killian replies.

I glance at Finn. He gives me his "I don't know what the fuck to do" expression. It doesn't make me feel any more confident, but I'm not sure what other option we have.

"I vote to unlock one of the back doors," Nolan says.

Declan shakes his head in frustration at Nolan. "Yeah, because if the Baileys attack us, it's not like they won't have thought about coming in from behind."

I pace the roof. I can't see over the walls. It really is the perfect surprise escape, assuming the helicopter still flies and Crazy Keith doesn't kill us. I turn back to Leppy. "Make sure Keith is ready."

Killian's eyes widen. "You're serious?"

"There aren't any other options unless you have another idea?"

He stays quiet.

"That's what I thought. Now, does anyone else have any other ideas or things we need to check out while we're here?"

My cousins all stay quiet.

"Then let's get out of here."

We leave and reassess all the checkpoints on our way out again. More acid curls in my stomach, thinking about what could happen and wondering what Rory will say. I want to give orders to take him out as he comes into the meeting, but if I do, there will be an all-out war in the streets, not just from the Baileys and Ryans but from other mob families. There are rules to obey. My father was very clear on this, and I'm not so naive to think my actions won't have consequences. If I give the order and attack the Baileys during this requested meeting, I might as well put a death warrant on every O'Malley.

It's three in the morning when we get to our hotel. I refrain from contacting Hailee, knowing she's going to ask questions I won't answer. I don't fall asleep for hours. When I finally crash, I sleep hard and don't wake up until noon. I go into the hotel's gym, get a workout in, then meet my cousins in the restaurant. I attempt to eat, but I'm too nervous.

My father's words—to keep quiet and use my head and gut—are on replay in my mind. The problem is, all I see are Hailee's blue eyes staring at me. So all day, I struggle to separate my desire to kill Rory from following one of the few rules of mob code.

Nighttime comes. It turns dark, but we wait until midnight approaches. We arrive at the warehouse but not too early. Within minutes, the Baileys arrive.

Three black SUVs arrive. Two are ours and one belongs to the Baileys. It's as it should be, but my heartbeat never slows down. I hit the recorder my father gave me, inside my coat pocket. My cousins and I stand in a line, with the other O'Malleys circling us with guns drawn.

Leppy holds his firearm and shouts, "Out! Now! Hands up!"

Slowly, the doors to the SUV open. When Rory steps out, my chest tightens. It's been fifteen years since he put a plastic bag over my head and tried to kill me. The smell of his breath rushes to my nostrils just by looking at him. His long leather coat is almost identical to mine. Hatred and cockiness fill his expression. He steps ten feet in front of me and stops. I want to slap the smug smile off his face. I know it all too well. His eyes dart from me to Finn then the Irish accent I will always know as his, says, "Feels good to be out, doesn't it, boys?"

We say nothing.

He laughs then steps closer to me. His brother Mack steps up next to him.

"Go any closer, and I shoot you," one of my guys warns.

His expression morphs from arrogant to disgusted then into what I think the devil himself might look like. His eyes turn to slits. "You have what's mine."

My pulse accelerates. I can't help myself and jab, "Yeah. I'm rather enjoying what no longer is yours."

He licks his lips, attempts to keep calm, but the vein in his neck pops. "I don't see your father here. Did he die yet?"

My heart stammers, but I don't allow myself to flinch. "He said to tell you he's looking forward to seeing you in Hell."

"Guess he'll be warming my seat up, won't he?"

I sniff hard. "Did you come to discuss my father? Or is there a point to all this?"

He lunges toward me, and my cousins and I all draw our guns. Rory and the rest of the Baileys aim theirs at us.

Rory orders, "You crossed a boundary. You'll deliver my wife and four daughters to me in forty-eight hours."

Rage consumes me. I struggle to maintain my composure. "No. You crossed the boundary. You're leaving Chicago. All of you."

"Forty-eight hours. You deliver them to me. If you don't, we'll take this to the streets," he seethes.

My veins race with horror. When two heads of crime families get together, threats aren't empty. An all-out war will destroy one of our families, but whoever is left standing will also be severely harmed. You can't have a war in the streets without casualties.

I fire back, "You have twenty-four hours to get every Bailey out of Chicago."

Through gritted teeth, he sneers, "My daughters are Baileys. So deliver them to me, unless you want to make another deal."

The hairs on my neck stand up. I grind my molars and force myself not to press the trigger aimed at his head. "I don't need to make a deal with you. They're O'Malley property now. And you know this, don't you? Because any Bailey or Ryan who steps foot in Chicago is in O'Malley territory. And since they have both families' blood, they're now ours. As a courtesy, I'm giving you twenty-four hours to leave Chicago. I suggest you take it."

A sinister smile develops on his lips. "Do you remember when I held that plastic bag over your face?"

My insides quiver, and I say nothing.

"I determine what happens in this world. Not you. If I could get to you there, I can get to you out here," he claims.

Finn snarls, "You might want to remember how that ended. Unless you have something else to say, I recommend you get back in your vehicle and return to North Carolina."

Mack speaks up. His face twists into an evil smirk. His Irish accent sends a chill down my spine. "Still looking for Brenna?"

My stomach lurches. I swallow down bile. I do everything in my power not to take my eyes off of Rory and look at Finn. Silence fills the warehouse.

"Do you think she's still alive?" Mack taunts.

I pull my other gun out of my back pocket and aim it at Mack. I step closer to them and command, "Meeting's over. Two seconds to get in your car, or I shoot both of you."

Rory grunts. He warns, "Forty-eight hours. If you don't deliver my family to me, you'll suffer the consequences."

"Twenty-four. Leave Chicago, or you'll see the wrath of the O'Malleys," I warn him again.

They slowly back up, the Baileys all get in the SUV and our vehicles escort them out of the warehouse. When I can't see the taillights or hear the motors, I turn to Finn. "He only said that to fuck with you."

The crazy look I saw in his eyes the night I met him at his hotel after he killed our financial guy is back. He walks toward our SUV and opens the door. "No one kills Mack. Not until I've had my chance to get every bit of information out of him regarding what he knows about Brenna."

"He's lying," I claim.

Finn spins. "What if he's not? He's friends with Judge Peterson."

I don't answer. There isn't anything I can say. It is a possibility Mack would know.

Killian and his brothers get in one vehicle, and I get in the other one with Finn. We ride in silence for a long time. Finn eventually turns toward me and says, "What are you going to do? You know Rory doesn't make threats he doesn't intend to keep."

There's no analyzing the situation. There's only one option. "I'm going to find a way to kill them before they kill us."

28

Hailee

I WAKE UP TO A TEXT.

Liam: *I'll pick you up to take you to school this morning.*

Me: *You're back?*

Liam: *Yeah. Want a latte?*

Me: *Sure. Are you okay?*

Liam: *Yes, you don't need to worry. I'll see you in an hour.*

Me: *Okay. Love you.*

Liam: *Love you, too.*

I breathe in relief when Liam walks into Boris and Nora's penthouse. He sets a container with five drinks on the counter then wraps his arms around me. He murmurs in my ear, "I missed you."

I squeeze him tighter. The bad feeling I had while he was gone never left. "I missed you more."

He grunts, kisses the top of my head, then releases me. His eyes travel down the length of my body. "You look nice, little lamb."

I reach up and stroke his cheek. His eyes are bloodshot. "Have you had any sleep?"

"Not last night."

I sigh. Nothing I say will change his situation, but I worry about how running the O'Malley clan is affecting his health. I can see it almost on a daily basis. "Promise me you'll sleep today while I'm at school."

"That's the plan."

I stand on my tiptoes and kiss him. He glides his hand through my hair, firmly holding my head, and deepens our kiss until I'm out of breath, craving more and feeling like jelly in his arms.

"We better go, or you'll be late," he mumbles against my mouth and slides his tongue against mine again.

"Get a room," Nora teases.

He pulls back and circles his arm around my shoulders. "Brought you a latte. Thanks for letting Hailee stay."

"No problem."

Gemma walks into the room. She glances around, and her eyes widen. "Where's Nolan?"

"He'll be here later."

"He's okay?"

"Yeah."

She takes a deep breath and nods.

"We have to go, Hales," Liam reminds me.

I hug Gemma and Nora goodbye. We leave, and Liam hands me my drink. He kisses my head and wraps his arm around my waist, tugging me close to him.

I glance up. "Are we going straight from school to Skylar's grand opening tonight?"

"I'm glad you reminded me. I forgot about it," he admits.

"I'm sure you have other things to worry about," I tease, but my stomach flips when I say it. I hate knowing he's doing dangerous things. I dislike I'm in the dark about what they are, but Liam has always made it clear he won't ever tell me anything that could harm me. So it's something I've come to accept.

He says nothing, just kisses my head again. The elevator opens. He guides me into the car, and we don't say much. The driver pulls up to the school, and I kiss him goodbye. I cup his cheek. "Go get some sleep, Liam."

"Do you have a lot to catch up on from being out?" he asks.

"Yeah. Plus, I have a team meeting after school."

"Okay, little lamb. I'll pick you up at five thirty." He kisses me and squeezes my ass.

"Get sleep," I repeat and get out of the car.

My day goes by quickly. Before I know it, it's time for the kids to go home. I take them to the bus, release the children who walk home, and lead the remaining kids in the latchkey program to the gym. I meet the other teachers and principal in the conference room and try to concentrate on all the upcoming changes the administration wants to implement for the following year.

The room erupts in groans about all the new testing standards and changes in curriculum. They did the same thing last year. I try to stay positive and not make any negative remarks, but Liam's promise to give me my own school pops into my head. It's still something I can't comprehend. I wonder if it's possible. The costs would be outrageous, and I wouldn't want to start a school unless inner-city kids could go for free. They have the fewest resources, and their success rate to get to graduation is the lowest. If Liam was going to give me a school, that's who I would want to help.

The principal adjourns the meeting. It's after five. I rush back to my classroom to finish a few things and pack up before Liam arrives. When I walk into my classroom, the door slams shut, and a black-gloved hand goes over my mouth.

My heart almost stops, and my chest tightens. I struggle to breathe and attempt to fight back, but the cold, familiar Irish accent growls in my ear, "Fight me, and I'll kill you right now."

Tears well in my eyes, and I freeze. I never wanted to hear that voice again. Flashbacks of my mother crying and bloody fill my mind. My father screaming all kinds of horrible things while hurting her fly at me. Dreams I've had for years and tried to escape play like a movie reel.

My father spins me and grips my cheeks with his hand so tightly, I wince. His cold blue eyes send more chills down my spine. "You've betrayed me. You're not an O'Malley. Your last name is Bailey. The blood running through your veins is mine. And you're going to prove your loyalty to me, or the entire O'Malley clan, plus your sisters and that whore of your mother will all be destroyed."

His face blurs from my tears. I take short, shaky breaths, paralyzed and unable to move, except for the quivering in my stomach.

He leans closer, and his stale breath invades my nostrils. "You will bring your mother and sisters to me. Midnight. Tonight. If you don't, the next time you lie down with that O'Malley bastard, I'll slice both of your throats. And know this, dear daughter. No one, and I mean no one, can protect you from me."

He releases me and steps back. "Keep your phone on. I'll send the location later tonight. And if you bring any O'Malleys with you or tell them about this conversation, I'll blow every one of their houses up. Then I'm going to blow this school up, just for fun."

He opens the door, walks out, and I quickly shut and lock it. I collapse on the floor against it. I hug my knees to my chest and attempt to stop my tears and regulate my heartbeat. The smell of his musky cologne, I can't seem to shake.

My phone rings, and I glance at the clock.

Five forty. Liam will be waiting.

I rise on weak knees and dig into my purse. I pull my phone out and text Liam.

Me: *I'll be out in a few minutes.*

I go into the adjoining bathroom, attempt to clean the makeup off my face, put some more on, and debate about what to do.

My father doesn't make empty threats. He follows through on them. I know this about him. I experienced it as a child. His words to blow up the O'Malleys and the school tear at my heart.

I close my eyes and take several deep breaths. I pull the settings on my phone up, double-check my microphone is still off, and wonder if there is any way he could be listening to my conversations.

I grab a notepad and pen, put it in my purse, then leave. I avoid looking at anyone and go straight to the car. When I get inside, Liam's eyes turn to slits. He holds my cheeks and says, "What's wrong, little lamb?"

I put my trembling finger to my lips and pull out my notepad. I write:

Don't talk. I'm scared my father is recording us.

Liam's eyes grow wide. He tugs me closer to him. He mouths, "Why?"

My writing turns into scribbles as my hand tremors intensify.

He was in my classroom. If I don't take my sisters and mom to him at midnight, he's going to kill me and blow up O'Malley houses and the school.

Liam sniffs hard. A scowl erupts on his face. He takes the pen from me.

Are you okay? Did he hurt you?

I crumble in his arms and sob while shaking my head. He pulls me tight to him and shushes me. He reaches into my purse, does something on my phone, then checks his. He says, "Hold on a minute," releases me, then dumps the contents of my purse. He examines it with his hands and eyes then pats down my hair and clothes.

"No one is listening, little lamb. Did he hurt you?"

"No."

Green flames of rage build in his eyes. He seethes, "I'm killing him. Tonight."

I blurt out my biggest fear, "What if you die instead?"

"Shh." He tugs me back to his chest, stroking my head. "I'm not dying."

Liam's phone rings and he sends it to voicemail. It immediately rings again, and he answers it. "This isn't a good—" His body stiffens, and his face turns white.

The driver pulls up to Skylar's office building.

"Jesus. Call my cousins." Liam hangs up and swipes his screen.

"What's wrong?" I ask.

He holds his finger in the air and closes his eyes. He barks, "Where is he?"

I begin to panic. *Please don't let anything happen to my sisters or mom.*

"How many men are with him?" Liam barks.

Oh God! Please, please, please.

Liam hangs up.

"Are my sisters and mom—"

"They're fine. Selena's ex-husband kidnapped her. Listen to me, Hailee. I'm taking you inside. You stay with the Ivanov women and their security. Understand," he orders.

My relief is brief. Selena and I have become good friends. I only have an inkling of what her ex did to her, but I know he's a nasty, dangerous man.

"Okay."

Liam's eyes morph into the crazed expression I've only seen a few times. "When I get back, I'll take care of your father."

Fear for Selena, my family, and that something will happen to Liam overpower me.

Liam cups my cheeks. "I need you to be strong right now, little lamb."

I nod. "All right."

He opens the door, guides me into Skylar's office, and Obrecht rushes toward us.

He seethes, "Do you see what not taking care of loose ends does?"

I step out of the way, and Liam holds his hands in the air. He says, "She's at his house."

Obrecht throws another death glare at Liam, and both of them, along with the rest of the Ivanovs, head outside.

Skylar, Aspen, Kora, Nora, Anna, and Gemma all huddle around me. They look as scared as I do.

I study Kora. She knows more about Selena's situation since she was her divorce attorney. I deal with the elephant in the room. "He's going to kill her, isn't he?"

She shuts her eyes then turns away. Her face scrunches. "He's an evil man."

A few hours pass. Kora's phone rings. She answers, "Sergey. Is she okay?"

I hold my breath.

Kora puts her hand to her mouth then tears fall. "Good. Thank you. Be safe." She hangs up and turns to us. "They have her. Obrecht is taking her home."

"Oh, thank God," I say as my friends all do the same.

More time passes. I glance at my watch, and my gut drops further. It's ten o'clock, and my father's threat stays on the surface of my mind. Gemma and I go into Skylar's personal office and sit on the couches.

Finn comes storming into the room. His face is red, and he barks, "Where is Liam?"

"I-I don't know. He's not back yet. No one is," I answer.

"What's wrong?" Gemma asks.

Finn's demeanor doesn't change. "When you see Liam, you tell him I'm looking for him."

"Finn," Liam says from the doorway.

I jump up but freeze. The two men pin an intense gaze on each other.

"I told you not to touch Mack," Finn growls.

Mack? My father's brother?

Gemma grabs my arm.

"I didn't. Obrecht did. It happened before I could stop him," Liam claims.

"Is he dead?" Gemma asks.

Liam closes his eyes then clenches his jaw. He stares at Finn. "Yes."

"And Jack?"

"Ivanov garage. Obrecht gave me his word he'll wait."

Finn shakes his head in disgust at Liam then shoves past him.

"You can't go right now. I need you to finish this off," Liam calls after him.

Finn spins. "What are you talking about?"

He points for him to go back into the office.

Finn reluctantly returns.

"Rory threatened Hailee in her classroom today," Liam informs him.

"What?" Gemma cries out.

"He's texting her a location. There are no more options. We take him out. Tonight."

Finn glances at me. "Are you okay?"

I nod. "Yeah. But he's going to blow up O'Malley houses and the school if I don't bring my sisters and mother to him at midnight."

"Hailee! What the hell? Why didn't you tell me this?" Gemma accuses.

Finn looks at the ceiling then says, "I'll be outside. I need some air. I'll let you know when I can think again."

29

Liam

Finn finally comes inside when the Ivanovs return. Guilt plagues me about Obrecht taking Mack out. I should have at least attempted to warn Obrecht, but it didn't occur to me. I think Mack was lying about knowing anything about Brenna, but now we'll never know. Finn nor I will forget this mistake anytime soon, and it's apparent in his expression.

Although, I'm not sure it would have mattered if I said anything to Obrecht. The only reason Jack Christian is still alive is because I went to his penthouse and begged him to wait to kill him until Jack's company goes public. Selena stepped in and told him he isn't allowed to touch Jack until after the deal goes through, and I have to send her daily pictures of Jack in a cage. I'm more than happy to do that and relieved Finn's and my plan hasn't been destroyed, but it still doesn't help us get closer to finding Brenna.

Regardless, I can't dwell on tonight's mistakes. Time is running out. I tell Maksim, "I need your men."

His icy-blue eyes drill into mine. "For what?"

Acid curls in my stomach. Admitting to myself what Rory could do to my family is tough enough. Having to declare it out loud is another blow to my ego, but this isn't the time for pride. "If I don't take Rory Bailey out tonight, he's going to take us out."

Maksim's face hardens. He exchanges a glance with his brothers and Adrian then studies the women. "Our women go to my penthouse and stay there with security. Have you talked to Darragh?"

I swallow the bile crawling up my esophagus. "No. He's not doing well."

Sympathy floods Maksim's face. "Do you have the ability to direct all your men and access to all weapons?"

"Yeah. My father turned everything over to me."

Maksim pats me on the back. "Take us to your arsenal so we can see what we're working with. I'll have our guys meet us there."

I take Hailee's phone off her, direct her and Gemma to go with the Ivanov bodyguards, and leave. I climb into the SUV and send a text out to the clan to meet at the warehouse. When we get there, I punch the code to open the door to the weapons room.

Maksim mutters, "Jesus."

"There's enough in here to blow up the entire city," Dmitri states.

"O'Malleys don't fuck around," Killian boasts.

"Still prefer my knife," Boris mutters.

Hailee's phone vibrates. I remove it from my pocket, punch in her security code, and read the message. I groan. "Figures. Gary, Indiana. Whatever happens, we don't have the police chief to cover shit up." I hand the phone to Declan.

"I assume these are untraceable weapons?" Maksim asks.

"Yeah."

Declan calls out, "The number the text came from shows he's there."

"It could still be a trap," Finn says.

"I don't get it. Why did he meet with us last night and give us a forty-eight-hour deadline to turn the women over if he's demanding Hailee bring them tonight?" Nolan asks.

My father's voice calls out, "Because you retaliated with a twenty-four-hour one."

The hairs on my neck rise, and I spin.

My father raises his eyebrows. "I listened to the recording you left."

My gut drops. "So this is my fault?"

My father's eyes meet mine. "Yeah. And Rory is going to be prepared for either situation to occur."

UNCHOSEN RULER

The confidence I've built over the last few months waivers. I ask my father, "What should we do?"

"You know what needs to happen, son."

Silence fills the air. I stare at my father in his tweed cap, his green eyes bloodshot and layers of clothes on his deteriorating body, which still doesn't hide the muscle or fat he's lost. He arches an eyebrow, waiting for me to do what he's done his best to prepare me for.

I spin. "Nolan, pull the map of Gary up."

We go into the next room, which has several large screens. Nolan pulls up the aerial map of the city that's full of abandoned factories.

"Put last night's footage on the other screen," I demand.

Years ago, my father installed a system that records coverage of Chicago. Since Gary is close by and lots of crime occurs there, he also has surveillance on it.

The side-by-side version of the two maps shows every difference between last night and now. I point on the screen. "That has to be the Baileys. Mark the address Rory sent."

Nolan types something, and an X comes on the screen. It's in the middle of his men, which doesn't surprise me.

My father steps next to me. "Locate his exit points."

We spend several minutes reviewing all the footage, and I gather my men. "O'Malleys lead. Ivanovs will trail."

"That's no fun," Boris mutters.

I ignore his comment. "Take them out. Leave no Bailey alive. Declan and Nolan will assign each of you a target on the way. Use the walkie-talkies. We need to go now."

The room clears, and I step out into the cool night air. My father gets in the car next to me. I ask, "What are you doing?"

He lights up his pipe. "I'm going to shoot some Bailey cocksuckers. What do you think I'm doing?"

I push down the emotions filling my chest.

He takes a long drag of his pipe and cracks the window. I watch him blow the air out, and he sighs. "Your mother won't stop bitching about me smoking in the house."

I stifle a chuckle. "That shit will kill you, you know?"

"No shit? Huh. Guess I'll have to look into that." He winks and takes another drag.

Several minutes of silence pass. I finally ask, "I shouldn't have given him a twenty-four-hour window, should I?"

My father turns to me. His green eyes glow in the dark, and amusement floods his face. "Depends on if we live or die tonight, son."

"Fuck," I mutter.

He pats my thigh. "There are no rules, Liam. I'm not sure what I would have done in that situation."

"Really?" My father always seems to know exactly what to do.

"Yeah. If you haven't noticed, I'm not always right."

"Really? Since when?" I ask.

"I wasn't right about you going after Adrian's shooters, was I?" he admits.

I sit speechless.

He takes another long drag, blows it out, and adds, "I doubt you'd have over one hundred Ivanov men trailing ours right now if you hadn't done that. It was a smart move."

Surprised, I ask, "You aren't still mad?"

"Nah. I have to say, though, I never thought your woman would be a Bailey or a Ryan."

My protectiveness over Hailee overpowers me, and I defensively blurt out, "She's not one of them."

An arrogant grin fills my father's face. "Still has their blood."

"Dad, don't—"

"She worth all this?"

I jerk my head back. "She's worth ten times this."

His eyes turn to slits. "Good. Make things right between your mother and her, then."

I sigh. "I am."

"Your mother is my heart. I expect you to take care of her when I'm gone."

I stare at the ceiling, grinding my molars, attempting to calm my insides. "I will."

"Good. You know your mother is going to be a pain in the ass when you get married."

I groan.

"I hope Hailee isn't a bridezilla because your mother will be. You'll need to manage that. And you *will* have a Catholic wedding. Like all O'Malleys, you'll go to confession before you say your vows. So will Hailee."

I scrub my face. "There's no saving me, Dad. You know this."

"Probably not. But it'll make your mother sleep better at night. So, when are you making Hailee into an honest woman?"

My pulse races. "After the deal goes through. I don't want to have nothing to offer her."

My father shakes his head. "Son, sometimes you know when to use your heart, and sometimes you don't."

"What does that mean?"

He studies my face. "You're Liam O'Malley. It's the *only* important thing you give her."

I think about his words then ask, "Why didn't you give me hell about staying with Hailee when we found out she's a Bailey and Ryan?"

He grunts. "I'm a dying old man. The only time I see you smile is with that girl. I also trust in your judgment. So, if you're confident she never knew and wants nothing to do with them, then it's good enough for me. Besides, I kind of like sticking it to Rory that his daughter prefers an O'Malley."

I snort. "Guess I get my warped side from you."

"Well, it's not from your mother."

Gunshots ring in the air, and men's voices begin coming through the walkie-talkie. We're taking them out from all sides, so there is nowhere Rory can run.

"Zone A cleared."

"Zone D cleared."

"Zone G cleared, but we've got a man shot."

"Shit!" I cry out. I press the button. "Status?"

"Arm only. I'm pulling out. Backup is coming in."

"Replacing zone G," a Russian accent comes through the device.

More cleared zones come in, more men hit, gunshots get closer and more frequent.

"It's a fucking war zone!" my father cries out and pumps his fist in the air.

I look at him in horror. "You shouldn't be enjoying this."

He huffs. "You lie in bed for months with your mother worrying about you. Judge me after that."

I shake my head, and Killian's voice fills the car. "Main target moving your way."

The shots lessen, and there are four more big booms. An SUV spins out a hundred feet in front of us.

"Got him!" Killian shouts.

"Make him get out. Shoot the glass," I instruct.

Gunfire fills the air, and the SUV's glass explodes. The door opens, and Rory and another man attempt to find cover while shooting their weapons.

The driver goes down with a bullet to the head. Rory crouches next to the flat tire and keeps firing. When I'm confident he's out of rounds, I stick my gun out the window and shoot near him to see if he'll fire back. He attempts to, but nothing comes out.

"Got you," I mutter.

"Careful. Never get cocky," my father warns.

"Noted." I pick up the walkie-talkie. "Don't take him out. Check no one else is in the vehicle."

Nolan and Finn cautiously search the SUV and nod it's clear.

I step out of the vehicle and keep my gun aimed at Rory. His smug scowl is on his face. But for the first time, I see fear in his eyes. I pause, taking in the man I've hated forever. The one who tried to suffocate me and almost did. The man whose blood courses through my little lamb's veins, yet he still threatened her life.

I kick him in the head with my boot.

He yelps, and blood spurts everywhere. I kick him again several times. Then I crouch in front of him, with my gun aimed at his bloody head.

"Just do it," he barks.

I laugh. "I'll do it when I'm ready."

"You piece of shit." He spits on me.

"There's only one thing I want you to know before I send you to Hell."

"I'll see you there," he growls.

I grunt. "You will. And your daughter, she may have Bailey and Ryan blood in her. But she's the queen of the O'Malleys. *My* queen. And she chose it and me."

He starts to say something, and I shoot him in the head. He flops to the ground. I rise, kick him once more, then turn.

My father's lips twitch. He pats my back. "I can die a happy man now."

30

Hailee

No one is sleeping, except Shannon. Everyone is sitting at the table, except Skylar and me. The two of us are pacing.

Aspen rises. "I think we need to open a bottle of wine."

"Don't you mean several?" Kora teases.

"Count me out," Skylar says then yawns.

Sympathy fills me. She's worked so hard for her own fashion line. This should have been an awesome night for her. I comment, "You must be exhausted from entertaining everyone while all this was going on. I'm sorry your grand opening got ruined."

She freezes. "Actually, that's not why I'm tired."

"No?"

She shakes her head.

"Are you going to fill me in on your secret?"

She grabs my hand and drags me to the table. "I'm pregnant."

We all congratulate and hug her. She beams, and Kora says, "All night you kept this from us?"

Skylar winces. "Sorry. There was just so much going on. And I'm still trying to wrap my head around Hailee and Gemma being mafia princesses."

"Ugh. Don't call us that," Gemma groans.

"Yeah. Besides, Hailee isn't a princess. She's Liam's queen," Nora teases.

"Nora!" I reprimand her.

"What? It's true. Now you two just need to get married, pop out some babies, and continue the O'Malley lineage. No pressure," she states.

I groan. "I'll just wave my magic wand and make that happen, okay?"

Nora winks then turns to Gemma. "What's up with you and my brother?"

Anna laughs. "Nora's keeping it real like always, I see."

Nora turns to her. "What? My brothers always interfered in my love life. Seems fair that I at least get to know what's going on in theirs."

"Nothing is going on," Gemma claims, but her face turns crimson.

Nora tilts her head. "You're a bad liar."

"Nothing is going on. What you should ask Nolan is what is up between him and Molly."

Surprise fills Nora's face. "Molly?"

Gemma smirks. "Yeah. She's constantly bringing him food and sending him messages. And how many times can a person really have laptop issues?"

Nora winces. "She tends to make bad decisions and usually finds herself in some sort of pickle."

"Yeah, well, I'm sure some of it she creates so Nolan can save her," Gemma asserts.

Confusion fills Nora's face. "I thought her brother Colin sorted her out?"

Gemma rolls her eyes and reveals, "She's still obsessed with Nolan."

"For someone who says nothing is going on with Nolan, you sure seem annoyed by it." Kora raises her eyebrows.

Gemma rises. "I'm not. I'm going to the restroom."

She goes down the hall, and Nora asks, "Do you know what's going on between them?"

"No." Gemma still hasn't disclosed anything to me. While I'm pretty sure something is going on, I'm not going to throw my sister under the bus. For whatever reason, she doesn't want to talk about it.

I return to pacing, and Gemma comes out of the bathroom. She says, "You're making me nervous."

I stop moving and stare at her. "Sorry. I...seeing him today..." I don't need to say our father. She knows who I'm talking about.

Gemma swallows hard. "When Orla made me visit him in prison, I didn't understand how we could have his DNA in us."

"I know."

Her face turns dark. "I hope Orla is there tonight and they take her out, too."

I put my arm around Gemma and tug her tight to me. "I'm so sorry she came after you. I wish she would have picked me."

Gemma shakes her head. "No. I'm glad she didn't. But, Hailee, I swear to God, if they don't take her out, I will."

I freeze. A chill runs down my spine. "Gemma—"

"I can't deal with it anymore. She's ruined my entire life. I lost my career, my home, and everything I thought I knew about myself. I-I don't sleep at night. She keeps breaking the firewalls Nolan puts on my phone and texting me. Every time he adds something, it only takes her a few weeks to bypass it. He's stopped giving me new phones. It doesn't matter. She still seems to find me. Sometimes, I think I'm going insane," Gemma admits.

"All this will end soon. I promise," I vow to her.

She sarcastically laughs then wipes her face. "I hope it's before I end up in a straitjacket."

"Gemma—"

"Everyone safe and sound?" Adrian's Russian accent fills the air.

I spin and run over to Liam. He wraps his arms around me, and I close my eyes, listening to his heartbeat. He kisses the top of my head.

I glance up. "Is he—"

"They're all dead."

"Orla, too?" Gemma asks with hope in her voice.

Liam's face falls. "We don't have any proof she was there. We'll have to wait and see if she was in any of the cars."

My sister shuts her eyes and walks out of the room. Nolan follows her.

"I'm sorry. I wish I could give her an answer," Liam states.

I cup his cheek. "It's okay. But my father is dead?"

His tone is cold. "Yeah. Let's go home."

Relief fills me. I don't remember ever feeling anything good surrounding my father before I knew he was a Bailey or after. The fact I don't have to worry ever again about him or his threats brings me great comfort. Maybe I should feel some morsel of pain he's dead since he's my father, but I don't.

We say our goodbyes and get into his SUV. It smells like smoke. "Was your dad with you?"

Liam smiles. "Yes. I just dropped him off."

"He was okay to leave the house?"

"I guess so."

"That's good. I told your mom we would go over for dinner tomorrow night."

Liam pulls me onto his lap. "Thanks. It's going to be hard for her when my dad passes. I need to be there for her."

"Liam, I don't hate your mom. And I want you to be there for her," I tell him.

He strokes my head. "I know your mom doesn't trust me and hates my family, but I think now that your father is dead, we should try to have some sort of relationship with her."

Tears fill my eyes. I've stayed away from my mom. There's so much I feel betrayed by. "I don't know—"

"She's your mom, Hales."

A tear drips down my cheek. "I'm not sure how to mend things with her."

He deeply inhales and wipes my tear. "We'll take it a step at a time, okay?"

I sniffle. "Okay." I lean into him. "I'm so glad you're safe."

He holds me until we get home, and we stay up all night talking. I take the next few days off work, and things start to sink in. My father and his brother are no longer a threat. Orla isn't confirmed dead, but the shoot-out was all over the news. The police are still confirming bodies. But Gemma hasn't received any new text messages.

A weight seems to lift off Liam's shoulders. We spend more time with his parents. I have a good talk with his mom, and we both apologize for things. I try to talk to him about his dad's health, but he avoids it at all costs. Two weeks after the death of my father, it's Selena and Obrecht's wedding day. After the ceremony, we eat dinner, and Liam pulls me onto the dance floor.

"It's about time I got to dance with you at a wedding," he says, pulling me closer to him.

I smirk. "Are you complaining we left Nora and Boris's wedding early?"

He laughs. "Nope."

I don't mention Sergey and Kora's wedding. It's in the past, and I don't want to think about our fight.

In the middle of the song, Liam's phone vibrates. He pulls it out of his jacket. "Let me turn—" The color in his face drains.

"Liam, what's wrong?"

"My mom said my dad's at the hospital."

Goose bumps break out on my skin. "Let's go."

We leave without saying anything to anyone. The ride to the hospital is quiet. I hold Liam's hand, and he stares out the window. When we pull up to the entrance, we quickly go inside.

His mom sits in a chair. Her bodyguard is several feet away, giving her privacy. She's quietly saying the Rosary, clutching Darragh's tweed cap. Tears stain her cheeks.

"Mom!" Liam quickly is at her side.

She looks up, and her face crumples. Liam pulls her up and into his arms. She sobs, "They're putting him on a ventilator so he can have last rites. Father Antonio is coming to deliver them."

Liam's jaw trembles, and he sniffs hard. He avoids looking at me and focuses on the ceiling.

"Ruth." A bald man wearing a priest's collar approaches us.

She pulls away from Liam. "Father Antonio."

He embraces her, and she sobs all over again.

I wipe my face and slide my arm around Liam's waist. He puts his arm around my shoulder but doesn't look at me.

Father Antonio releases Ruth and shakes Liam's hand.

A nurse comes out and says, "You can go in now."

We solemnly walk into Darragh's room. He's hooked up to a ventilator, and it's beeping. Ruth and I keep crying. Liam's face hardens. He picks up one of his father's hands, and Ruth holds the other. Father Antonio administers the last rites, and both Ruth and Liam spend a few moments alone with Darragh.

Ruth signs paperwork to remove the ventilator, claiming it's what Darragh wanted. The hospital staff remove it then we all go back in the room and wait.

Several hours pass before Darragh takes his last breath. He never opens his eyes. Liam never cries, nor does he look at his mother or me. He keeps me close to him, with his arm around my shoulder, but continues to avoid me. Father Antonio stays the entire time next to Ruth.

We offer to spend the night at his mom's house, but she claims she wants to be alone. When we get home, it's after midnight. It's only once we get into bed that Liam breaks down.

And it's the only time he ever cries.

31

Liam

A few weeks later

"To Darragh," Declan shouts, raising his shot of whiskey high in the air.

"To Darragh!" the clan repeats, mimicking his motions.

I toss the liquid in my mouth and force myself to swallow it quickly, feeling the burn travel down my stomach and forcing myself not to get emotional. I nod at Declan, grateful he made a speech and I don't have to. I can't talk about my dad. It's too painful. Everyone is already looking at me, assessing whether I'm going to be as good of a leader as my father was.

"Stop questioning shit," Finn mumbles and hands me a Guinness.

I turn to him. Like my entire adult life, he can tap into my mind and know what I'm thinking.

Finn takes a big swig of his beer. "Jack's company went public. When Obrecht gets back from his honeymoon, he's going to want to finish him off."

I shrug. "Let him." I chase the burn of the whiskey with the cool stout.

"The stock hasn't gone up enough yet. Better to keep the status quo the same until we reach the correct level and can place our short positions, don't you think?"

I close my eyes. "Finn, I promised Obrecht he only had to let him live until his company went public."

"We lose a billion if we do it right now."

I sigh. "You deal with it. I did everything I could to keep that bastard alive. If you want to extend his life, you convince Obrecht."

"I will. He owes me after shooting Mack," Finn claims.

Hailee puts her arm around my waist, and I turn. She rises on her tiptoes and kisses me. She gives me a small smile and softly says, "Hey."

"Everything okay?" I ask.

"Yeah. You?" Concern fills her face. It's an expression I wish I could take away from her. I hate her worrying, but I know it's because she loves me.

I force myself to smile. "All good. By any chance, have you seen Nora?"

"She's in her office trying to get Shannon down for a nap."

"I need to talk with her quickly. I'll be right back, okay?"

Hailee nods. "Sure."

I give her a chaste kiss and go into Nora's office.

She gently places Shannon in the bassinet and looks up. A sad, sympathetic smile forms. She whispers, "Everything all right?"

I take the seat across from her. "I'm dealing."

She tilts her head. "It sucks, doesn't it?"

"Yep."

Silence fills the air. There's always been loss in the O'Malley family, but nothing has ever hurt as much as losing my dad. But I also know I need to move forward. I clear my throat. "Are you free tomorrow?"

"I can be. What's going on?"

Flutters fill my stomach. "I want to pick out a ring for Hailee, but I don't even know where to start. I was hoping you'd come with me so I don't screw it up?"

Nora's face lights up. "Ummm, yeah! And no matter what you get, you won't screw it up, Liam."

"Thanks. Does eleven work?"

"Sure."

"Great. I'll pick you up then." I get up and glance in the crib. "She really is adorable."

Nora beams. "Yes, she is."

"Thank God she looks like her mom." I wink and leave. I find Hailee. She stays by my side the entire time, and we spend the rest of the wake talking to different clan members. At the end of the night, we drop my mom off, then go back home.

The next day, I pick up Nora. When I walk into the penthouse, she points to the couch. "Sit down."

"Okay, boss," I joke.

She sits next to me and hands me a small box. It's Kelly green and faded. There's a gold Celtic symbol embossed on the lid.

"What is this?" I ask.

"Open it."

I lift the lid, and my heart stammers. I trace the gold trinity knot with emeralds and diamonds then glance at Nora. "Nana's necklace?"

She smiles, and her eyes glisten. "The night of the pub reopening—the same night you met Hailee—your dad gave this to me. He said Nana gave it to him before she died. She told him she prayed every day you would get out of prison and find a good lass to make you happy. She also wanted your wife to know she was welcoming her into our family. Even though she wouldn't be here in body, she would be here in spirit." A tear falls, and Nora wipes it. All my cousins and I were close with our nana, but she and Nora had an extra-special relationship.

I stare at the necklace in shock, once again, holding back the overwhelming feeling of grief I can't seem to shake. I take several deep breaths, pulling it together before I look at Nora again. "The last thing she ever said to me was after I got arrested. She said I shattered her already-broken heart."

"She loved you, Liam. Besides me, you were her favorite," Nora teases, but we both know it's true.

"I think Nana had this pipe dream I wouldn't become who I am," I admit.

Nora puts her hand on mine. "She wouldn't like either of us involved in what we are. It is what it is. And it's our lives to live. But she loved you to pieces, Liam. She'd be thrilled you found Hailee."

I study the necklace I remember my nana wearing anytime there was a special occasion. "I think Hailee will love this."

"She will," Nora insists.

I put the lid back on the box. "Thanks for giving this to me."

"It was an honor to hold on to it. Your dad said I was the only granddaughter Nana trusted," she says, smiling at the memory.

I glance at the window, staring at the waves of Lake Michigan, blinking hard. I quietly say, "I miss him. I'm not sure how to do all this."

Nora sniffles and squeezes my hand. "I do, too. But you're already doing it, Liam."

I compose myself and rise. "We should go."

Nora and I spend several hours at the family jewelers. I finally settle on a princess-cut diamond with a Celtic pattern on each side and a matching band. I have them engrave on the engagement ring, *My Little Lamb.* On the wedding band, I have them engrave, *My Forever Queen.*

I drop Nora off, pick Hailee up from school, and go to dinner. I don't eat a lot. I'm too anxious about when or how to ask her. I wanted to be able to give her a school before I proposed. Jack's company has gone public, but there are more moving pieces I didn't anticipate. I don't know how long it will take to start seeing the money. It should be soon, but there are no guarantees.

My father's voice never leaves my head. *"You're Liam O'Malley. It's the only important thing you give her."*

Hailee grabs my hand across the table. "Liam, are you okay?"

I pick her hand up and kiss it. "Yeah, little lamb. You ready to get out of here?"

She glances at my plate. "You've hardly eaten."

"I'm not hungry." I rise and throw cash on the table. We leave and go home.

The dozens of things I could do or say don't seem right or even quick enough. I finally step in front of her, fist her hair, and kiss her.

When I pull back, she holds my cheek. "I love you."

I stop analyzing how or when. I drop to my knees and glance up.

She runs a hand through my hair.

"I don't have all the things yet that I'll someday give you. Most days, I don't know if I'm making the right choices or not. The only decision I've ever been sure about was you."

Tears fill her blue eyes. She smiles and strokes my cheek.

"I'm going to make one promise to you. No matter what, I'll always give you me. You know my faults and strengths better than anyone. And you still stand by me. So I always want you by my side. Forever." I pull the ring out of my pocket and hold it up. "Will you marry me?"

She puts her hand over her mouth, and her eyes dart between me and the ring. She whispers, "Liam."

My heart feels like it's going to beat out of my chest, waiting for her to answer. I finally say, "You need to answer, little lamb."

She blinks and dips close to my face. "Yes."

"Thank God. You about gave me a heart attack."

She laughs, and her tears drip on my face. "Sorry!"

I slide the ring on her finger and kiss her, happier than I've ever been, knowing she's my forever.

"I have something else for you," I murmur in her mouth.

She glances at the ring. "Besides this stunning, most perfect ring ever?"

I smile, relieved she loves it, and pull the necklace out of my pocket. "Nora gave this to me today. It was my nana's. My nana said she wanted my wife to have it so she knew she was welcoming her into the family."

Hailee gapes at the necklace. "Liam, this is gorgeous."

"You like it?"

Hailee studies it closer. "It's amazing."

I unclasp it and put it around her neck.

She touches it and smiles. "Thank you."

I rise, kiss her again, then say, "I'm going to go sit on the couch. You're going to strip out of everything but your jewelry."

She softly laughs. "No. Not out here."

"Why?"

Her eyes brighten, and the naughty expression I love forms on her face. "I have something for you."

"What is it?"

"Close your eyes and don't open until I say you can."

I obey her.

She takes my hand, pulls me into the bedroom, and says, "Okay, you can open now."

"Wow! Is that the chair?" I ask.

"Yep. Do you like it?"

I run my hands over the ornate wood. The plush padding is Kelly green with a gold Celtic pattern. "I can't believe you did this. It's amazing."

She smiles and orders, "Sit."

I take a seat, and she straddles me. "Do you like our new bedroom accessory?"

I arch my eyebrow. "You aren't going to sell it?"

She leans into my face. "No. The king of the O'Malleys needs his own throne. Now, tell me to strip."

EPILOGUE

Hailee

Two Months Later

"Liam! Oh God!" I scream as my body convulses with tremors.

He holds me tighter, thrusting faster, with our glistening skin sliding against the other's. Liam murmurs in my neck, "So good, little lamb."

I whimper, adrenaline consumes my cells, and my eyes roll.

"Fuuuuck," he growls in my ear, coming hard inside me.

We don't move, trying to catch our breath. Liam finally lifts his head out of the curve of my neck. His arrogant expression turns me on more. "One hundred and fifty points. That takes me past five hundred. You better get the treat box ready."

I smirk and boast, "The treat box is always ready."

He drags his finger down my neck, and new tingles erupt. "After our appointment with the wedding planner, I have a surprise for you."

"What is it?"

More cockiness fills his face. His lips curve up, and he nibbles on my ear. "I got chains, little lamb."

My heart races faster. "You did?"

"Yeah. I'm going to chain you up, lick that sweet pussy of yours until you get hoarse begging me, then I'm going to—"

"Liam!" Nolan's voice shouts.

I jump beneath him. "What the heck is Nolan doing in our house?"

"All my cousins have an emergency key," he says, as if it isn't a big deal.

"What? Wait! Why?" I ask.

"It's better than Nora's fake rock," he claims.

"Liam!" Nolan barks.

"Chill. Give me a minute," Liam yells back and rolls off me. He grabs his shorts off the floor and puts them on.

I slide down under the covers farther. "Has your family not heard of calling before they come over? Is it lost manners or something?"

Liam bends down and gives me a chaste kiss. "You're cute, little lamb. Now, after I deal with whatever this is, make sure the treat box—"

"Liam!" Nolan hollers again and opens the door.

"Nolan, what the hell! Get out of here," Liam orders.

I pull the sheets up to my neck. "Seriously, Nolan?"

He ignores us. "Hailee, have you talked to Gemma?"

My pulse quickens. "Not in a few days. Why?"

Nolan's jaw clenches. In a cold voice, he claims, "Orla contacted her."

I sit up and hold the sheet to me. "When?"

"Last night. She was up all night, and I couldn't calm her down."

"Why didn't you call me?" I accuse.

"It was two in the morning," Nolan says.

"So what?"

Nolan scrubs his hand on his face. "Liam, we need to go, now."

"Go where?" Liam asks.

"To get Gemma. I was in the shower, and she left. She ditched security."

"Why would she do that?" I frantically ask.

Nolan's face hardens. His eyes blaze into mine. "She took my gun. She's going to kill Orla."

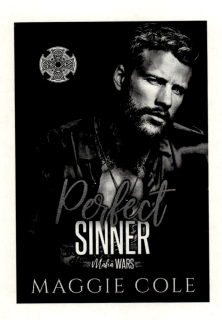

I'm the mafia princess Nolan O'Malley hates to love.

The moment we collide, he wants to destroy me.

He should. My blood is that of his arch enemy.

I'm unsure if the war raging inside him or me is stronger.

Instead of running away or ending me, he keeps me close.

He watches my every move, and monitors each threat my estranged family delivers to me.

The close quarters we share only get smaller until there is no more distance between us.

Yet I still am who I am.

Time and again he saves me from every dark demon.

When we think the one person who wants to ruin me is dead, she isn't.

This time, she won't win. I'm coming after her.

Except my actions have unintended consequences.

And I should have known he'd come after me.

After all, he's my perfect sinner.

READ PERFECT SINNER - FREE ON KINDLE UNLIMITED

GEMMA O'HARE
PERFECT SINNER PROLOGUE

Gemma O'Hare

They say every person has a breaking point. I never gave it much thought. I assumed I was mentally tough and too strong and independent for anyone to mess with me. That was before my half-sister, Orla Bailey, stalked, harassed, threatened, and even physically hurt me.

Anything I cherished, and things I didn't even think about, she stole from me. My freedom to go wherever I wanted disappeared. I can't step outside without worrying about my safety. The ability to live on my own and get a good night's rest evaporated into thin air when I woke up with rodents and bugs crawling all over my body. When I do sleep, it's not uncommon for me to wake up screaming and crying with sweat coating my skin.

My entire life, I was carefree and confident. Those traits eroded until they were nothing but a mere memory of who I used to be. Orla's determination to ruin me affected everything, including my career, which I loved and was great at.

Now, I no longer know who I am. Most days, I believe I'm going crazy. There just isn't any way to escape the unhinged thoughts going through my mind.

Except when I'm with Nolan.

Everything about him makes me weak-kneed, even when we're fighting. When I'm with him, I feel like a piece of my old self has returned. The times he leaves and I can't go with him, everything inside me feels off. And the fact he hates the Baileys, my blood relatives, as much as I do, seems to make me crave him more.

I don't know how he does it, but all I've lost seems manageable when I'm with him. The crazy feelings I have go away, and life becomes hopeful again. The notion I could have a future and not stay stuck in this world of fear and spiraling thoughts ignites and grows.

Then Orla finds her way back to me.

No matter what Nolan does to keep her away, she always maneuvers back into my life. Each time, the desperation to end her life or mine grows. And now, I'm kicking myself.

I got comfortable. Too much time passed without hearing from her. Maybe my mind needed the break from the anxiety, but the longer she stayed away, the more relaxed I became. I hoped she was somehow in the shoot-out and the police just didn't report it. After all, they still haven't reported the death of my father. Nolan promises me he saw Liam shoot my father in the head. He insists my father bled to death on the street. And Liam claims that the police often keep mafia activity under wraps due to different dynamics.

So the possibility Orla was in one of the cars and got shot isn't out of reach. The fact my father wasn't reported dead gave me too much hope she died as well.

Yet, I should have known better than to let my guard down.

Now, her threats aren't about hurting my sisters or mom. She decided to redirect her wrath to someone else. And if I lose this person, I will go crazy. I'll end up in a straitjacket or give in to the temptation to end my life.

Last night, when I saw the text, I couldn't breathe. Anxiety rushed back in, squeezing my heart. But this time, Orla's pushed me too far. She's set her evil sights on killing Nolan. So when this is over, I'll be the one pulling the trigger.

It's ironic, really. My father wanted me to step into my role in the family. I claimed it wasn't who I was and never would be. But that was before I ever laid eyes on Nolan.

Orla may be a mafia princess, but the blood swirling in my veins makes me just as much of one as she is. The only solution is to dig down and pull out all the evil that's inherently in me, then finish her off. In the end, only she or I will be standing.

She succeeded and broke me. But I won't let her destroy the only good thing I have left in my life.

READ PERFECT SINNER - FREE ON KINDLE UNLIMITED

ALL IN BOXSET

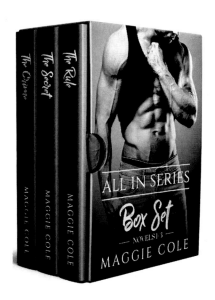

Three page-turning, interconnected stand-alone romance novels with HEA's!! Get ready to fall in love with the characters. Billionaires. Professional athletes. New York City. Twist, turns, and danger lurking everywhere. The only option for these couples is to go ALL IN...with a little help from their friends. EXTRA STEAM INCLUDED!

Grab it now! **READ FREE IN KINDLE UNLIMITED!**

CAN I ASK YOU A HUGE FAVOR?

Would you be willing to leave me a review?

I would be forever grateful as one positive review on Amazon is like buying the book a hundred times! Reader support is the lifeblood for Indie authors and provides us the feedback we need to give readers what they want in future stories!

Your positive review means the world to me! So thank you from the bottom of my heart!

MAGGIE COLE

MORE BY MAGGIE COLE

Mafia Wars - A Dark Mafia Series (Series Five)

Ruthless Stranger (Maksim's Story) - Book One

Broken Fighter (Boris's Story) - Book Two

Cruel Enforcer (Sergey's Story) - Book Three

Vicious Protector (Adrian's Story) - Book Four

Savage Tracker (Obrecht's Story) - Book Five

Unchosen Ruler (Liam's Story) - Book Six

Perfect Sinner (Nolan's Story) - Book Seven

Brutal Defender (Killian's Story) - Book Eight

Deviant Hacker (Declan's Story) - Book Nine

Relentless Hunter (Finn's Story) - Book Ten

MORE BY MAGGIE COLE

Behind Closed Doors (Series Four - Former Military Now International Rescue Alpha Studs)

Depths of Destruction - Book One

Marks of Rebellion - Book Two

Haze of Obedience - Book Three

Cavern of Silence - Book Four

Stains of Desire - Book Five

Risks of Temptation - Book Six

Together We Stand Series (Series Three - Family Saga)

Kiss of Redemption - Book One

Sins of Justice - Book Two

Acts of Manipulation - Book Three

Web of Betrayal - Book Four

Masks of Devotion - Book Five

Roots of Vengeance - Book Six

It's Complicated Series (Series Two - Chicago Billionaires)

Crossing the Line - Book One

Don't Forget Me - Book Two

Committed to You - Book Three

More Than Paper - Book Four

Sins of the Father - Book Five

Wrapped In Perfection - Book Six

All In Series *(Series One - New York Billionaires)*

The Rule - Book One

The Secret - Book Two

The Crime - Book Three

The Lie - Book Four

The Trap - Book Five

The Gamble - Book Six

STAND ALONE NOVELLA

JUDGE ME NOT - A Billionaire Single Mom Christmas Novella

ABOUT THE AUTHOR

Amazon Bestselling Author

Maggie Cole is committed to bringing her readers alphalicious book boyfriends. She's been called the "literary master of steamy romance." Her books are full of raw emotion, suspense, and will always keep you wanting more. She is a masterful storyteller of contemporary romance and loves writing about broken people who rise above the ashes.

She lives in Florida near the Gulf of Mexico with her husband, son, and dog. She loves sunshine, wine, and hanging out with friends.

Her current series were written in the order below:

- All In (Stand alones with entwined characters)
- It's Complicated (Stand alones with entwined characters)
- Together We Stand (Brooks Family Saga - read in order)
- Behind Closed Doors (Read in order)
- Mafia Wars (Coming April 1st 2021)

Maggie Cole's Newsletter
Sign up here!

Hang Out with Maggie in Her Reader Group
Maggie Cole's Romance Addicts

Follow for Giveaways
Facebook Maggie Cole

Instagram
@maggiecoleauthor

Complete Works on Amazon
Follow Maggie's Amazon Author Page

Book Trailers
Follow Maggie on YouTube

Are you a Blogger and want to join my ARC team?
Signup now!

Feedback or suggestions?
Email: authormaggiecole@gmail.com